LOST

Lost in Thyme

Lilas Taha

دار جامعة حمد بن خليفة للنشر
HAMAD BIN KHALIFA UNIVERSITY PRESS

Hamad bin Khalifa University Press
P O Box 5825
Doha, Qatar

www.hbkupress.com

ISBN: 978-9927129582

Printed in Beirut-Lebanon

Qatar National Library Cataloging-in-Publication (CIP)

Taha, Lilas, author.

Lost in thyme / by Lilas Taha – Doha : Hamad Bin Khalifa University Press , 2018.

Pages ; cm

ISBN: 978-9927-129-58-2

1. Palestine -- fiction. 2. Family -- Fiction. II. Title.

PJ7816.A517 T343 2018

892.73–dc23   201827085880

To the warm heart of my mother,
Nawal

CHAPTER ONE

Kuwait, 2016

This must be a mistake. He was not the one who should be here.

Sami Amara eased onto the backseat of the black Mercedes-Maybach S600. He studied a lost luggage receipt and gritted his teeth. He couldn't bear being caged in this car for long, no matter how luxurious the interior. The driver's slow exit from the airport added to his misery. Stuffing the receipt into the breast pocket of his suit jacket, he stretched his legs as far as he could in the limited space.

Several car horns blared from behind.

Everything around him objected to his presence. He buckled his seat belt, freed his trapped tie and loosened it.

His mobile phone buzzed. He searched his pockets until he discovered the phone had slipped out of his trousers and lay on the seat beside him.

He eyed the caller ID and answered his brother's call. "What's wrong, Fareed?"

A red Ford truck in the farthest lane to the right cut sharply into the left lane and screeched ahead of the Mercedes. Sami's driver slammed on the brakes.

Sami's seatbelt locked and dug into his chest. The Ford sped off. Cars in other lanes honked, burying whatever Fareed said. Sami unlatched his seatbelt and fumbled to adjust it. "Say that again?"

"We really need to get to work."

"Hell, I just landed."

"I can't sign or do anything in Houston until you finalize things with this Haddad woman in Kuwait."

Sami's eyes followed the Ford squeezing its way between cars. A bright yellow Maserati speeding up from the left sprayed sand onto his window. He shuffled to the other side away from the dirtied glass and latched his seatbelt. "Don't worry. I'll get to the bottom of this."

Fareed exhaled into the phone. "Who the heck is she? Where did she come from?"

"I have no idea. Haven't seen anyone yet."

"Vaughn didn't meet you at the airport?"

"He sent a limo service. I'll call you as soon as I have something." Sami ended the call and braced himself.

Once they reached the highway, the limo driver surprised Sami with his skill, weaving away from careless motorists who drove as if they owned the road.

Sami's sight adjusted to the yellowness of his surroundings. Small patches of trees and sand-dusted shrubs sprinkled sides of the road that cut through the desert—a black ribbon floating on a sea of sand. Villas and houses, some the colour of dried mud, dotted the horizon in the shimmering distance, their architectural designs varying in degrees of complexity. Lonely palm trees poked their heads above high walls. A concrete one-story cube with small windows stood out. The car turned into its parking lot and cruised to a stop.

Sami planted his feet on the hot ground and gripped the door's inside armrest to keep his balance. The asphalt under the soles of his leather shoes felt viscous. His sunglasses fogged, and he took them off to check he wasn't sinking into the molten surface. He used his necktie to clean his lenses, adding smudges with the sweat-soaked silk. He slipped his glasses into his shirt pocket and took in a long breath, inflating his lungs despite the heat, tolerating its swift burn.

This hostile environment did not matter. He could take it. He could take anything but being confined in that car for another minute. He watched the Mercedes drive off and shook his head. His torturous ride was an oddly fitting way to top-off a miserable twenty-three hour trip from Houston.

Sami entered the office building, noting the big sign overhead that spelled Amara & Sons Construction Company in bold red letters. The same was written in Arabic next to the company emblem. Walking into the chilled interior, he faked a cough to hide a shiver brought on by the sudden temperature drop. Where were the restrooms? He felt a sudden urgency.

"Mr. Amara." A stout, white-haired man met him in the lobby and offered his hand. "Allan Vaughn, chief legal counsel. We spoke on the phone?"

"Right." Sami matched Vaughn's strong grip. "Everyone calls me Sami."

Vaughn clasped Sami's elbow with his other hand. "Wish we'd met under better circumstances. Your father will be greatly missed."

Sami gave a curt nod and freed his arm. He had no desire to waste a single minute on small talk. He needed to finalize this business as quickly as possible. He shrugged off his jacket, rolled up his sleeves and told his bladder to calm down. "I'd appreciate an update."

"Of course." Vaughn led the way to his office.

The industrial fluorescent lighting and low ceiling pressed onto Sami. He fought the need to hunch his shoulders and headed toward the only window in the room. If he opened it to this sweltering heat, he would look like an imbecile. His eyes sought the air-conditioning vent between the white ceiling panels, and he imagined the ventilation duct opening to the outside world at the other end. He willed his nervous heartbeat down a notch.

Over the years, he had mastered a couple of tricks to suppress his claustrophobia. Up to a point. And today was proving to be a hellish trial. He had endured the arduous flight on tightly-sealed planes to sort out the mess his father had left for him in this place. His control over his body slipped from his grasp.

"Kuwaiti heat getting to you?" Vaughn said in a condescending tone. "You've worked in harsher climates than this, haven't you?"

Out in the open, Sami wanted to say. He clenched his jaw and let the snide remark roll over him. "Just a little tired from the flight. So, where are we?"

"I have the documents ready." Vaughn produced a folder from the massive desk. "All you need is to have Mrs. Haddad sign them." He motioned toward one of the leather chairs. "Drink?"

"Water's fine." Sami stayed rooted to his spot by the window. Heat radiated from the glass pane and gave him a strange measure of comfort. He took the icy water bottle Vaughn offered. "Have you contacted her?"

"We'll meet with her tomorrow at nine. Thought I'd give you time to rest. Get over the jet lag."

Sami decided against taking a sip of water, to appease his bladder, and placed the bottle on the windowsill. "We're meeting here?"

"I advised her to hire a contract lawyer. Recommended someone I know. She declined and chose someone else." Vaughn checked a business card on his desk. "Rida Al Faisal. He arranged for the meeting to be at his office downtown."

"And she has no idea what this is about?"

"Only that it concerns her father. She asked me questions. I had no answers." Vaughn tapped his index finger on the folder. "Do you?"

Sami shook his head. "I'm in the dark, too." He pointed at the folder. "I'd like to see those sealed envelopes Dad left in his will." He studied Vaughn, trying to gain the measure of the older man. Vaughn had come into the company two years ago to oversee the Kuwaiti branch. His eyes shifted like a ferret and landed everywhere except directly on Sami. Would he prove trustworthy?

Vaughn sauntered over, a white envelope in each hand. "Since your father stated you both need to be present to open them, I saw no point giving this woman a heads-up over the phone."

Sami examined the seals and the handwritten names. Was this his father's handwriting? Working on construction sites, his occasional correspondence with his father was through emails and typed documents. At thirty-two years of age, he struggled to remember what his father's handwriting looked like. When was the last time they had spoken? Last summer when he was on assignment in Costa Rica. And what was it about? Nothing personal. He had discussed business details to assure his father the resort project was completely under his control. Ever since the Chile disaster early in his career, Sami scrutinized contractors and worked hard to regain his father's trust. He had quickly learned to depend on no one.

Sami handed back the envelopes. "Did you find out who this woman is? Is she any relation to Dad?"

"Nothing I could find in any records. Her father Waleed Saba and your father went to the same high school before your father left Kuwait for America."

"That was more than forty years ago. They didn't keep in touch?"

"It doesn't seem so." Vaughn shrugged. "The school was destroyed during the first Gulf War. No records remain. And your father didn't elaborate, told me to find Mr. Saba's daughter."

"Haddad is her husband's name, I take it?"

"Therein lies the problem." Vaughn raised his hand. "Her mother changed her name to Clayton when they moved to the States. When she died, a spinster aunt adopted Petra, and she became Petra Keats. Then she married and returned to Kuwait as Petra Haddad." Vaughn shook his head. "I spent a number of billable hours searching for Petra Saba."

"How much time?"

"Since March. Your father asked me to search for her soon after he was diagnosed."

Vaughn finally looked Sami in the eye. He let his sentence hang in the air for several heartbeats.

Sami maintained eye contact and didn't flinch, certain Vaughn had known long before he did about his father's illness. Vaughn had watched his father draw

13

his last breath. Here in Kuwait. Away from his sons, his family. What other secrets did this guy possess?

"And her mother?" Sami asked.

"Deborah Kirkwood was from Milwaukee. Died of breast cancer when Petra was seven. Like I said, the sister adopted her. That's all I could gather." Vaughn scratched his head. "As far as I know, Petra never met your father."

Vaughn went to the long row of metal filing cabinets opposite his desk and pulled out a manila folder. "Everything my detectives discovered is here." He waved the file in the air, a faint smirk on his face, daring Sami to abandon his spot by the window.

Sami turned his gaze toward the dancing leaves of a lonely tree at the edge of the parking lot. "What line of work was her father in?"

"Partner in an import export company. Mainly household appliances. He inherited the family business as an only son." Vaughn flipped open the folder. "Company records were destroyed during the war, and nothing else is registered in his name. In May 1990, Petra's mother reported her husband missing to the American Embassy in Kuwait."

"Wait, Petra's father disappeared three months *before* the Iraqi invasion?"

"That's right. His wife took Petra to her family in Milwaukee. She was four at the time."

Sami leaned his shoulder against the window and folded his arms. "When did Petra return to Kuwait?" He stopped shy of asking why.

Vaughn checked the folder. "2013. She teaches at the American School. Math, I believe. One son. Her husband was a teacher, too."

Sami arched his eyebrows. "Was?"

"Oh, I didn't mention she's a widow? Her husband died in 2014. Something to do with his heart."

"Was he old? Could he be the recent connection to Dad?"

"He was thirty-four. A couple of years older than you. Odd, isn't it?" Vaughn slanted his pale lips into a side smile. "My sources didn't find a single connection between her husband and your father. I believe the woman is the common factor here." Vaughn gathered the folders and slipped them into a leather briefcase. "You can go over these tonight after you've rested. My driver will take you to your hotel."

Vaughn held out the briefcase for Sami. "Your father gave me clear instructions on how to do this. I don't understand the reasons behind his decisions, but it's my duty to see them through as he directed." Vaughn placed his hand on Sami's shoulder. "I know you were never involved in the logistics side of the company. Your father made it clear he wanted *you* to oversee this transaction instead of Fareed."

15

Sami grabbed the leather briefcase. "What are you talking about?"

"You'll understand once you read what's in there."

Showered and wrapped in the plush hotel bathrobe, Sami grabbed a bottle of Perrier from the room's mini-fridge to settle his upset stomach. He lounged on the bed, leaned his head to the headboard and closed his eyes. Before he tackled the contents of the briefcase, he promised himself five minutes rest, only to awake hours later, his neck stiff and his feet cold. If it hadn't been for the bellman delivering his lost-and-found luggage, he would have slept on through the entire afternoon.

He stretched and headed into the bathroom. His thick dark hair flattened at the back of his head and shot out on both sides of his face. He ran wet fingers through his hair.

The luxurious bathroom had no windows, and the marble walls seemed to move closer. Sometimes, his eyes played tricks on him. He lifted his arms to his sides, gaining a good sense of the empty space. To compound his phobia, his more than average height made him perceive enclosed places as smaller than they actually were. He waved his arms around and tried to shake off the illusion.

He checked his laptop for work-related emails. Nothing required immediate attention, and he went through his mobile phone messages. Six were from his brother, his tone escalating in levels of urgency.

He dialled Fareed's number. "Did I wake you?"

"I'm already up," Fareed whispered. "It's five in the morning here."

"Where's here?"

"Hold on. Let me get out of the bedroom. Don't want to wake Lora."

"You're still in Houston? I thought you were going to Dallas after the funeral to seal that deal tomorrow?"

"Couldn't. The twins came down with a cold. I didn't want to leave Lora by herself." Fareed yawned aloud. "Besides, everything is frozen until you settle matters."

Sami spread the files on the table before him. He had to hand it to his younger brother. Fareed was a devoted father, never letting work come before his family. "You sounded more frantic than usual in your last message."

"Did you find out anything?"

"I have in my hands the file Allan Vaughn prepared about the woman. You've dealt with him. What's your read on the guy?"

"Dad trusted him. And you know how Dad was when it came to assessing people."

Sami rubbed the bridge of his nose. He knew nothing about his father's attitude toward people. He didn't know much about his father's attitude toward many things.

He scanned the file. "Let's see. Petra Haddad, born in Kuwait in '86, moved to Milwaukee with her mother in 1990, master's degree in accounting from UW, married in 2010, returned to Kuwait in 2013 with her husband. He died a year later."

"Wow. That didn't last long."

"That's about it. Nothing stands out." Sami rifled through the rest of the file looking for a picture and found an old, out of focus image. Interesting.

"Could she be . . . family?" Fareed asked.

"Hell, I don't know." Sami flipped through another folder, scanning legal documents drawn up and signed by Vaughn.

"Can't see Dad having a mistress, being unfaithful to Mom." Fareed drew in a long breath. "That would destroy her."

"Keep Mom out of the loop for now. Until I find out more." Sami's eyes landed on a particular document. He rose to his feet. "Oh, shit!"

"What is it?"

"Look, I'll get a better idea after I meet this mystery woman and open the sealed letters." He swallowed. "I'll call you tomorrow as soon as we're done."

"Wait," Fareed barked.

His raised voice must have woken the twins. Sami heard loud cries in the background and welcomed the interruption. He didn't know how to explain what he held in his hand.

"Go take care of your kids, Fareed. I got a handle on this. I'll call you tomorrow."

Sami set his phone on the table, reached for the grainy photo and studied the hazy image, which looked as if it had been cropped from another snapshot. Vaughn and his detectives couldn't provide a better picture of this woman?

Sami flipped open his laptop and went online, searching for her name, in all its variations. The same goddamn image popped up on the UW website graduates' list, showing her standing in a group. He searched social media outlets. Nothing. He slammed the laptop shut. Who in this day and age didn't have their pictures plastered all over the Internet?

He flopped onto the bed and tossed the photo on the nightstand. Reaching for the lamp switch, he muttered, "Until tomorrow, mysterious Mrs. Haddad."

CHAPTER TWO

Petra ran to catch the elevator before the doors closed. She edged next to a woman in one corner and dug into her bag for her lawyer's business card to check the floor number. Twentieth. She addressed the tall man blocking the keypad.

"*Eshreen, law samaht.*"

Dressed in a finely tailored black suit, the man ignored her request.

Had she not correctly pronounced the Arabic number? Petra connected eyes with the other woman, who asked for the fifth floor.

The man stepped to the side and faced them with unmistakable nervousness, jaw muscles pumping fast, eyes shifting from side to side.

"Sorry! Could you say that again?"

His voice sounded coarse, as if something was stuck in his throat. Judging by his accent, the man was American. Seeing that floor number twenty was already pressed, Petra waited for the other woman to repeat her request in English. She did so, he obliged and the elevator jolted upward. The American inched closer to the doors, his nose almost touching the reflective surface, hands tapping the sides of his thighs. His stance reminded Petra of Elias on his way to a birthday party, ready to bolt from the car as soon as it came to a stop. She winced at the foolish thought, comparing the grown man to her six-year-old son.

Petra shifted her gaze to the woman beside her to see if she, too, sensed something was off with this man. Clad in an Yves Saint Laurent head cover that matched her bag, the woman kept her eyes fixed on her mobile phone. Petra looked down at her aching feet and suppressed a groan. She must have scuffed her left shoe when she got out of her car. She had bought the pricy pumps just yesterday. No point fretting about it now. She tried to relax.

Over the past two days, she had considered numerous possibilities for this meeting. Ever since receiving a phone call from the Vaughn fellow, she had dug through her father's papers to figure out the connection. At first she thought it a case of mistaken identity, but when Vaughn insisted on a meeting with her and a lawyer, she felt that she couldn't afford to brush him off. Vaughn might have news of her father. Was it possible he was alive after all these years?

The elevator stopped at the fifth floor. The American dashed out while the doors pulled apart. He lifted his head and inflated his chest, unclenching his jaw in obvious relief. He stretched out a hand to stop the doors from closing and waited for the other woman to exit.

Petra hid her surprise by feigning interest in her bracelet. He must have been holding his breath the entire time. She dipped her nose to her shoulder and sniffed her cotton dress. She had dabbed droplets of rose water fused with a mix of aromatic oils behind her ears this morning as usual. The mellow scent lingered. And that woman wore oud wood essence, for sure. Many affluent Kuwaiti women used the aroma-rich oil to perfume their clothes and hair. Petra recognized the sweet exotic fragrance as soon as she entered the elevator.

What offended the American's senses, then? Why did he hold his breath?

He stepped back in and let the doors close. This time, he kept his dark eyes on the ceiling fan. Petra couldn't look away, fascinated to see if he would hold his breath to the twentieth floor. Small beads of sweat gathered on his creased forehead below short, dark bangs. His Adam's apple bobbed up and down, stretching tanned skin with a copper tint, not the dark brown shade she was accustomed to seeing on most men here. Lighter shades spread out in thin lines from the sides of his eyes, suggesting he spent too much time outdoors without sunglasses.

He pulled back his broad shoulders and stiffened, stretching his white shirt enough to show tight muscles underneath. His build defined raw masculinity. He must have made the gesture to show off. This fellow knew how to highlight his assets. He flexed his hands a couple of times before shoving them into his trouser pockets. The trousers wrapped round him well.

Fearing her cheeks were about to flame, Petra snapped her gaze to her feet. She jerked her bag open and pretended to search for something. Good thing that ceiling fan fascinated him so much—perhaps he hadn't noticed her shameless gawking.

Why was this elevator so slow? And what was wrong with her today, acting like a lustful teenager? She was a thirty-year-old mother. A respectable teacher, for heaven's sake.

The doors parted at the twentieth floor. She shot out and hurried down a long hallway, looking for suite 2026. She was a good half-hour early. She picked up her pace anyway, trying to distance herself from the intriguing male specimen behind her. Her senses were on high alert and she needed a clear head for this meeting.

Entering her lawyer's office, she came face to face with a young woman. Pitch-black hair pulled back from unblemished creamy skin in a tight bun. Kohl-framed dark, intelligent, questioning eyes stared steadily, not a hint of a smile on her stunningly beautiful face.

Petra introduced herself using the few Arabic words she had so carefully practiced. "*Sabah elkhair. Ana Petra Haddad.*"

"You are early." The woman spoke English in an accusatory tone. Dismissing Petra's good morning wishes, she checked her computer screen and clicked the mouse several times. "We are not ready." She rearranged a stack of papers on the desk. "Do you want to drink something?"

"No thank you," Petra mumbled, deflated after the effort she had put into correctly pronouncing the difficult Arabic words. This was not her lawyer. She had talked to a man over the phone, and he was nicer, not so bossy.

"I'll be back." Petra left the office and followed signs to a public restroom. She checked her reflection in the longest mirror. Nothing out of place. The blue cotton fabric of her dress was thick enough, none of her lingerie showed beneath. The pencil-cut dress was modest and simple, it did nothing to accentuate her figure. Twisting her arm behind her, she felt for the zipper, secure in its place. She never wore makeup during the day, so no mascara, and no eyeliner ran under her eyes. If only she could carry a small bottle of perfume in her bag like every woman she knew, but her allergies deprived her of such indulgence. Her sensitive nose and skin could only tolerate aromatic chemical-free oils, and she smelled the fragrance of her special blend clear enough on her clothes and hair. Using her fingers, she combed down her bangs, making sure they completely covered her forehead. If that woman found offense in what she saw, that was *her* problem. Petra gave her reflection a firm nod and returned to the office.

Not bothering to hide her rolling eyes, the woman ushered Petra into an inner office this time around and introduced her to the head lawyer. Mr. Faisal fit the image in Petra's head. Old, fat and loud. He spoke English with a proper British accent. The authoritarian woman turned out to be his assistant. When she left the room, Petra breathed a sigh of relief. She took a chair and followed instructions to sign representation documents explaining how she should deal with Vaughn and his client Sami Amara.

At exactly nine o'clock, two men walked into the office. Petra bit the side of her lip. Sami Amara turned out to be the intense man she had encountered in the elevator. That might explain his odd behaviour. Was he dreading this meeting as well? And what kind of name was Amara?

He extended his hand. "Thank you for meeting with us on such short notice."

She shook his hand and found herself anticipating the moment he would clear the scratch in his throat. The moment never came. That was his voice, rough and weathered.

Things grew stranger after the introductions. While the lawyers exchanged papers and talked business for several minutes, she withstood Sami Amara's blatant stare. He didn't try to hide his visual examination of her, and she squashed her irritation. She had done the same to him during their ride in the elevator. It was only fair to give him a similar chance.

She swept her eyes upward from his polished leather shoes to a slightly oversized silver belt buckle. His tie matched the exact charcoal shade of his Armani suit. This man seemed well put together, but he was far from composed. He radiated tension, and her feminine antennae did not have to be finely tuned to pick it up.

She met his gaze, daring him to back down. She inserted her sunglasses through her hair to pull back her bangs, exposing all of her face, freckles included. Nothing to hide.

A heartbeat passed.

Sami clamped a fist to his mouth and dashed out of the office.

Petra arched one brow at the closing doors. What was that all about?

CHAPTER THREE

Sami cupped his hands under running water and splashed his face, trying to get a grip. He held the edges of the sink and let water drip down his nose. He had finally done it. Lost control.

A little girl of no more than five ran between the sinks giggling, her voice ringing like bells in the tiled room. Frozen to his spot, his eyes chased her until she ducked under his sink and flashed him a bright smile. Freckles on her left temple aligned in an arrow and pointed to big hazel irises. The red dots on her forehead stood out, prominent in her round face.

His hand shaking, he reached out to trace the arrow with his thumb.

Vaughn stormed through the door. "What the hell just happened in there?"

The girl put a chubby index finger to her lips and faded into the tiles.

Sami straightened and loosened his tie. "Had to get out of there."

"You're sick? You should've told me. I would've rescheduled the meeting." Vaughn approached from behind. "You know how rude you were in doing that?"

"Couldn't help it." Sami snatched paper towels and dabbed his chin. He was not insane, after all. The girl with the arrow birthmark wasn't a visiting apparition. She was real, and she sat in that office a few steps away from him. Nature's stamp branded her, made her unique. Now he could give a name to the images which had plagued his world ever since he was a child.

A home video of him chasing the little girl around a dining table played in his head, he a boy of seven or eight. A memory? Or was it his imagination inventing the event to make sense of her sudden appearance? Who was she? And why had she stuck to his soul and muddled his mind all those years?

Vaughn checked the calendar on his mobile. "I'll see if they can meet this afternoon."

"No don't. I want to get this over with." Sami balled the towels and dumped them into the trash bin. "Must be something I ate on the plane. I'm sure they'll understand." To shut Vaughn up before he had a chance to ask questions, he left the restroom and hurried back. He wouldn't waste any time. He wanted to know more about Petra. Did she have a memory of him?

Sami pulled the office door open, bolted inside and almost knocked Petra off her feet. He shot a hand to her arm until she regained her balance.

"Sorry! Didn't see you there." He dropped his hand. "You okay?"

"I was on my way out." She lifted the strap of

28

her bag onto her shoulder. "Obviously—this was a mistake."

"Allow me to explain." He stepped aside to give her more room and crushed something under his shoe. They both looked down. In the commotion, her sunglasses had slipped off her head. Shit! He had destroyed them.

Vaughn caught up with them and addressed Petra. "This is about the legal will of this man's deceased father, and you are mentioned by name."

"Sorry about that." Sami collected the mangled frame. Pieces of broken lenses dangled from the splintered plastic. "Please come back inside. The livelihood of many people is on hold until things are finalized."

Her lawyer stepped in. "You have moral and legal obligations to hear Mr. Amara's last wishes, Mrs. Haddad."

"Half an hour." Petra glanced at her watch. "Then I'm gone."

They returned to the big office. Petra eased into a chair, keeping her back stiff and straight.

Sami deposited her broken sunglasses on the coffee table and stood by the window opposite to where she sat. "Allow me to apologize for my behaviour. I'm afraid airplane food doesn't sit well with me."

Petra crossed her legs, careful to tug the hem of her dress over her knees. "Where did you fly from?"

"Houston."

"If you don't mind me asking." She brushed hair off her eyes, exposing the tip of her arrow. "What sort of name is Amara?"

"Palestinian. My father is ... was from Ramallah, originally. My mother, as well."

His slip must have caught her off guard, for she winced. "My condolences for your loss."

"You're very kind." He tried not to stare at the part showing her natural tattoo. It sat higher on her temple than the child's in his mental images, the redness less sharp with the passing of years.

"My father's family is from Palestine, too. Nazareth."

"I see." Sami filed their mutual background as a clue to the puzzle that was Petra.

"Have you been to Palestine?" she asked.

"Not yet."

"I hope to go someday."

"When I was a child, my father talked about taking me and my brother every summer. Never happened. And I haven't had the chance myself." Focused on trying to find out if she possessed any memory of him, Sami kept his position by the window. He gave her ample time and a clear view to recognize him.

"I'm certain I've never heard the name Amara before. Am I supposed to have known your father?"

"I honestly don't know. This is the first I've heard of you." He released a long breath, disappointed and uncomfortable with his statement, even if it were the truth.

He knew her—a young version of her.

Vaughn cleared his throat, reminding Sami there were other people in the room. "Mr. Amara was adamant on how to do this. He left two letters. You are to open them at the same time." Vaughn handed Petra one of the sealed envelopes first, then gave Sami his. He turned to her lawyer. "Mr. Faisal and I will go over other documents while you read your letters."

The female assistant marched into the room and opened a connecting door to a spacious conference room. She motioned with her hand. "This way."

Clutching her unopened letter, Petra strode over and sat at the head of a long, polished table. Sami went straight to the window and drew the mini blinds open, letting sun rays brighten the room.

A young man from South Asia in a white uniform stood behind a side bar. He set a water jug and glasses on the big conference table.

The assistant closed the doors and pointed at the office boy. "Coffee? Tea?"

Petra shook her head, turning the envelope in her hands.

"This is fine. Thank you." Sami filled two glasses with ice-cold water, set one before Petra and emptied the other in a single gulp.

The assistant dismissed the office boy and stepped into a glass cubicle at the other end of the room. She sat at a small desk, offering privacy, yet not leaving them alone.

Sami glowered at the assistant. In this conservative society, there were rules and restrictions to adhere to. He wanted to be alone with Petra, to grasp a sense of the kind of person she was in the hope it might trigger more memories. His discomfort grew disproportionally to the space around him. He took in deep breaths and tried to brush aside creeping anxiety. This was no time for his aggravating condition to strike. He had business matters to focus on rather than worrying about circulating air and seemingly shrinking rooms. He needed to find out who this woman was.

Petra waved her envelope in the air, looking serious with her brows knit together. "Shall we?"

Sami sagged to a chair two seats away. "On the count of three." He tried to dilute the heaviness that descended on him with a buoyant tone, "One, two, three. Go."

They opened their envelopes and started reading. Sheets of paper shuffled and landed on the table one after another. Several minutes passed in silence.

Petra gasped and slammed her hand to her chest.

Sami jumped to his feet, shoving his chair against the wall. A sound escaped his throat, guttural and contorted. He faced Petra.

"On my father's grave, I swear I knew nothing about this."

CHAPTER FOUR

The words blurred before Petra's eyes. She blinked, spilling droplets onto the letter in her hand. She looked at Sami, his face distorted through her tears. "How could this be?"

Sami placed both hands on the table, crumbling a page in his fist. "I don't know what to say."

"All those years." Petra rose out of her chair. Sheets of tear-smudged paper fluttered to the floor. "Do you know the kind of life my mother had? What she suffered?"

His voice came out strangled. "I'm so sorry!"

"What she could have done with that money?" Petra raised her voice, losing control and not caring one bit. Images of her mother's frail body shrinking in agony flooded her mind. "My mother couldn't afford treatment. I . . . saw her twist in pain. I . . . c—c couldn't hold her." She placed her hands on her ears. "Had to block her screams."

Sami raised the hand clutching the page and offered it to Petra. "Dad couldn't find her."

"My mother died!" Petra shrieked.

Before her, Sami's body oscillated in sync with the paintings on the walls and the furniture. She gripped the edge of the table. She was the one who was shaking, not her surroundings.

Her shriek sent the legal assistant scrambling to her feet in the glass cubicle.

Petra wrapped her arms around her ribs, afraid anger would eject her heart out of her chest. "My aunt took me in." She forced her voice down, and the assistant halted at the glass door.

Sami fumbled through his letter. "Dad wanted to make things right. He didn't know about your mother's half-sister and spent his last days looking for you." Sami pointed at the closed doors leading to the lawyer's office. "They're going over legalities as we speak."

Petra couldn't breathe. A savage storm whipped through her and dumped despair into her lungs. Anger ignited a torch in her chest, bringing more memories of her mother's torment. Who was this man? And how dare he throw her back to that miserable time?

She snatched her bag and trotted toward the door. "No."

Sami beat her to the door and placed his hand on it. "What do you mean, no?"

"I cannot accept this. Any of it."

"Mrs. Haddad, it's the truth. Think about it. Why would my father invent something like that on his deathbed?"

She sidestepped him and reached for the door handle. "I don't know."

"Look, you're in shock. I'm having a hard time processing this, myself." Sami tapped the back of one hand to his open palm, just as she did when she wanted to dumb down a concept to her students. "The way I see it, my father borrowed money to start his project from your father. When he was in a position to pay it back, your father had disappeared and your mother didn't leave a trace. She even changed her name." Sami tapped his hands again. "Like it or not, we can't ignore these facts."

"Oh, I can. And I will." Petra opened the door, not caring that she was acting childishly. "I'm leaving."

Vaughn rose from his chair. "I have a duty to see this through, Mrs. Haddad. Everything is in order. Your lawyer and I went over every detail."

Mr. Faisal looked up from the papers on his desk. "Once you sign, it is all yours. And it has to be done by the end of business hours the day after tomorrow."

Sami advanced past Petra. "Where does that deadline come from?"

"If Mrs. Haddad doesn't accept her shares within seventy-two hours of opening the letters," Vaughn said. "Your father stipulated that one third of the company's net worth goes to a boarding school run by the church."

Sami stiffened with an unreadable expression on his face. "Any specific school?"

Vaughn checked his folder. "The Bright Beacon Academy in Chicago. Your father didn't mention it in his letter to you?"

Sami exhaled. "No."

Petra sought Mr. Faisal. "He would deprive his family because of me?"

"Your shares are less than a third. Worth only the company assets in Kuwait," her lawyer stated. "I spoke to Mr. Amara's Kuwaiti partner, and he is in agreement. Mr. Sulaiman has no objections to the transaction. He much prefers you as a partner instead of ending up entangled with the church." Mr. Faisal produced a document from a stack of files on his desk. "Mr. Sulaiman has signed and notarized his affidavit."

"I told you I had everything in order," Vaughn interjected.

Mr. Faisal shot him a sideways glance before leaning closer to Petra. "It is in everyone's interest if you accept. Mr. Sulaiman has offered to buy you out if you prefer cash."

"I won't take what's not mine." Petra pushed past the men. "I need to go."

Sami followed her. "My brother has children, Mrs. Haddad. Refusing this arrangement will mess with their future. Please don't do that."

Petra's steps faltered. She would fight dragons if they threatened her son's future. She faced Sami, unable to mask the hesitation that crept into her voice. "And you? You don't care about losing so much to a complete stranger?"

A muscle ticked under his right eye. "I want my father to rest in peace."

The anguish in his voice struck hard. She knew all about that compelling urge. Had her father gone to his final resting place? Had it been peaceful? She straightened her shoulders, lifted her chin in defiance, and fought the inclination to soften her attitude. "I need time to think, look things over. I'll give you my answer tomorrow."

The assistant appeared and handed her a thick folder. "Copies of all the documents."

Petra hurried out before anyone had a chance to object.

As the doors closed, Sami Amara's rugged voice exploded into an elaborate chorus of curses.

***

Petra made it to the faculty and staff meeting on time. With two weeks left before classes started, her workdays were busy with curriculum updates and lesson plans. The session ended earlier than expected, and she had no idea what the outcome of the meeting had been, her mind stuck on Sami Amara and his dead father. Could she believe this revelation, despite the fact that her mother had never mentioned the Amara name? It didn't appear on any of her father's surviving documents, either. Did her aunt know about the loan?

She should not have gone to that meeting with the lawyers by herself.

Stubborn woman.

Mouzah had offered to accompany her and she should have accepted. Her friend would have marched past those men and got her out of there before she came unglued, screaming like a little girl. Simple words on a sheet of paper had sent her spinning out of control. Her world anchored by numbers and mathematical logic, she had never truly appreciated the power of the written word. Until now.

Forced to grow up fast in the early absence of parents, she had come a long way and done well considering the circumstances. What an illusion. This bombshell of the past exposed the truth. Lord help her, she was still grieving—not her parents, not her husband, but her lost childhood.

A need to inflict pain took over. She hurried into the restroom to avoid talking to other teachers. She gathered her hair into a tight ponytail and pulled the strands as hard as she could. Her scalp throbbed with a deep twinge. She fought tears and stifled a groan. Years of skirting a path through her aunt's household as an unplanned addition to it had prompted her to ease anxiety with strange practices, and those old tactics lingered. She was a grown woman now, a mother. No room for unbalanced behaviour. Taking deep breaths, she let go of her hair and set aside the pathetic little girl hungry for parental affection.

Activity died down in the hallway outside the restroom. Petra slipped out and left the school. She got in her car, rolled down the windows, and blasted the A/C. Careful not to touch her back to the hot leather seat, she waited for the first assault of steamy air to blow over. Whatever had possessed her husband to buy this car, decked out in leather, was evil. Bassam hadn't factored in the effect of sweltering heat on leather seats. The Honda Civic did have an excellent A/C unit, though. She could be thankful for that.

Through the glare of the windshield, she spotted the school principal dismiss a group of teachers and head her way. She slapped the gearshift into reverse and started to pull out of her parking space when he called for her. She bit her lower lip and stopped the car. This better be quick. She needed to pick up Elias from Mouzah's house before heading home to make her investigative calls.

"My son's waiting on me, Mr. Frost."

Richard Frost draped his arms over the top of her car and yanked them back with an audible yelp. "Why so formal, Petra?" He rubbed the scorched spots on his forearms. "There are no students around. Just Richard, okay?"

Two of her colleagues passed by, and she caught their sly glances. She injected a good measure of formality into her tone, "What can I do for you?"

Richard leaned in and stuck his face through the open window. "You seemed distracted today. Anything I should know about?"

Richard had sad eyes, no other way to describe them—there was no lustre in those swamp-water irises. Widowed years before she lost her husband, he conjured a shared connection. But every time she came into his proximity, the fine hairs on her arms shot upward. An instinct screamed to watch out. She had no clue why. Since Bassam passed away, Richard had been kind and supportive, and he paid special attention to Elias. Every six-year-old boy needed a role model.

"Lots of things on my plate now that I'm teaching an upper grade." Petra forced a smile. "Nothing I can't handle."

"The son of the Minister of Finance will be in seventh grade this year. I want him to have the best math teacher in the school."

She wasn't looking forward to the added pressure of a high-profile student. The kind of facade she would need during parent meetings alone would be aggravating, not to mention having a spoiled brat for a student. As if dealing with teenagers all day wasn't trying enough.

She released a long breath. "I hope I won't disappoint you."

"You never have, Petra."

"There are more qualified teachers. I'm not sure I'm the best fit for this."

"You have advantages others don't have."

"I do?"

Richard tested the edge of the window with his fingers before gripping it with both hands. "Youth and beauty. Never underestimate their power."

She flinched, annoyed by his mischievous tone. If he meant to flatter her, he didn't just miss the mark, he crashed over the edge. Grappling for control, she fumbled with her bag on the passenger seat, hunting for nothing in particular. It kept her away from Richard's face glistening with sweat.

"I might need to stop by more often to check on things. No reflection on your work, of course. I have no doubt you'll do a great job."

She should be pleased by the professional confidence he showed in her, but damn it, there was a ton of wrong in the way he said it. "Thanks."

He reached for the A/C vent by the driver's window and adjusted the blades to blow cool air in his direction, further invading her personal space. "I'm available any time, Petra. Remember that. Whatever you need."

She snatched her mobile phone and waved it in his face, forcing him to step back. "I really must go. Is there anything else?"

Straightening, he clasped his hands together. "Meeting tomorrow at nine. Say hello to the little guy."

Petra closed the window, spun her tyres in reverse and drove out of the parking lot as fast as she could manage. She could worry about Richard and his unflattering, adolescent crush later. Right now, she had a muddled past to unscramble.

CHAPTER FIVE

Back in his hotel room, Sami Skype-called Fareed and brought him up to speed on the details of their father's will. Easing away from the laptop screen, Sami watched his brother's face recover from the shock. Fareed's mouth opened and closed without uttering a word. A twisted sense of relief descended on Sami. His brother didn't know anything about Petra. The little girl with the red arrow birthmark remained his secret.

"The church?" Fareed finally asked.

"Just the school. Our school."

"I don't get it. Mom always complained about the outrageous tuition fees the school demanded from Dad. Why would he give it more money?"

"I guess he liked the way we turned out." Sami couldn't prevent bitterness from marring his words. He coughed behind a clenched fist, hoping Fareed didn't catch it. "It shows how much Dad wanted to pay back his debt."

"So why not give this woman her money?" Fareed exploded. "The original loan plus a good percentage for the lost years. And donate to the church, for heavens' sake. Why go about it in this twisted way?"

"To force my hand. This way, I have to make sure she accepts her shares."

"Dad putting *you* in charge of sorting out this mess says a lot, Sami. He trusted you to do the right thing."

"Yeah?" Sami brushed invisible threads off his trouser leg, shielding his eyes from Fareed's stare for a moment. "I don't think he ever forgave me for what happened in Chile."

"You're still hung up on that?" Fareed raised his voice again. "It's been years. That son-of-a-gun contractor cut corners. Fortunately no one was hurt and insurance covered our losses. Dad came to understand it wasn't your fault."

"I hired the thief contractor. Dad made sure to remind me of that at the beginning of every project from then on." Sami's knuckles knocked on the surface of the desk. "This is not about Dad trusting me. He knew I'd never let a penny go to that school."

"I'll never understand why you drifted away from the church." Fareed laced his fingers together under his chin. "Maybe he's helping you find your way back."

Something rumbled in Sami's chest, an entity too angry and volatile to unleash. His brother had got it wrong. He hadn't *drifted*. He had run, as fast and as far as he could.

"You have a good life, Fareed. I won't mess it up." Sami scooted forward and stuck his face inches away from the laptop screen. "You have my word, I'm not going to let this woman deprive your kids of their rightful inheritance, no matter what Dad intended."

"All I'm saying is . . . I'll go along if she decides to walk away. I don't want you to feel guilty . . . like you failed to convince her or any nonsense like that." Fareed unlaced his fingers and fiddled with his keyboard. "Lora . . . the twins . . . we'll be fine, no matter what."

Sami's throat tightened. Fareed was a decent man, put together right from the inside, no missing pieces. Unlike him, big chunks of his soul carved out by the school his little brother was so eager to donate to. Could he blame him? Fareed's experience at the school differed from his, Sami had done his best to make sure of that. He had the scars to show for it. He stretched out his legs and arms to maximize the space his entire body occupied, a ridiculous reflex whenever he thought of that school.

He sat back and joined his hands behind his head. "I wish I had more time. I need to see Mom. Find out if she knows anything about Petra and her father."

"Then you'd better fly home. I'm not going to try."

"How is she these days?"

"Took up painting again," Fareed said.

"That's a good sign."

Fareed shook his head. "The paintings? All black. Not a dab of colour. Like being in a tomb."

"Shit! The beginning of another cycle. Tell Rosa to watch out."

"Don't worry! Everyone's on guard. I asked Rosa to stay weekends for a while. Have to pay her overtime, of course. She'll keep Mom in check." Fareed knit his eyebrows. "Can't you see?"

"What?"

"If Dad hadn't sent us away, I doubt we would have survived Mom. That school kept us alive."

In what shape? And at what price? Sami clamped his mouth shut. Old habits were hard to break. He wouldn't shatter the safety of his brother's perfect world. How much weight did the truth put on a heaven and hell believing soul? Let Fareed live with his delusions if they made him happy.

Fareed drummed his fingers on the surface of his desk. "Did you rule out the possibility Petra is our half-sister?"

"For sure. The timing is totally off. Besides, Dad would have assigned her shares with no stipulations or conditions if that were the case. No, she's not his." Sami's voice faltered on the last words. Doubt hung about him and buzzed, an annoying fly that wouldn't shoo away. Under what circumstances had Petra become part of his childhood memories then? And why?

He rubbed his eyes, feeling the combined effect of tension and fatigue. "I'm meeting with Dad's Kuwaiti partner this evening. See where the guy truly stands."

"I talked with Sulaiman several times on the phone since we started the branch there. Shrewd businessman."

"Anything I should watch out for?"

"He might seem a bit dry and standoffish. But he's straightforward and honest. Did you know he comes from one of a handful of Kuwaiti families that are Christian?"

Sami hid a smile behind his closed fist. Did Fareed mean to add a measure of respect to the man's character by saying that? Fareed's delusions ran deep. Sami planned his own evaluations of the man's calibre, regardless of his professed faith. "Maybe he can help me nudge Petra into a favorable decision."

"And if she walks away? You'll be okay with the alternative?"

"No one refuses money. She has a son to take care of. Trust me, she's not going to walk away."

"Sami, don't use her child as leverage."

Sami's abdominal muscles contracted from Fareed's unexpected blow. So that was how his brother saw him—a man who would use a child to procure what he wanted. "Thanks for the reminder." Sami made sure his tone dripped with injured sarcasm.

"You know what I mean." Fareed waved a hand in the air and brushed aside his harsh comment, either choosing not to see how deep it cut into Sami, or genuinely oblivious to its cruelty.

"I'll call as soon as I have something solid." Sami closed the laptop and slid it to the far edge of the desk, needing the physical distance to disengage from the

46

mess of emotions Fareed had stirred. He rose and paced his hotel room. Space shrank with each step.

The hotel overlooked a beach, and the sea beckoned with its openness and caressing breeze. Sami grabbed his wallet and headed out. Once he brought his breathing to normal, he would consider ways to leave Petra no choice but to accept what his father forced him to offer.

Sami took off his sandals and dipped his feet into the waves breaking upon the shore. The warm water didn't fit the scene around him. The late afternoon sun ready to hide behind the horizon created a restful and calm vibe. Had the water been cool on his skin, tension would have drained from his system, washed away with the retreating waves. He experienced none of that serenity. His mind hopped from one thought to another, chasing childhood memories of the little girl with the arrow birthmark that eluded his grasp.

A young boy ran waist-deep into the water and dived head first into an oncoming wave. His laughter drowned out his mother's voice. She halted at the shoreline a short distance from Sami, slightly lifted the hem of her long black robe with one hand, and swung a towel with the other. The boy waved and yelled something in Arabic. The mother laughed, took a glance at Sami, and let go of her robe allowing the fabric to get soaked. She took tentative steps forward

47

and called out for her son. The boy dived and swam further away, his green shorts rising and dipping under the water.

Sami set his wallet and watch on the dry sand and prepared to dash after the boy if he didn't heed his mother's calls.

The mother threw the towel aside and slammed her hands to her thighs, screaming louder. The boy switched direction and started to swim to the shore, his arms slicing the surface with obvious confidence and skill. Reaching shallow water, he prodded toward his mother with a sheepish grin on his face. His shorts sagged on his slim frame.

Yelling non-stop, the mother wrapped the towel around his shoulders and shook her finger in his face. The boy nodded his head several times and pulled free from her grip. Holding firm, she yanked him to her side, kissed his wet hair, and walked him toward a car parked on the street.

Sami watched, relief mixed with resentment in his chest. The interaction between mother and son triggered an unwelcome memory. He was around that boy's age cradling his baby brother in his lap and clawing with his bare fingers at the insides of a hardwood box, screaming for Mother to let them out.

Fareed was too young to remember that incident, and the many that followed until their father shipped them off to boarding school. His brother was right.

Fareed wouldn't have survived Mother's distorted brand of love. But *he* did. For eight years. He mastered techniques to contort his growing body into mother's cramped, airtight, cedar chest at the foot of her bed.

And when Fareed arrived, he found ways to nestle his small body in with his to keep from crushing him. A lump of clay stuffed into a mould, those years of *mothering* had shaped him with such finality and set his life on a complex path filled with fear, loathing and loneliness. His mother *made* him the perfect target for bullies at that school. It wasn't enough being harassed for his Middle Eastern background; cruel boys used his specific fear of tight places to showcase their ignorance and impose dominance. Teachers turned a blind eye, let it all happen, and instructed *him* to toughen up, be a man. And as he grew bigger, he grew meaner; made sure Fareed didn't suffer the same treatment.

Now he had to endure these flashes from the past, exercise mental games to control panic attacks and hide certain realities from Fareed—the little brother who so casually expected him to use a child as leverage.

A warm breeze ruffled the tails of Sami's linen shirt. He gulped for oxygen, sensing none of the open space before him. Was he destined to stay trapped in that box for the rest of his life?

He retrieved his sandy wallet and picked up his sandals. Perhaps he shouldn't dig into Petra's past. Let buried truths remain buried, lest they trigger more unpleasant memories that threatened to spin him out of control.

CHAPTER SIX

Petra rang the doorbell to Mouzah's house. A young maid opened the door, hiding most of her body behind the stained glass. Petra didn't recognize her. She tried to put the timid woman at ease.

"You're new, right? I'm Petra."

The maid opened the door wide. "Madam is inside."

Petra followed her into the living room, her pumps clicking on the marble floor. Mouzah lounged on a long white sofa at the far end of the huge room. She scrambled to her feet when Petra walked in. Tall and slender, Mouzah in her floor-long yellow robe personified the Arabic meaning of her name—a single banana—hearty, soft and nourishing.

Mouzah's parents had chosen the perfect name for their daughter. Unlike Petra's, who named her after ancient Nabatean ruins carved from stratified rocks in the Jordanian desert. Nothing warm or welcoming about an old rock, no matter how colourful its composition. In a magazine, Petra learned a person's name affected personality. Was that the reason she stood firm and rejected change? Was she destined to remain out of sync with her turbulent life?

Petra stepped forward to embrace her friend. Close up, she distinguished the embroidered Arabic letters in brown thread decorating the collar of Mouzah's robe—a ripened banana.

Withdrawing from her affectionate hug, Mouzah slammed a hand to her chest. "*Haww! Ya hafith!*"

Petra sank into plush cushions. "English, please."

Mouzah slammed her chest again. "Oh! Dear Keeper!"

Petra suppressed a smile. Her friend's attempt to translate Kuwaiti expressions literally always amused her. Somehow, the English words didn't convey enough of Mouzah's dismay. "Do I look that bad?"

Mouzah dropped next to her. "Your face is very . . . white." She lifted the ends of Petra's hair. "What have you done to your hair?"

"It's been a long day."

"*Yalla*, tell me." Mouzah crossed her legs and snapped her fingers. "From *Ta'a Ta'a* to *Salamulaikum*."

"I have no idea what that means."

"You never heard this expression before? I think it is Egyptian." Mouzah waved her hands in a wide circle. "I want you to tell me every detail. From the minute you knocked on the door to the instant you told them goodbye."

Petra shook her head. "I'd like to see Elias first."

"He is swimming with the boys. Don't worry, Khalid is with them. He knows not to let Elias grow too tired."

"I thought your husband would still be at work?"

"He came home early. He wants to hear what happened with you and his lawyer friend."

Petra rested her head back on the cushion. "I must thank him for the referral. Mr. Faisal was very helpful."

Mouzah addressed the maid. "Bring small boy here."

"Yes, Madam." The maid went through French doors leading to the patio.

Petra hid the sting she felt at Mouzah's description of her son; though she was sure Mouzah didn't mean to refer to his size, rather his age. Elias was the youngest boy here, and he was small for his years, his growth stunted by a weak heart.

She decided not to correct her friend and tilted her head toward the door the maid had left from. "Who did she replace?"

"No one. Indonesians work in the kitchen and do the cleaning. I brought Tria to help with the children. *Philipinieh.* Better."

Never comfortable with the constant presence of maids, Petra tried to guess at the meaning of Mouzah's ill-spoken words to understand their implications. Mouzah was the most affectionate person Petra had ever encountered. The woman had drawn her and Elias into her family with the strength of blooming flowers attracting bees. Ever since she had met her in college while Khalid was pursuing his MBA degree, Petra saw an older sister in Mouzah, and she clung to the missing familial connection. If only Petra had a grasp of the Arabic language, she would have caught the connotations in Mouzah's speech, and perhaps found her words less objectionable.

Petra ventured, "Tria is from the Philippines? Easier to communicate with since she speaks English, right?"

Mouzah nodded. "Well educated, too."

Wrapped in a beach towel, Elias dashed in and threw himself in Petra's arms. "Mama, I don't want to go home now."

Petra held him as long as she could before he wiggled away. A squeezed sponge, Elias deposited wet blotches on her dress. When she let go, he absorbed her weariness in return. Thoughts of Sami Amara and his company retreated to the back of her mind.

"Elias, will another half hour be enough?" Petra raised her hands and wiggled ten fingers. "That's three tens. Thirty minutes."

Elias bobbed his head and hurried outside. The maid tried to hold his hand. "No running. You slip and fall on wet floor."

"See? I didn't have to tell Tria to do that." Mouzah touched Petra's forearm. "And you are not leaving here before we have lunch with Khalid." Mouzah winked. "*Machboos*. You like it."

Petra licked her lips. "*Daggoose*, too?"

Mouzah drew her brows together. "Of course. You can't have *Machboos* without its hot sauce!"

Petra didn't dare refuse the invitation. The traditional spiced rice and chicken dish was something she only dreamed of cooking, although Elias loved it.

Over a cardamom-flavoured cup of tea after the meal, Petra went through the details of her meeting. Khalid studied every sheet of paper in the folder she gave him, including Mr. Amara's letter.

"So what do you think?" Petra gathered the scattered documents.

"Illy ma ya'arif el sager yishweeh."

Petra counted to ten. When would her friends realize she didn't understand much Arabic, and the Kuwaiti dialect in particular? She cleared her throat.

Mouzah volunteered her interpretation abilities. "That means he who does not know a hawk might grill it."

Dumbfounded, Petra bit her tongue to stop from screaming in frustration. "I'm sorry. I don't understand how a hawk comes into play here."

Khalid's bushy brows created a deep groove over his nose. "I'm in the oil business, Petra. And this is an architectural construction company. I have no idea how to advise you. They do have a good reputation is all I know."

"But do you think this could be true?"

"I have no doubt. All the documents are legitimate and are in perfect order with the regulations here. Didn't the lawyer check all that?"

Petra nodded. "Mr. Faisal said as much."

"I trust Faisal." Khalid ran his fingers down his moustache and goatee. "That is why I sent you to him. I would heed his advice if I were in your shoes."

"What about this partner?" Mouzah interjected.

"Sulaiman Enterprise is a solid name in the market. I don't know the man personally, but for him to agree to this arrangement speaks well of his goodwill." Khalid poured more hot tea for everyone. "Looking at it from a purely business angle, I understand why a successful entrepreneur doesn't want a third party meddling in his company. Especially not one affiliated with a church."

Khalid pointed his finger at Petra. "Having you for a partner protects the Amara brothers too. Sulaiman must have had a good relationship with Sami's father."

"The lawyer said Mr. Sulaiman offered to buy my shares if I wanted cash." Petra took a sip of her tea.

"Legally, and based on Faisal's evaluations, I would say you are in the clear."

Mouzah tapped the table. "Why should she sell now? If the company is doing well, she should hold on to her shares and collect profits every year. She cannot pay Elias's increasing medical bills on a teacher's salary alone."

"I've been doing fine so far." Petra's knee-jerk reaction brought a flush to her cheeks in embarrassment. She rearranged sugar cubes in the sugar bowl. The genetic defect in her son's heart would require more tests and intervention as he grew older. Mouzah's honesty was dead on, a sharp reminder of Elias's only inheritance from his father.

Khalid rubbed his goatee. "That is something to definitely consider. I cannot advise either way. Like I said, I don't know the business." He flipped open the folder again. "Want me to ask Faisal to check the company stocks and track record to give you a better idea?"

"Please." Petra checked her watch. Time to go home. She was the worst math teacher when it came to Elias. The half hour ultimatum had turned into over two hours.

A maid came in and cleared the tea service. She put down a plate heaped with *lugaymat*, Petra's favourite dessert. The marble size fried pastry balls dipped in hot syrup weakened her resolve to leave. "I don't know. It doesn't feel right to me. Accepting any part of the company share, much less the money."

Mouzah scooped sticky balls onto Petra's plate. "You came to Kuwait to be closer to your father, right? To find a thread that would lead you to him? Well, here it is."

"I never imagined this . . . kind of connection."

"You expected to find him alive, not sending you an inheritance."

"Mouzah!" Khalid scolded his wife.

"What?" Mouzah shrugged. "I am only saying the things Petra will not put into words."

Fearing she might cause a problem between husband and wife, Petra popped a sweet ball into her mouth and pretended Mouzah's words didn't faze her. She swallowed bitterness injected by the harsh reality her friend articulated. At times like these, she wished this candid woman lacked her barbed tongue.

"You have a point. As unexpected as this is, it tells me things about my father I didn't know before. I could readjust my perspective."

Mouzah leaned closer to her husband. "Khalid, invite Faisal and Sami Amara for lunch tomorrow. You can evaluate the man and give Petra your opinion."

Petra rose. "Thanks, but there's no point in that. I don't care what sort of man he is, I just want to check if any of this makes sense."

Khalid and Mouzah exchanged a strange look, its meaning lost to Petra. She glanced away, ashamed to acknowledge jealousy pricking her. During her short-lived marriage, she couldn't remember passing unspoken messages to Bassam or his picking up on them.

Khalid got to his feet. "Actually, that is a good idea. If you decide not to sell, Sami Amara will be your partner with Sulaiman, and you will have to deal with him at some point. Better gauge his character. *If* you trust my opinion."

"Of course I do. Who else do I have here to watch out for me other than you two?"

"I will arrange everything with Faisal and invite Sulaiman to join us at our *Deewaniah*."

"Do you think he will come at such short notice?" Petra gathered the contents of the folder. "I imagine Mr. Sulaiman is a very busy man."

Khalid scowled. "A smart businessman wouldn't refuse an invitation to a *Deewaniah* meeting. It is *the* place to discuss matters of interest here." Khalid headed out of the dining room. "Trust me, Sulaiman will come."

"Thank you for a fabulous meal." Petra picked up her bag and beamed at Mouzah. "Can you call Elias, please?"

Mouzah poked her head into the kitchen and spoke to her maids. She turned, hooked her elbow in Petra's and walked her through the entrance hall. "You said Sami Amara is *philistinee* raised in America like you?"

"He is of Palestinian origin, yes." Petra did a double take. "I think he doesn't know Arabic, either. So be careful tomorrow, please."

"And he is Christian?"

"From Ramallah."

Mouzah slowed her pace. "Tell me, is he a handsome man?"

"I suppose some women would say that."

"Is he married?"

"I didn't see a wedding band." Petra stopped. "Where are you going with this?"

A mischievous expression hovered over Mouzah's face for a split second before it was replaced by a slow spreading smile. "*Halat el thoub rig'ateh minnah ow feeh.*"

"For the love of God!" Petra rolled her eyes. "I give up."

Elias trotted in with Mouzah's youngest son, preventing her from understanding what Mouzah said. Bader was only a year older and the two boys got along very well. Petra was thankful for that bond. Elias needed a normal childhood. She knew about growing up with neither a father nor siblings to lean on. Having a close friend was the next best thing to family. She took a look at her son, eyelids droopy, shoulders hunched, beyond tired.

Good.

They would collapse into bed as soon as they arrived home—Elias exhausted from swimming, she from thrashing about in an emotional sea. Wave after wave of reality threatened to change her life once more. She scooped Elias into her arms.

Mouzah opened the front door.

"What time should I come over tomorrow?" Petra asked.

"Any time you want. But this is a men-only affair."

"Women don't go to the *Deewaniah*?"

"You and I will talk to Khalid after the men leave."

Petra stepped out. "Wait, what was it you said in Arabic earlier?"

Mouzah ruffled Elias's hair. "The beauty of a mended robe lies in the patches made from its own cloth."

CHAPTER SEVEN

Dressed in khaki trousers and a white shirt, Sami removed his shoes and followed Vaughn into a spacious air-conditioned room filled with colourful rugs. He had ditched the suit, a wise decision, he thought, noting the seating arrangement of long divans pushed against curtain-covered walls. A charcoal burner on a huge brass tray commanded the centre of the room.

Khalid greeted Sami and Vaughn and introduced them to his two teenage boys. Khalid gave Sami an appraising look before he gripped his hand in welcome. Sami steadied his gaze and returned a firm handshake. Good thing the room was laid out with not much furniture clutter. He could breathe with ease and remain calm. Before him stood Petra's champion—a man older than him, a married man and a father, with enough weight in Kuwait's business world to merit her trust. He needed Khalid on his side if he wanted Petra to play along.

Sami exchanged greetings with Sulaiman, comfortable with the no-bullshit man after their brief meeting the evening before. The businessman struck him as an intellectual who didn't waste time with small talk.

In plain words, Sulaiman had expressed his admiration for his father's scrupulous action in giving Petra what he deemed her inheritance, acknowledging the Amaras' right to do whatever they wanted with their assets as long as it wasn't illegal. No fuss and no complications. Sami liked that about the man.

Faisal arrived as the welcoming greetings were dying down. Khalid received Petra's lawyer in a less formal manner. It was obvious to Sami that the two were friends as well as business colleagues.

Sami settled next to Vaughn on the thick comfortable cushions and faced the three men across the room. Khalid, Faisal, and Sulaiman wore traditional Kuwaiti white robes, which reached their bare feet. White trousers showed underneath when they sat down. A white cloth with the sides flipped back onto the shoulders covered every man's head. A black ring of twisted rope kept the head cover in place. Sulaiman and Faisal had worn business suits when Sami had met them yesterday. Now they looked different, foreign and intimidating.

Over talk of local politics and recent events in the Middle East, a South Asian man in starched white trousers and shirt entered the room. He lifted the brass pot off the charcoal burner with one hand and grabbed a stack of small cups in the other. One by one, he served Arabic coffee and followed with a large tray piled high with dates. He took a seat by the door.

The bitter coffee, laced with a spice Sami didn't recognize, stung his throat. As soon as he swallowed his last sip, the server returned and refilled his cup. Not wanting to be rude, Sami drank, noticing the others didn't get a second serving. Sami was about to place his cup on the low table by his knees when the server picked up the coffee pot again and headed his way.

Sami shot his hand out. "Thank you. No more."

The server fidgeted, looking confused, his eyes seeking his employer.

"I'm afraid it's a taste I'm not used to," Sami added.

Vaughn leaned over a round tube of a cushion that served as a hand rest. "You need to shake the cup in your right hand to signal you don't want more."

"Would you rather have Turkish coffee instead?" Khalid asked, unsmiling.

"Not used to that taste, either."

"Nescafé?"

"Thank you, but I'm fine."

Khalid signalled to the server to return to his spot by the door.

Sami started a list in his head of reasons he resented Vaughn. At the top of it, was Vaughn holding his father's confidence during his last days instead of him. Dragging him to this *Deewaniah* meeting without explaining its purpose sat at number two. Not telling him about proper etiquette involving Arabic coffee in this traditional setting trailed at number three.

Concentrating on the men before him, Sami tried to follow the others' conversation about problems in the Kuwaiti Parliament and the suicide bombing of a mosque that had shaken the country. He found the three men highly educated, casually expressing themselves in proper English. Sami ventured his thoughts when the topic expanded to uncontrollable violence in the entire region, especially the war in Syria and the latest Israeli air strikes on Gaza. Sami kept his guarded comments universal and vague, unable to gauge where each man stood on some of those topics.

Khalid finally addressed him with a personal question, "Is this your first visit to Kuwait?"

"Yes, hopefully not my last."

"Your father grew up here, did he not?"

"My grandparents immigrated to the States in the mid-seventies after my father graduated from high school. He tried, but never returned to Kuwait until he established the company branch here two years ago . . ." Sami broke off, weighing what to say next.

Vaughn scooted forward. "Your father told me it wasn't easy for him to return—given the uh . . . negative uh . . . attitude in Kuwait," Vaughn stumbled on, "against Palestinians after Saddam's invasion?" He flipped out his thick hand. "You know, Arafat appeared to have uh . . . sided with Saddam. That caused a lot of animosity."

Oblivious to the weight his words delivered, Vaughn looked at Faisal, then Sulaiman, and finally arched an eyebrow at Khalid. "Am I right?"

Khalid gave a stiff nod. "Arafat conveniently forgot Kuwait was the birthplace of the Palestinian resistance movement."

Feeling the bite of a misplaced accusation, Sami decided on complete honesty if he had any hope of gaining the men's approval. "Arafat's poorly calculated move ruined a long-standing relationship between our people." Sami flattened his tone, making sure he sounded like someone stating a fact, rather than projecting an opinion. "Through no fault of their own, Palestinians who considered Kuwait their second home became estranged by association."

"But they weren't treated uh . . . fairly to begin with, right?" Vaughn drew his lips into a smug line. "I mean before the war. Always seen like outsiders by Kuwaitis, here to take." Vaughn raised his palms in the air. "That's what I keep hearing."

Sami's back stiffened. Vaughn's malicious comment stung his ears. Vaughn had lived in Kuwait for two years; could hardly claim ignorance of the historic and prevailing vibe toward Palestinians. Stressing political and social friction in this meeting was intentional on his part. Vaughn was not oblivious. The jackass knew what he was doing, sabotaging Sami's image before these men. What the hell was his motive? And why choose this setting to display his total lack of diplomacy?

Vaughn fiddled with his tie and opened his mouth.

Looking Khalid in the eye, Sami clamped a hand on Vaughn's arm and interrupted him. "Palestinians helped establish Kuwait's infrastructure, medical, and educational systems since the early fifties. They worked hard for the life they created in Kuwait. They didn't take. They *gave* everything they had left after they were forced out of their homeland at gunpoint, during ruthless wars and massacres. They didn't ask for charity. They wanted only to be treated with dignity."

The men stared at Sami, stone-faced. Did they not expect him to know the country's history? Assume him young and ignorant of the past? Or did they agree, and hold their tongues out of civility?

Vaughn licked his lips, ready to stoke the fire, no doubt. Sami faked a cough behind his fist to keep the devious fool quiet. Sulaiman and Faisal shifted their gazes to Khalid. So *he* was the dominant figure here. He was their host, after all. Was there another reason to wait for Khalid to respond? In this gathering, Faisal and Sulaiman stood lower on the hierarchical scale.

Convinced by his analysis of the sociopolitical setting around him, Sami counted to ten in his head. If no one followed with a comment, he would drop the subject. Move on to something personal to prevent Vaughn from saying more damaging things.

No one said a word. Khalid signaled for the server to start another round of coffee.

Sami wanted to accept the offering to gain some time, but that would make him appear flaky after declaring he didn't like the taste. He thought fast. He should establish a level of familiarity. Why would they trust a son who had never visited his father during the last two years? They didn't know he spent every free moment of his time at home taking care of his mother to relieve Fareed and Lora's burden. Having them live with her while he finalized his last project in Costa Rica added volumes of pressure on Fareed's small family. These inquisitive men didn't know that his father left behind an unbalanced wife in order to search for Petra.

Sami picked out a plump fleshy date and separated it from its pit. "Dad told me stories about his life here. School was unbearably hot without air conditioning. He talked about the sea and said he had a good time growing up. Formed good relationships with people from all over the Arab world. Uncomplicated life, he called it."

He chewed the date, giving the men a chance to ask questions. They remained silent. This was harder than he expected. A construction engineer, he bounced from one site to another, came to a group of men as the overseer, and to be effective at his job he had to remain socially distant from the people he supervised. He didn't have to establish trust, it was granted by default once he took care of his employees. He didn't need to talk about himself to obtain favourable opinions.

The intense sweetness of the date made his tongue stick to the roof of his mouth. Where was that bitter coffee now? Was there a signal to indicate he wanted some? He grew uncomfortable under the men's direct gazes, and the green curtains covering the walls floated closer. He swallowed.

"The nature of my job kept me away. And with the little time I had at home, I took care of family matters." There, introducing family into the picture should make him seem normal, shouldn't it?

"You are first generation Palestinian American?" Faisal asked.

"Born and raised in the U.S.A. Yes, sir."

"Your mother is also Palestinian, I understand." Faisal picked up on Sami's desire to switch direction. An attentive man, this lawyer. He just might like him a little.

"That's right."

"But you don't speak Arabic."

"My brother and I grew up in a boarding school. I'm afraid my spoken Arabic is very poor. I took classical Arabic classes in college. I can get by reading basic stuff."

Faisal's eyes lit up. "You attended the same boarding school endowed in your father's will?"

69

"The Bright Beacon Academy. I never lost sight of my Arab roots. In fact, some boys at that school made sure to remind me as often as they could."

"That was way before nine eleven," Vaughn said. "You were targeted then?"

"Prejudice against Arabs didn't start with nine eleven, Vaughn. Racism has no place or time. I looked different, and I had a funny name. That was enough for some of those boys. Their bullying didn't go on for too long, though."

Vaughn arched his bushy eyebrows. "What happened?"

"I bet he grew big and fast," Khalid said, dismissing Vaughn and levelling a piercing look at Sami. "You couldn't pick up Arabic when you went home on holidays?"

"It was difficult." That was more of an accusation than a desire to know him better. Sami squared his ankle on his knee, rejecting the veiled rebuke. "Dad worked hard, and my mother isn't always on top of things. She has a . . . delicate nature."

Khalid and Faisal exchanged uncomfortable glances.

Sami hid his satisfaction by tugging on the tails of his shirt. A sure way to end this trail of questioning—hint at a mentally-ill mother.

"You are Christian like Sulaiman," Khalid carried on, undeterred. "What church do you follow?"

"My family is Eastern Orthodox."

"So is Mrs. Haddad."

"Around half of Christian Palestinians belong to the Orthodox Church of Jerusalem." Sami spit out the statistic without hesitation, noting the formality Khalid used when he mentioned Petra. "Have to admit, I had no idea there were Kuwaiti Christians." Sami offered his honest thought with a note of caution.

"Fewer than a dozen families," Sulaiman stated.

Khalid turned toward him. "Not if you count the naturalized Christian Arabs who came to Kuwait in the fifties and sixties."

"I'm talking about native Kuwaitis who have been here from long ago."

"But you all stick together, anyway." Khalid's tone hovered between admiration and criticism. "You attract each other, like magnets."

"Isn't that true for all minorities?" Sami suggested. "I mean that happens by necessity everywhere in the world, no matter what the faith."

Sami had no idea where the talk about religion was leading. Sulaiman hadn't mentioned it in their meeting last night. There must be a reason for Khalid to bring it up now. An evaluation tool? The man had no idea how ineffective that would be in Sami's case. He decided to divert the focus away from himself. "Is your family native, Sulaiman?"

Sulaiman adjusted the white cover on his head and checked to see if the middle crease was in line with his nose. "My family hails from Iraq. Happily settled in Kuwait over a hundred years ago."

Sami brought down his raised ankle. Wrong heritage in light of the war history between the two countries.

"And how about you, Khalid?" Vaughn asked.

"Muslim. Sunni. And, yes, native." A slight twitch of Khalid's moustache exposed displeasure. "Originally from *Najd* in Saudi Arabia. My family established a residence here in the early eighteenth century, if you want to be specific."

"Like the ruling family," Vaughn said. The expression on his face showed how pleased he was with his contribution.

Sami tried to shake the feeling that Vaughn managed to make both Khalid and Sulaiman uncomfortable with his casual reference to Kuwait's rulers. And why were the men talking about religion, anyway? What difference did it make to his problem?

Faisal coughed into his fist. "You haven't asked me about my background."

Sensing a trap, Sami remained silent.

"Do tell us," Vaughn chipped in, taking the bait.

Faisal's lips broke into a sideways smile. "I am also considered native, although my family's roots are Iranian. Settled here at least a hundred and fifty years ago. Shiite, of course."

A tense calm hung over the room. Sami pushed his back onto the cushions and stretched his legs. "Interesting history."

Vaughn crossed and uncrossed his ankles, loosened his tie, and opened the button of his collar. He looked borderline terrified rather than embarrassed.

The three men stared at Vaughn for several heartbeats, their faces solemn and serious. Khalid burst out laughing, Faisal followed, and finally Sulaiman.

"You look worried, Vaughn," Khalid said between chuckles.

Vaughn wiped his brow with his palm. "I thought any minute, you'd tear each other apart."

"The sectarian tensions propagated and exaggerated by your western media are nothing but nonsense. Divisions exploited by foreign powers." Khalid's tone turned serious. "We have lived together side by side for many years. Sunni, Shiite, and Christian. No problems." He leaned forward. "Only the uneducated and the weak fall prey to the hatred invading our societies." Amusement danced in Khalid's voice, revealing his satisfaction at Vaughn's rising discomfort.

Sami rolled his armrest closer. "Unfortunately, there are many weak-minded people on all sides of the political spectrum. And they're not only gaining traction—they're gaining momentum."

Vaughn pointed at Sami. "That's what I uh ... meant."

Khalid released a long breath. "Our gathering here is an anomaly these days, I give you that. And back to your point about holding a grudge against Palestinians."

73

Khalid ran a hand down his goatee. "Yes, that was the case for many years after the liberation. But lately, we've seen a favourable shift in people's attitude and even government policy toward the Palestinian people who had nothing to do with what happened."

Sulaiman nodded. "The cruel destiny of Arabs is to suffer the foolishness of some of their leaders."

The conversation died. Sami watched the three men drink more coffee and chew on dates. Were they serious? That was the shortest, most polite political discussion he had ever witnessed. And though he hadn't been to a Gulf state before, he had travelled around the world, seen more political differences than he could count. No one talked that way, expressed opinions as if reading articles from newspapers. No matter how well-educated or enlightened these men were, the differences between them created too many complications, yet they brushed them aside as insignificant and foreign. No one mentioned ISIS or Trump, either. The region around them was exploding, and they chose to ignore the deafening boom.

Who were they kidding? They acted roles, exercised constraint, and extended courtesy. There must be a reason. Was it Vaughn's presence, the American with no Arab roots who forced them into amiable pretence? Was that their way of telling Sami they did not trust Vaughn?

Sami clasped his hands in his lap. Now what? When would Petra join them? He arched his eyebrows at red-faced Vaughn and mouthed Petra's name in silent question.

Vaughn shook his head. Sami kept his mouth shut. The men switched talk to sports. Football, in particular, and once he realized they meant soccer, he had nothing to say about that. Khalid's boys became animated, speaking in Arabic. Their Kuwaiti dialect differed from the Arabic Sami was used to. It sounded a foreign language with longer vowels; the *j*s turned into *y*s and *k*s into *sh*s in the words he could make out. Every now and then, the boys would say something in English—brief phrases in an American accent. Sami recognized a few players' names: Ronaldo, Zidane and Messi, legends as he recalled from sports programmes.

Faisal brought the talk back to English. "What is your sport?"

"Basketball. When I have time. My work schedule gets very hectic." Sami appreciated Faisal's efforts to include him. "When I'm done with a project, there's usually a lull period. I catch up on things, including sports."

"You are older than your brother, yet he ran the business with your father," Sulaiman said. "Usually the oldest son becomes the right hand."

"My brother and I reached an agreement. I don't like being cooped up in an office all day. Working outdoors on construction sites suits me better." Sami locked eyes with Sulaiman. "I have full confidence in

Fareed's abilities to run the business. I'm sure you've seen the finances."

"We've never had an issue we could not resolve to our mutual satisfaction. The government is pushing to rebuild the country and an investment in a construction company is proving to be very beneficial." Sulaiman pointed at Sami. "You have not yet handled a project here. I've learned about your excellent time-management skills, and I respect your thoroughness. I tried to convince your father to bring you on board for the Marina project last spring. We are so far behind schedule that I just fired the chief engineer."

"I was tied up in Costa Rica." Sami saw an opening for what he really wanted to talk about. "But I happen to be in-between projects. I'd be happy to review your development plan and give an opinion." Sami paused, measuring the man's interest. Sulaiman didn't give an indication if he would value a second opinion or not. Sami continued, "If Mrs. Haddad accepts her shares in the company, I will need to stay here and make sure the transition goes smoothly. . . you know, coordinate with the mother ship in Houston."

"And if Sulaiman buys her out?" Khalid asked. "Would you consider taking over the Marina project anyway?"

"In all honesty, it would be difficult. Fareed has a number of proposed projects in the works. I go where he sends me. If I stay, I will certainly give the Marina project serious consideration."

"Perhaps I should consider withdrawing my offer to buy her shares, then." Sulaiman half laughed out his words.

Sami found it difficult to gauge the man's sincerity. It was against his policy to acquire a project mid-construction, not to mention one languishing behind schedule, but if this opportunity jumped at him, he might grab it, as homage to his father. He didn't intend to push Sulaiman into a corner, and he had serious doubts the man was ever pushed into anything. There were undercurrents at play in this meeting, bordering on an orchestrated conspiracy, no doubt planned by Khalid. Sami couldn't see the blueprint with clarity, but he detected the big picture. Khalid was on his side, didn't think Petra should refuse or sell her shares.

A thought struck Sami and he sat up. He wanted Petra to stay on as a partner for another reason that had nothing to do with his father's will. It would be an excuse to see her again, interact with her, solve the nagging mystery of her childhood visits. Perhaps then, the branded little girl would leave him alone, stop her frequent intrusions into his consciousness and allow him to live a normal life, free of hallucinations.

Khalid landed a hand on Faisal's shoulder. "What do you think, my friend?"

"Mrs. Haddad is my client. I will discuss things only with her." Faisal rubbed his belly. "When will we eat?"

The meal ended the meeting. No further talk of business or mention of Petra took place over food. Sami followed the unspoken rules, taking his cue from Faisal, not Vaughn, whose presence he barely noted.

Khalid resumed his interrogation. "You are single?"

"Absolutely!" Sami regretted showing his exhilaration at the idea. Perhaps they gave more weight to a married man, or one who *wanted* to be married. A family man would be more trustworthy and dependable. He toned down his response. "I haven't been fortunate enough to find the right woman, yet."

"The right woman will not fall in your lap out of the sky. You have to seek her, find her."

"No time for romance."

"What about children? Don't you want any?"

Sami took a long sip of water to steal a moment. He didn't want to be insincere with men trying to look after Petra's best interests. But how could he explain his fear of passing on his mother's damaged genes to his children? Fareed had failed to see the full picture, fallen in love and plunged into family life without reservation. He, on the other hand, was handed a different looking glass, a magnifier, and his heart was void of the blind courage that came with love.

Sami put down his glass. "I don't think it's fair to have children at this stage in my life. Me being away from home most of the time is not a good formula for a healthy family."

Khalid hugged his boys to his sides. "Are you content living alone?"

"I have my nieces. Twins. They're absolutely amazing. I love being the spoiling uncle when I'm home."

Khalid switched the conversation to weather and fishing. Sami rode the wave with reserve. Had he passed the man's tests? He gave up on expecting Petra to join them mid-meal, realizing the male-only nature of this gathering.

At the door to the *Deewaniah*, separate from the main house entrance, Khalid shook hands with his guests. Sami walked out with Faisal. Vaughn went to the car.

"I will discuss matters with Mrs. Haddad and give you a call in the morning." Faisal shook Sami's hand.

"Wouldn't that be cutting it close to the deadline?"

"If she agrees, you will come to my office tomorrow morning. I will have a public notary witness her signatures. Trust me, everything will be ready."

"And if she doesn't agree?"

"Vaughn will trigger the necessary arrangements for the alternative."

"Any chance I could talk to Mrs. Haddad?" Sami hesitated, feeling silly asking permission to see the woman. "In person?"

"If she wants to talk to you, she will call you."

Sami headed to the car. He hated indecision and waiting for something to happen. And he hated waiting for a stranger to make a decision that would affect his family's future to a significant degree. What was to stop him from showing up on the woman's doorstep?

He got into the car with Vaughn and buckled his seatbelt. "You have her address, right?"

"Mrs. Haddad?" Vaughn frowned. "We can't go to her place."

"We'll call ahead."

"That won't matter. It's just not done here." Vaughn eased the car into traffic. "She lives alone with her son in an apartment. She has neighbours. We can't visit if there isn't a male relative present."

Sami exhaled. "Fine. I'll call and invite her out for coffee."

"That won't work, either. To be seen in public alone with a single man is also unacceptable."

"You'll be with us."

"I'm another man. A foreigner. That's worse."

Sami slammed his fist to the dashboard. "Goddamn it, I must talk to her."

"There are ways. If she is accompanied by a family or a couple." Vaughn drew out his words, as if formulating the plan while he spoke. "I know she doesn't have family here. Khalid, Sulaiman and Faisal are out of the question. I'm sure she has close friends she could rely on."

"What's her number? I'll call."

"You have your eye on her?" Vaughn shook his head. "Bad idea."

"What the hell are you talking about?" Sami hated losing control, and this man pushed at his limits. So now the asshole was an expert on social standards in Kuwait? What a cruel joke. "I want to explain things, that's all."

Then it hit him. Why did Vaughn say that? What else did he know about Petra? Sami forced himself to calm down. "Timewise, I've ruled out the possibility she's my half-sister. Am I wrong?"

"You're not. Your father made that very clear to me when I voiced my suspicion. That's not the reason I'm advising you to stay away. We should concentrate on business."

"That's what I plan to do," Sami said in a firm tone that could not be misunderstood.

"Let me call her, then. I got her to agree to the meeting in Faisal's office, remember? It's less personal that way. More professional. You can trust me on this."

Sami chewed the inside of his cheek, adding another item on his list against Vaughn. He had sat like a piece of furniture in the meeting, and when he spoke, spewed nothing but provocations. Now he decided to assume control? Trusting Vaughn was the last thing he intended to do.

"Never mind. It's best to wait until tomorrow." Sami ran his hand through his hair. "Let her lawyer handle it. Don't overwhelm her today. She has a lot to think about."

Vaughn nodded. "Good. Until tomorrow, then."

Sami entered his hotel room, grabbed a bottle of water and looked out of his window. Trees lined the streets below. He had stretched the truth to those men in the *Deewaniah* meeting. His father hadn't talked much about his early life in Kuwait, or perhaps he had and Sami didn't recall the stories. In the very few father to son talks he remembered, his father had painted a bleak picture of a desert city without much greenery. These flourishing trees presented a strange alternative to the scene he had imagined before setting foot in Kuwait.

The little girl with the arrow birthmark showed up in his window. She put her hands over her eyes and counted aloud numbers out of order—one, two, seven, ten, four. She removed her hands, twirled in circles, and chimed, *Pita Bread is coming to get you!*

Sami blinked. The little girl smiled. He smiled back and traced the dotted arrow on her forehead with his finger. The little girl giggled and disappeared.

Sami took a long sip of water and concentrated on a small array of stars clustered north of the crescent moon. He didn't require Vaughn's interference or finesse. Other than a taxi, or better yet, a rental car, everything he needed to reach Petra was in the folder Vaughn had given him.

CHAPTER EIGHT

Elias blew into the white foam blob on his arm. "Mama, what are bubbles made from?"

"Soap and water." Petra sat on the floor by the bathtub and blew into a wand dipped in soap solution. Big colourful spheres saturated the bathroom.

"This soap is sticky and yucky." He grabbed at a big bubble floating above the faucet. "Bubbles are light. They fly, mama."

"That's because they're full of air." She pulled the plug. "Bubbles don't fly, Elias. They float." She held a bath towel out for him. "Come on. Bath time is over."

Elias got to his feet, froth stuck to his legs from the knees down. "How does air go inside them, mama?"

She used his Spiderman cup to wash his legs, wrapped him with the towel, and carried him out of the tub. "Didn't you know?"

"What, mama?"

She rubbed him dry and helped him into his pyjamas, loving the way he always started or ended his speech with the word *mama*, as if there were other people in the room and he needed to call her to get her attention.

"Bubbles have magic powers, they trap air inside."

"Like a prison, mama?"

She ran the towel over his wet auburn hair. "Set air free and pop those bubbles on your way to the kitchen. It's dinner time."

Elias swiped a hand at a huge bubble the size of his head. "Mama, what's for dinner?"

"Mac and cheese."

"Mac and cheese? Mac and cheese!" He squeaked and hopped to the door, his excitement too exaggerated a response for the mundane meal. But he did that every time she served it, taking away some of her guilt for the artificially-coloured, nutrition-lacking dish.

Elias had napped on the way home from Mouzah's place, waking with a burst of energy once they arrived. He kept her busy throughout the afternoon. Now she needed to put him to bed to contemplate Mr. Faisal's recommendations and Khalid's assessment of Sami Amara.

She had spotted Sami leaving the *Deewaniah* from Mouzah's living room window after lunch. Casually dressed, he seemed younger and less burdened than the man she had met the day before. Khalid spoke of him with reserve, but she could tell he had a favourable view of Sami's character. Khalid said it was refreshing to meet an honest man, one who cared about moral commitments more than money. A man who saw matters with the clarity of a hawk's eye.

She served Spiderman-shaped pasta and added steamed broccoli. It made her feel better, although

Elias would not touch the vegetable. After several bites, Elias rolled his head from side to side and teetered on the edge of his chair.

She grasped his shoulders. "Are you dizzy, *ya albi*?"

"I'm a prisoner inside a bubble. I'm not your heart, mama."

Having had her mother for so little time in her life, Petra treasured the few things that stuck in her memory, including those Arabic terms of endearment denoting her mother's heart, life, and soul. Her mother learned very little Arabic from Petra's father and called her by those expressions instead of using her name. Petra cherished the safety generated by that form of speech. It filtered into her way of addressing Elias, and she loved that he took it literally.

She poked his forehead. "There, I set you free."

He bolted off the chair and waved his hands in the air. "Mama, where does air go when it's out of the bubble?"

"To brush its teeth, of course." She pointed to the bathroom. "I'll come tuck you in once you're done." She wiggled two fingers. "Remember, flip the sand clock twice while you brush."

Petra cleared the table. The phone rang. She cradled the cordless handset by her ear to finish washing dishes.

"Good evening, Mrs. Haddad. Sami Amara here."

Jolted by his scratchy voice, the phone handset

slipped and she caught it before it plunged under the water. She put it to her ear again. "Mr. Amara?"

"Did I call at a bad time?"

She turned off the water and stepped away from the sink. "It's fine."

"I need to talk to you before you make any decisions. Can you meet me for a cup of coffee or tea—anywhere you choose?"

"I can't." She went into the bathroom and checked the sink faucet. Elias ran out of the bathroom and almost tripped on the runner in the hallway.

"I'm told this is slightly non-decorous," Sami said. "I mean no disrespect. Half an hour is all I'm asking for."

"I don't know who told you that, Mr. Amara. It's not that backward here." Petra waved at Elias to slow down and go to his bedroom. "I can't meet you anywhere on account of my son."

Elias lunged under the blanket on his bed, curled into a ball, and rolled from side to side. "Mama, look. I'm catched inside a bubble. Come pop it again."

She smoothed the edges of the scrunched runner on her way to catch up with Elias. "I'm about to put him in bed, Mr. Amara."

"My apologies for the inconvenience. I'm downstairs in the entrance hall of your building. May I come up?"

Petra stopped in the hallway. "Mr. Amara, whatever you have to say to me can wait until we—"

Elias rolled off his bed and smacked his head on the bedside table. She dropped the phone and ran to pick him up. Blood covered his face and dripped off his chin.

"Elias! Oh, God! Elias!" Hands shaking, she bundled him with the blanket and dashed to the front door and outside onto the landing.

Sami skidded to a stop before her on the landing. "I heard you scream," he panted.

"My son's hurt." She pushed past him, no time to wait for the elevator. "I need to get him to a hospital."

Sami bolted ahead. "I'll drive. Just tell me where."

He opened the door to his car and waited for Petra to climb in. She cradled her son's limp body on her lap. Elias made a choking sound. His eyes rolled back in his head.

"No!" she screeched.

Sami lifted Elias higher in her lap. "Keep his head elevated and his airways clear."

Warm blood soaked her boy's hair and face. "I can't see . . . where the blood's coming from."

Sami yanked off his dress shirt, bundled it, and pressed it to the top of Elias's head. "There. Keep the pressure on."

"Please hurry! First exit after the fire station gets you to the freeway." She rubbed Elias's neck and shoulders to keep him warm and tried to control her panic. Street signs blurred behind her tears. She couldn't direct Sami to the right turns.

Sami made a sharp U-turn and slammed the breaks before a hospital entrance.

"Keep driving." Her voice shook. "They won't take us in this hospital."

"Sure they will. There's an ER."

"This hospital is for Kuwaitis only," she screamed. "There's another one south of here. Please go."

"I don't fricking believe this." Sami took off. He arrived at an intersection. "Left or right?"

"Left." She looked around, confused. "Wait, no. I think—"

"Never mind. I see it." Sami turned right, stopped the car, and jumped out. He lifted Elias from her hands and ran into the emergency room. She ran after him.

Hospital staff took Elias and disappeared through metal doors. Yelling, Petra pushed at the doors. "I'm his mother. He needs me."

A nurse came out from a side door and spoke in Arabic.

Petra grabbed her hand. "Please. I don't speak Arabic. Please, I need to be with my son."

"You cannot go in now." The nurse freed her hand and patted Petra's shoulder. "They will stop the bleeding, then a doctor will come out to talk to you." She retreated behind the door.

Petra clutched the door handle before it closed. "He has a heart condition." She slipped a medical bracelet off her wrist and handed it to the nurse. "I must explain it to the doctor."

The nurse took the bracelet and examined it. "I will tell the doctor, don't worry." She looked past Petra toward Sami. "*Iza mumkin*, wait here."

Sami held Petra's elbow. "Let them do their job." He led her to a chair. "Does your son have a specialist you can call to communicate with the doctors here?"

"Oh, God! Yes. I must call doctor Iman."

Sami sat by her side and handed her his phone. She misdialled a couple of times, her fingers trembling, stained a deep red. She burst out crying mid-conversation, and Sami took the phone to tell the doctor which hospital they were in.

The tense wait became unbearable. Good thing Dr. Iman had suggested that both she and Elias wear the medical bracelet at all times. Most of the medical staff members were not used to this alert method, and they might have missed the one on his wrist. Petra wrapped her arms around her waist and bent forward, trying to keep herself calm. Where were her shoes? Had she run out of the apartment barefoot to Sami's car? She turned to the quiet man at her side, feet planted apart, elbows on his thighs, his white undershirt stained with her son's blood.

"Than—" She cleared the lump in her throat, "thank you."

"Boys are more resilient than mothers think. Your son will be all right."

She shook her head, trying to clear the image of Elias's blood-soaked face. "Why won't they let me in? Elias is only six. He must be very scared."

Sami nodded. "At least your child is not by himself." As soon as he said the words, Sami drew a sharp breath and jerked upward in his seat. "Elias is surrounded by doctors and nurses who will—"

Dr. Iman stepped in and Petra ran to talk to her. She followed her to a nurse's station at the end of the hall and listened to her confer on the phone with the doctor tending to Elias. Petra lost track of Sami. When Dr. Iman went inside to check on Elias, Petra remained behind once again, relieved her son's cardiologist would handle his treatment.

This was a private hospital, one she hadn't been to before, and she didn't know any of the staff. No one to give her feedback about her son's condition. Shivering, she slumped on her chair and closed her eyes.

Should she call Mouzah? Her friend would come over. Knowing her brutal honesty, Mouzah would spell out Elias's poor condition using some colloquial saying Petra couldn't understand. She didn't have the energy now to swipe aside negative remarks. What she needed was unconditional support, a shoulder to lean on, a family member who would hold her and comfort her. She had no one.

She opened her eyes and was struck to see Sami sitting opposite her.

"You're still here?"

"You looked like you were in prayer or meditation. I didn't want to disturb you." He opened a plastic bag by his feet. "I got you slippers from the gift shop." He held out a pair of fuzzy yellow slippers with orange duck beaks. He winced with a crooked smile. "Maternity section."

She hugged the slippers to her chest, crying aloud at this point. He took the slippers from her hands and knelt down. "These go on your feet." He slid the shoes over her cold toes. "Head injuries bleed a lot because blood vessels under the skin don't have the protection of a fat layer. It doesn't necessarily mean the injury is bad."

"How do you—" her voice broke, "—know that?"

Returning to his seat, he pushed back his short bangs and exposed a two-inch scar close to his hairline. "Houdini stunt gone bad. I was seven." He opened a tub of wet wipes and pulled one out. "Alcohol based. May I?"

She stared at him, confused.

He pointed at her hands. "To wipe off the blood stains. So you can hold your son when he wakes without scaring him?"

She extended her hands. He took his time scrubbing them clean, his gentle motions a massage distracting her from watching the clock. Her shaking subsided. "How did it end?"

"Excuse me?"

"Your Houdini stunt."

He let go of her hands. "My father rescued me."

The side door opened. Petra jumped to her feet. Her slippers quacked.

Dr. Iman approached with a smile on her face. "Elias is doing very well in the recovery room. He has nine stitches." She ran her fingers along the top of Petra's head. "Here. His face is swollen and there are bruises around his eyes from the pressure and the trauma. There should be no lasting damage."

Petra placed her hand to her chest and opened her mouth. Dr. Iman cut her off before she asked anything. "No complications because of his heart. They will keep him in overnight to watch for signs of a concussion. I have to leave now. Elias is still sedated, but you can see him." The doctor glanced at Sami. "Your friend can go in, too."

Without hesitation, Petra grabbed Sami's hand. "Please come with me."

CHAPTER NINE

Sami leaned against the wall, careful to steer away from switches and medical equipment in the small room. His heart drummed madly, and he concentrated on one of the beeping monitors to tame it. Avoiding cramped places was a challenge, but denying this woman's request for his support was impossible. To alleviate his angst, he imagined himself standing by the seashore, nothing but blue water and open sky before him.

Petra approached her sleeping son with caution, sliding both feet along the floor to keep from making noise. Her delicate fingers swiped hair off the boy's forehead, avoiding the bulky bandage around his head.

The nurse they followed into the room parted a heavy curtain concealing another bed. "This is Doctor Musa. He looked after your son."

The doctor turned away from the adjacent patient, who seemed to be asleep. Dr. Musa barely made eye contact with Petra and directed his gaze at Sami. "You have a very *b-e-rave* boy. He has a surface cut on his scalp *th-e-ree* centimetres long." Dr. Musa spoke English with an Egyptian accent, stressing his 'r's and constantly inserting 'e's where they didn't belong. Sami's college roommate his sophomore year had been from Egypt, and he recognized the particular musical inflection.

"The stitches we used should dissolve on their *ow-e-n* in a week. We will-*e* remove the bandage the day after tomorrow in the *k-e-linic*." Dr. Musa flipped open a chart, wrote something, and handed the chart to the nurse. "*Doctorah* Iman and I consulted over his condition. I will *p-e-rescribe* something for headaches that does not interfere with his other medications."

Petra rubbed her son's hand. "How much longer before he wakes up?"

"Very soon. I gave him a *mild-e* sedative after I was done stitching the wound. I needed him to be alert as *much-e* as possible." The doctor shook his head and addressed Sami. "No signs of concussion. So you can take him home."

"Tonight?"

"Yes. Yes. Your boy is fine. Keep the bandage *d-e-ry* until it is off."

"Thank you." Petra bent over the bed and held her boy's hands, her eyes never leaving his bruised face.

The nurse held the door open for the doctor. On his way out, he stuck his hand out for a handshake. Sami shook it, but the doctor didn't let go and signalled with his head for Sami to follow him out of the room.

"How did this happen?" Dr. Musa asked as soon as the door closed behind them.

Sami had no idea. Shit! The doctor's tone was suspicious. Although Sami hadn't seen what happened, he was sure Petra hadn't harmed her son. She had been on the phone telling him she was getting the boy ready for the night.

He looked the doctor in the eye. "Jumping on the bed."

Dr. Musa scratched his thick beard. "You should *child-e* proof his room. He will do it again no matter how many times you tell him not to. Believe me, I know. I have *th-e-ree* boys." The doctor headed down the hall and threw over his shoulder, "bring your son on Thursday to take *off-e* the bandage."

Sami blinked. *Your son?* No, no, no. He should set the doctor straight. But Dr. Musa was gone. Sami looked through the small rectangular window in the door. Petra remained frozen over the bed in that awkward position—arms extended around her son, back arched, and head thrust forward. The florescent light overhead reflected off shiny equipment and cast a strange bright white halo around her.

Sami tilted his head to one side and the circle of light disappeared. Great! As if his hallucinations of her as a child weren't enough to make him view himself a lunatic. He rested his forehead on the cold glass. What the hell was he doing here? This wasn't his affair. He knew nothing of the kind of agony a mother went through in such a situation. Petra needed support, and he was in no position to give it—the wrong man to provide help on so many levels. He pulled away from the window. A mother with a sick child shouldn't be alone, he knew that much.

He looked at his blood-stained undershirt. At the gift shop, there had been nothing other than women and baby stuff. No menswear. Dropping the shopping bag to the floor, he lifted the tail of his undershirt out of his trousers, slipped his arms free, and turned the shirt around so the blood stain rested on his back. He eased into the room as quietly as he could manage.

Petra ignored him, or perhaps she didn't notice him, her full attention pinned on her son. Sami checked his watch. Ten minutes passed. Elias made a sound. Petra shot her hand out behind her. "Look. He's waking up."

Surprised by her calling him, Sami grabbed her hand. She drew him closer to the bed and let go. The boy groaned and opened swollen eyelids.

"You're in the hospital," she whispered. "You hit your head on the nightstand."

"Mama, it hurts."

Petra patted his hand. "I know, *ya rohi*. Your head will hurt for a while."

"First day of school, mama."

"You won't miss it. You'll be well enough when school starts. Don't worry, *ya rohi*."

Elias slanted his lips in an attempt at a smile. "Mama, I'm not your soul. I'm your son."

Tears ran down Petra's face. She nodded. "You're both."

At a loss, Sami stared on, bracing himself for the emotional train speeding his way. The obvious relief this boy showed the instant he saw his mother struck hard. Sami had blocked most of his twisted childhood events, but the accompanying feelings were always present—sharp, persistent, and screwing with his life. He never sought his mother's comfort, never experienced serenity in her company. He shifted in his spot, annoyed by his emotional regression—a grown man missing his mama. He had lost track of Petra's conversation with her son.

Elias looked up at him. "Are you a doctor?"

Sami glanced at Petra, wondering how to respond. "I'm a friend of your mother."

"A teacher like mama?"

"Mr. Amara is . . ." Petra arched her eyebrows at Sami.

He completed her sentence, "An engineer."

"What's that?" Elias asked.

"I design . . . uh, put things together to make buildings and other stuff."

"He helped me bring you to this hospital." Petra winked at her son. "You should thank him."

"Thank you." Elias's lips quivered. "My head hurts, mama."

As if on cue, the nurse walked in with a needle in her hand. "Time for medicine."

Fear gripped Elias. His puffy eyelids closed, his jaw clenched. He turned away from the nurse.

Petra kissed his hands. "Time to be brave. The needle will hurt a little."

"I know," the boy choked.

"It'll be fast and the medicine will take away the pain in your head."

Elias started to cry.

Sami held his hand out to the nurse. "Can you give us a minute?" He leaned in to face Elias. "Who is your favorite superhero?"

"Spiderman."

"Spiderman is great. Mine is Batman. You know why?"

Elias sniffed. "He has a Batmobile?"

"That, and because he doesn't have super powers like his friends. He's a regular guy who faces danger when he goes after bad people. A brave man. Thinking of him helped me when I was little and hurt like you."

"Do you have sick pieces in your heart, too?"

"No, but I got in trouble all the time." Sami dug a stuffed Batman from his shopping bag. "Can you try to be brave like Batman for the nurse?"

Elias freed his hands from his mother's grip and hugged Batman to his chest. "Okay." He turned to the nurse. "I am ready now." He scrunched his face and held his breath.

The nurse worked fast. "You can take him home after you've completed papers and finalized payment."

Petra kissed Elias on the cheek. "I'll be right back." She tucked a strand of hair behind her ears, exposing more of the arrow on her forehead.

Sami drew a long breath, seeing her birthmark, his secret beckoning. It demanded his full attention, not that it needed to. He was already attuned to every move, every sound Petra made.

"May I borrow your phone again?" Grabbing the mobile, she headed out of the room.

Sami hurried after her before the door closed. "Please allow me to cover the hospital bill. You don't have your bag and whoever you're calling will take time to get here. I'm sure you want Elias home sooner rather than later."

Petra's hand hovered over the keypad. "I couldn't possibly let you do that, Mr. Amara."

"Sami. Just Sami." He leaned his shoulder on the doorjamb, keeping the door ajar with his foot. "Let me help."

"You've done a lot." She punched numbers and put the phone to her ear. "I'm calling Khalid. He can probably settle this over the phone." Several seconds passed, and she ended the call. "Straight to voice mail. I'll try his wife's number."

Shuffling in her duck slippers, Petra did complete circles where she stood. The hem of her ruffled skirt billowed around her ankles, making her resemble a Sufi Turkish dancer whirling in a trance.

"No answer." She stopped, checked her watch and looked past Sami through the open door. "It's late. If I call the house, I'll wake up the children." She pursed her lips to the side, talking to herself. "I'd rather not call Richard."

Sami straightened. Who was Richard? And why did he care to know?

"Consider it a loan?" he offered.

Elias called out for her.

Petra handed Sami the phone. "I'll pay you back as soon as I can get to the bank in the morning."

Sami lifted drowsy Elias out of Petra's arms and waited for her to leave the car. An old woman rushed over. "I saw you from my window running out earlier. I called many times."

"Elias had an accident, Maryam. We took him to the hospital." Petra patted the woman's shoulder. "He's okay."

"*Hamdillah*. I was so worried. What happened?"

"He hit his head on the nightstand." Petra reached for Elias. He groaned, buried his face in Sami's neck, and hugged Batman closer.

"Who is this?" Maryam asked.

"Sami Amara is a family friend." Petra dropped her hands. "This is my neighbour, Madam Maryam Fua'adah."

"Ma'am," Sami nodded down at the old woman. Her head barely reached his waist, and he felt like a giant standing before her. Bald spots hidden by her thinning hair shone under the full moon.

"Family? I see." The woman put her hands on Sami's waist and tried to push him. "Well, come on. Let us put this boy in bed."

Sami tried to keep a straight face. Maryam's efforts did nothing but tickle him. He connected eyes with Petra. She nodded and went into the building.

Sami shifted Elias in his arms and headed to the stairs. "You two take the elevator. I'll meet you upstairs."

"We can all fit, *chéri*." Maryam kept the doors open. She waved a wrinkled hand. "*Vien ici*. Come, come."

He gritted his teeth and squeezed in with them.

"So what is the family relationship?" Maryam asked.

"He's not family," Petra said.

"Yes, I understand he's family, *chéri*. Is he your cousin?"

"Not. *Not family*, Maryam." Petra raised her voice and Elias stirred on Sami's shoulder.

"Oh, your mother's family?" The woman insisted. "So he must be American." She looked up at Sami. "My eldest son lives in Chicago. Dr. Fahmy Fua'adah. Do you know him?"

"No, ma'am."

"He keeps asking me to go to America and live with him. I stayed for six months. They were enough for me.

Never liked that kind of fast life." Maryam waved her hand, dotted with big brown patches. "Always busy, running after the dollar. And the snow . . . too much snow. Perhaps you've heard of him? Fahmy is the president of the American Lebanese Medical Association chapter in Chicago."

"Mr. Amara doesn't live in Chicago." Petra's effort to show patience was obvious in her tone, though she kept her voice down for her boy's sake.

"Yes, Chicago. Close to Milwaukee. Your mother's family is from Milwaukee, right?"

Petra sighed and nodded, evidently abandoning the idea of setting the woman straight about Sami.

"And when did you come to Kuwait, young man?"

"Recently," Sami resigned himself to leaving hard-of-hearing Maryam in the dark. If Petra had given up on correcting her, he would keep his mouth shut. Crowded in the small space, he was struggling to maintain a steady heart rate to begin with, and the old woman's one-sided conversation was not amusing. The elevator doors opened and he followed Petra into her apartment, Maryam right after.

"This way, please." Petra headed to a room and switched on the light.

Sami stood at the threshold. This wasn't the boy's room. It was hers, with a queen size bed, a matching dresser, and a stand-alone mirror.

Petra snatched a black nightgown off the bed and peeled back purple covers. "Set him down here, please.

103

I want to keep an eye on him through the night." She tucked in Elias and his Batman and placed a couple of pillows against the nightstand by his side. "He turns a lot in his sleep," she whispered.

"Should I pull back the nightstand?"

"That's a good idea."

Sami dragged the heavy nightstand as far as the space allowed. A silver picture frame fell face down. He set it right to see Petra in a wedding gown standing arm in arm with a burly man sporting a full beard.

"Oh, *mon Dior*! Look at this mess," Maryam said from the hallway behind him.

Sami ignored the old woman. "Maybe you should put pillows on the floor in case Elias rolls off?" he offered, knowing he should leave Petra to it, but he couldn't make himself walk out.

Petra opened her wardrobe and pulled out a couple of pillows from the top shelf. "I won't fall asleep. You're right, though." She spread the pillows on the floor. "Better be safe."

Scanning the room, he caught small details—private and intimate. Scattered on the dresser: a glass fish-shaped figurine draped with hair ties, a clear spray bottle, hairbrushes, and a blow dryer. Colourful belts and scarves dangled off the corners of the stand-alone mirror. A book lay open face down on the other nightstand. He tried to read the upside-down title: *Something* Heights.

Petra sat on the bed and kissed her son's forehead, whispering something. Elias reached for her, and she slipped under the covers next to him.

Sami backed out of the room into the hallway. He followed droplets of blood to the boy's room. Maryam was stripping Spiderman linen off the bed.

"Help me, young man. These old hands don't work fast anymore."

Sami did his best to help and mopped blood off the floor, all the while wondering why he was still there. He should leave. In the kitchen, he stuffed the soiled towels and linens into a plastic bag. Maryam's hands tickled his waist again.

"Your shirt has blood stains. Take it off."

He tried his best to be polite and step out of her reach. "It's fine."

Petra walked in. "He's finally asleep. Thank you for cleaning up. You didn't have to do all that."

Maryam tried to push Petra out of the kitchen. "Go bring him a clean shirt, *chéri*. Don't you have any of your husband's tucked away?"

Petra froze.

"I'd better go." Sami passed the women and headed to the front door.

Petra caught up with him. "I can't thank you enough, Mr. Amara."

"No need." His hand paused on the door handle. "And please call me Sami."

"You came here tonight wanting to talk about your father's will. Is there more I need to know?"

"Don't worry about that now. We have time." He stepped out. "I left my personal number on the fridge. Please don't hesitate to call should you need anything."

"I'll be at Mr. Faisal's office at nine to go over everything."

Sami hesitated. He searched her tired face, pale and smudged with tears. "You sure?"

She nodded. "My son . . ." She swallowed and took a deep breath. "It could have been worse. I want to give thanks."

"I just happened to be here at the right time."

"I'm giving thanks to God." Petra started to close the door. "Mercy should always be reciprocated in acts of kindness."

CHAPTER TEN

Petra signed the last document and slid it across the table to Mr. Faisal. He added it to a stack in a file and handed the folder to his assistant. From the moment she had stepped into her lawyer's office, Sami was silent. He stood by the window and listened to legal jargon. This must be very hard on him, transferring a good portion of his father's company in Kuwait into her name.

Every now and then, she noticed him staring out of the window. No matter how noble his desire was to honour his father's wishes, this must sting. Yet, he didn't put up a fight. Were other, more compelling reasons driving him? What skeletons did this man hide?

Mr. Faisal shook Vaughn's hand. "Everything is set in motion now. I will have a notarized final copy delivered to your office before noon."

"Very well." Vaughn turned to Petra. "You've made a wise decision, Mrs. Haddad."

Mr. Faisal nodded. "A sound investment."

Sami peeled his shoulder off the windowpane. "A kind act." His rough voice mismatched his words.

Petra uncrossed her legs and smoothed her skirt. Was he mocking her? She hid a pang of discomfort by checking her watch. "If nothing else is required, I need to go."

"I'll walk you to your car." Sami held the door open and turned to Vaughn. "Email me a copy of those finalized documents. I want to read them before you file."

"Don't worry," Vaughn huffed, advancing. "I'll take care of everything."

"I'm new to this side of the business." Sami placed a hand on Vaughn's shoulder. "Indulge me."

Petra walked out to the hallway, paying attention to the obvious mistrust between Sami and Vaughn.

Sami closed the door behind him to join her. "How's the brave boy?"

"Elias had a rough night. But he's better this morning. Maryam is keeping an eye on him."

"Sure that's a good idea?" Sami scratched his head. "I don't mean to interfere in your business. But the woman can't hear a darn thing."

"He's watching Batman cartoons in bed. It's fine for an hour. I'm heading home."

Sami pointed at the hallway behind them. "I appreciate your cooperation on the shares transfer. It makes life a lot easier for many of our people."

"I hope so."

They reached the elevators and waited for the doors to open. She studied Sami's profile, jaw clenched, skin darkened by unshaven stubble. He was so approachable and kind last night, but miles away today. Stepping into the elevator, she dug into her bag and pulled out an envelope.

"Thank you for your help yesterday. This is what I owe you for the hospital bill. Kuwaiti dinars."

"You didn't need to bother so quickly."

"I'm not used to having debts. If you'd rather I pay in dollars, I'd be happy to make an exchange."

Sami slipped the envelope into his jacket pocket. "It's fine. I have something for you, too." He produced a wrapped rectangular gift box.

"What's this for?"

"To replace your sunglasses. I didn't know which brand they were, so I chose something similar." He extended his hand. "I, too, don't like to owe anyone anything."

"But I can't—"

The elevator doors opened, and a group of men joined them. Backing into a corner, she slipped the box into her bag. The men crowded them, speaking fast in Arabic, as if arguing. With Sami's head several inches above the others, she could see his deep scowl. His forehead glistened with perspiration. Did he still have a stomach ache from that airplane meal?

The men left at the ninth floor. Sami briefly closed his eyes and exhaled.

She searched for something to distract him from whatever caused his misery. "You said your father never mentioned my father's name. Did he ever say anything about my mother?"

Sami pressed his hands to the walls on either side of him and lifted his head toward the ceiling. "No."

Her mobile rang as the doors opened to the lobby. She answered the call, walking fast to keep up with Sami striding out of the building.

"Are you on your way?" Richard's tone was urgent.

"To school?"

"Ten o'clock meeting. Remember?"

She slowed her pace and cupped a hand over her other ear to block traffic noise. "I'm afraid I won't be able to make it."

"But the minister's wife is on her way to check out the school. She expects to meet her son's teachers. You've got to be here, Petra."

She checked the time. Making it to school across town in morning traffic could take another hour. Too long to leave Elias alone with Maryam. She softened her tone and dropped the formalities, resorting to that feminine power her principal had no problem praising yesterday. "I really can't, Richard."

Sami stopped, and she almost bumped into him.

Richard exhaled into the phone. "Forget the general staff meeting. Just come to my office to see the minister's wife. Ten minutes, no more. I'm counting on you to be here."

"Let me call you back."

Sami shoved his hands in his trouser pockets. "Something the matter?"

She shook her head. "Work."

She returned inside the building to escape the heat, Sami on her heels. She dialled Mouzah's number.

"Salam, Petra," Mouzah's cheerful voice greeted. Loud humming and swishing noises overlapped in the background.

"I can barely hear you," Petra said. "Where are you?"

"I'm on a boat to Failaka... mother-in-law... party."

Petra raised her voice. "Failaka, the island?"

"Yes. Bad reception. Khalid's mother... birthday. Spending... day there. *Aloo?* Can you hear me?"

"Have fun. Call me tomorrow."

"Wait, how did it... with Faisal?"

"Everything's done. Tell Khalid I'll fill him in later. Enjoy your time."

Petra chewed her lip. She should have informed Mouzah about what had happened to Elias last night, but she didn't want to come out whiny and pathetic. Now her friend was inaccessible. She dialled home and waited through several rings. "Come on, Maryam. Please pick up."

"She probably can't hear the phone," Sami said.

Petra gave him her back. The machine beeped. Maryam talked through the greeting message. "*Aloo? Aloo?*"

"It's Petra."

"She is not available."

"Maryam, it's me, Petra."

"You sound so different, *chéri.* "

"It's because of the answering machine." Petra pulled on her ponytail. "Ignore it, Maryam. How's Elias?"

"He is not playing with any machines. Elias is watching TV."

Breathing a sigh of relief, Petra walked out to the street again. "I'll be home soon."

"Take your time. I'm going to lie down for my nap, now."

"Please don't do that, Maryam. I'm on my way." She hung up and hurried to the garage, Sami still on her heels.

Her phone rang again. She skipped the greeting. "Richard, it's not going to happen. Tell the minister's wife I'm sorry, I can't come in."

"This could cost us the endowment."

"Fine! Fire me if it'll make her happy." She ended the call and tried to shove her mobile into her bag. The phone clattered onto the cement and split into several pieces.

"Oh, shoot!" Petra stopped in her tracks.

Sami collected the scattered parts. "Take it easy."

Worried and thrown off balance, she half-screamed, "I don't have time to deal with this."

He touched her elbow. "Just hold on a moment. Tell me what's going on. I can help."

"I'm a horrible mother—that's what's going on. I left my sick child in the care of a woman who can't hear him if he cries and she's about to take a nap! The only friend I trust is miles away on an island."

"And this Richard guy? What does he want?"

Petra waved a dismissive hand in the air. "Richard Frost is my principal." She fumbled with her car keys. "He wants me to meet the wife of the minister of finance, today—at school. Their son's going to be in my class this year."

Her hands shook, the keys jingled against the car door. Richard's quest for her support was starting to grow tiresome, he whined as if no one else mattered in this world other than the minister's precious son. She expelled a lengthy breath. Why wouldn't the car door open? And why was she telling Sami all this?

Sami put his hand over hers. "You drive a Honda Civic, right?"

She blinked, then nodded.

"This is a Toyota." He pointed behind her. "I think your car is parked over there."

"Oh, God!"

"Listen. You go to your meeting. I'll stay with Elias and Maryam until you're back." He took her keys. "You have little reason to trust me with your son, so I'll make sure the old woman stays awake."

"I . . . it's not that. I can't . . . ask you to—"

"You're not asking. I know what it's like. To feel trapped." He gave her his phone. "Here. I'll call you from your place when I get there. Stay with Elias on the line the whole time you're gone so you can hear everything." He opened her car door and returned the keys. "I already feel horrible for making you leave your son to attend to business. I'll never forgive myself if you lose your job over this."

She shook her head. "Richard won't fire me." It wouldn't come to that. She calmed down a notch and weighed her options. She needed the minister's wife on her side when she dealt with the woman's teenage son, considering her principal's eager-to-please attitude.

And Sami had showed tenderness toward Elias last night. He would be more attentive than Maryam. This man stood before her, clearly concerned about her and her child. How long had it been since she had that?

Petra slipped behind the wheel. "Two hours are all I need. Hopefully less." She removed her house key from the keychain. "Here. In case Maryam doesn't hear the doorbell. I'll call her to let her know you're on your way."

"Let's hope she picks up. I don't want to walk in and scare her."

Before and after her meeting, Petra kept Elias on the phone until he asked her to hang up so he could play with his new friend. Arriving home, she rang the doorbell and waited. Elias's laughter rang louder than the doorbell.

Maryam let her in. "Good! You are home. I have been dealing with two children, not one."

Elias hopped over to give her a hug. "Look, mama. Uncle Sam and I made a Batmobile from Legos." His excitement matched his reaction to her mac and cheese. He dragged her through the living room. Sami's suit jacket lay crumpled on the couch, and she resisted stopping to drape it over properly. By the window, Sami lounged on the floor propped on one elbow, shoes off, sleeves rolled up and necktie loose. He rose to a sitting position and leaned against the wall.

Elias snapped several pieces off the top of a strange construction with wheels. "When I do this, it turns into a motorbike. See, mama?"

"How clever." Petra smoothed her skirt and knelt down. Elias showed her other things the Batmobile could turn into. Ignoring Maryam's clatter in the kitchen, she avoided looking at Sami. The idea of this man relaxing in her living room and playing with her son confused her. She didn't know how to act.

Sami modified a number of Lego pieces, his nimble fingers with well-groomed nails working fast. Fine dark hairs covered his arms.

She peeled her gaze away and concentrated on Elias rummaging through a pile of Lego blocks. "Airplane needs wings, mama."

"Of course." Summoning courage, Petra arched one eyebrow at Sami. "Uncle Sam?"

He winced and nodded toward the kitchen. "Maryam's words. Your meeting went okay?"

"All is well."

Something banged in the kitchen, and Maryam came out. "Will you set the table, *chéri*?"

Petra got to her feet. "What're you doing, Maryam?"

"I found chicken in your fridge and knew you wouldn't mind." The oven timer beeped. "Casserole is ready." Maryam went into the kitchen.

Sami slipped on his shoes and picked up his jacket. "Glad everything worked out. I'm off."

Elias hugged his leg. "But we haven't finished the Batmobile, Uncle Sam."

"You're almost there." Sami squeezed Elias's shoulder. "Just keep working on the wings."

"Please join us for lunch." Petra approached Sami. "It's the least I can do."

Elias sat on Sami's shoe. "You said you was hungry."

Sami flashed an embarrassed smile. "I only said that to give Maryam something to do and keep her from falling asleep."

"I insist." Petra took his jacket and draped it on the back of a dining chair. "You can't miss a chance to eat Lebanese food. Maryam is a fabulous cook."

Maryam poked her head out of the kitchen and pointed at Sami. "Help me carry the casserole to the

116

table. It's too heavy." She waved a spatula at Petra. "*Aller, chéri*. Change into something more comfortable. Uncle Sam and I got this."

"It's settled, then." Petra kissed Elias on the cheek. "Go wash your hands, please. Soap and water." She dipped her head at Sami. "Will you excuse me?"

"Of course."

She went into her room and dropped her bag on the bed. She quickly washed her face and changed into jeans and a blouse. Exhausted from lack of sleep and having gone through the emotional roller coaster of this morning, she lay on her back, promising herself it would only be for a minute to get her bearings.

Having Maryam for a neighbour was an exercise in forgiveness and tolerance. The meddling woman watched her every move from her windows and invaded her privacy on countless occasions.

At first, Petra wished she had never leased this apartment. Not today. Not when Maryam's presence allowed her to spend time with Sami. And she wanted to know this man, needed to find out more about him, discover his connection to her father. That was the source of her interest in Sami, wasn't it? She couldn't afford it to be anything else. She sprang upright.

Her bag fell off the bed and spilled out her wallet, pens, keys, and the gift box she had forgotten about. She sat on the floor to unwrap it. Dumbfounded, she stared at a pair of elegant sunglasses nestled in a velvet case. The ones Sami had crushed came from a pharmacy store she found soon after she moved to Kuwait. Sami chose the latest Burberry style to replace them.

The mobile phone rang. Startled, she picked up the call then realized it was Sami's phone, not hers. Too late. A woman's soft voice purred in her ear.

"Hey handsome! When will I see you again?"

CHAPTER ELEVEN

Sami went round the dining table and helped Elias distribute cutlery and napkins. Maryam drizzled olive oil over a bowl of tabbouleh. Struck by how comfortable he felt in this domestic setting, Sami moved with ease, breathed at a normal rhythm and forgot to gravitate toward the window. He kept eying Petra's closed door, waiting for her to join them. He hadn't experienced this buoyancy indoors for a long time. Where had his anxiety disappeared to? Not that he missed it.

Elias tugged at his hand. "Can I go play now, Uncle Sam?"

"That's not a good idea." He lifted Elias to a chair. "Your mom will be upset, don't you think?"

"It's okay. I'm brave like you and Batman."

"Brave. Not stupid," Sami chuckled. "I never disobeyed my mom, at least not on purpose."

Maryam took a seat at the head of the table. "Listen to Uncle Sam."

Petra came out of her room. His heart kicked an extra beat. Damn! She looked fine in jeans—tiny waist, curvy hips, taut thighs.

She handed him his phone. "I'm so sorry. I answered without realizing it wasn't mine." As she shook her head, loose auburn strands tumbled over her shoulders. "Someone's asking for you."

He put the phone to his ear. "Amara here."

"Have you forgotten about me?"

"Who's this?"

"Arenal Hotel in Florés? Don't tell me you can't recognize my voice, you handsome devil."

"Hi, Adriana." Sami gripped the back of his chair and threw a nervous smile at Petra. She went to her son's side to check his bandage. He should let her know that Adriana was one of the local liaisons for the company he had dealt with during his stay in Costa Rica. He had endured a rough relationship with sexy Adriana and a tougher break-up. From the sound of it, Adriana was ignoring the fact they broke-up. How could he make Petra understand that? And why in God's name did he care?

He switched the phone to his other ear. "What's this about?"

"Seems I called at a bad time. I can call later."

"If there's a problem at work, I'm sure our team in La Fortuna can work it out. Got to go, Adriana."

"Always on the move. Where in the world are you? Any chance you will make a stop our way?"

"Highly unlikely." He twisted sideways and dipped his chin to his chest, lowering his voice. "You made it quite clear I wasn't needed any more, remember?"

"We had a misunderstanding. Can't you see I—"

"I see very clearly." He cut her off. "Shoot the team leader an email. She'll manage whatever is needed. Take care, Adriana." He dropped his phone into his jacket pocket. "Sorry about that. Work. My latest project in Costa Rica." He caught Petra roll her eyes before she slipped into a chair. What the hell had Adriana said to her when she answered the phone?

Maryam touched his hand. "Sit, *chéri*. Sit and eat, before the chicken is cold."

Distracted by Adriana's call, he hadn't noticed how much food Maryam had piled onto his plate. Taking a hint from Petra's comment about Maryam's cooking skills earlier, he sampled the food and licked his thumb to praise Maryam. The women talked of ingredients and spices during the meal, and he tried to find an opening to prod Petra about her past without sending the old woman off on a tangent.

"You said your brother has children?" Petra asked.

He nodded. Yes. He could talk about that. "Two nieces. Twins. The most beautiful creatures I've ever seen."

"How old are they?"

"About to turn three. They babble nonsense, and I can't understand a word. Their mother does. How, is beyond me. They have Fareed wrapped around their little fingers."

Petra smiled, amusement danced in her eyes. "And I'm betting there's nothing you wouldn't do for them."

"Guilty. It drives Lora crazy."

Maryam dumped another serving onto his plate. "Your brother's wife is crazy?"

"No, Maryam," Petra sighed and raised her voice a notch. "Sami doting on his nieces drives their mother crazy."

"Children can drive a saint crazy if they are not disciplined right. Ask me, I raised four."

Sami ignored Maryam and pointed at Petra. "I believe we met when we were children."

"Really? When?"

"I remember us at a dining table. You were too young to remember, I guess."

Petra waved her fork. "Where?"

"At our house in Houston."

"I didn't know you lived in Texas, *chéri*," Maryam said.

Petra shook her head. "I didn't. Sami must be mistaken."

He touched his temple at the same spot where Petra's arrow birthmark sat on her forehead and dropped his voice. "I'm pretty certain the little girl I chased around the table was you."

Maryam darted her eyes back and forth between them. "A man has the right to lift his engaged cousin off the camel, you know."

He caught Petra's cheeks flush before she hid them behind her napkin. What the hell did a camel have to do with anything? He eyed the piece of meat on his plate. It looked like chicken, tasted like chicken. Please, let it be chicken.

Petra caught his attention with a dainty, graceful *ehmm*. "You said you'd never heard my name before."

"I called you by a nickname, though for the life of me I don't know why I chose it. It's weird."

She lowered her fork onto her plate. "It wouldn't have to do with something edible, would it?"

"Pita Bread."

Elias giggled, spilling milk on his clothes. Petra wiped his mouth and chin with her napkin. "That name stuck with me most of my school years. I never knew how it started."

"You want pita bread?" Maryam asked, getting to her feet.

Sami shot his hand out to stop her, but Petra beat him to it. "It's in the freezer."

"I know where you keep your bread, *chéri*. I'll warm some in the oven. Finish your meal. You hardly eat anything anymore, so skinny and delicate."

Maryam went into the kitchen, and Petra raised her eyes to the ceiling, praying for patience, no doubt. He sure did.

"Mama, I finished my food. Can I go play now?"

Petra patted Elias on the shoulder. "Go ahead."

Elias shot out of his chair and made for the Lego pile.

"Wash your hands, *ya rohi*."

"Yes, mama." Elias trotted to the bathroom.

Petra tilted her head sideways. "What else do you remember about me?"

"Honestly, that's about it." Sami exhaled. "I'm hoping to learn more from my mother when I go see her. She might have something to add."

"My birthmark triggered your memory?"

He nodded. He couldn't tell her the birthmark had remained with him through the years, imposing illusions and images he couldn't shake off. She would think him insane, never trust him again, not with her son for sure. He flicked his hand toward the kitchen. "I know we're not cousins. Dad didn't have siblings, and I know Mom's family tree very well. Shouldn't you set Maryam straight about that?"

"I will. If you learn more from your mother, will you please let me know?"

"Of course. Perhaps your aunt can shed some light, too?"

"My aunt passed away my freshman year in college. I have no one from my mother's family I could ask." Petra broke eye contact and pushed food around her plate. "My father's relatives in Nazareth don't know anything about his life in the States or Kuwait. He was very private, sort of secretive. I'm alone in this." She took a bite and chased it with a sip of water.

Sami remained silent, not knowing what to say to that. And he thought he had problems.

"I came to Kuwait to follow my father's trail. Three years and you're the closest connection so far."

"Are you in touch with your late husband's family?" Sami emptied his drink, hiding behind the tall glass his face and his surprise at blurting out the question. Why did he ask that? She was talking about her father, not her son's father.

"Bassam was an only son. His parents passed away. Strange isn't it?" Petra flashed an expectant smile, as if Sami knew what she meant.

Sami set his glass down. "What's strange?"

"Most Palestinian families are big with plenty of children, right? I married into one of the few that isn't."

"You're right. Most Palestinian families I know have at least four or five children." Sami filled his spoon with the last bits of rice on his plate. "I never thought about it."

"Even my mother's family of Irish descent didn't follow the tradition of spawning lots of offspring." Petra twisted her lips sideways. "I try to keep in touch with Bassam's cousins as often as I can. Unfortunately, they're not close. I want Elias to know he has relatives. Scattered all over the world, but family nonetheless." She waved her fork in the air. "You know, Palestinian refugees. I want to raise Elias Palestinian as my mother tried to do with me to honour my father. My aunt did her best, involving me with Arab families to pick up the culture." Petra slanted her gaze sideways. "But I always felt like a—"

"An intruder?" Sami blurted, then cleared his throat, regretting the impulse.

Petra gave a firm nod. "One day, I will take Elias to Palestine. A boy needs to feel his roots. Keeps him steady. It's hard for me to accept that most of my roots have shrivelled and died." Her eyes narrowed with determination. "Searching for my father gets me going. Keeps me hopeful. I don't want Elias to end up like a lonely tree." She snapped her gaze back to Sami. "It's a huge responsibility growing a boy into a man."

Sami stopped his loaded spoon halfway to his mouth. This woman knew what was at stake, having to raise a boy on her own. He matched his tone to the seriousness of Petra's. "I couldn't agree more."

Maryam returned with a breadbasket. "My son Ali eats rice with bread, too. I will never understand how you can eat two starches in one bite."

She handed Sami a warm pita. He had to accept it, and he had to eat it with the spoonful of rice. The sticky bite lodged in his throat. He refilled his glass from the pitcher and gulped water to push it down. He couldn't dislodge what stuck in his head. His entire life, he had been running away from the past, and Petra had spent years chasing after hers.

Sami slipped into his jacket and was surprised to see Maryam open her arms to him. He stepped into an awkward hug. "Thank you for a great meal."

"Visit again, but make it in the evening. You can meet Ali." Maryam touched Petra's arm. "You invite him, *chéri*."

Petra put on a patient smile and pointed at the couch. Elias had fallen asleep clutching his Lego Batmobile to his chest. "Thank you again, Sami. I really appreciate it."

"Anytime." Sami headed to the door, happy that Maryam didn't follow them. "Do you need me to go with you to the clinic on Thursday? To remove his bandages?"

"Oh, no. We'll be fine. You've done more than enough. And you really didn't have to replace my sunglasses. Thank you."

His steps faltered. Usually, he couldn't wait to go outdoors, now he couldn't make himself open the door. He stalled. "The camel Maryam mentioned at the table." He whirled his index finger in the air by his head. "Is she that far gone?"

Petra winced. "She was referring to the cousin's first right of refusal thing."

"What's that?"

"Ancient practice in some bedouin Middle Eastern cultures. A girl was frequently intended for one of her cousins for protection. He had the right to stop her from marrying a stranger. Even bring her back from the wedding procession toward her husband's tent on her wedding day." Petra opened her palm to one side. "Hence, lift her off the camel."

"Never heard of it."

"I have. A couple of times, so I researched it. No record of anyone practicing it, though. Literally, I mean. Of course first cousin marriages were, and to some extent still are, acceptable in many parts of the world." Petra played with her medical bracelet. "Old women like Maryam use the reference as a saying to stress responsibility and accountability. She thinks we're cousins, and she heard the word *chase* when you were talking about your memory of us as children. Her mind filled in the blanks of what she didn't hear." Petra put her hand on the doorknob. "I'll explain who you are when I have her full attention. And she wears her hearing aid."

Petra's move brought her a step closer, and he was hit by a wave of her fragrance—different to anything he had smelled on a woman. He inhaled. Her scent was unusual, youthful and... invigorating. Comforting. What else could he do to delay leaving?

"That hospital you had me pass," he said. "Is it really dedicated to Kuwaiti nationals only? I find that hard to believe."

"Ah, yes. That hospital. It's a very sore issue here. Lots of Kuwaitis are against the recent government decision. I'm not sure the law has taken effect yet, but I didn't want to risk wasting time."

"Good call. I'd like to see Elias before I fly to Houston. I feel bad leaving while he's asleep without saying goodbye."

"I'm sure he'd want to show you his progress with the Batmobile. When do you leave?"

"Friday."

"So soon?" She tucked hair behind her ear, exposing a blush creeping up her neck. "I thought there are things you needed to work out here after the new business arrangement."

"I have to tie ends with headquarters first. I'll be back next week." Why was she blushing? And how on earth could this woman smell so engaging? God, she smelled sweet with . . . a touch of fire. He must be losing his mind. He should leave. His feet refused to move.

"When can I see . . . Elias?"

Petra opened the door. "I'll call you."

***

Sami dived into a wave and let the sea strip away his weariness. He had spent two days glued to a desk, forming a clear picture about the company's business. He followed Fareed's instructions to dig for specific data and send him reports.

Finished with his brother's requests, Sami conducted his evaluations of the Marina project, his area of expertise.

He informed Sulaiman it was salvageable, and he would begin working on it as soon as he returned. Cleaning up the mess created by an incompetent engineer was bound to be a wretched affair. Sami considered sending his top engineer to take on the task, but he had given his word to Sulaiman to oversee the project personally. The company would not suffer another Chile failure on his watch. It would take six months to get work back on track. That wasn't too bad. He wouldn't mind if it took longer. A chance to figure out this Vaughn character. More time to research the woman from the past.

Sami floated on his back and willed his muscles to relax. The late afternoon sun was soothing, its heat tempered by lukewarm water. He let go, allowing the waves to rock him. A deep sentiment settled in his core, foreign, yet greatly missed.

He peered at the sun playing peekaboo with a billowy cloud. Petra wasn't the one who had called. It was Khalid who invited him for a *family* lunch at his house earlier today. Petra sat across from him, reserved and distant, her focus on Elias the entire time.

The boy looked fine without the bandages. Strangely enough, Sami missed having Maryam flutter about. He could have communicated his concern to Petra without drawing attention, tried to find out why she seemed . . . sad. Khalid's wife was all ears, a drone hovering over Petra, zooming in and interrupting whenever he opened his mouth.

Sami left the surf, water dripping from his relaxed shoulders. He dried off watching a seagull perched atop a flag post fly toward the sinking sun. One week. He would return in a week and settle here for the remainder of the year. Plenty of time to get to know Petra, the little mirage from childhood and the woman.

CHAPTER TWELVE

Petra wiped the whiteboard clean and set down the eraser. Done with teaching, she would use this last free period to prepare for the following day until the final bell rang and Elias ran into her classroom. Hopefully, she would be spared a Richard visit today. He had made far too many stops at her classroom since school started for her to find an official reason for them. And he almost always caught her at the end of Tuesdays, when she was alone waiting for Elias, basically trapped.

There were many ways a woman could politely let a man know she wasn't interested. She had tried them all. Principal Frost ignored every effort. Perhaps it was time to switch to a different tone—a harsh one that cut deeper. She couldn't claim sexual harassment, for Richard hadn't *done* anything, suggestive or otherwise, but he loomed over her, made her self-conscious about everything she said or did in his presence.

Her colleagues would have to be blind not to have noticed his persistence. If she didn't put a stop to this, she would be the main subject of gossip in the teachers' lounge.

She removed a packet of wet wipes from her desk drawer and scrubbed her hands. Elias had bounced back from his accident, but Dr. Iman suggested that a colleague pediatric specialist in Chicago review his case. She had jumped at the opportunity and urged the doctor to send Elias's medical file. According to this specialist, there was a good chance Elias would qualify for a new breakthrough procedure available only at the Children's Hospital in Boston and the DeBakey Heart Center in Houston.

Petra tossed the used wipe in a small wastebasket and sighed. She had hoped her son wouldn't need further surgery this soon. She had planned to work for a couple more years to save enough for additional treatment. Even with her medical insurance, the co-payments for tests alone would drain what little she had set aside. She had nothing to offer as collateral to secure a sufficient loan, not until now.

Willing or not, Sami presented her with an opportunity, and she needed to act fast. She would approach him upon his return to sell her shares. What good was owning part of a big company if she couldn't give her son the best treatment available? Had Dr. Iman told her earlier about this new procedure, she wouldn't have signed those papers and accepted her shares in the Amara business. She would have worked out a settlement, taken cash and let go of the whole mess. Anything to get Elias to either of those heart clinics, once she learned which one would accept his case.

She eased into her chair and arranged test papers in two neat piles on her desk. Mr. Faisal had explained in great length that by accepting the business shares, she met the condition stipulated in Mr. Amara's will and shielded the company from the complications of a church-affiliated involvement. She could sell her shares whenever she wanted. It was only fair to give Sami the first option to buy them before she approached Mr. Sulaiman.

Holding a red pen, she worked fast to grade one pile of papers—top students in her first period class. She always started with the best to lift her spirits. Three weeks had passed and she hadn't heard from Sami. When she brought herself to ask Mr. Faisal about him, he said Sami was still in Houston. Sami had sent someone in his place to oversee the company business in Kuwait. That person would not be authorized to make decisions about selling or buying shares. Mr. Faisal added that Mr. Vaughn had left ten days ago without saying a word. What was going on?

Perhaps she should call Sami. Would he ignore her? A business proposal shouldn't be discussed over the phone. She should have Mr. Faisal send an official email or letter indicating her desire to sell her shares. That would grab Sami's attention.

She moved on to her next stack of tests. Her spirits dropped and she slumped in her chair. Too many mistakes. The red ink would bleed dry by the time she was done with this pile. She couldn't get these students to where they needed to be.

Most of the students were really trying, especially the minister's son. Fahad was a quiet, awkward young man, withdrawn and introverted, not the flamboyant, defiant teen she had expected. She had interfered twice to shield him from the cruelty of four of his classmates, privileged sons of prominent families who had no regard for the value of a good education.

They tried to pressure Fahad into conformity, egging him on to behave as they did, disrespectful, arrogant, and downright defiant. But Fahad resisted and withdrew further into his shell. It tore at her heart to see the bright young man struggle that way. She would bring the matter to Richard and let him inform Fahad's parents of his struggles, though she had a feeling the mother knew. A mother always knew what kind of child she raised.

Elias ran into her classroom, his backpack pumping up and down his back with enough noise so that she heard his approach from the hallway. She gave him a hug and eased the bulky bag off his shoulders.

"How was your day?"

"Mama, I had a green apple today!" he beamed. "Miss. Amal said I didn't talk lots and she put a green apple sticker on my folder."

"Your first this week. I'm impressed." Petra opened a drawer and took out a pack of Oreo cookies and a drink. "Let's have a small celebration. You can have these while I finish my work. Ten minutes, max. Are you tired?"

Elias shook his head, chose a desk, and became busy pulling apart chocolate discs and licking the cream filling.

Petra returned to her tests and tried to ignore the slurping noises Elias made. His backpack was too big for his small body. She had tried to convince him to use a rollaway one, but he said the boys would laugh at him, peer pressure already starting. How could she protect him from what was coming? He would always be smaller and weaker than other boys his age. She needed to build his self-esteem, boost his confidence, and raise him to be strong, resilient. He needed role models, and super heroes were not a healthy way to go.

Richard Frost had been kind and attentive to Elias, yet he called him *little guy*, emphasizing his disadvantage. Sami, on the other hand, taught him how to be brave and creative. No wonder Elias hadn't stopped asking about Sami since the day they spent together.

Elias slept every night with the stuffed Batman Sami had given him. His Batmobile, looking more like a monster than a car, sat in the middle of the coffee table in her living room, a centrepiece worthy of display for Sami when he visited again.

She lifted her eyes to Elias. He was arranging Oreo discs in a pile, squinting this way and that as if to examine his structure from different angles. He hadn't shown interest in building anything with the Lego set until Sami's visit. Elias was hooked, and spent hours constructing a world of his own. What sort of man would her son turn out to be? Mouzah's sons were closer to their father by her own admission and Khalid was a strong figure in his boys' lives. Elias had no one. No one except her, a woman who grew up without a father. She knew little about the world of boys.

Living with her childless, unmarried aunt gave her a roof over her head, but fell far short of creating a real home where a child felt loved and protected. Petra had none of that, sensing her aunt tolerated her presence out of necessity, leaving her to fumble her way through confusing teenage years. She tried not to fault her aunt for lacking the uninhibited compassion of a parent.

You can't give what you don't have in your possession, Bassam had said to her once when she told him about her dry, lonely upbringing, her fears of becoming a mother. What of her shortcomings? What kind of deprivation was she inflicting on her son? How could she offset her deficiencies, when there was no strong male presence in his life? Bassam had left life too soon after his son was born. Elias didn't remember him at all.

Petra shook her head to focus. She gathered her things and escorted Elias to the car, elated that she had escaped Richard. First, she would have Mr. Faisal inform Sami this afternoon of her desire to sell.

Second, start the ball rolling about travel and treatment arrangements. And finally, let Richard know she was leaving, so he could find a substitute teacher.

Stepping out of the shower, Petra heard the phone ring. She wrapped a towel around her and hurried into her bedroom to answer the call.

"Petra? It's Sami Amara."

"Oh, hello." She tightened the towel over her chest. That was quick. Mr. Faisal must have sent the email as soon as she had finished her phone conversation with him earlier. "Are you coming back to Kuwait soon?"

"That's why I called."

Sami sounded strange, as if he was swallowing something. "It'll be some time before I do." He paused. "I . . . want you to know something . . . so you won't . . ."

Keeping the cordless handset to her ear, Petra opened the wardrobe to grab a robe. Sami didn't pause mid-sentence, he stopped talking altogether. Several breaths passed in silence. Was he eating? How rude could he be to have a conversation while he was chewing?

"Know what?" she snapped, making sure he heard the irritation in her tone.

"My brother is dead."

She froze. The robe dropped, covered her feet. "Oh, God!" She leaned against the wardrobe door and slid to the floor. "What happened?"

"Car accident . . . Fareed *and* Lora."

"The twins?" She squealed the question with a burst of air that emptied her lungs.

"Safe."

Sami wasn't rude; he was choking on his words. He went on with long pauses between broken sentences. "I ... stayed home with the girls. Told Fareed to take his wife ... out on a date. His battery had died and ... I ... gave him my car." Sami's voice contorted on the last words, coming out scratched, painful to hear.

Petra pressed her hand over her mouth. She knew only too well the inescapable slippery track surviving loved ones slid on, the *if onlys* that snared them away from logic, made them suffer through each possible scenario, and threw them into the pit of self-blame.

"I'm so sorry," she whispered.

"Heavy rains that night. Should have checked the tyres." He exhaled into the phone. One, two, three long, nasal breaths. "Front tyre blew out ... car slid off a bridge ... plunged into a creek."

"It was an accident." Petra rocked back and forth. What else could she say? Nothing would make this better. Nothing would lessen his pain. Unwelcome thoughts drenched her with cold sweat and sent her back in time, to the moment her entire world collapsed. She should have paid closer attention to Bassam. He had told her he wasn't feeling well that night. She should have backed off, allowed him to rest. She should have learned how to perform CPR, shouldn't have panicked and watched her young husband take his last breaths before her eyes.

"Petra, are you there?"

"I'm here."

"I handed Fareed my goddamn keys."

"It wasn't your fault, Sami."

"I can't . . ." He stopped talking again.

Petra recognized his need to withdraw. She waited, listening to his laboured breath. The clock by her bed ticked louder with each passing second. If there was one thing she could do for him, it was to listen, give him a chance to articulate his misery. His wound was too fresh, though. He wouldn't talk about it with her—a stranger to his life, a nobody. When Bassam died, she had had no one but God to unload on, and she wasn't on good terms with the Almighty to begin with. Her gut told her Sami was in a similar spot.

"I know how hard this is, Sami."

"Faisal told me you want to sell your shares?"

Water dripped onto her lap. She tried to brush aside her wet hair, but it was tucked under the towel she had twisted at the top of her head. Those were tears landing on her knees. "Don't worry about that now."

"We haven't told anyone about . . . what's happened. Only Sulaiman knows. I asked him to keep it quiet until Vaughn and the rest of our legal team figure out what to do. How to proceed."

"Of course." Her knees glistened with more tears. "This is not the time."

"If you're strapped for money, I mean if that's why you want to sell, please let me offer you a loan until we pin down legalities." His voice grew stronger, more controlled. "Faisal said it has to do with Elias? Some new medical procedure?"

She nodded stupidly, unable to form words. Good. Let Sami talk business to get his mind off horrible reality.

"Petra?"

"I just heard this morning. A hospital in Houston accepted Elias's case."

"Oh, here? That's good. We have one of the best medical centres in the country."

"It'll take time to process his papers. If I'd known what happened, I wouldn't have bothered you now." She took a deep breath. "God, I feel terrible."

"Don't. You're looking out for your son. I want to help."

"This isn't your problem, Sami. I'll figure something out."

"When did they tell you to expect to travel?"

"Six weeks at the earliest. There's so much to work out."

"I can give you a loan from the company, with your shares as collateral. Please, it's very important not to mess with the company structure at this time. We need to keep our image intact given . . . the circumstances."

"I understand. But really, you shouldn't think about this now."

"How much do you need?" He insisted, his tone hinting at impatience.

She threw her head back. He was probably eager to end the call and move on to the other zillion things that required his attention. "A couple hundred thousand, maybe? If they accept Elias onto the new treatment programme, the insurance will cover a fraction, if anything."

In the background, a door slammed, followed by a woman's voice addressing him as Mr. Amara. Then complete silence. He must have covered the mouthpiece with his hand.

"Petra, I've got to go. I'll send Sulaiman a word about our arrangement. Faisal and Vaughn can finalize things when you're ready. Does that sound reasonable?"

"Thank you."

"Call me directly if you need anything else."

Sami ended the call. Just like that, before she could ask how the girls fared, or how his mother took the news of her son's death days after losing her husband. Before Petra could offer help, whatever that might be.

She pulled herself to her feet, kicked her crumpled robe out of the way and trudged toward the bed. Tears clouded her eyes and she sagged to a corner of the mattress. She hung her head and said a silent prayer for the deceased couple, the orphaned children, the deprived mother, and for Sami to remain on his feet.

CHAPTER THIRTEEN

Sami headed home at noon. He had bolted out of the office before he exploded in front of everyone. Lawyers, accountants and loyal employees guided him through the complicated process of taking over the business, expecting him to fill his father's and brother's shoes in a meagre span of days.

Having a moment alone was nearly impossible. Everyone wanted his attention. He needed to separate himself from them, step back and disconnect in order to hear his own thoughts, breathe right, regain balance. But he couldn't afford to do that. Not when he saw a cadre of eager-to-please opportunists setting their sights on possible personal enrichments. They waited, expecting him to fail rather than shoulder their responsibilities. And Vaughn circled, a jackal ready to attack, licking his lips and hiding his motives.

Sami looked forward to the innocent company of his nieces before returning to the office. With that excuse, he convinced himself that he wasn't checking on the household, showing up when not expected. He fought against a sense of guilt, having to rely on his brother's in-laws to watch the twins.

Lora's parents had looked after the girls since the day they arrived from Cleveland for their daughter's funeral. For the benefit of their grandchildren, they set aside their grief, allowing him to spend long hours at the office. But the girls weren't used to their grandparents, wouldn't fall asleep without him holding them, rocking and singing to them every night, especially Deena. More animated than her twin, Deena was highly sensitive to her surroundings and transferred her uneasiness to quiet, amenable Leena.

Lora and Fareed had never explained why the relationship with her parents was not close. The old couple seldom visited their daughter, rarely spent any time with the twins. He suspected they had refused to accept Fareed into their family. Regardless, Sami appreciated their help, welcomed it and made use of them as much as he could. How long would their benevolence continue? How could he manage work and be there for the girls when their grandparents returned to Cleveland?

He strode into the kitchen. His stomach muscles clenched, killing his appetite.

His mother sat at the table feeding little Leena in her highchair. Mother wore a white lacy dress, her shoulder-length hair perfectly coiffed, her beautiful face made up to conceal her age. She was in denial, refusing to process that her son was gone. The passing of his father had pushed her into a dark corner. Fareed's

145

death flipped her to a complete opposite, where she no longer displayed any signs of mourning.

Sami ruffled Leena's dark curls and kissed her forehead. "Where's everyone?"

"Rosa went to the grocery store." Mother wiped Leena's mouth. Leena lifted her arms to him. He grabbed her little hands and dotted them with kisses.

"And Lora's parents?" he asked. "Are they taking care of Deena?"

"Margaret said something about needing to return the rental car, took her mouse of a husband with her." Mother inflated her chest. "I told them I'd watch the girls."

Sami went round the huge kitchen, his insides coiling tighter with each step. "Where's Deena?"

"They're always around, son," his mother whispered. "Watching."

He froze at the other side of the wide island. "What did you do with Deena, Mom?"

"I hid her so they couldn't hear her and take her away."

An image of his mother shoving him into a cabinet to hide him from *The Watchers* when he was a boy flashed before his eyes. She wore that same pleased look today. He sprinted forward, lifted Leena into his arms, and tried to control his panic so he didn't push his mother to the defiant stage where she shut down and refused to cooperate. He swallowed his fear and modulated his tone, as if having a casual conversation.

Calm, remain calm, he repeated in his head.

"Wood muffles sounds. I'm sure *The Watchers* won't hear Deena if you hid her well."

Mother gazed at him, her face full of pride—misplaced and utterly wrong. "I taught you well, didn't I, Sami?"

Dread ignited rage in his chest. He stroked Leena's back to keep his hand occupied, fearing he might thrust it to his mother's throat. At moments like these, Sawsan Amara wasn't the woman who birthed him, but a dangerous stranger.

He tried one more time. "Mom, you were an excellent teacher. You didn't hide Deena in the kitchen if *The Watchers* were looking over Leena, right?"

Mother nodded. Her casual smile slowly spread into a grin, transforming the look on her face into a smug expression—too familiar . . . too cruel.

Sami backed out of the kitchen, bolted up the stairs and into his mother's bedroom. He sat Leena on the rug and checked the wardrobe and closets. Deena wasn't there. He looked into the cedar chest and the bathroom bottom cabinets. Nothing. His heart knocked against his ribs.

Leena wobbled out to the hallway. He picked her up again and went into Fareed and Lora's bedroom, searched their bathroom, all the while calling for

Deena. Regressing to his childhood years, he gulped for air. Minutes had passed as long as hours for him back then, in the dark, the smell of damp wood crawling up his nose. How long had Deena been imprisoned? Why wouldn't she answer his calls? Had Mother put her in a dry place? He searched the other rooms. Deena was nowhere to be found.

He stood at the end of the hallway, opened the window and tried to subdue his heartbeat. Could Mother have hidden Deena outside the house? Hell, could she be in that dreadful shed at the farthest end of the property?

Leena started crying, mirroring his anxiety. He kissed her hair. "Sweetheart, do you know where your sister is?"

A giggle came from behind. He turned.

The little girl with red hair stood at the other end of the hallway. She ran up the stairs toward the attic. He followed, Leena in his arms. The redheaded girl pirouetted on top of a big trunk in the middle of the attic. He was fast losing his grip on reality.

Sun rays shining through the circular window reflected off the girl's hair. Her arrow birthmark glowed bright and clear on her forehead.

He blinked twice.

She smiled and disappeared.

He hurried closer. There was Deena, asleep behind the trunk, on a bed of blankets sucking her thumb. He lifted her onto his other shoulder, keeping her sister secure in his arms.

He stumbled downstairs. Let him have his mother's defective DNA. Let him be touched by the spirits, guided by whatever entity that ruled the unseen world. Let him be crazy, enlightened or damned. At that moment, he did not care. His own phantom, the Petra child visitant, had helped him find Deena. Hugging the twins tighter, he went into the living room, sat on the couch, and waited for his fury to wither.

His mother sauntered in. "See? *The Watchers* didn't find her."

"Go to your room, Mother." He couldn't control his voice, and his command came out ugly. "You need to rest."

Unperturbed, his mother touched the sides of her hair with the tips of her fingers. "Yes, I think I will. Send Rosa up when she comes in, will you?"

"Go on, Mother."

He would send Rosa packing, that's what he would do. Soon after Father left for Kuwait, Fareed had moved his wife and children into the family house to keep Mother company. Sami had hired Rosa to ease the load, giving her clear instructions not to leave Mother alone with the children.

When Lora and Fareed were around, Rosa's compliance was never tested. But things had changed. There was no one to protect the twins anymore. He was alone in this. If he had any hope of maintaining a level of normality for his nieces, he needed to take charge. He would contact the best agency in town to find a suitable nanny. And Mother? He needed to hire a more competent assistant, someone who shadowed her day and night.

Dictating instructions to his secretary, Sami reluctantly delegated work to his team and spent the rest of the day at home. He made phone calls and scheduled interviews to hire a live-in nanny and an assistant to replace Rosa. Frustrated with how time-consuming the process was, he reflected on his situation.

He couldn't fire Rosa as he had planned. She understood Mother's moods and expertly managed her needs. Pouring his anger and frustration onto Rosa when she returned from her errand was a mistake. The kind woman absorbed him, realizing the predicament he faced. This was not the time to replace her.

Later that night, Sami tiptoed his way out of the twins' room. He kept the door ajar and went down the hall to his room. His muscles were stiff from the near hour he had spent on the wooden rocking chair between the two cribs, extending his arms to hold each girl's hand until they fell asleep.

He massaged his neck, checked the baby monitor on his nightstand and dropped onto the bed. This mustn't go on. He had slept a handful of hours since the dreadful night of the accident. He closed his eyes, inviting sleep to give him relief. Perhaps God would grant him this single favour, having taken so much, so quickly.

He slipped off his shoes and turned to face the window. What was he to do with Mother? Her therapist had warned that a sudden shock would snap her into a blurred reality and could lead to her committing an unpredictable, possibly violent, act. After the events of today, how could he hide the details of her condition from Lora's parents? Seeing her as merely artistic and fragile, they didn't understand the danger she represented.

Lora and Fareed had insisted on keeping her parents in the dark about Mother's mental illness, and he needed to respect their wishes now that they had passed. Besides, it wouldn't be right to let Lora's parents return to Cleveland with the extra burden of fearing for the safety of their grandchildren after they had lost their only child.

Should he consider the doctor's suggestion to move Mother into a facility if her mental state deteriorated— something he had sworn to his father not to do? But Father wasn't here, nor was Fareed. Everything was down to him now. He would do right by his brother's children, no matter what the cost.

He inhaled deep. He would start by replacing that torturous rocking chair with the Lazy Boy from his own apartment. Get rid of the bachelor's pad altogether.

Sami avoided eye contact with his mother the following morning over breakfast. He didn't want Lora's parents to pick up on his lingering resentment. He waited until his mother had left the kitchen, filled his thermos cup with coffee, and got to his feet.

"I'm off to the office, but I'll be working from home this afternoon. A number of candidates are coming in for a nanny position. I'd appreciate your input, Margaret, if you'd join us in the study."

"Sami, George and I need to talk to you." Margaret placed her knife and fork at right angles on her plate. "About the girls."

George laced his fingers over his belly. "It's important."

Sami sat back in his seat. Since George had arrived, Sami could count on one hand the number of times the man had opened his mouth. Margaret was the engine in her family, the communicator, planner, decision maker. Several years older than Mother, frail and delicate with her raised veins and almost transparent skin, her appearance contrasted with her feisty nature. Sami had sensed it the instant he met her. He hated to see the couple leave, but knew it had to happen.

He steadied his gaze on Margaret. "Is it time? To go back to Cleveland?"

"It is. George can't leave his store for too long."

Sami nodded. "You're always welcome in this house, anytime you want to see the girls. And I'll bring them over this Christmas. You have my word."

Margaret and George exchanged a strange look—reluctant, worried.

Sami hid his apprehensiveness by pretending to check the lid on his thermos cup. They couldn't have heard what happened to Deena yesterday. By the time they had come back, everyone was settled: Mother tucked away in her room, the girls safe and happy with him.

He shook his head, a good measure of confidence in his voice. "Don't worry about the twins. I'll take good care of them."

Margaret raised her faded eyebrows. "How? By paying some stranger to watch them while you're at work?"

"I will *employ* a trusted, highly recommended, live-in nanny from the best agency in Houston. A professional educator. I'll spare no expense, you can count on that."

"I have a better solution. One that's more practical." Margaret went to stand behind her husband, placed her hands on his shoulders. "We take the girls with us. Raise them in our home."

Sami pushed back his chair. "That's not going to happen."

"Excuse me?"

"As much as your sentiment is appreciated, you will *not* remove the girls from their home. Away from me. They need continuity and stability."

"You talk like you know what you're doing. You're a single man. You've never been a parent." Margaret

153

raised her voice. "How much attention can you give them? Let us have them."

He rose from the table and stretched to his full height. "For how long, Margaret?"

"Forever."

"Be realistic."

"I am. You will always be their uncle. Visit whenever you want."

Sami towered over the old couple and softened his tone. "Forever might not be that far ahead."

"How dare you?"

"I dare because I'm thinking of the best for my nieces. It's inevitable. And then what will happen to the girls? Move them back here? Have them go through another drastic change in their young lives?"

Margaret stepped closer. "The girls need mothering. *My* mothering. But I can't stay here."

"Look, you know I'm right. What you have to offer will diminish over time. I, on the other hand, can provide a promising, brighter future."

Margaret poked his chest with a bony finger. "Not as a single man. We'll challenge you in court. No judge will favour a bachelor's environment over the grandparents' stable home."

Sami blew a long breath. "I can't believe this. Are you serious?"

"I want to raise my daughter's children." Margaret shifted back her shoulders. "It's my right."

"I understand your pain. I really do. But you can't expect the girls to replace Lora." Sami connected eyes with George. "Are you on board with this?"

George left his chair and stood by his wife's side. "You wanna be realistic? You ain't married. You have your hands full with your weird mother and gypsy-like work schedule. Your lawyer, Vaughn, told me you come home a couple a months a year. That's it." George readjusted the Browns cap on his head. "You don't even have close friends. Other than them people I seen at church, no one stops by, offers help. I can't believe my daughter didn't have more carin' friends here."

Sami fiddled with his cuffs. George sure had lots to say. Vaughn told him? So George had been poking around, asking questions. Had he found out it wasn't Lora who lacked social skills? People stayed away from the house because of Mother. Sami exhaled. Time to do some damage control.

"I'm CEO of the company now. Staying in Houston. My days as a gypsy on construction sites are over. As for Mother, she's . . . fairly independent. If anything, she'll enrich the girls' education. And I don't plan on staying single for long." He shoved his hands in his pockets, not believing he had actually uttered those words. "This is the twins' home. A place that's familiar, comforting. Don't deprive them of that after they've lost so much."

"All the more reason to give them a fresh start," Margaret said, her voice harsh. "We plan to leave tomorrow. We've booked seats for the girls and everything."

"And you are informing me of that? Is that it?" Sami shot back, unable to remain collected. He would not lose his brother's children to this old pair. He would not lose Fareed's girls, period.

"We thought you'd see things the way we do, young man. You're carin' enough. I don't doubt you mean well." George tried to pacify him, as if he were a customer negotiating a deal to buy new tyres from his store. "But you ain't got enough experience. Raisin' children calls for discipline, structure, a firm hand."

Sami stiffened. Was that what had ruined Lora's relationship with her parents? Quiet George's firm hand? No way in hell would he let him take the girls. At least Mother's actions weren't premeditated, rationalized or reasoned with the intention to cause harm. She had never laid a hand on him or Fareed. Hell, he should have the girls' pediatrician examine them as soon as possible, to make sure George hadn't already "disciplined" them.

Damn it, how could he have missed that? If Lora had been more open about her parents, he would never have allowed them to be alone with her daughters.

The windows behind George shifted closer. Sami resisted the need to stick out his arms. Fatigue made him more susceptible to the tricks his eyes played on him. Perhaps Lora had talked about her upbringing with Fareed, and it was Sami who was kept out of the loop, as he was a roadrunner who whizzed through their lives every now and then.

Could he have read too much into George's words? Was he so cynical that he saw threats to children in everyone? He squinted to focus and mentally pushed George, his wife and the approaching windows further back.

"I will not allow you to take my nieces."

Margaret grabbed her husband's hand. "Then we'll see you in court. And we will win, Sami." They strutted toward the stairs in unison. "We *will* have custody of our daughter's children."

CHAPTER FOURTEEN

Petra gazed at the city lights below and tried not to concentrate on a single spot. Though the revolving café at the top of Kuwait Tower crept round at a barely detectible speed, the idea that she was dining with Mouzah while scanning the city and sea shoreline every thirty minutes from four hundred feet above did nothing to alleviate her headache.

A waiter served their salads, and her temples throbbed. She moved the salt and pepper shakers next to the white ceramic vase in the middle of the table. The trio formed a replica of the three landmark towers of Kuwait City: a white slender tower, another tower which held a blue water tank, and the third main tower carrying two blue spheres, one above the other. The lower and bigger sphere housed a restaurant and the upper sphere, a café.

The first time Petra laid eyes on the towers, she thought of her aunt's knitting yarn balls. The blue-tiled spheres looked as if they were pierced by long white needles and planted on a promontory in the Arabian Gulf.

Mouzah played with a flower in the vase. "I think you should call him."

"Call who?" Petra asked.

"Sami Amara. As a courtesy."

"I already thanked him for the loan. Honestly, I have no idea how I'm going to pay him back." Petra rummaged through her handbag searching for something to relieve her headache. "Even after I sell my shares in his company, I have so much to cover."

"Khalid and I will give you the money. Don't worry."

"I can't pay off one debt by adding another."

"It will be our gift to Elias. Petra, what are you looking for in that shabby bag?"

"I have a massive headache. Do you have any Tylenol?"

Mouzah pulled out a bottle from her Fendi bag. "I only have *Aspireen*. You should come with me to the mall to find you a bag *al mouda*."

"Bassam bought this for me on our last anniversary." Petra took two pills.

"It's so old style," Mouza said.

"I like my bag. And I appreciate your offer to pay my debt. But there's no way I'd accept your money."

"You think about money too much." Mouzah shrugged. "We can afford it."

Petra suppressed a groan. She thought about money because she didn't have much. Unlike Mouzah, she wasn't born into a wealthy family, nor had she married into one. Never wanting for anything, and despite all her efforts to learn about the world, Mouzah remained oblivious to the struggles of working people living from pay cheque to pay cheque.

"You know me. I can't accept such a generous gift." Petra mellowed her voice to let her gratitude show, "not even from you, my friend."

"We are here for you whenever you need us." Mouzah sighed, tabling the offer.

Petra hid her smile. This was not the first time Mouzah had tried to cover her expenses. "Thank you."

"It would be nice to let Sami Amara know you are going to Houston. It will be good for you to know someone there. I wish I could go with you. The boys' school, you know?"

Petra stared at her friend. "You don't have to worry about me so much. I've been on my own most of my life. Elias and I will be fine."

"I wish your life was easier." Mouzah tasted her salad. "I can't imagine what Sami is going through right now. You should offer your condolences to his mother."

Petra moved around croutons on her plate to postpone taking a bite until her headache subsided. "I should?"

"In person, I believe. Maybe you can ask her about your father." Mouzah fiddled with the many bracelets jingling around her wrist. "Did Sami ever tell you what she remembers about him?"

Petra shook her head. "There wasn't time. I guess everything came crashing down on Sami soon after he arrived home. It would have been extremely poor taste to ask under the circumstances."

The revolving café reached the half point of its turn and the city lights behind Mouzah disappeared. Petra saw only blackness under the moonless night. "It's not that important to me anymore. I have to concentrate on Elias."

"Elias will be fine. A month at the most and you will have him back here in school. Do not worry."

"I may have to stay longer. Depending on how Elias fares after the procedure. Richard Frost won't appreciate that."

"If you do, Khalid and I will bring the boys for the National Day week's break in February to keep you company. And your principal would be a donkey if he causes problems. You found him a substitute teacher, so now he should be quiet."

"Mr. Frost holds my job in his hands." Petra hid her amusement at the way Mouzah described the stubborn Richard. "I can't afford to lose my position, and I need him on my side. I may resign the school here and find a job in Houston if... Elias has to go through more surgeries."

"He will not," Mouzah said with confidence, jerking down her head once.

"I'll need a good recommendation letter from my principal if it comes down to that."

"You can't think about what may or may not happen. It is all in God's hands."

A couple took the adjacent table. Mouzah openly gawked at them. She flicked up her head in quick acknowledgement to the woman, who returned the same gesture before she slipped into her chair. Mouzah leaned across the table. "See those two? Recently married. She was a young widow." Mouzah lowered her voice, though not low enough. Petra was sure the woman heard every word.

To add to Petra's consternation, Mouzah pointed a finger at the man. "He was married and got a divorce early this year. Many forces worked to bring them together."

"I don't see how this concerns us," Petra whispered. She kept her eyes on her plate, mortified and feeling sorry for the couple.

Mouzah touched her hand. "*Illi fi aljider, yitalle'a almallas.*" She withdrew her hand and sat back, a smug expression in her kohl-framed eyes.

"Should I ask what that means?"

"It means, my friend, what is at the bottom of the pot will be brought up by the ladle." Mouzah winked. "You wait and see."

Petra sipped water to stay quiet. All her life, she had waited for God to show her what was in His other hand, prayed it would be better than what she had been dealt. Yet, it had not helped.

***

Elias's excitement at taking the Airbus monster plane from Frankfurt faded after the second movie he watched on the entertainment system. His Lego set kept him busy for another hour or so, then he shifted between games on Petra's iPad and colouring superheroes in a comic book. He fidgeted in his seat when boredom took full hold. It was a challenge to keep him restrained by his seatbelt. Finally, he dozed off a couple of hours before landing. Petra didn't have the heart to rouse him.

Struggling to keep Elias in her arms, she dragged her suitcase behind her. She cleared customs, exited through the main doors, and looked for the taxi stand. The apartment she had leased was on a metro line which went straight to the Medical Center. According to her real estate agent, she might never need a rental car, an expense she could do without.

A tall man in a black suit and cap approached her. "Mrs. Petra Haddad?"

Petra blinked, then noticed the white sign he held with her name on it. "Yes?"

"Imperial Transportation Services. I'm to drive you to your place, ma'am."

"I uh... didn't book a service."

"I was hired by Mr. Sami Amara?"

"Oh, I see."

The man moved to take her suitcase. "This way to the car."

Exhausted and barely managing to keep Elias on her shoulder, she followed the man through a huge garage and crossed a wide walkway until they reached a black SUV. She buckled Elias into the child car seat. He grumbled, rubbed his eyes with his fists, and went back to sleep. Petra slipped in next to him.

This was better than taking a taxi on her own at night.

"There are water bottles and refreshing towels for you back there." The driver started the car. "Trip too long for the young man?"

Petra sighed. "For both of us." Though thirsty, she opted not to grab a water bottle. She hadn't used the restroom before they left the airport because of Elias, and she wouldn't risk the call of nature.

"Do you know where we're going? It's an apartment building near the Methodist DeBakey Heart Center." She dug in her bag to find the paper with the address.

"Yes, ma'am. I know where that is. We'll be there in about forty-five minutes."

She checked the address with the driver and sat back. Mr. Faisal had arranged for the month-long lease on a furnished apartment through a real estate agency, and he had evidently communicated the details to Sami. Why, she didn't know, and she couldn't try to guess. She was too tired and sleepy to think. All she cared about right now was reaching the very affordable apartment, use its hopefully clean bathroom, and get settled close to the hospital where Elias would undergo treatment.

Elias woke when the car cruised into the parking lot. Fully rested, he bounced out and followed the driver through an impressive lobby with a marble floor. A huge vase with a massive flower arrangement stood in the centre and filled the air with the pungent smell of fresh gardenias. A security guard behind a desk verified Petra's ID and handed her the apartment keys.

"Everything is arranged." The driver gave her suitcase to the security guard. "Have a pleasant stay, ma'am."

"Thank you." Petra pulled out her wallet. "How much do I owe you?"

"It's been taken care of, ma'am." He touched his cap. "Welcome to Space City and have a good night."

The security guard motioned toward the elevators. "Shall we?"

On the way up to the seventh floor, Petra half-listened to the guard listing the available amenities: swimming pool, sauna, home cinema, catering services and something about recycling. Despite herself, she yawned.

The guard gave her a fatherly smile. "Pamphlets and schedules are in the apartment. Kinda letting you know what to look for, that's all."

"Sorry. We've been travelling for almost twenty-four hours."

Elias looked up at the older man. "Are you a policeman?"

"Private security, son."

Elias pointed at the man's hip. "But you have a gun."

"To make sure everyone here is safe and happy."

"You keep the bad guys away?"

"You bet." The guard walked them into the two bedroom apartment. "This is prime location, Mrs. Haddad. Close to the Medical Center, the museum district, Montrose artistic area, and the Zoo."

"Zoo? Does it have gorillas?" Elias asked, his eyes sparkling with energy.

"Gorillas, tigers and . . ." the guard paused before he added, "alligators!"

Elias jumped onto the pristine white couch. "Mama, did you hear that? Can we go see the alligators?"

"Of course." Petra slipped off his shoes, her mind crunching numbers. She had paid five hundred dollars for this exquisite, high-end, strategically located apartment. She didn't know much about real estate, but she had enough sense to realize how valuable this location must be, and the luxurious furniture alone was an indication of the apartment's quality.

"Careful, there," the guard eased Elias away from a leather bench with a barbell above it. Weight discs of different sizes lined the wall next to it.

"Excuse me," she called the guard's attention. Had he ever given her his name? She couldn't remember. She squinted to read the name badge on his chest. "What company owns this complex, Roy?"

"Each apartment is privately owned, ma'am. The grounds are managed by Apex Estates." Roy pointed at the phone mounted on the wall in the kitchen on his way to the door. "Anything you all need, just dial zero. There's someone at the front desk twenty-four seven. I come in after nine pm."

"I sorted out the details of this lease through a realtor. I'm curious to know who owns this particular apartment."

"A young man. He hardly ever uses it, though. Good thing he decided to lease it."

Petra held the front door and her breath. "His name, please?"

Roy stepped out to the hallway. "Sami Amara, ma'am."

CHAPTER FIFTEEN

Sami stared at the stack of papers in his hands, his eyes fixed on the top line. Mentally, he had checked out soon after the meeting started. He had already finalized the details last night. This meeting was merely a formality to inform the players in his recognized team who would be responsible for each project. His presence in the conference room was to emphasize his new position of power, especially for those who expressed doubt in his ability to command. Vaughn, the most vocal critic, strolled in late.

There Sami sat, at the head of the long mahogany table, in the same seat his brother and his father had occupied before him. He listened to his managers spell out details, stress deadlines. Every now and then, he looked up and glared at the doubters to let them know he was onto them. *Question my authority, fail to follow my directives, and your careers end in tatters.*

Towards the end of the meeting, as discussions moved past milestones, his assistant Robert walked in and whispered that he had unscheduled visitors. Before Sami could ask who they were, the director of the Design and Development Department demanded his attention.

"Show them to my office, Robert. I'll be right there." Sami dismissed Robert and obliged the director with the consideration she deserved.

"So why the delay?" Sami asked. "I signed off on your proposal last week."

"Yes, but Vaughn said we should wait for his authorization," the director said. "I don't understand why. The project was approved by the legal department before it reached your desk."

"Get started, then. I'm CEO of this company and I gave you the go-ahead." Sami hid his anger at Vaughn, letting out just enough in his tone as a warning to the director. "Are we clear?"

"Crystal clear, Mr. Amara."

Sami turned to give quick answers to several questions from others, then went into his office.

Petra stood before him with Elias in her arms. They were examining one of the miniature models mounted on platforms by the windows. Petra graced him with a demure smile and lowered Elias to the floor. She wore a dress the colour of unclouded summer skies.

"These are fascinating. Are they all projects your company completed?"

"These are a few samples. My favourite ones, sort of. More are displayed in a special viewing hall."

He approached, hoping his face didn't betray surprise. She spoke as if they were mid-conversation, like they had just parted an hour ago and she hadn't

169

dropped into his place of work from halfway across the world. Not knowing what to make of this, he extended his hand to Elias.

"Hey there, brave boy."

Elias thrust his arms around Sami's waist, forsaking a handshake.

Sami ruffled the boy's hair, the same deep auburn colour as his mother's. "How was your flight over from Kuwait?"

"Boring." Elias stepped back, eyes wide with awe and wonder. "Can I see the other models, Uncle Sam?"

"If it's okay with your mom, my secretary can show you."

"Can I go, mama?" Elias hopped up and down. "Please? Please, mama?"

Sami threw a questioning look at Petra. Damn! Why did he feel this awkward? Moments ago, he had intimidated powerful characters with one stare, yet he failed to connect eyes with this woman without being shaken.

Petra nodded. "If it's not too much trouble."

Sami took Elias's hand and walked him to his secretary's office. He could have summoned the secretary over the phone, but he opted to leave Petra's presence briefly, hoping to get centred. This was not good. Not good at all. He was a mess when it came to this woman. He returned to the office and clamped his mouth shut.

Petra drew in a long breath. "You're probably asking yourself what in the world I'm doing here. I should have called ahead." She exhaled, slumping her shoulders. "I really don't know why I didn't."

"You have a right to check out the company anytime."

"That's not why I came." She turned her gaze to the windows. "Thank you for sending a driver to the airport. You didn't have to do that."

"Would've picked you up myself if I could have. It's daunting to arrive late at night in a big city like Houston and not find someone waiting for you." He shoved his hands in the front pockets of his trousers. "Did you find the apartment to your satisfaction?"

"I didn't know I had leased *your* apartment." She faced him. "Mr. Faisal never mentioned that. I can't understand why he didn't tell me."

"Would it matter if he had?"

"I'm paying less than a quarter of what it's worth on the market." She squared her shoulders. "I won't accept charity."

Sami waved his hand to the side and chuckled. "There's your answer."

"Excuse me?"

"That's probably why he didn't tell you, thinking you might see it that way. The fact is, you're doing *me* a favour by leasing it."

She crinkled her eyebrows "How is that?"

"You won't throw wild parties, destroy my furniture. I've seen how neat you are in your place."

She crossed her arms over her chest, adding a *don't con me* expression to her stance.

"Look, I have no idea why Faisal did what he did. I put him in touch with my realtor when we finalized the loan agreement, and he took it from there. Didn't give it much thought." Sami stepped closer. "I certainly don't need the money, and I imagined you wouldn't make use of the apartment free and clear even though you're on a tight budget, so I threw out a number."

"I think you gave your real estate agent a heart attack. She couldn't stop saying how lucky I was to rent the place for next to nothing."

"When did helping someone become so unacceptable?"

Petra unlocked her arms, relaxed her shoulders. "I'm not used to . . . needing—accepting help."

"It's no big deal. I've moved into the family house. Too many changes happened in my life. I'll eventually sell the apartment, but in the meantime, it's the perfect place for you and Elias."

Petra's face crumbled. "Oh God!" She dropped onto one of the leather chairs and covered her face with her hands.

He hurried to her side. "What's wrong?"

". . horrible," she mumbled.

He took the chair opposite hers. What the hell had he said to upset her? He touched the back of her hand. "What happened?"

She dropped her hands. Her face reddened, the birthmark pronounced and unavoidable. "This is not the conversation I imagined. I wanted to ask about your nieces and mother when Elias left because I didn't want him to know . . . what happened."

She shook her head. "I don't know how I ended up selfishly talking about the apartment and . . . money." Her lips slanted sideways in a shy smile. "I think I'm a little nervous."

Sami sat back. A level of satisfaction settled in his core, quaint and embarrassing. So he wasn't the only one whose nerves were thrown off balance by this visit. He curled his fingers into his palm to keep from reaching over to trace the arrow on her forehead. Did it emanate heat?

His phone rang. He snatched the handset and put it to his ear. "Hold my calls, Robert." He placed the handset back. "You're worried about Elias. That's perfectly natural. When does he start treatment?"

"He'll be admitted this coming Monday."

"Best team of doctors in the field, definitely the right place for Elias." Sami tried to sound confident and knowing. In the back of his mind, he speculated more reasons for her nervousness: going through the medical ordeal, being in a big city, new place, and having no one around to confide in. Dare he consider the added effect of seeing him? He scratched his temple, dismissing the arrogant thought.

"Everything will work out fine. Elias looks healthier and stronger than when I last saw him."

Petra nodded. "The doctors are optimistic. I've gone down this road before." She raised her hand and wiggled two fingers. "Twice. The wait during the long surgeries is what kills me, not the tests, not the recovery and all the pain he has to endure." She laced her fingers over her knees. "It's the waiting room, where folks talk to distract themselves and the TV chattering constantly. I discovered I need silence." She raised her eyebrows. "So how are they?" Her voice turned soft and sincere. "Your mother and nieces?"

"Mother is still struggling to acknowledge what happened." He blurted, then sucked in a sharp breath. Petra had shared something personal, private. She had forced him to reciprocate. He could have said that his mother was fine, or sad, or moving on, or for God's sake, anything but the truth.

"That's understandable," Petra said.

He exhaled slowly, resigning himself to the ridiculous idea that he was under some spell to give a detailed report. "The twins miss their mother the most, I think. Especially at bedtime. But I figured out that if I can get Deena to calm down and relax, Leena usually follows." He stopped himself before he began to talk about his struggles to entice them to cooperate with their nanny and eat something other than rice. He turned the pencil holder on his desk so that the company emblem faced him. "I doubt they understand what's going on and probably won't remember it later. I guess I should be thankful for that."

"How old are they?"

"They'll turn three in October."

"Elias was a few months older when Bassam passed away. He doesn't remember his father at all. But I have to tell you this." Petra leaned over to touch Sami's balled hand resting on his knee. "Elias remembers he was loved. If you can call it a memory. A sense, is more like it. Children are so pure, they pick up the vibe early on. They will remember the way their parents' love made them feel." She patted his hand before she withdrew it. "The twins know you care deeply about them, too."

"How can you tell?" His rough voice sounded more rugged than usual. He resisted the urge to clear it, fearing Petra might sense his unease. How did she know about his craving to hear the things she was saying?

"It spills from your eyes and voice when you talk about them. If I can see it, I'm sure the girls sense it. It'll help make them feel safe. It's what they need the most right now. Everything else will follow." Petra tilted her head sideways. "I had to figure it out on my own. That's what I came here to tell you, Sami. I know you didn't ask for my wisdom, but that's what you get for helping me." She left her chair, adding a bright smile. "A single mother's simple musings, if they're worth repeating."

He rose, unable to respond. She made light of her words, but her tender eyes showed a weightier measure of sympathy. Did she know how powerful, how important, her words were? He coughed behind a closed fist to steal a moment.

"I wanted to visit your mother to pay my respects. I couldn't find your home address anywhere."

"It's not listed. May I ask how you got here?"

"I rented a car this morning." Petra produced car keys out of her bag. "Thank God for GPS. I thought I wouldn't need a car, but this city is huge and so spread out." She winked. "I can afford a rental car since I'm saving on the apartment."

His heart pounded faster.

"Thank you again for your generosity. If I have to extend my stay another month, I insist on paying the fair price, agreed?"

"Okay." Damn! Was that all he could say? The woman had quelled his biggest doubt. He *was* doing right by the girls, keeping them with him, giving them all the love he could muster. Furthermore, she offered to connect with his mother. Dare he risk that?

"I've taken too much of your time." Petra sounded hesitant.

He stood before her, expressionless, a rigid shell

hiding a mass of emotions he didn't know how to handle.

She did a swift turn and headed to the door. "Could you please call for Elias?"

"I'll walk you over to where he is." Sami beat her to the door, held it open and waited for her to pass. "I'm glad you came, Petra."

His assistant jumped to his feet behind the desk. "Mr. Amara, you have a—"

Sami held up his hand. "Back in a moment, Robert." He escorted Petra through the main hall. "I can show you around if you wish, give you an idea about the scope of the company."

"Another time, perhaps. I promised Elias a visit to the Natural Science Museum today. He's discovered dinosaurs." She tucked hair behind her ear. "I'm trying to get most of the sightseeing out of the way before he's trapped indoors. The zoo tomorrow. I've read we can spend a whole day there."

"May we tag along?" Sami surprised himself more than Petra by his request. "The girls would love a day at the zoo, and I certainly could use a break from . . ." he waved his hand around, "here." He imagined Robert snapping a bundle of pencils once he learned of his intention to take Friday off with all the work scheduled for that day, and the girls' nanny doing a joy dance for the unexpected holiday.

Petra stopped and bowed her head.

He couldn't see her face. She remained quiet for several seconds. Disappointed, and taken aback by how much her silent rejection bothered him, he backtracked. "I don't want to intrude, of course."

"Any dietary restrictions?"

"Excuse me?"

Petra lifted her head. "Do the twins have any food allergies?"

"No."

"I'll pack us a light lunch. Elias and I will be ready downstairs in the lobby. You'll have the girls buckled in their car seats so no need to come up. How does eleven o'clock sound?"

CHAPTER SIXTEEN

Sami fumbled with the twins' bumblebee backpacks and double-seat stroller. The twins insisted on walking with Elias to the zoo entrance. Pushing the clunky stroller, Sami kept up with them. He couldn't remember a day in late February with nicer Houston weather—sunny with a temperature in the mid-sixties.

He hired one of the red wagons provided by the zoo. The girls climbed in and Elias took charge of pushing it. Every now and then, he stood on an iron rod at the end of the wagon and rode along, letting his mother know he needed a break.

Elias connected with the girls quite easily and they let him boss them around. Sami saw a glimpse of himself in the boy, in the way Elias sometimes assumed the role of their guardian and instructor. Elias dictated who sat at the front, when to switch, even tried to lift the girls onto a bench to see the elephants better.

And Petra?

Petra emanated softness and feminine charm. She had her hair tied in a loose ponytail and wore dark jeans under a baby blue button-down shirt. Blue seemed to be her favorite colour. She made him think of a flowing stream. She moved with similar fluidity, calm and serenity, and a peaceful smile never left her lips. Warm and approachable, she repeatedly touched his arm or shoulder as they walked side by side and talked about everything but the past.

He didn't know what to make of that, and he sure as hell didn't mind it. Bathed in her special scent, he imagined it rubbing off on his skin, and experienced a level of innocence he hadn't felt in a long, long time. Her birthmark did not distract him much, and he relaxed enough to enjoy her soothing company. Quite a contrast to the mess he had been in the day before. For the first time since the tragic accident that had taken his only brother, he felt hopeful. Spending the day outdoors may have been a major reason for the carefree feeling he relished. He appreciated Petra's tranquil presence, nonetheless.

The girls interacted little with Petra. She monitored them with reserve and a compassionate eye, but the girls kept their distance and it was obvious that Petra noted it. The one time Leena hesitantly approached Petra, babbling something in her special language, Petra simply held on to Sami's forearm, kneeled to Leena's level and smiled. No hugs, no kisses, no closeness. It baffled him and he was unsure why he had expected differently. She was a loving, caring mother to Elias, surely she could draw in his sweet, adorable nieces.

The girls cried inside the enclosed Gorilla Quarters. Sami thanked his lucky stars for their fear of the intimidating primates. He took them outside and filled his lungs with fresh air, leaving Elias and Petra to watch bored gorillas staring back through the glass divider.

At the petting Zoo, he trailed Petra among bleating goats, letting the kids play with the docile animals. Deena tugged on ears and tails, Leena patted backs and hinds, and Elias tried to entice a goat to follow him by waving a bundle of straw.

They ate lunch at a picnic table in the toddlers' playground. Sami deliberately postponed eating his peanut butter sandwich until the kids were done.

"Do you think you can watch the twins while your Mom and I finish our lunch over here?" He asked Elias, counting on the idea that the boy would welcome the chance to assume more responsibility.

"DeLeenas, come." Elias invented the mashed name to address them both at the same time. They scurried after him. He helped Deena crawl over a massive colourful turtle slide and go down its short tail. Leena copied her sister with Elias's encouragement.

Sami slowly munched on his sandwich, while keeping an eye on the kids. "I can't believe how great Elias is with them." He shook his head. "DeLeenas. Now, that's clever."

"All his life, he's been *the little* one. At school, with Mouzah's boys. He's in a different situation with the girls, so he's spreading his wings." Petra twisted open a water bottle. "It's important for a boy not to feel disadvantaged once in a while. It grows character."

"He's sweet and caring. You've done well with him."

"So far." She took long gulps from her water bottle, tilting her head back.

Sami watched tiny freckles dance up and down Petra's outstretched neck each time she swallowed. Was her entire body dotted like that? She brought down the bottle, and he slanted his eyes to the turtle.

"Elias takes after his father, actually. I believe it's in his nature. My influence is limited."

"Not true. You're being modest. A mother's power is very strong in shaping her child's character." Sami heaved a heavy sigh. "Believe me, I know what I'm talking about."

He regretted steering the conversation in that direction and readied himself for her to ask about his mother. Would she still be interested in paying a visit? It might be the trigger to snap his mother out of her phase of denial. Or if Mother wasn't ready to talk about Fareed, or even acknowledge his death, perhaps she could talk about Father once she saw Petra, reveal more about his past. Although that might backfire and throw Mother into another fit.

Petra let his comment pass. She remained quiet, that thoughtful smile on her lips.

He finished his sandwich and switched direction. "I fear I'm going to ruin the girls' lives."

She lifted her sunglasses to rest them on her head. "Why do you say that?"

"I didn't have what you call a normal upbringing. I spent my growing up years with my brother at a boys' boarding school away from home." He squinted against the sun. "Most of the time, I don't know what I'm doing. They're . . . girls."

"They're healthy and seem happy, Sami. They're behaving normally."

"Healthy, yes. According to their pediatrician. But happy? How do you get that? They haven't exactly warmed up to you."

"They don't trust me. Why should they? I'm a stranger."

"I thought you'd . . . I don't know. Because you're—"

"Because I'm a woman? You thought I'd win them over with my motherly aura?" She shook her head. "It doesn't work that way. I hope you didn't get the wrong idea. If you've noticed I've come . . ." She dropped down her sunglasses, blocking him from reading in her eyes what she wasn't articulating. "I've come too close to you throughout the day. Invaded your personal space, so to speak. Touching your arms and shoulders?"

"Oh, I've noticed."

"Yes, well. It's one way to establish trust with the girls, showing them I am . . . okay, acceptable. They pick up their cues from you, and you tolerate my touch, so they might accept it later on when I offer it."

183

"I see." Sami stared at his reflection in the dark lenses of her sunglasses. Was that a valid approach in the world of child rearing? Or was Petra bullshitting him? And how in the world could he tell the difference? He knew nothing about child psychology. He knew very little about her. He crumpled his sandwich wrapper. "And here I was, thinking you were flirting with me."

A fire started between the open top buttons of her shirt and a blush flared to her neck. "I should have explained my actions from the start. I acted on impulse, I guess. When I saw how apprehensive the girls were from the moment I got in the car, I thought I should hold back until I can establish trust." She watched Elias chase the girls around a huge red mushroom and waved them over. "Not sure it's working, though."

"It might explain why the girls didn't take to their nanny as well as I expected. With all her glowing credentials and expertise, Mrs. Madigan hasn't established a warm connection with them yet. It's been two months since I hired her. She takes very good care of them, don't get me wrong." He ran a hand through his hair. "In all honesty, I hadn't thought about gradually introducing her to the twins. I trusted she knew what she was doing."

"Give her time." Petra rose and brushed crumbs off her jeans. "If she's as competent as you say, she'll figure out how to break the barrier." Petra gathered the leftover fruit in Ziplock bags and the juice bottles and returned them to Elias's backpack.

Sami threw away the trash and returned to the bench. He stuffed the girls' snacks into their bumblebee bags. "By the way, I don't *tolerate* it."

"Sorry?"

"Your touch. I don't tolerate it."

Petra's lips parted with an audible short exhale.

"I welcome it."

A bottle slipped from her hand and fell off the table. She watched it roll away. He watched her; that bashful fire crept up her neck again.

Elias went after the runaway bottle. "I got it, mama."

Deena ran into Sami's legs and wrapped her arms around his knees. He sat her on the table to fix her shoelaces, and turned to grab her sister. With a questioning look in her big dark eyes, Leena raised both arms to Petra.

"Let's do something about those crazy shoes." Petra lifted Leena and seated her next to her sister. Before she let go, Leena wrapped her short arms around Petra's neck. Petra returned the hug and waited until Leena dropped her arms before she pulled back.

The red laces in Sami's hands turned to rubber and he couldn't tie them right. Either that, or his fingers suddenly became claws. Damn! The woman knew what she was doing. Leena finally reached out to her, and it had taken Petra only half a day to gain her trust. So, did he have to entice stocky, broad-shouldered Mrs. Madigan to give him full-blown hugs? He shuddered at the thought.

Elias retrieved the bottle and pointed behind Sami. "I want to do that."

Sami carried the girls off the table and set them down. He turned to see what Elias was pointing at and read the sign: Prairie Dog Tunnels.

A huge glass bubble encircled a dirt mound. Several small clear cylinders jutted out from the dirt pile under the dome. Children poked their heads into the cylinders and saw the animals run around.

"Mama, can we go in there?" Elias tugged on Petra's hand.

"Sure." She let Elias drag her to the tunnels' entrance and waved at Sami to follow. "Bring the girls. This should be fun."

Sami hesitated, eying the narrow entry to the tunnels. Deena ran after Elias and Petra, Leena followed her sister. He had to go along, gritting his teeth. Hunching his shoulders, he ambled through the tunnels until they opened out into an artificial cave with dim lighting.

Elias wiggled into a plastic tube, Petra right after him. Their laughter echoed through the enclosure. The girls crawled into another tube, mimicking Elias.

As if diving head first, Sami held his breath and squeezed his body after them. They poked their heads into the cylinder at the end of their tube. Petra and

Elias waved from their cylinder. The girls pounded on the glass, laughing.

Sami connected eyes with Petra and lost it. He withdrew as fast as he could from the tube, gasping for air, forced to leave the girls behind.

Petra met him outside her tube. "What's wrong?"

He clutched his chest. "Can't do this." He panted and pointed behind him. "My girls. Please," he managed between gulps.

"Go. I got them."

Finding his way out from the cave and tunnels, he stumbled to a spacious area away from trees. He closed his eyes, stretched his arms to his sides and moved them in a wide arc over his head to get a sense of the void surrounding him. He filled his lungs with deep breaths and lifted his face toward the sun. Dread peeled off his body bit by bit like a mummy's rotten shroud. To passers-by, he must seem like a lunatic, but he had learned to ignore stares a long time ago. He dropped his head with a sudden realization. How on earth was he to look after the twins with this condition? A fool, he was nothing but a fool to think he could look after them better than Lora's parents.

He opened his eyes. Petra approached with the kids and there he stood before her—a pathetic weakling, vulnerable, handicapped.

Petra had a strange expression on her face—neither worry, nor sympathy. Some other countenance he was in no condition to interpret. Her lips moved, but all he could hear was high-pitched ringing in his ears. He bent down and rested his hands on his knees, allowing more blood to rush to his head. The ringing subsided.

Elias hopped around him. "Did you see the prairie dogs, Uncle Sam? They ran around us."

Sami straightened, shaking his head. "Sorry, I didn't."

"See those chickens over there by the white fence?" Petra addressed Elias. "Walk DeLeenas over there? Don't let go of their hands. We'll be right there."

"Yes, mama." Elias walked the girls a few steps over.

Petra handed Sami a water bottle. "What happened?"

Sami squeezed water over his head and neck. "I don't do well in cramped spaces." He scrubbed his face.

"Claustrophobic?"

"Yeah." He took long sips of water and watched her study him, tapping the sunglasses in her hand against her thigh. He crushed the empty bottle in his fist. *Don't ask. Please don't ask how this condition was spawned.* He flung the mangled bottle into a nearby recycling bin. "It was stupid of me to go in there."

"Yes, it was." Petra threw back her head. "Thank God!" She passed him quickly to reach the kids.

What the hell? She was relieved at his stupidity? He strode after her, stood aside when she swung the gate open to let the kids go into the coop and run around with the chickens. She closed the gate and dangled her arms over the white fence.

He joined her, determined to set her straight. "I had no choice but to follow my girls into that torturous exhibit."

"Not true. You could have told me. I'd have spared you the pain."

He scratched his ear. She had a point. "I'm not used to talking about my . . . condition."

"A perceptual problem." A wide smile took up most of her face.

"You're pleased?" Sounding light and nonchalant, he kept his annoyance and embarrassment hidden. "Glad to be of service."

She dropped her smile. "When I saw you clutch your chest, I thought . . . this can't be happening. Not again."

"Again?" He tried to remember when she saw him freak out before.

"The odds of me coming across another young man with a heart problem should be very slim."

"You thought I was having a heart attack?"

"Do you recall what I told you about remembering a certain feeling, your body experiencing it rather than your mind knowing the incident that caused it? Well, it was like that in the tunnels. For a second, I experienced the same anxiety." She shook her head. "Nothing compared to what you were going through. You really thought you couldn't breathe in there?"

"Right." Hadn't he just said he didn't want to talk about his problem? For someone who was so good at interpreting children's social signals, she pretty much failed at reading his. Better switch the focus of the conversation onto her.

"Were you there when it happened to your husband? Were you with him?"

Petra pushed off the fence, hooked her thumbs in her back pockets and shifted her feet.

Sami would have kicked himself if he could. To self-preserve, to avoid talking about his complex, he had dragged this emotionally fragile woman to a painful memory.

He reached for her elbow. "Sorry. I shouldn't have asked."

She twisted away and stared at her feet. "Sometimes when I have a moment to myself, truly alone, I go there in my mind. I'm in our bedroom, frozen at the foot of the bed, watching Bassam convulse, sheets twisted between his feet."

Sami swallowed. "Jesus!"

She lifted her head. Tears shimmered, trapped behind long eyelashes. "Thank God Elias was asleep in his room." She blinked, freeing the tears. "What happened to Bassam rearranged me. I'm not broken, just misshapen."

Sami opened his mouth. *You're perfect*, he wanted to say, convinced he would be stating a fact rather than paying a compliment. But his lips wouldn't move, his tongue a puffer fish filling his mouth. He was the one deformed, and he was playing with fire. This widow with a sick child deserved far better. Why in hell had he invited himself today? Why inflict his twisted life on this delicately poised woman?

Petra's lips sagged in a sad smile. She wiped under her eyes with the tips of her fingers. "You know, ever since I met you, I've been trying to figure out something."

With a dry throat, he managed, "Yeah?"

A rooster flapped his wings fast and scared Deena. She shrieked and fell onto her backside. Sami jumped over the fence and scooped her into his arms. She wailed and clung to his neck. As if a trigger had been released, Leena's lips quivered, getting ready to lose it. He picked her up, too, and got out of the small pen. Petra called on Elias to follow.

"Let's clean up." Petra helped Sami scrub the kids' hands with wet towels. Leena reached for Petra's dangling hair strands as she bent forward. Petra let her play with them.

"Why is that chicken bigger than the others?" Elias asked.

"It's a rooster." Sami wiped Deena's smudged face after she had calmed down. "A daddy chicken."

"He's mean." Elias hugged Deena. "He scared her."

"He was protecting his turf. His home," Sami explained.

"I'm surprised the zoo keepers let it be in there," Petra said.

"Mama, do we eat rooster eggs?"

"A rooster doesn't lay eggs."

"What does he do, mama?"

"A rooster and a hen, a mama chicken, make baby chickens. They're called chicks and they hatch out of eggs when they're ready."

"But, mama, we eat eggs."

Petra shook her head. "Those we eat are not special. They don't have chicks in them."

"How do you know that?" Elias's voice trembled.

"The farms that send eggs to grocery stores make sure of it, *ya albi*."

"But how?" Elias had difficulty holding back tears. "How do they know without breaking the eggs?"

"Hens lay eggs without the rooster's help too, and those eggs don't turn into chicks. Farmers know that, you see?"

Elias cupped his small hands in front of his face. "How do chicks get inside their eggs, mama?"

Sami took Leena from Petra's hands to let her focus on her son. Somewhat entertained, he waited to hear what Petra would come up with.

"When the rooster helps a hen, she lays special eggs. She sits on them to keep them warm and comfy. Chicks grow inside and when they are big enough, they pick at the egg shells from the inside with their little beaks."

Petra hooked her index finger at the tip of her nose and pecked the wooden table.

The girls giggled.

Petra stretched and flapped her arms to her sides. "Then the chicks are *born* and they spread their wings."

"But what does the rooster do? How does he help?"

Petra went down on one knee to Elias's eye level. "You remember when I explained that you have a part of your Daddy in you?"

Elias bobbed his head. "My wee wee."

Sami covered his surprise with a fake cough. It drew Petra's eyes to him and she flashed an embarrassed smile.

"Well, it's kind of the same for chickens." Clearly exasperated, her thinning patience showed in her voice. "The rooster gives a part of himself to the hen to make eggs that have chicks."

"How does he do that, mama?"

Sami stepped in, feeling sorry for Petra. "Want to see the alligators now, Elias?"

Elias hopped in his place. "Can we? Can we Uncle Sam?"

Sami raised his eyebrows at Petra to gauge her reaction at his interference. Relief poured out of her eyes. "We sure can." Sami sat the girls in the wagon, thinking he should have suggested seeing docile giraffes instead. If Elias thought the rooster was mean, what would he think of alligators? The boy was in for a big surprise if they arrived during feeding time.

Elias took off with the wagon.

"Please slow down, Elias," Petra called out.

Sami fell into step with Petra behind the children. "He's very excited."

"I don't want him to exhaust himself. He forgets his condition and gets carried away."

Sami stuck two fingers in his mouth and blew a piercing whistle. Elias stopped and turned around. Sami walked his fingers in the air. "Don't run, buddy. I'm tired."

"Yes, Uncle Sam."

"Thank you for cutting Elias off earlier," Petra said. "I was taken off guard. I haven't thought about how to explain those things to him, yet."

Sami winced. "He seems to have a strange idea about his father's role."

Blushing, she tucked loose hair strands behind her ear. "I needed him to know his father is forever part of him. I started explaining about male and female chromosomes, and ended up making a mess of it. That's what stuck in his head, I guess."

"I suggest you work on coming up with clear answers very soon. I was seven when I found out what my parents did to conceive me."

She touched his arm. "Oh my God! You were that young?"

"Dad spelled things out when Mom started showing her pregnancy with my brother." Sami halved his palm

194

with the side of his other hand. "Clear cut. Correct terminology. No hesitation. Dad had that way about him. I couldn't sleep for days. Then Fareed came soon after. Unlike me, he looked so much like Dad, and that's when it clicked in my head."

"I can't see myself doing that to Elias at this age. It's too soon. He still believes in Santa."

"You're probably right. I'm not saying it was the correct approach." Sami shrugged. "What do I know?"

Petra tilted her head to one side and winked. "I'm finding out you know plenty, Sami Amara."

The afternoon sun suddenly came too close; its heat flushed Sami's face. It had to be the sun because he couldn't be blushing, for heaven's sake. He shoved his hands in his jeans' front pockets. "You said you were trying to figure out something about me?"

"You seem so . . . straight."

He tripped, checked under his feet and pretended to kick a pebble. Shit! Did she think he was gay?

Petra kept going, ticking her fingers one at a time. "You honoured your father's wishes despite the disruption they caused the company—your family's legacy. You've been extremely generous with me—a stranger. Kind to Elias—connecting really well with him. And you've shouldered tremendous responsibility after your family's tragedy, taking very good care of your nieces, worrying about your mother." Petra slowed her pace. "I thought, there has to be something wrong with this guy. No one is that good."

Sami stopped. "There's plenty wrong, Petra." He would not allow her to entertain the slightest illusion about his distorted composition. Not for a single minute. "Trust me on that."

"Well, now I know." She hooked her arm in his and nudged him forward. "You're a normal guy, Sami Amara."

He had no idea how to respond. What sort of world did this woman live in? How did she define normality? He let her drag him along, savouring her closeness and ignoring the honorable thoughts that had silenced him earlier with reasons to distance himself from vulnerable Petra. Walking away would be the right thing to do, gentlemanly, decent. One thing his mother's illness had taught him was never to take a woman's trust for granted. If Petra brought down her guard thinking he was no threat, she was surely mistaken.

He slowed down to make sure the kids were out of earshot and unhooked his arm from Petra's. "I'll have you know, I'm not gay."

Her face flamed red, up to her birthmark and to the roots of her pulled-back hair. "Excuse me?"

"I don't want you to have the wrong idea about me."

She overlapped her hands on her chest. "Have I done anything to imply I thought you were gay?"

"You said I *seemed* straight."

"Straight as an arrow. On the right path. Decently responsible." Her blush deepened. "That's what I was talking about."

He bit his tongue to keep from cursing out loud. He had stepped in it, hadn't he? The hell with decency. He was buried knee-deep in crap when it came to dealing with Petra. He gave a confirmation nod. "Glad we cleared that up."

They reached the alligator area. Elias's excitement quickly faded after they had watched alligators sunbathing on the creek banks for three minutes.

A wooden bridge crossed the creek. Sami waited with the girls at one end while Petra walked Elias over to get a better view of the largest alligator lounging on the other bank. They returned, disappointment unmodulated on Elias's face.

"I'm tired, mama." Elias yawned. "Can we go home now?"

"What do you say, Sami?" Petra asked.

"The girls are about to fall asleep, too." Sami motioned for Elias to hop onto the wagon. "Let's go."

They headed to the gates. Sami pushed the kids, making sharp turns now and then. Their collective screams and laughter kept them awake.

Petra leaned closer to Sami and lowered her voice. "I have to ask you something."

He dipped his head. "Yes?"

"Outside the tunnels, when you stood in that strange position for a while, moving your arms like that . . ." She pressed her lips together and hesitated.

He straightened. So she was intent on making him talk about his disorder no matter how many signals he sent. "It helps me get a real sense of space."

"Where did you learn to do that?"

"I've done it ever since I was a child. I don't know who taught me. Why do you ask?"

"My mother called it her special pain controlling technique. Before she became too sick, she stood exactly that way every morning."

CHAPTER SEVENTEEN

Petra brewed chamomile tea and took her steaming cup to the living room. She lounged on the couch, hoping for a restful night. Elias had barely tolerated a quick bath after dinner and had fallen asleep watching a Disney movie on the king-size bed.

Since her first night in the apartment, she hadn't slept in Sami's huge bed by herself, knowing she was being silly and unreasonable. It just didn't feel right. It was better to share the master bedroom with her son and forego the twin-size bed Sami had thoughtfully installed for Elias in the den.

She picked up her book and flipped to the bookmark. Halfway down the page, thoughts of Sami invaded her mind. She set the book aside.

Sami had fallen quiet in the car, distant. When Elias asked how the arching bridges hung over wide interchanging roads, she had expected Sami to respond. He seemed not to hear Elias, and she offered what she thought were reasonable answers to keep her son from asking more.

The twins stayed awake. Petra fretted the entire drive home on how to turn Sami gently down if he asked to come up to the apartment. But once they arrived, Sami threw a half-hearted smile, a quick goodbye and drove away. Though relieved, she was irritated at his sudden withdrawal.

Whether he meant to or not, Sami made her feel normal, less of a misfit. Something she hadn't experienced in a long time. She lost her inhibitions and reservations in his presence, ignored the restrictive filters and social checks in her head. She let go. Did she even flirt a little? She sure did. She was drawn to Sami. Any healthy woman with a decent set of eyes would be. By any measure, Sami was an attractive man, quick mood shifts, claustrophobia and all.

Petra blew into her cup. Sami was probably involved with some gorgeous, model-like, high society woman, if not an actual model. Miss saucy-voiced Adriana from Costa Rica, for example. Most likely with a perfect tan and birthmark-free. Handsome successful men were never alone.

She sighed. Time to be realistic. With her unsophisticated personality and blemished skin, she didn't stand a chance of catching Sami's eye. If it hadn't been for his father's will, he wouldn't have given her a second look, certainly wouldn't have spent an entire day at the zoo with her and her kid.

She took a sip of the herbal tea and burned her tongue. She teared up with the pain, then the tears kept coming. What sort of mother was she? Her focus should be on Elias and the trying time he would go through in the hospital. Instead here she sat, thinking of Sami. It felt good to be around him. He didn't ask specifics about Elias's condition and for a few hours she had stopped worrying about her son's malfunctioning heart.

She blew her nose on a tissue and eyed the twirling tiny cloud above the teacup. Talking about Bassam's death was a mistake. She must have appeared needy and desperate. No wonder Sami couldn't wait to dump her and Elias. He had probably left the girls with their nanny and gone to the model waiting for him at her childfree place.

Her phone buzzed with a WhatsApp call. Anticipating Mouzah's voice, she was surprised when she heard Maryam's instead.

"*Bonjour, chéri.* Is it too early? I hope I didn't wake you."

"Good morning." Petra calculated the time difference. Six a.m. in Kuwait. Better not correct Maryam about time zones. It would only confuse her— something she should avoid at all cost while having a phone conversation with her hard-of-hearing neighbor.

"I wanted to let you know I'm alright," Maryam said as if Petra had asked for the reason for the call.

"I'm glad."

"The car is gone, but the apartment is okay, considering."

"Car? Whose?"

"Yes, *touz*. It lasted most of the afternoon. I never saw anything like it. Ali knew what to do, but he didn't have time to do the same for your apartment."

Petra rose, frustrated at not knowing the meaning of the Arabic word Maryam used. She raised her voice. "What did Ali have to do? What happened to my place?"

"It's covered. The beds, living room furniture, the kitchen. Red sand everywhere, even inside the cabinets. You should have sealed the doors and windows with sponge before you left. That's the only way to keep sand from getting into everything. I'm going to hire a cleaning team for this, *chéri*. I can't do it on my own."

"Yes, of course. Please do. I'll cover the cost. And thank you for checking on things."

An incoming local call beeped with an unknown number. Petra ignored it. Whoever it was could leave a message.

"*Aloo? Aloo?* Is that your alarm clock?"

"Someone is calling, Maryam. Never mind the beeping." Petra dropped back on the couch. "I've heard of sand storms hitting the region, but there haven't been any since I moved to Kuwait."

"You're wrong, *chéri*. We didn't have *touz* last year."

Petra tapped her foot and decided to let Maryam be with her misunderstandings. "Thank God you're okay. Tell me about the storm."

"It happened almost instantly. We had a few minutes of warning. Ali was home, so he was able to seal the windows in my apartment. People trapped in their cars on roads suffered the most. Ali says your car's engine is not working. He will fix it, don't worry."

"Any casualties?"

"Cashews? I didn't check the snack canisters in your kitchen, *chéri*. It's best to throw everything away."

Petra pulled on her ponytail to stop herself from cursing. "Yes, do that."

"*Aloo?*"

"I'm listening."

"Will you turn off your alarm? It's very distracting."

Petra silenced another incoming call from the same number. "There, it's off. So what was it like during the storm?"

"We barely breathed." Maryam sounded irritated. "It reminded me of the times I spent in shelters in Beirut, especially during the last Israeli attack in two thousand and six. You would think spending half your life in wars, you get used to the horror. You really don't."

"Was it that bad?"

"*Oui.* The sound of the howling wind was as frightening as the alarm sirens and bombings."

"The most important thing is that you're fine, right?"

"We are thankful. Tell me, when is Elias's surgery?"

"Tuesday."

"I'm praying for him. Five times a day, you know. It adds up. Did you find a church nearby? Are you praying?"

"Yes." Petra struggled to remain composed. If only prayers were enough.

"God listens to mothers, *chéri*. Muslims, Christians, Jews, it doesn't matter. When it comes to children, there's only one religion. Motherhood. God listens to old women in particular. I've been through enough hardship not to be ignored."

"I hope you're right," Petra choked.

At times, Maryam drove her to distraction, but the old *chéri* was caring and loving, as close to a grandmother as Petra could ask for Elias.

"Is it open heart surgery? Similar to what they did to the downstairs neighbor, Abu Ahmad?"

"Oh, no. It's a low-impact procedure, minimally invasive. They'll implant a cardioband to fix the leaky mitral valve without opening Elias's chest."

"Oh, I don't know what that means, but it sounds less scary. Please call and let me know when he is out of surgery."

"I will. Stay safe."

Petra dragged herself into the kitchen and dumped the remainder of her herbal tea in the sink. Nothing more effective than a phone conversation with Maryam to drain whatever energy she had and send her to bed.

A soft knock sounded at the front door. Petra checked her watch, half past ten. It must be the night guard. Had she parked in someone's spot again? She snatched her night robe, slipped it over her pyjamas, and hurried to open the door.

"I didn't move my car today, Roy."

Sami filled the doorway, looking haggard. "It's me."

He was still in the T-shirt and jeans he had worn to the zoo. Petra pulled her robe together and partially hid behind the door. "What are you doing here, Sami?"

"I called. You didn't answer."

Petra's eyes flew to the couch, where her phone sat on a cushion. She had forgotten to check her messages. "That was you? I didn't recognize the number."

"Oh! That's my local number. The one you have is for the phone I use when I'm travelling. I left that one at home." He rubbed the nape of his neck. "Sorry about that. I've been driving around since I dropped the girls. I didn't wake you, did I?"

"What's going on?" Her voice broke, exposing her unease. Sami didn't just look haggard; he was troubled. "Are the girls okay?"

"They're fine. I need to talk to you." He placed his hands on the door frame. "And I'm running out of time."

CHAPTER EIGHTEEN

Petra let Sami in and closed the door.

He remained just behind her. His faint scent hung in the narrow hallway, something clean and crisp.

"Is Elias asleep?" he asked, keeping his voice low.

She turned to face him. The rough scratch in his voice was more obvious than it had been earlier in the day. She nodded. "Since seven."

She was wrong. Sami had on a different T-shirt to the one he had worn at the zoo. This one was a shade darker and freshly washed, smelling of trees and heavy rain. He said he had been driving around for some time. Did he keep a change of clothes in his car? Whether that was true or not, the notion that he had made an effort to put himself in order before he saw her pleased her.

She moved toward the living room.

Sami went straight to the window, withdrew the mini blinds and leaned a shoulder on the glass pane. Under the bright lights, he stood there in contrast to the white furniture. Stubble darkened half of his face, his eyes were red and restless, his stance far from casual, as though he needed the window to support his weight.

"Have a seat."

"I'm fine right here."

"Will you excuse me for a minute?"

"I shouldn't have come this late. But I saw your lights were on and I couldn't—"

She cut him off. "It's alright, Sami." Late hour or not, she would *not* have a conversation clad in her pyjamas. "I'll just be a moment."

She hurried into the bedroom and, as quietly as she could so as not to wake Elias, changed into yoga leggings and a white T-shirt. If that didn't give the image of a relaxed and confident woman, she had no idea what outfit would. Perhaps Sami was too engrossed in whatever predicament had brought him to notice her nervousness.

She returned to the living room to find him staring out of the window, his arms crossed hard over his chest. "Can I get you anything to drink?"

"No, thank you." He unlocked his arms. "I like what you've done to the place."

"Everything is as it was when I moved in." She approached, hesitant and apprehensive. "I didn't change anything."

"Yes, I see." He spread his lips into a smile that didn't reach his eyes, making him look more miserable. He pointed at the weight-training bench covered with a white sheet. "Eyesore?"

"I didn't want Elias to be tempted and hurt himself."

"I should've moved it out of here before you arrived."
Sami shook his head. "Didn't think that far. I'll send
someone to pick it up if you want."

"Only if you need it. And I'm not saying that you
do." She bit her lower lip, surprised by her forwardness.
Did he know how sexy he looked with that rough, yet
vulnerable vibe? And what in God's name was in that
tea bag that made her senses so heightened tonight?

He flashed a hesitant smile, no doubt confused
by her subtle flirting. "I don't have time to work out
anymore."

"Elias knows not to go near the weights. So it's
really no trouble leaving it." She balanced herself on
the couch's wide arm. Enough with the small talk.
Why was he here? She forced her foot to stop swinging,
fearing her flip-flop might fly across the room. "What
couldn't wait until the morning, Sami?"

He turned his face to gaze out of the window again.
"Did your mother have red hair?"

"My mother? Why?"

Sami's long exhale fogged the glass pane. "Please,
Petra. I'd like to know."

"Hold on." She went to the kitchen counter that
opened into the living room and dug into her bag for
her wallet. She slipped out a picture and returned to
Sami's side. "Here, see for yourself."

Sitting on the windowsill, he took the slightly
wrinkled photo and gazed at it for several minutes. He

seemed to have gone down his own private memory lane, somewhere far away and not so pleasant. His face contorted with the recollections.

"My mother's lips were blood red. She never wore lipstick." Petra tried to bring him back to the present. "Strange the things that get stuck in our heads, right?" An anxious giggle escaped her. "As you can see, the only things I got from her are the freckles. I managed not to pass them on to Elias."

"I'm pretty sure I met your mother when I was a child." Sami's voice came out dreamy, sombre. "I remember a red-haired lady teaching me to manage a panic attack. Those moves you saw me do at the zoo? When you said your mother used to do the same, it hit me."

He ran his thumb over her mother's face and long wavy hair, a caress that went straight to Petra's heart.

"I remember her standing in our upstairs hallway," he continued, "holding my arms out and stretching them above my head. Morning sun from the window behind her highlighted the redness in her hair. In my panic, I remember thinking her head was catching fire."

"Before she became too sick, she let me brush her hair every night as part of our bedtime routine. She never lost it, you know."

Sami looked up. "She never lost what?"

"Her fiery hair. She never lost it. No chemo."

"She kept telling me *feel it, it's there. It's always there.*"

"Her hair?"

209

He shook his head. A single word came out heavy with his ragged voice, loaded with emotions, opposite to the meaning it carried, "emptiness."

He handed her the photo, slid his hands over his thighs and rested them on his knees. "That's the only memory I have of her."

"How old were you?"

"I must have been eight or nine. Fareed was little. I remember hearing him in the background—crying."

Petra turned away from the window and returned the photograph to her wallet on the kitchen counter. She took her time to process the information. Sami had a pleasant memory of her mother, a private one that stayed with him and affected him as a man. It irritated her. As if he had stolen something valuable, a mother and child moment that was her privilege, hers alone.

Ashamed of the irrational jealousy, she shoved the wallet into her bag with more force than necessary. Where was she in that memory? If he was eight at that time, then she was around five. That was after her mother had left Kuwait and moved to Milwaukee.

How had her mother ended up with Sami's mother in Houston? The women couldn't have known each other before their husbands entered their lives considering that each couple met years after the men had left Kuwait. Her mother and Sami's mother must have been introduced to each other through their husbands.

Petra lifted the folder onto the counter that contained all the documents Mr. Faisal had given her. She flipped it open and looked for Mr. Amara's letter. Scanning it in a hurry, she read his claim that he had lost all contact with her father after he moved to the States. Had Mr. Amara lied to his son? She glanced at Sami, who was silent, head bowed, staring at his feet.

Or was Sami lying to her?

She cleared her throat to draw his attention. "I'm certain your mo—"

"I need to know who you are," he interrupted. Pressing the heels of his palms to his eye sockets, he half-shouted. "Who *are* you?"

"You know who I am." The intensity of his tone and his obvious frustration raised alarm bells in her head. "I'm not the one hiding anything."

"What's that supposed to mean?" He pulled away from the window. "I've told you everything I know."

"Your mother can clear up all this."

"That's why I came here." He moved to the middle of the living room, softening his tone. "I want you to meet my mother."

Petra pressed her lips tight, summoning patience. That's what had him twisted out of shape, unable to wait for the morning? An invitation to visit his mother?

"I know this is a bad time for you," he continued. "You're completely focused on Elias, and I'm being selfish. But I want to get to the bottom of this as soon as possible."

"Why now?" She wanted to know the exact nature of their connection, yes, but this urgency irked her. "What's so pressing?"

Sami opened his mouth to answer, seemed to change his mind, and clamped it shut.

Noticing his hesitation, the alarm bells in her head turned into sirens. He *was* hiding something.

"You said you were running out of time. Regarding what, exactly?"

"I don't want to bother you during Elias's treatment. That leaves us this weekend."

"I have a feeling something else is going on."

He worked his jaw, clearly conflicted. He stared on, eyes haunted.

Going against instincts of caution and self-defence, she ignored the blaring in her ears and strode past him to the chair by the window. If she was right, Sami was tethered to windows—his comfort zone. If he felt physically at ease, he might open up and spill whatever he was trying so hard to keep down. She held out her hand.

"You've helped me in many ways, Sami." She followed with an encouraging smile. "Will you let me return the favour?"

As if she had pulled on that invisible rope which kept him anchored to windows, he shuffled forward and dropped onto the chair opposite hers. He sought the lights outside. Several minutes passed and Sami still sat there before her, his mind a thousand miles away.

She studied his profile, his Adam's apple jutting out at a sharp angle. That might explain why he had that scrape in his voice, there was little room for his vocal cords to vibrate. Close to his T-shirt collar line, his copper tan faded into a lighter shade. The same tan line peeked from under his short sleeves when he moved his arms. What would he look like without his T-shirt?

She sucked in a sharp breath at the shameful thought. The man was in turmoil, and what was she thinking about? His bare chest! She dropped her head and pretended to look at something outside, letting her hair drape over part of her face to hide an embarrassed blush.

Sami snapped out of his pensiveness. He leaned forward, rested his elbows on his knees, and locked his fingers together. "I received bad news today when I got home."

"How bad?"

"Fareed's in-laws are taking me to court. I could lose custody of the girls to their grandparents."

"Oh! Can't you work it out without having to go to court?"

"I've been trying to appease the old couple. Sent them pictures and videos of the twins almost every day to show how happy they are, that they're well cared for.

I try to Skype them every evening so they can chat with the girls. But they rarely accept the calls."

"Perhaps if they came to see for themselves—"

"I bought them open tickets to use any time they want. They never came. Not once since they returned to Cleveland after Lora's funeral." He unlocked his fingers and sat back. "I thought they'd realized it was for the best and decided to let it be. But they've filed for custody and a court hearing is set now. I can't let them steal Fareed's girls from me." He shook his head. "I won't."

"When do you have to be in court?"

"On the sixteenth. I have three weeks to somehow convince a social worker and then a judge that I can provide a stable and nurturing environment."

"That's what you've been doing for the past two months. That's easy to prove." Petra edged forward, her apprehension gone. This was a man fighting to keep his brother's children, a parent in the making. He *wanted* to care for them, not because he had to. Her aunt had taken her in after her mother's death, but she hadn't needed to fight anyone over her. One day, when the twins were old enough, they would realize how much a difference that made in their lives, to be *wanted*.

"And you're young, Sami. Surely that's better for the girls than being cared for by an older couple."

"It's not their age I'm worried about. Lora never took the twins home to see her parents. That says a lot." Sami ran a hand through his hair. "I have a bad feeling about her father. Call it a gut feeling. I don't know much about parenting or children, but I know men. And that man is dangerous."

"You're good with the girls, Sami. Good *for* them."

A vein pulsed in his left temple. "Am I?"

"You *are*. I've seen how well the girls respond to you. I'm sure the judge will see that."

"Wish I had your confidence," Sami whispered. Doubt reflected off his entire body like sweat. She could almost see the dull sheen.

"So you have issues. Who doesn't?" She laid a hand on his knee. "When I first found out I was pregnant with Elias, fear overcame me. I was terrified that with all my baggage, I'd ruin an innocent life. I suspect you're at that stage." She withdrew her hand. "You, Sami Amara, are pregnant."

He arched his eyebrows and blinked several times.

Sticking to her ridiculous analogy, she forged forward. "You don't have nine months to adjust emotionally. To ease into the idea. Your babies are here."

"When does it go away? That fear?"

"It never does. You do your best despite that fear. It puts you on guard. As long as you know what your shortcomings are, you work around them. You can do this."

He nodded sharply. "God! I want to. I really do."

"What do you need to make it happen?"

"My lawyer says two major things are against me. Time is one of them."

"And the other?"

"I'm not . . . a family."

"You have your mother living with you, right? She's the girls' grandmother, too. That's a family."

Sami winced. "Yeah, about my mother. She's . . . unreliable. I can manage the social worker visits. Keep Mom under control at home. The minute she sets foot in the courtroom, the judge will discover her issues." Sami shook his head. "I can't risk it."

"Unreliable how?"

"Mom lives in her own bubble." Sami turned to the window again. The torment in his voice was inescapable. "Sometimes she's so far gone, I can't reach her."

"If there's anything I can do to help, please don't hesitate to ask."

Sami bit his upper lip and slowly released it, a plan taking root in his head. He faced her, his forehead creased in a slight frown.

Petra recognized that expression. Like her, Sami was not used to being helped. He probably didn't know how to ask. Unsure why she was so compelled to ease his pain, Petra pushed, "I mean it. Anything I can do."

"Come for lunch at my house tomorrow. Talk to Mom about your parents. See what she has to say. It might draw her out to talk about the past, about Dad. I can explain my situation. Get her on board." Sami left his chair and extended his hand. "What do you say?"

Petra grabbed his hand and rose to her feet. "Can we make it an afternoon coffee, instead? I promised Elias to take him to the Health and Science Museum during the day."

"There are interesting places other than museums, you know. Fun things to do. I bet he'd enjoy a visit to NASA. Kemah has a great amusement park close to the pier. I think most rides are appropriate for his age."

"I read that one can walk through a massive heart in the museum." She let go of Sami's hand. "I thought it'd be a good idea to show Elias how things work from the inside."

"That *is* a good idea."

"I'll use a NASA trip as an incentive, something to look forward to once he's back on his feet."

Sami nodded. "Sounds right. Let's make it dinner, then. Pick you up at six?"

"I'd rather bring my car."

He pulled out his phone from his pocket. "I'm texting you my home address. Need directions?"

"GPS." Petra guided him to the door. "It shouldn't be a problem."

Sami stepped out. "Good night, then."

"See you tomorrow." She kept the door open and watched him walk away, his shoulders relaxed. The weight he carried had shifted.

He started heading down the hallway then stopped. "Please remember to bring your mom's picture with you."

CHAPTER NINETEEN

"You okay, Mom? Need anything?" Restless, Sami paced from the living room window to the front door.

"I'll go for a glass of red wine."

"You've already taken your meds. Cranberry juice?"

"I'll spend most of the night in the bathroom." Sawsan crossed her legs. "Will you settle down? You're making me dizzy."

Sami switched on the outside lights. He should thank Rosa for picking out his mother's black dress; it was less than a month since they'd buried Fareed. Rosa made sure Mother looked subdued, like a grieving widow and mother. If left to her own devices, she would have chosen a bright red dress, the mood she was in.

A car came down the driveway. Sami nodded to his mother. "Remember what we talked about?"

"This is important to you, I get it." Sawsan rolled her eyes. "It's not that you haven't brought girls home before, Fareed."

"You're right. Fareed's the one who brought girls home." Sami bent over his mother, keeping his voice gentle. "I'm Sami, Mom."

"I know who you are."

He kissed her forehead. "I told you, remember? Petra is an important friend. Please, please be nice."

"Of course I will, silly. I'm always nice to your friends." She reached up and caressed his cheek. "You be nice to mine, okay?"

"Sure." Straightening, Sami wondered where his mother had disappeared to, and if he would ever get her back. Delusional, weird, it mattered not. The woman before him seemed to think she had met his friends. He had never brought any home. And, as far as he could remember, she never cultivated friends of her own.

The doorbell rang. Taking a deep breath, he shifted his focus to the evening ahead and opened the front door.

A pristine-looking man in a dark suit holding a bunch of flowers smiled at him. "Good evening."

Sami frowned at the middle-aged man with unnaturally dark hair jelled to one side of his small head. "Can I help you?"

"You don't remember me?" The man stuck out his free hand. "I'm *Khoury* Dahood. Your mother invited me."

In his mind, Sami placed the priest next to the coffins of his father and brother. Familiarity struck. Same face, bald head, however. So this was the friend his mother had mentioned. When had she invited him? And why tonight, of all nights?

He took the priest's hand. "Of course." Sami prolonged the handshake. "Sorry! I didn't recognize you . . ." What could he say? He hadn't recognized him with that hairpiece glued to his scalp? He went on to say, "with those flowers." He let go of the priest's hand, ignoring the nervous look the man shot his way. What did he expect? Did he really think he could pass off that hideous pelt for hair? Sami stepped aside. "Please come in."

Sawsan rose and accepted the flowers with grace and reverence. "*Aboona*! You honour us in our home."

"Thank you for inviting me, Mrs. Amara."

"I hope the security guard at the gate didn't give you any trouble."

"No, not at all. He had my name on the visitors' list."

"Good. You remember my eldest?" She passed the flowers to Sami.

Khoury Dahood addressed Sami. "I hoped to see you in church more often." He spread his lips into a yellow smile, the kind of smile that goaded one into admission of guilt. Sami knew that smile all too well. The teachers at the boarding school used it to extract confessions about one mischief or another without seeming aggressive. It worked on every boy in the school. *Almost everyone.*

"It's good of you to finally visit, *Aboona*." Sami threw the veiled accusation in the man's face. Since Fareed's funeral, the priest hadn't stopped by to offer solace to a member of his congregation after tragedy had struck. Apparently, he had to be invited by Mother.

Looking at the flowers in his hands, Sami reined back his resentment. He was overreacting, projecting his bitter school experience onto this priest. For all he knew, *Khoury* Dahood was a decent member of the clergy and rumours about Mother's unpredictable behaviour were reason enough to keep him away.

Sami offered a tight smile. "Drink?"

"I'll have whatever Mrs. Amara is having."

"Call me Sawsan, *Aboona.*" Mother chimed. "I hope you can tolerate cranberry juice."

"Well, if our Lord turned water into wine at Cana, cranberry juice would be fine with me." *Khoury* Dahood beamed, as if expecting a laugh.

Sawsan tilted her head and chirped like a teenage girl. "I have faith in your ability to turn cranberry juice to wine, *Aboona.*"

Sami had nothing to offer, intrigued with his mother's transformation into another woman, vaguely recognizable, almost normal. At ease with the priest, she spoke about choir performances, church events, and asked about women—names Sami had never heard.

He caught Rosa waving at him from the kitchen doorway. "Excuse me." He went into the kitchen, flowers in hand, and closed the door behind him.

"I'm sorry." Rosa wrung her hands. "I don' know when Mrs. call him. I stay with her all day, cookin' and everythin'. 'Cept when she take her bath."

Sami laid the flowers on the counter and pulled a bottle of Ocean Spray from the fridge. "Do you know if she's called him before?"

"*Sí*. Many times."

Sami slammed the fridge door shut. Bottles clanged. "How many?"

"I don' know, Mr Sami. *Cinco*?"

"And you didn't think it important to tell me that bit of information?"

"I don' . . . know," Rosa stuttered, her lips twisting.

Sami set the juice bottle on the counter. "Did he come over before?"

"No, Mr. Sami." Rosa took a vase from a top cabinet and filled it with water.

"Anyone else comes to the house when I'm not here? Or calls?"

"A lawyer." Rosa scratched her head. "Mr. Car . . . no, Mr. Van."

Sami scowled. "Vaughn?"

"*Sí*. He call." Rosa fussed with the flowers. "Monday." She paused, lifted her head. "No, *Viernes*."

"Vaughn called this Friday?"

"*Sí*. That when he call last time."

"Listen, I know it's difficult to stay with Mom every minute of the day." Sami gently touched Rosa's shoulder. "I don't expect you to do that, as long as you're with her when the kids are around. But, please keep me informed of phone calls or unexpected visitors. *Bueno*?"

"*Sì*, Mr. Sami." Rosa moved to set glasses on a tray, still looking dejected. "I bring drinks."

"Where are Mrs. Madigan and the twins?"

"Games room."

"Thank you for choosing that dress for Mom, Rosa. It's perfect."

The doorbell rang. Sami hurried out of the kitchen, but not before he saw Rosa's smile. Keeping Rosa happy was important. He needed her. Especially tonight.

"That must be your friend, Sami." His mother said as he crossed the living room to open the front door.

Elias threw himself into a hug. "Uncle Sam!"

"Hey there, brave boy!"

"Hello." Petra beamed in a short sleeve navy dress and baby blue shawl draped over her arms. A small bag dangled from her elbow. Her auburn hair, styled in wide waves, flowed down and parted around her shoulders—a lazy creek shimmering under summer sun. The hairstyle exposed the entire birthmark on her forehead. She held a box tied with the distinctive Godiva ribbon.

"Come in." Sami walked backwards with Elias clinging to his waist. Petra glided into the hall. Her fresh scent delivered a teasing caress. She must have heard his deep inhale, for she did a double take and stumbled to a stop.

"Sorry I'm late. The car's GPS insisted on taking me off the highway."

"Fix the settings." Sami froze. Jesus! Did he just say that? And in that commanding tone? He tried to recover. "It's only been fifteen minutes. That's not late in my book."

Frowning, Petra held out a hand to Elias. He let go of Sami and went to her side. She gave the chocolate box to Sami, practically shoving it at his chest. "For Mrs. Amara."

"Mom loves chocolate," Sami blurted. Shit! Who doesn't love chocolate? He led the way to the living room, his steps stiff and awkward, in direct contrast to Petra's gracefulness. What a great start to this evening. He couldn't say *don't worry about it,* or *thanks for coming over,* or *you look lovely, tonight.* No, he had to tell her—order her—to correct the goddamn settings on her GPS.

As soon as Petra stepped into the living room, recognition gleamed in his mother's eyes. She stopped mid-sentence and fixed her gaze on Petra. Sami did the introductions.

"You have a beautiful home, Mrs. Amara." Petra's hand hung in the air, her attempt at a handshake unreciprocated.

Khoury Dahood grabbed Petra's hand, covering the awkwardness. "A pleasure to meet you, Petra. A lovely and very interesting name."

Gratitude filled Sami, replacing his earlier resentment of the priest. Aiming to give his mother time to recover from her apparent shock, he followed the priest's comment. "I bet there's a story there."

"Not really," Petra shrugged. "My mother visited Petra in Jordan and was fascinated by the carved Nabatean ruins in the rocks. She gave me the ancient city's name."

"I've been," *Khoury* Dahood said. "Natural colourful sand waves cover the interior walls of caves. I tell you, they drew me into the chambers like a sorcerer's summons. I didn't want to leave. Extremely captivating."

Just like that arrow on her forehead, Sami wanted to say, but he held his tongue.

"It's interesting to hear you describe it that way." Petra rested her hands on her son's shoulders and turned him to face her, obviously trying to break Elias's stare at the priest's makeshift hair. "I've always thought of my name as hard and dry."

Mrs. Madigan came in with the girls and broke the stiffness in the room.

Elias ran over and hugged the twins to his little chest. The affectionate embrace changed the mood in the room.

Petra kissed the girls and touched the pink ruffles around their tiny waists. "Oh, what adorable tutus! Are you ballerinas? Will you show me a dance?"

The girls put their bent elbows to their sides and flipped their hands down. They hopped around the room like bunnies, wiggling their behinds.

"We have a long way to go," Sami said with a crooked smile. Worrying his mother might snap any minute and say or do something nasty in front of the children, he placed his hands on his knees and bent to Elias's eye level. "I have a collection of model airplanes. Would you like to see them?"

Elias lifted questioning eyes to Petra.

Sami addressed her. "Do you mind if he goes with Mrs. Madigan and the twins to the games room upstairs?"

"Not at all." Petra smiled at the nanny. "I must warn you, he asks a lot of questions."

Mrs. Madigan held out her hand to Elias. "Well, young man, I happen to have a lot of answers."

Elias egged the girls on. "DeLeenas. Let's go."

Sami turned to his silent mother, genuinely concerned. He tried to pull her out of her trance. "Mom?"

Sawsan approached Petra and, with a trembling finger, traced the arrow on her forehead. "Dear girl! Look at you!"

Petra froze.

Sami's insides coiled with anticipation, and a little bit of . . . envy.

Sawsan dropped her hand and pulled Petra into a tight hug. "Welcome." She stepped back, sweeping Petra head to toe, giving her a once-over. "They let you go."

227

"Who?" Petra asked, her voice soft.

"*The Watchers*," Sawsan whispered. She ran her hand over Petra's hair. "What did they do to you?"

Petra's eyes flickered to Sami's for a fraction of a second, enough to show him she caught on to his mother's weirdness. Her lips broke into a kind smile, conveying sympathy and respect at the same time. "They took care of me."

"Oh! *Nushkur Allah.*" Sawsan turned to the priest. "I had to do it, *Aboona.* So they wouldn't snatch my boys too."

Khoury Dahood raised his eyebrows. "*The Watchers*, you mean?"

She nodded. "I tried to explain that to her. She wouldn't listen. She made me show her." Sawsan cradled Petra's face in her palms. "That's when they took you. I'm so sorry, honey."

"It's okay, Mrs. Amara. As you can see, I'm fine."

Petra's soothing tone had the opposite effect on Sami. He held his mother's elbow and urged her to face him. "Who made you show her what, Mom?"

His mother blinked, her eyes glazed and distant.

"The woman who didn't listen to you. Who was she?"

"Deborah was her name."

Petra staggered back a step and breathed out, "My mother."

"She was stubborn. Wouldn't listen to a word I said. She went crazy, yelling, searching the house." Sawsan wrapped her arms around Sami's neck. "She found you and . . . and threatened to offer you to them. I had to do it, son. I had no choice."

Sami could stomach it no longer. He nestled his mother in his arms. "What did you have to do?" His voice shook.

"I gave them—" Sawsan loosened her locked arms and rested her cheek on his chest, "this girl, instead."

Petra drew a deep breath. "Who's *them*, Mrs. Amara?"

"I told you! *The Watchers*." Sawsan pulled away from Sami and dropped onto the couch. "But I couldn't protect my boys any more. My husband had to send my sons to a place where they would never find them."

His patience evaporated, Sami kneeled before his mother. "Is that what you think? Dad sent us to boarding school to hide us from *The Watchers*?"

"It was our best option. He said so himself."

Sami rose, his legs shaking. He wanted to scream, *Dad sent us away to protect us from you!* He glanced at Petra, instead. "You remember anything about that day?"

She shook her head. "Nothing."

Khoury Dahood sat next to Sawsan on the couch and held her hands. "Tell me, what did *The Watchers* who took Petra look like?"

"I don't know, *Aboona*. I never saw them."

"Then how do you know *The Watchers* were there?" *Khoury* Dahood's voice remained calm, pacifying.

229

"Deborah said she saw them coming and if I didn't tell her where her daughter was, she would have them snatch my boys. She forced my hand, *Aboona*." Sawsan looked over her shoulders and brought down her voice. "It's strange, you know? They never visit when others are around. But they did when Deborah came over."

Sami cursed under his breath and turned to the window, seeking a way out of this madness, which intensified by the second. His head hurt and his lungs laboured to fill with air.

Petra approached him, whispering. "She's not making sense. Let's give her a break."

"You don't understand," he whispered back. "This is as much sense as you'll get from her."

"I want to know what my mother was doing here." Petra pressed her lips together. "Why did she come to this house?"

"Perhaps we can talk later," *Khoury* Dahood offered. "When Sawsan has had some rest?"

Sami observed his mother being comforted by the priest. He exhaled a frustrated breath. "Let's have dinner."

Sami's coiled insides prevented him from eating anything. He admired *Khoury* Dahood's efforts to bring his mother back to earth from whatever planet she was on. The priest hit the right note by discussing her paintings that lined the dining room walls. He offered to arrange an exhibition at church. Engaging Mother and giving her something to look forward to might connect her to reality for longer periods.

If he were a believer, he would attest to *Khoury* Dahood's divine inspiration. The man had a stabilizing effect on Mother. Did she know that? Was that why she had invited him tonight, knowing Sami needed her to be . . . all there? And was he then, her son, the volatile factor in this strange equation?

Sami pressed a closed fist to his lips. The odd realization delivered a blow to his insides. That could explain why Mother had sunk deeper into her strange world after his father and Fareed died. With his defective genes, he was too much like his mother. They needed someone—a catalyst—to restore balance to their skewed family. *Khoury* Dahood was the right element.

Across the table, Petra quietly pushed food around her plate, the look on her face a mix of confusion and preoccupation. She seemed to follow the conversation between Mother and *Khoury* Dahood with very little attention, perhaps revolving more questions in her mind?

Sami opened the topic again. "Mom, do you remember what Deborah was doing here that day?"

"She came to talk to your father."

"My mother knew Mr. Amara?" Petra's attempt at keeping her tone casual failed. Anxiety spilled out with every word.

Sawsan shrugged. "Deborah told me they'd never met."

Sami pushed his untouched plate away. "And what did Dad say to that?"

"Nothing." She waved a dismissive hand in the air. "Deborah left before he came home."

Petra dropped her fork onto her plate with a loud clang. "But what did he say when you told him about my mother's visit?"

"Dear girl, I didn't tell him."

"Why not?" Petra snapped, losing her composure.

"I didn't need to. Deborah called him before she left." Sawsan wiped her mouth with her napkin. "Let's have dessert on the patio, shall we?"

Sami locked eyes with Petra, hers screaming in frustration, his begging for patience. He helped his mother push back her chair. "What did Deborah say to Dad?"

"I didn't hear their conversation. I was busy calming Fareed down. He was crying and she ran downstairs to make the call. I'm guessing she told your Dad about *The Watchers*, because not too long after that day he sent you and Fareed off with that man from church." Sawsan turned to *Khoury* Dahood. "Maybe you know him, *Aboona*. His name was Hanna . . . something. He had a Greek last name."

Khoury Dahood slowly got to his feet. "Vanyos? Hanna Vanyos?"

"Yes. That's it."

"Who's this guy?" Sami asked.

"A friend of the church. Kind of a... problem solver," *Khoury* Dahood said. "I've heard his name many times since I moved here. He left years ago."

"My husband trusted Hanna with the boys while he dealt with Deborah and her husband."

Petra sprang from her chair. "What do you mean? What about my father?"

Sawsan arched her eyebrows, undeterred by Petra's obvious distress. "What about him?"

"My father went missing when I was a child."

"Oh! Well, isn't that interesting?"

"Jesus Christ, Mom!" Sami swung his mother around so abruptly, he feared he might have hurt her. "Are you saying Dad had something to do with her father's disappearance?"

"Your Dad never discussed his business with me." Sawsan checked her hairdo. "Now, be a dear, and tell Rosa to bring dessert to the patio." She batted her eyes at *Khoury* Dahood. "A little bird told me you're fond of *Hilbeh*, *Aboona*. I baked a tray of it. You'll never have anything near its rich taste outside Palestine."

"I haven't had *Hilbeh* in years." *Khoury* Dahood licked his lips. "With almonds on top?"

"Of course," Sawsan said, pride audible in her tone.

"*Hilbeh* is a mix of fenugreek, semolina and condensed milk, right?" *Khoury* Dahood followed with his flattering inquiry.

233

"Yogurt. Not condensed milk." Sawsan dropped her mouth open and sucked in a sharp breath. "Now, *Aboona*, you're not trying to trick me into revealing my secret recipe, are you?"

The priest threw his head to one side with a forced laugh. "I thought it might work."

"Well, whenever you fancy having it, all you have to do is let me know." She turned to Sami. "Remind Rosa to drizzle more syrup over the whole tray, please." She extended her hand to *Khoury* Dahood. "Shall we?"

The priest sent a sympathetic look toward Sami, took Sawsan's hand and walked her through the French doors to the backyard.

Petra dropped on her chair. "I don't believe this."

The paintings on the walls came alive before Sami's eyes. Bright oversized flowers were plucked out of their fields and darted toward him. He remained on his feet. His chest hurt, and he realized he was holding his breath for fear of smelling those god-awful flowers.

"I need to get out of here." He pointed toward the living room and beckoned Petra. "Please?"

They walked through the living room and stepped out to the front porch. Sami inflated his lungs and tried to tame his erratic heartbeat. The kids' laughter rang from the games room's open window above. Sounds of innocence, happy and ignorant of the past, added an extra squeeze to his heart. He studied Petra by his side.

"You okay?"

"Your mother turned my world upside down." Petra rubbed her hands over her arms. "I'm definitely *not* okay."

"If it's any consolation, I believe your mother saved my life. I think she got me out from the hiding place Mom stuffed me into that day. And whatever your mother said to Dad, it prompted him to action. Got me and Fareed far away from Mom before she did more damage."

"Your Houdini stunt gone bad."

"Excuse me?"

"When Elias was hurt in the hospital in Kuwait, you showed me a scar from when you were a boy." Petra pointed to his forehead. "You said your father got you out. That's how it started? Your phobia?"

Sami looked into the distance past Petra. Pearly moon rays reflected off her rental car parked in the driveway and illuminated her silhouette. Her shoulders were shaking. "Mom was inventive in her efforts to hide me from the fu—fricking *Watchers*."

He stuck his hands into his back pockets to stop himself from wrapping his arms around trembling Petra. "You cold?"

Petra ignored his question. "How can she be so far removed?"

"She's flirting with a priest right before us. Mother's not removed." Sami blew a long breath. "She's unhinged. That's what I've been trying to tell you."

"Has she ever been diagnosed?"

"Some form of schizophrenia. She's convinced those *Watchers* are after children." Sami rocked on his heels. "Thanks for playing along. Mom thinks her *Watchers* took you. I wonder if seeing you alive and well might convince her *The Watchers* aren't that bad. I'll let her therapist know. See where it leads."

"That stuff about my father's disappearance? She made it all up, you think?"

"It's hard to isolate the truth. This is the first time I've heard her talk about Dad that way. It might explain his obsession to find you. The strange stipulation in his will." Sami ran his hand through his hair. "Hell! I don't know."

"I wonder if that had anything to do with my mother changing our last name after we moved to the States. I couldn't find out why. My aunt never wanted to talk about it."

"I've got to find that Hanna Vanyos guy and see what he says."

"I think I'll leave, now." Petra took a couple of steps toward the house, creating more distance between them. "Please get Elias for me."

"I'll have Mrs. Madigan send him down." Sami didn't blame Petra for her repulsion. He trudged his way to the front door.

Petra followed. "I'll say goodnight to Sawsan and *Khoury* Dahood."

Holding the door open, Sami exhaled his frustration. "I'm so sorry, Petra. I didn't expect this can of worms."

"I have my son to worry about. The past is not that important." Before she passed him, Petra halted on the threshold. "Maybe it's best for you not to dig too far."

The concern in her voice took him by surprise. After what his mother had said, he had expected Petra to push hard to find out what happened to her father. Instead, she pretty much asked him to let it be. Was it possible she wanted to protect him from whatever truth he might discover about his father's involvement?

"I'll get to the bottom of this." He leaned toward her, intent and sincere. "I promise."

"There's something more important for you to do."

"More than figuring out my father's past?"

"The girls, Sami." Petra touched his arm. "You have to keep your mother away from the girls. You don't want them to face the same things you went through with her."

He shifted his shoulders back, indignant and slightly hurt. "She's never alone with them. I make sure of it. You think I'd risk their safety?"

"I don't know what to think, anymore. Your mother is unpredictable. Even with the best intentions, you can't control what you cannot foresee."

CHAPTER TWENTY

Petra trudged into the hospital waiting room and chose the farthest chair from all the family members waiting for their loved ones to come out of surgery. She had held it together so far and hadn't broken down crying when she kissed Elias before they rolled him into the operating room. Though he was older than when he had gone under for his previous operation, it was harder to let his hand slip away today.

Fear showed in his eyes. Elias understood what was at stake this time and knew what it meant to have his heart operated on, no matter how minimally invasive the procedure. Her son was scared and she couldn't be at his side to comfort him.

Sitting alone, detached from her boy, helplessness crippled her. She spread a blanket on her lap and turned off her mobile phone. Mouzah had been in constant contact since Elias was admitted into the hospital. But right now, Petra couldn't handle a conversation with her. She had nothing to say. Her friend would understand her need to disconnect from the world.

Petra closed her eyes to block the TV screen and everyone else and braced for the long wait. Time crept by. Her agitation grew with the noise level rising around her.

Someone sat on the chair to her right, a man, judging by a subtle scent of leather. Petra gritted her teeth and kept her eyes shut to thwart conversation. The man seemed to get the hint and stayed quiet, though making plenty of noise typing on a keyboard. Fast strikes at the keys tapped at her nerves.

What time was it now? How many hours had passed? She dared not check her watch.

A loud laugh rang around the room. A woman's voice. She must have heard good news. An omen? Maybe the person sitting next to her would go and talk to the woman and leave the space near Petra. She sensed no movement from the right, however. Another high-pitched laugh forced her to open her eyes.

Sami sat next to her, in dark slacks and a white shirt, working on a laptop balanced on his knees.

"What are you doing here, Sami?"

He lifted his eyes from the screen, a sombre, serious expression on his face. "Working." He handed her a shopping bag. "And to give you this."

"What's this for?"

"Silence."

Petra couldn't believe her ears. Had he just told her to shut up?

Sami nodded at the bag. "I hope it helps."

She dug into the bag and lifted out a box containing a pair of Bose headphones, the kind that go over the ears to block noise.

"Don't worry. I won't talk to you," Sami said. "I plan to catch up on some emails." He returned to his laptop.

Dumbfounded, she stared at him for several heartbeats. So he had remembered what she told him about this time, about her need for silence. She had heard nothing from him since she left his house Saturday evening. And here he was once more, giving her what she needed.

She took out the headphones and figured out how to use them. Slipping them over her ears, she settled under her blanket. Chatter disappeared.

Several minutes passed.

A strange calm engulfed her. Her breathing slowed down to normal and her mind emptied of negative thoughts.

Elias would come out of this okay. She couldn't explain it, but she slowly became sure of it. Almost too sure. Where did this confidence come from? She opened her eyes. Sami was still in his seat, typing.

A doctor in green scrubs came into the room. A woman rose and ran to him. They moved to a corner away from everyone. Petra tried to read the doctor's lips, moving slowly, explaining. The woman shook her head. The doctor patted her shoulder, sympathy poured out of his face. An older woman rushed to the woman's side and held her in her arms. They sobbed. Mother, grandmother, aunt, sister, friend? The pain was the same.

Petra closed her eyes to shut out the crying women. This had no bearing on her son. She didn't believe in omens. She was a rational, educated woman. Elias would be okay. Her heart thumped heavily and her breathing picked up speed.

A hand clutched hers.

She opened her eyes.

Sami gave her a soft squeeze.

She shook her head. She needed no comfort. There was no reason for it. Elias would be fine. She just knew it. In fact, Sami could leave. He must have better things to do than waste time here. She withdrew her hand.

Sami set aside his laptop and rose. His trousers crunched and creased over his thighs.

Panic flooded over her. No! Sami couldn't leave. Who was she fooling? She didn't want to receive news of Elias when she was by herself. Had Sami heard her earlier? Had she spoken out loud? She slid the headphones to her neck.

"Do you have to go?"

"Afraid so." He pointed at the large Styrofoam cup on the table beside his chair. "Too much coffee." He shook his legs, smiling. "I really have to go."

"Oh!" It dawned on her. "Restrooms are across from the elevators."

"You need anything? I can stop at the cafeteria and grab sandwiches, drinks."

"You go ahead." Relief settled her nerves. Sami planned to return. "I'm not hungry."

Sami shifted on the spot, concern streamed from his dark eyes. "I don't know what to do here, Petra. I want to help. I'm not sure how." He sucked his upper lip. "Will you tell me what you need?"

"Stay," she blurted. "Please."

He dropped on the chair.

"No, no. Go to the restroom." She touched his forearm. "I meant stay with me. I don't want to be alone."

Sami jumped to his feet again. "I'll be right back." He darted from the room.

Petra slipped the headphones over her ears, closed her eyes and leaned her head back until Sami patted her shoulder.

"Petra, it's time."

She opened her eyes to see him hovering over her. "Is the doctor out?"

"A nurse said he'd come in shortly." Sami handed her a cup of coffee. "Here."

Petra took a sip and tried to perk up. She had dosed off. For how long? She inspected her surroundings. The waiting room was empty except for one young couple.

"Why didn't you wake me?"

"You need rest. It's okay, you didn't miss anything."

She unfolded her legs and stretched, guilty and horrified. It had never happened before, falling asleep while she waited for news of her son's condition. How could she be so relaxed? What was wrong with her?

Elias's doctor came in with a woman in a grey suit.

Petra scrambled to her feet.

"Elias's vitals are very good," the doctor said. "Surgery went well. It took a little longer than I anticipated, but I was able to put the cardioband firmly in place."

"Thank God." Petra wiped sudden tears, her chin trembling. She took the doctor's hand in both of hers. "And thank *you*."

The doctor removed a colourful bandana from his head. "If Elias continues to improve, we won't keep him in ICU for long. We'll transfer him to a room soon. That's when you can see him."

Petra released the doctor's hand. "How soon?"

"A couple of hours. He's under observation now. A nurse will come for you when it's time." The doctor smiled with an overabundance of energy. Then his cheeks drooped and he looked as if he might fall on his face. He pointed at the woman by his side.

"Mrs. O'Donnell is a hospital administrator in charge of patients' affairs. I've asked her to join us."

Petra went numb. "Oh?"

"There's something I need you to do, Mrs. Haddad." The doctor rocked on his heels. "We video recorded the procedure."

Petra swayed backwards and landed on Sami's chest.

Sami steadied her with a strong grip of her arms. "She doesn't need to see you cutting into her little boy."

"Of course not." The doctor ran his hand over his cropped hair. "I'm sorry. That's not what I meant. The procedure was textbook perfect. It'd be great if I could use the video as a teaching tool for surgeons."

The administrator opened a folder. "Consent forms. We can't use the images without them."

Sami moved Petra aside and stood in the doctor's face. "And you have to have it right now?" he asked, agitated.

"A colleague in Boston is scheduled to do the same procedure tomorrow. I'm hoping to send him the digital records today." The doctor tried his weak smile again. "We can wait, of course."

"I agreed to this." Petra snapped back to life. She eased from Sami's grip. "I signed a stack of forms when Elias was admitted."

"A couple were missing. My mistake," Mrs. O'Donnell said. "Do you mind, Mrs. Haddad?"

"I'll sign whatever you need."

"Mrs. O'Donnell will walk you through it." The doctor bowed, almost bending over. "Lots of children will benefit from this. Thank you." The doctor shuffled away.

Mrs. O'Donnell spread the forms on a nearby table. She explained each document briefly. Petra understood little, but didn't care. Elias was fine. His chance of a healthier life was greatly improved. Anything else was insignificant.

As she was about to sign the first form, Sami stopped her. "Want me to go over these real quick before you sign?"

"Could you? I can't concentrate."

"Sure." He gathered the papers and signaled to the administrator. "Give us a few minutes, please."

"Of course, I could use a cup of coffee." Mrs. O'Donnell withdrew.

Sami pulled two chairs toward the table and waited for Petra to take one before he sat down. He took out a fountain pen from the breast pocket of his shirt and started reading. She watched him study the forms, thankful for his diligence. Sami must have a zillion things to do at work, and with his complicated family situation, he must spend every free minute taking care of things at home. Yet he had stayed the entire day, making sure she wasn't alone.

Petra looked out of the windows. Darkness descended. Why was Sami so intent on helping her? He couldn't be thinking he needed to compensate for his father's actions. There was no proof of any wrongdoing. She had no idea what Mr. Amara had done, if anything at all, to her father. Could Sami ever be free from the shadow his mother hung over his head? It wasn't fair. Could there be another reason for his caring attitude? Dare she guess? Hope?

Sami slid a paper across the table and pointed at a clause, interrupting her thoughts.

"If you sign this, you give the hospital permission to freeze Elias's tissue for future experimentation. You okay with that?"

"If it helps others, yes."

"It's better to initial the line that specifies tissue harvested from this particular procedure, Petra. You can't leave it open that way."

She took the pen from Sami's hand and initialed where he pointed. "I can't remember the last time I used a fountain pen."

"This was my father's," Sami said softly. He kept his eyes cast down and flipped to the last page. "Over here, you have the option to let them use the recorded operation without disclosing Elias's full name."

"That's good, right?"

"For damn sure. They have an excellent policy to protect patient privacy. I don't see a problem." He rubbed his chin. "How about I send this to our legal department to be certain?"

"It's okay, Sami. I want the doctors to benefit from this. Help another child."

Sami nodded. "Initial that clause, then."

Petra finished signing the forms in time for Mrs. O'Donnell's return. Handing them over, Petra caught Sami checking his phone. He scowled at the screen. Displeased? Or worried? She waited for him to respond to the message that had upset him. Time for her to release this kind man.

"You should go home."

Sami flinched. "My girls are fine."

He looked disconcerted by her swift dismissal. Did he think she was implying he neglected the girls? He was touchy about this. She couldn't take back what she said.

"I'm fine now. Really, I've kept you away from home too long."

"Everything's under control, Petra." Sami pumped his jaw, showing irritation. "I planned for today."

"Will you stop by tomorrow? Elias would love to see you." Trying to soothe the man was pointless. She had already pushed him away.

"I have a couple of important meetings early morning. I'll try to drop by at ten." He rose from the table and packed up his laptop, the look on his face intense and distant. "Do you have everything you need for tonight?"

She lifted her backpack off the floor. "I'm set."

"Call me if you need anything. No matter how late."

She couldn't let him leave without clearing things up. She hadn't meant to hurt him, for God's sake. She was letting him go, untangling his complicated life. Didn't he understand that? He would probably be relieved to distance himself from her problems. He had enough of his own.

She pointed at his phone. "Bad news?"

"That was *Khoury* Dahood. He's helping me locate Hanna Vanyos." Sami headed for the door and threw over his shoulder, "Hanna is in Bethlehem."

CHAPTER TWENTY-ONE

Petra spent the night on the big recliner in Elias's hospital room. Elias slept through the night, but she stayed wide-awake, watching his every twitch and squirm. It was the ideal time to update Mouzah and Maryam. Both were bombarding her with detailed questions. She responded to an email from Richard inquiring about her son's condition, surprised at his impeccable timing since she hadn't told him when the surgery was scheduled.

Sami popped in at nine in the morning and Petra completely missed him. She had snuck down to the chapel while Elias was asleep. The nurse told her of Sami's visit when she returned and showed her the bag he had left in the room, full of toys and books. Petra contemplated calling Sami, then decided against it. Not a good time to mend fences.

Sami showed up again in the evening, the twins with him. He held back the excited girls.

"Gentle, okay? Elias has a booboo on his chest."

The girls looked baffled.

Elias peeled off his Superman-patterned gown. "Four holes. See?"

Deena pointed at the bandages covering Elias's chest. "*Boobee*," she gibbered.

"That's a *booboo*, sweetheart." Sami gently poked Deena's chest. "Can you say *booboo*?"

"*Boobee*," Deena insisted, and Leena, poking her own chest, echoed, "*Boobee*."

Elias burst out laughing.

Petra pulled Elias's gown together at the shoulders and tied it. "That's enough, now." She dragged the adjustable table to the bed and opened colourful play dough tubs Sami had included in his gift bag. The girls went at it, kneading, shaping, trying to follow Elias's instructions.

Sami remained close, engaged with the girls. From the moment he stepped into the room, he avoided eye contact with her, focusing on Elias. Although thankful for his attention to her son, she couldn't help being annoyed.

She retreated to the window, certain Sami would eventually drift there. It didn't take him long. He stood next to her and gave her his profile, keeping an eye on the kids.

"Elias looks good, better than this morning," Sami said in a hushed voice.

"The doctor is very pleased," Petra whispered back. "I think he's a little surprised at Elias's quick progress. He said we probably won't have to stay past the weekend."

"Yeah? That's great news."

"Thanks for stopping by earlier. And for the gifts."

"I tried to find you, but it's a maze down there in the food court. I was short on time."

"I understand."

She straightened the bouquet of flowers by the window. Sami hadn't found her in the food court because she wasn't there. She decided not to correct him, nervous as a traitor. Where did that uneasiness come from?

Sami kept his face turned away. Why wouldn't he look at her? Was he that hurt by the way she had sent him off yesterday? That would be childish and immature. It didn't fit the kind of man she was coming to know. Something else must be going on.

"I'm glad you brought the girls."

"We had to go through screening at the visitor's unit downstairs to be cleared."

"That's good. Elias needed a break from me."

"Do *you* need anything?"

She gave Sami a silent shake of her head, daring him to look at her.

He didn't budge. "It's possible you won't be able to reach me for a while, Petra. So if you need anything, please let me know now."

"What's going on? Is your mother okay?"

"The past couple of days have been rough."

"Because of me." Petra sucked in a long breath. "I'm so sorry."

"It's not your fault. *I* pressed her for more information after you left. She . . . lapsed into a dark corner in her head. She's fine now. Back to normal."

"Her kind of normal?" Petra caught herself. "Sorry, I mean . . ."

"It's all right." Sami exhaled. "Mom didn't say anything new, in case you're wondering."

"You shouldn't pursue this further. Let it be."

"I can't do that."

Petra frowned. As if pushing against his will, Sami's words came out strangled with his scratched voice.

"What good would it do?" she asked. "Whatever happened is ancient history."

Sami turned his head, finally meeting her eye to eye. "I don't need protection, Petra. Don't you want to know the truth?"

"Of course I do."

"Then let me find it. I need to go see Hanna Vanyos."

"You're going to Bethlehem?"

"That's right." Sami switched his attention to the kids when their laughter rose. "I can't find a phone number for him."

A clump of play dough dropped to the floor. Deena dived head first after it. Sami sprinted to catch her before she fell to the floor. Petra recovered the ball from under a chair. Deena added it to a colourful pile.

"Are my girls helping you make the solar system, Elias?" Sami examined a red and orange ball on top of the pile. "This one looks like Mars."

"We're making people." Elias pointed at the reddish ball. "That's mama's head. The biggest one is yours, Uncle Sam." He spread a piece of blue dough on the table. "I'm working on your body. DeLeenas are making mama's body."

Petra pointed at Sami. "I don't know about you, but I'm flattered."

With her closed fist, Leena pounded on a pink blob.

Sami nodded, a serious expression on his face. "And flattened."

Petra toned down a laugh. She motioned for Sami to join her at the open doorway. Maintaining a watchful eye on the kids, she whispered, "You're seriously considering going to Palestine?"

"I am."

"Can't you send someone else to talk to Hanna?"

Sami shook his head. "I want to look the man in the eye when he tells me about my father."

"I understand the need, the drive to know firsthand. I really do." Petra clutched Sami's forearm. "But have you thought about the girls?"

"They're *all* I think about." He sounded angry and hurt. Again.

Frustrated, she dropped her hand and rushed to explain. "I mean the court date, Sami. What about the custody case?"

"I won't go anywhere before the case is settled."

He pushed up his shirtsleeves and crossed his arms, his stance spelling displeasure. Or was it disappointment? Did he think she viewed him as irresponsible and reckless? His knee-jerk defensiveness whenever she mentioned his care for *his* girls disturbed her. What was the matter with him?

"Sami, you told me you'll be unreachable for a while." She mellowed her tone. "I thought that's what you meant. That you're leaving."

"I am. To Cleveland. To see the twins' grandparents. I might stay through the weekend." He cracked a hint of a smile.

His quick mood shift puzzled her. She remained quiet.

"We may reach an agreement," Sami continued. "Their lawyer contacted mine. Seems they might drop their custody claim."

"Oh, that's wonderful!" She leaned against the doorframe, folding her hands behind her. "What made them change their mind?"

"Reality, I think. Perhaps the shock of losing their daughter wore off. I don't know. They asked to see me, so I'll go. I'm thinking of taking the girls. Not sure it's a good idea." Sami raised his eyebrows. "What do you think?"

"I'd jump on this chance if I were you. Take the girls. Let their grandparents know they'll be part of their lives even if you have sole custody." Petra cocked her head to one side and added, "It's the right thing to do."

A muscle under Sami's left eye twitched. Petra knew she had hit a nerve. This tip-toeing business when talking about his nieces exasperated her.

Sami unfolded his arms. "I hate to leave you at this difficult time, but like you said, I have to jump on this. My assistant has the necessary details. Ask him for anything while I'm away. Robert, you've met him at the office."

"That's very nice of you." Petra peered past the kids, savouring the warmth that Sami's concern spread in her chest. "You have enough on your plate. You don't need to worry about us."

Sami took out his phone and punched keys. "I'm texting you Robert's number. Just in case."

Slipping his phone into his shirt pocket, his face donned an ambiguous mask. "You and Elias *will* be all right, Petra."

His tone concealed something vague, something he rarely expressed, not with ease. What was it? Why couldn't she catch it?

She waited for him to elaborate, afraid to say something that sounded presumptuous. She could be reading him completely wrong. Everything that had happened in the past few days had thrown her off. This man nudged her off her centre.

"If things work out with Lora's parents, and after Elias is fully recovered," Sami stepped closer, "I'm going to ask you for a big favour. Provided you find it acceptable."

"Just name it." Petra hoped she hid her confusion well. "I owe you."

"That's not why I'm asking, Petra. It's just that I don't . . . trust anyone else with what I'll need done." He strode to Elias's bed and inspected the kids' creations spread on the table.

Petra blinked. That was it? No explanations? She followed him.

Sami held Leena's hands to prevent her from rubbing her eyes with play dough.

Elias presented his masterpiece with both hands. "Mama, can we put Uncle Sam's body in a place where it doesn't get mushed?" Long blue noodles dangled over Elias's fingers.

"I think I have a Ziplock bag big enough," she said.

Elias pointed with his elbow at a pink triangle flat on the table. "Do you have another one for your body and head, mama?"

"I don't think so, *ya rohi*. We can fit all the pieces in one bag for now."

Elias eyed his work, looking worried. "Make sure your body isn't squishing Uncle Sam's body, mama."

"It's time to go," Sami said.

"But we haven't finished mama's legs."

"Even brave boys need rest. We'll come again." Sami carried Leena. "Let's wash hands, okay?"

256

Petra handed Elias a Ziplock bag from her backpack. "Slide in the pieces gently." She picked up Deena and followed Sami to the bathroom.

Standing side by side, they washed the squirming girls' hands in the small sink in the tight bathroom. Petra's shoulder rubbed against Sami's a couple of times. He was definitely uncomfortable. In pain, even. He looked like he was holding his breath, biting the inside of his cheeks or something. Must be the cramped space and all that talk about bodies being squished.

She snatched a towel and stepped aside, giving Sami as much room as possible in a bathroom designed for children. Drying Deena's hands, she asked straight out, "What's the big favour, Sami?"

He lowered Leena to the floor and helped her out of the bathroom, passing Petra.

"I'll let you know when the time is right."

CHAPTER TWENTY-TWO

Sami booked a Hilton suite within a ten minute drive to the twins' grandparents' house. If necessary, he would spend the night at the old couple's place should they insist on keeping the girls during his stay. He wouldn't let the twins out of his sight. Having a backup plan never hurt, either.

Without Mrs. Madigan's help, taking care of the girls on the flight to Cleveland was far from easy. Thank God they were potty trained. Having to change diapers in the cramped airplane toilet would have killed him.

He hired a car and headed to the old couple's house without first stopping at the hotel. This way, he could use the excuse of the girls being tired, to leave early.

Crunching fall-coloured leaves underfoot, he walked the girls up to the front porch to greet their waiting grandmother.

"Well, isn't this a nice surprise?" Margaret held out her arms. "Come to grandma!"

The girls clung to Sami's legs.

"Give them a few minutes, Margaret." Sami lifted the girls in his arms. "The plane ride was rough."

"Yes, of course." Margaret's wrinkled face fell fast. Her murky-green eyes took on a rigid look. "Let's go inside."

In the house, the air was stagnant and heavy. The yellowed edges of russet wallpaper were peeling off in the corners of the living room. Intricate needlework covered brown sofa cushions as well as the back of two beige recliners.

Sami hated brown, in all its shades. This room repulsed him.

He stopped himself from barrelling out of there. Under his feet, carpet runners covered wooden floors which creaked with every step. Termite activity? Missing nails? No way would he let the twins wander around this house.

Ignoring the long sofa in front of a mildewed fireplace, he chose a chair by the window. He placed the girls on his lap and considered polite ways to leave as soon as possible. "Where's George?"

"At the shop." Margaret eased into a recliner. "He knows you're coming." She raised her dangling spectacles from her chest and checked her watch. "He'll be home soon."

Sami studied the grandfather clock facing him. The little hand lagged by a good three hours. Like the wooden box that encased it, time stood still here, trapped, a prisoner sentenced to linger in this house several decades ago.

Deena buried her face in the crook of his neck and peered at her grandmother with trepidation. She reflected his growing distress. If he didn't escape this house, he might soon burst some blood vessels.

"Take off their coats, Sami. It's too warm in here."

"How about we let the girls play outside?" Sami suggested. "They were fascinated by the fallen red leaves."

"Let's go out back." Margaret sounded annoyed.

Sami didn't give a damn. He shot to his feet and carried the girls through the kitchen, looking for the back door. "This way?"

Margaret took her sweet time easing out of the recliner. She grabbed a wool coat from a hook. Sami half expected to see moths swarm around the old woman's shoulders.

He let the girls go, red and bronze coloured leaves swirling around their feet in the cold breeze. Gathering piles of dry foliage, he threw handfuls above their heads. They laughed and went at it, kicking up a fall storm. He breathed fresh air and regained control.

Margaret shuffled next to him. "You shouldn't have brought them, Sami."

"Excuse me?"

"I'm not set up for children." Margaret's harsh voice turned sour.

"Don't worry. I booked a hotel." Sami hid his elation at not having to spend the night in this house. Thank God for small favours. "I thought you and George might appreciate the chance to spend some time with your grandkids."

"You should have warned me." Margaret pulled together the front of her drab coat. "I don't like to be surprised."

Sami nodded. "Fine. It won't happen again."

"I'm glad you came. Don't misunderstand me. How long do you plan to stay?"

"We leave tomorrow evening." Sami made the decision right then and there. Why should he stay longer if the old woman wasn't happy to see them? "I can't stay away from work for too long. I hope you understand."

Margaret kicked several bronze and yellow leaves toward the girls. "We better talk now, then."

"Shouldn't we wait for George?" Sami got ready to grab Margaret should she lose her footing.

She remained standing. "George must never know about our conversation. Promise me."

"What's this about?"

"Promise me." She laid her frail hand on Sami's arm and squeezed, anxious. "You will keep George in the dark about what I'm going to say."

Seeing Margaret vulnerable, her tough demeanour watered down, pity crept into Sami's chest. "Alright. Tell me what's going on."

Drawing a long breath, she withdrew her hand and straightened her back. "I want you to buy the shop. Offer George a deal he can't refuse."

"Why would I want to do that?"

"To keep the girls." Margaret puckered her lips, deepening the grooves around her mouth. "We'll drop the custody suit if you do."

Sami had never seen George's tyre store and had no clue how big the business was. Hell, he would buy it, no matter what the cost. "I'm in. How much do I need to offer?"

"Enough to get George out of debt and set us up with a comfortable retirement."

"How much?"

Margaret eased onto a rusty iron bench behind her. "When I insisted on having custody of the girls, I didn't know how much trouble George was in." Margaret lowered her voice. "George has always been such a gambler. I've managed to balance the finances, but I can't do it any longer." She shook her head. "At least, not alone."

Margaret lifted her glassy eyes. "Lora couldn't accept her father's addiction. That's what pushed her away from us."

Leena ran to Sami's legs. He brushed leaves from her hair. His instinct was right about George. Something *was* off with the man, though not as sinister as he had suspected. Destructive, nonetheless.

Leena joined her sister under the shedding maple tree.

"Give me a number," Sami said.

"I don't want George to have any access to the money. Buy him out and establish a trust under my name. He knows not to touch the house. We'll be set."

"A number, Margaret."

"Two hundred thousand for the trust."

"And how much is he under for?"

"Two hundred thousand. He took out a loan on the store for another three."

"Half a million? He owes half a million dollars?"

"Yes."

Sami dropped on the bench next to Margaret. "Half a million just to pull George's head above water? Add the trust you want, we're talking seven hundred thousand here."

"Will you do it?"

"What makes you think I have access to that much cash?"

"Oh, Sami, I'm sure you can come up with something. We will leave you and the girls alone."

"And if I don't?"

Margaret waved a hand in the air. "Well..." She dropped her hand, implying she would *not* leave them be. "Keep in mind, we *will* win the custody suit."

"I wouldn't bet on it if I were you." Sami tried not to sound smug. Armed with this new information about the couple's financial affairs and seeing the condition of the house, no judge would grant the old couple custody. If he challenged them in court, he would definitely win.

"George's financial problems are nothing compared to your mother's mental illness." Margaret arched a fading eyebrow. "You thought you could keep that a secret? That lawyer of yours, Vaughn... he told me a lot of things."

That goddamn jackass Allan Vaughn. Sami stretched to his feet. "What things?"

"Oh, things such as how unpredictable your mother's behaviour is. Being someone your father trusted and a lawyer, Vaughn is concerned for the girls' welfare."

Sami grappled for control. So this was how Margaret wanted to proceed? Even if she brought up Mother's condition in court, he would find a way around it. Place Mother with caring specialists in a separate home if it came to that. Shit! He would do anything to gain custody of his nieces.

As their grandparents, they would still have access to the girls, visitation rights and such. And they would ask for more money over the years. Margaret's callous greed made that clear. The girls would be old enough to know why their grandparents showed up now and then. How emotionally damaging would that be—knowing they were a meal ticket and little more?

He ran his hand through his hair. What a naive idiot he had been, trying to establish a healthy connection for the girls with their grandparents. So much for overlooking the road to hell paved with good intentions. He should have followed Lora's lead and kept her parents away from her daughters.

How could he get the couple out of the girls' lives? How could he guarantee this conniving woman wouldn't demand more?

The girls chased each other around the tree trunk. Their ringing laughter rose with Sami's boiling blood. This was blackmail, plain old-fashioned blackmail. The old woman wasn't vulnerable; she was calculating—a cold, heartless, bitch.

"Why don't you want George to know about this?"

"If he knew it was my idea, he'd never agree to it. He'd insist on having access to the trust money. I have to protect my future, whatever is left of it."

A car crunched pebbles on the driveway.

Margaret rose. "He's here. What do you say, Sami?"

"Will you and George sign a legally binding agreement not to have further contact with the girls? Abdicate your rights as grandparents?"

"You want to deprive us from our offspring?"

"I'll throw in another hundred thousand. How about it?"

"Make it an even million and you have a deal."

Sami staggered back a step. He had thrown in the suggestion to test Margaret's resolve. Her swift response, void of emotion and without hesitation, astounded him. This woman bartered her grandchildren as if she had landed a good deal on a Persian rug.

Hearing keys jingle in the background, Sami smacked his hands together. "Done."

On the way to the hotel, the girls fell asleep in their car seats. Thankful for quiet time during the short ride, Sami contemplated his situation. He needed to seal the deal fast. George followed his wife's plot with the eagerness of a threatened junkie sporting a black eye.

Sami opted not to ask about the identity of the debt holders. He would maintain his dealing with George and Margaret. No third party, loan sharks, or banks. Definitely, no Vaughn. Keep it simple and clean.

He would need someone trustworthy to oversee the tyre store. Determine if it was lucrative. Preferably someone local. He would have his lawyer handling the custody case set things in motion and draft the necessary papers. Sami would have to come up with the money on his own and not rely on company finances.

Too many changes had happened. He wouldn't jeopardize the livelihood of his employees. Besides, most of the company's cash flow was tied up in projects. He had around four hundred thousand in savings. Quickly selling valuable stocks in his portfolio might bring the lump sum past half a million. What would he do about the remaining amount?

Arriving at the hotel, he roused the girls to carry them out of the car. They cried and fussed non-stop for the next couple of hours. Nothing he tried calmed them down.

Frustrated, he called Mrs. Madigan for advice. She suggested a warm bath after dinner. By the time he had fed them, bathed them, and dressed them in their pyjamas, he was exhausted.

The girls got a boost of energy from their bath. They refused to settle down, wiggled out of his hands every time he tried to tuck them in. They used their full-size bed as a trampoline, bouncing on it and shouting. Fearing they might fall off the bed, he pushed it right against the wall and spread extra pillows on the floor on the other side.

About to lose it, Sami snatched his mobile and dialled Petra. The hell with Mrs. Madigan.

"Hey, Petra. I didn't wake you, did I?"

"Elias and I are watching a movie." Petra failed to hide the surprise in her voice.

"How is he?"

"The doctor had him walk around today and ran some tests. Elias keeps surprising him."

"Good. Good."

Deena shrieked and flipped on her back, wailing. It took Leena a second to mimic her sister.

"What's going on?" Petra asked. "Is everything okay over there?"

"I can't get the girls settled for the night. We're in a hotel. I've tried everything I can think of. Mrs.

Madigan suggested giving them a bath. That had the opposite effect. They're more stimulated and agitated."

"You're in a hotel? Not at their grandparents?"

"That's right. I don't know what's wrong with them. They can't be hungry. They had a good meal."

"Did *you* have a stressful day?"

He emptied his lungs with a long exhale. "You don't want to know."

"The girls are picking up your vibe. They sense you're stressed. And they're in a strange place and unfamiliar beds. Put the phone on speaker and free your hands."

"What for?"

At this point, he was willing to try anything. But if Petra had the power to lull his girls to sleep by speaking or singing to them on the phone, what did that say about his parenting abilities?

"Trust me," Petra said with a good measure of confidence.

"Fine." Sami put the phone on the nightstand and turned on the speaker. "Now what?"

"Hold them, Sami. Just hold them. They'll feel safe."

"I tri—"

"Shhhh. Don't talk. Lie on your back on the bed and hug them to your chest. Don't worry, you won't hurt them."

He did as instructed, half-convinced it was a waste of time. Leena wanted to flip onto her stomach, but he held her tight against his side. She quickly gave up and quieted down. Deena struggled and kicked him in the ribs. He let out a loud "oomph."

"Relax, Sami. Relax." Petra's voice soothed from the nightstand, calm, tranquil. "You got this. Take control."

Maintaining a good hold on Deena, he breathed deep and slow. Minutes passed. He imagined gliding through open seawaters to slow his heart rate. Then, the little girl with the red arrow birthmark appeared, floating, drifting further out to sea. He concentrated on catching up with her, rhythmically striking through the water surface.

Deena stopped pushing and nestled closer. Her little hand touched his cheek. A single word came out clear and loud, "Baba?"

Sami's throat clenched. His eyes burned. "Yes, sweetheart," he managed. "I want to be your Baba."

As if in response to a hypnotizer's snap of the fingers, Deena closed her eyes.

Warm and snug in his arms under the blanket, both girls finally fell asleep. He slipped out of their bed and moved onto his. Switching off the night-light, he picked up his phone, turned off the speaker, and whispered, "Petra, you still there?"

"I'm here."

"Sweet woman, it worked. Thank you and goodnight."

CHAPTER TWENTY-THREE

Sami threw himself into work after he returned to Houston. Confiding in his trusted assistant Robert, he tried to find a solution for his financial problem. He didn't explain why he needed the money and instructed Robert to liquidate some of his personal assets as quickly as possible.

Exhausted, Sami made sure to be home before the girls' bedtime every night. He settled for checking on Petra over the phone. He hid the details of his Cleveland trip, not knowing how to explain the agreement he had reached with Lora's parents. He told Petra he had found a way to keep them happy and offered no particulars. Petra didn't press for more.

Midweek, the doctors released Elias from hospital. Sami couldn't accompany Petra and her son home. Frustrated, he went into his study that night. Everyone in the house had gone to sleep, and he savoured the silence after his long day. He dialled Petra.

"Is Elias settled?"

"He's asking to go to NASA tomorrow." Petra huffed, as if out of breath.

"Is that a good idea? So soon?"

"The doctor said . . ." she panted, "Elias can handle such a trip."

"If you wait until the weekend, the girls and I can join you," Sami offered. What was she doing that caused her heavy breathing?

"Are you sure you can afford the time?"

Sami winced at the blow she delivered. "I'm sorry, Petra. I wanted to visit Elias again, but things got complicated at work. I couldn't break free at a decent time." His stomach lurched at the lie. Truth be told, he was avoiding her.

Something had happened to him that night at the hotel in Cleveland. His vision of Petra as a child had reminded him of his broken mind, tainted by his mother's defective genes. Though episodes of seeing her had become less frequent since the *real spectre* of Petra had come into his life, they hadn't completely disappeared. Like the firm clasp with which he had held his girls to break their resistance, Petra had a strong grip on him. There was no point in denying it.

"If you'd rather go during the week," Sami said. Better backtrack, give her a way out. "Don't let me stop you."

If he had a single decent bone in his body, he would remove himself from her path. She was a vulnerable mother with a sick son and he was a flawed man whose father may have deprived Petra of hers.

"It may be better not to keep Elias waiting," he stressed.

"I think," Petra blew air into the phone, "Elias would like you to come." Another huff followed. "If you can."

Sami took the chair behind his desk to check the NASA Visitors' Center's website. He could no longer take her heavy breathing. "What are you doing?"

"Umm... trying to remind you to keep your promise to Elias. He waited for you to visit again." She missed the meaning of Sami's question and blew another long exhale. "It's not like he has friends here."

Sami pushed his chair back. How had he missed that? Petra was lonely. She didn't know anyone in Houston. "Let's make it Friday. They have scheduled presentations at the Visitors' Center. Elias can meet a real astronaut."

"Oh, he would love that."

"You sound as if you're exercising. Careful with those weights."

She tickled Sami's ear with a ringing laugh. An open uninhibited laugh. "I'm cleaning the kitchen."

"Have the help desk send you someone. I already paid for the service."

"I want to do it myself. It's how I wind down. There, I'm done scrubbing the stove." The sound of running water followed. Petra stopped breathing into the phone. "I want to leave the place as spotless as when I moved in."

"With Elias's follow-up schedule, you have another month to worry about cleaning."

"I'm moving out of your apartment at the end of this week."

"No, you're not."

"I am, Sami."

"Please don't argue with me over this. You can pay whatever the going rate is for the lease if it makes you feel better." Sami pinched the bridge of his nose. "But really, it's the least of my problems right now."

"I'm trying to give you a solution."

"For what?"

"I asked your realtor. The sale of this apartment will bring you six to seven hundred thousand dollars. I don't know if it's enough for what you need, but it's a start."

"Who told you I need money?"

"Robert said you're looking to sell the place."

Sami pressed a fist to his lips, reeling from a powerful surge of anger. How could he be so stupid? He should have told Robert the apartment was off limits. "I'll find another way, Petra. Don't worry about it. It's my business."

"I can't sponge off you knowing you're strapped for money. I'm moving out as planned."

"You don't have to do that."

"It's done. I've booked a suite in an extended-stay hotel on Kirby Drive. It's close enough to the hospital and I can afford it. I'll also pay the two hundred thousand I owe you. A week at the most."

Sami couldn't stop himself from asking, "How?"

"That would be *my* business."

Petra's defiant tone broke something in Sami. Why in hell were they having this conversation? They should

273

be talking about her son's good progress and his girls, the good days that should follow. The hell with money. And damn George and Margaret.

"Why won't you let me help?" Petra's soft, earnest voice warmed him, as if she was nestling by his side.

He reclined in his chair until the back of his head met the wall. Perhaps this was it, the way to untangle Petra from his screwed-up life, give her a chance to walk away. "The loan I gave you was company money. If you pay it, that's where it'll go. It won't help me."

"Then the best thing to do is vacate your apartment." She sighed into his ear. "Sell it. It's yours, right?"

"Yes."

"I'm not stupid, Sami. I know it has to do with convincing the girls' grandparents to drop their custody suit." She paused for a moment. "They demanded money, didn't they?"

Shame swirled inside him. Should he tell her what the money was really for? Would that cause her to pack her bags and run? He knocked his head against the wall. "I didn't do the right thing."

"I don't understand."

"I talked Lora's parents into relinquishing their rights as grandparents. I... bargained for my girls. Struck a business deal about *their future*." He held his breath and waited to hear Petra's disappointment.

Several seconds passed and she said nothing.

"You know what kind of man that makes me?"

"You did what you had to do *for* those children, Sami. That makes you a true father."

***

Sami was all nerves on the way back from NASA, as Petra dosed in the passenger seat of his Lexus LS and the kids zoned out in the back. They had spent the entire day together, and yet he wasn't ready to part ways. He became buoyant in Petra's peaceful presence, a weightless astronaut floating in unknown territory. Her tranquillity spread over them all.

The twins, too young for such a trip, showed no interest in anything other than Dippin' Dot ice-cream and running after Elias. They obeyed Petra's instructions and behaved relatively well. It allowed Sami to pay close attention to Elias and bond further with him. Elias held onto his hand and talked non-stop. Meeting an astronaut in person enchanted the boy. He switched his superhero fascination to astronaut worship.

The gratitude in Petra's demeanor filled Sami with satisfaction and his blithe spirits soared higher. Somewhere on the tram tour, between the largest rocket model and the Space Shuttle replica, Sami suppressed his last speck of decency and came to a decision: he would not go away and let Petra be. He would venture closer, snuggle deeper under her comforting umbrella, and take shelter from his troubled life.

Approaching Petra's hotel, he slowed the car to a crawl and studied her, taking advantage of her slumber.

275

Streetlights passed over her face and neck in succession, caressing, teasing. If they didn't have the children with them, if they were alone, would she invite him to her room for a nightcap? He parked the car at the hotel entrance, killed the engine and waited as long as he could before gently rousing her with a pat on the shoulder.

Petra opened her eyes, smiling. "We're home?"

"Hmm," he murmured, silencing a quartet of violins bursting alive in his chest. What sort of woman wakes from an exhausting trip with the most captivating, serene smile on her lips?

"Elias, wake up, *ya omri*." Petra twisted her body and stretched her arm between the seats to rouse Elias, sandwiched between the girls' car seats. Her closeness entrapped Sami, filling his senses, confusing him. She smelled of something wholesome, spicy and woody with a hint of roses.

His voice an octave higher than usual, he asked, "How's your new place?"

"It's comfortable enough." Stretching further to unbuckle Elias's seat belt, she lifted off her seat. Her hip pressed against Sami's shoulder.

Sami held his breath. What was she doing? Why didn't she get out of the car to do that? And why in the world did *he* stay seated? He exhaled. "You have everything you need?"

"Oh, yes." Petra plopped down and opened her door. "Want to come up and see for yourself?"

Sami swallowed. "Now?" His eyes darted to the sleeping girls. "I don't want to wake my girls."

"How about you get them settled at home with Mrs. Madigan and come over for a cup of tea? Elias will be fast asleep."

Sami's tongue stuck to the roof of his mouth. Tea? Hell, he needed something stronger. An entire bucket of whatever. "You sure?"

"I want to show you something." She helped sleepy Elias squeeze between the front seats and pulled him onto her lap. "What do you say?"

"It'll take me two hours to get home, tuck the girls in bed, and drive back." Sami checked his watch. "It'll be close to ten, then."

Tilting her head to one side, Petra teased with a clouded smile. "I'll be waiting."

Sami missed the rush hour traffic and arrived home with the girls still asleep. Getting them settled with Mrs. Madigan's help went free of complications. He slipped out of the house as fast as he could, making it to Petra's in an hour.

In the hotel lobby, he hesitated to go up to Petra's suite, wondering if he should wait until ten o'clock. She might find him too eager. So what?

He took the elevator and stopped before her door to adjust the collar of his shirt. At least he had had the sense to grab a clean shirt before he dashed out of the house. Annoyed by his rising anxiety, he almost checked his forehead and nose for pimples. Damn it! It was high school summer vacations all over again. He had never honed a technique to go after a girl, and as the years seasoned him and he grew into a man, he had never needed to. Women gravitated toward him.

He knocked and took a step back.

Petra opened the door. "Good, you're early." Hair down and damp, she wore a turquoise tunic over black leggings and thick grey socks.

"Traffic wasn't as bad as I expected," he said, sounding sheepish.

"Come in." She stepped aside. "I'm making sandwiches. You hungry?"

"I can eat." Sami winced. He should've picked up something on the way. If only he had stopped to think for a moment, rather than hurry here. He stepped into a surprisingly spacious living room, furnished with a sleeper sofa, a lounge winged chair, a dining table with two chairs, and a decent-sized flat screen TV. French doors separated the bedroom, and a wall hid what must be the kitchen.

Petra pulled back one section of the curtains covering a wide window. Streetlights and neon signs cast her in multiple colours. Her damp hair glistened. "How did it go with the girls?"

"Smooth. They never really woke up." Sami helped her pull the other section, the desire to get a whiff of her freshly-showered fragrance as strong as his need to suppress his claustrophobia.

"I put them straight to bed." There was a trace of vanilla in her smell. And a tinge of alcohol. Had she been drinking?

"The girls had quite a day." Petra twisted her hair into a ponytail. "All that running around."

The birthmark on her forehead dared Sami to touch it, chart its tiny dots flickering with a bright ad sign outside. He stuck his thumbs in the back pockets of jeans, attempting to seem casual as he rounded the sofa to create more distance between them. He looked around for her possible drink. Nothing.

The French doors stood slightly ajar. From the narrow crack, he made out Elias asleep in a queen size bed. Or was he still awake?

Petra glided closer and pulled the doors shut. "Do you mind if we keep it down a little? I don't want Elias to wake up."

Sami licked his lips, suddenly thirsty. He removed his thumbs from his pockets, itching to touch her. "Is he okay?"

"Before he had the procedure, Elias wouldn't have lasted a day like today without lots of breaks," she said. "He's more than okay. And you made it all happen."

In a fluid move, she rose on her toes and kissed Sami's cheek. "Thank you." Before he could articulate a response, she slipped away and disappeared to the kitchen.

Sami remained stuck on the spot, arms dangling by his sides, hands empty. What was wrong with him? Why didn't he hold her? Return the kiss? Follow her?

Petra poked her head from behind the dividing wall. "Grilled turkey and cheese okay with you?" She sounded casual—as if she hadn't just planted a pile of quicksand under his feet.

"It's fine." He shuffled into a small kitchen, disgusted at his inaction. "Can I help with anything?"

Pressing sandwiches in a pan with a spatula, Petra motioned with her chin toward a tray on the short counter to her left. "Can you take the tea? These are almost done."

He edged in sideways to reach the tray, squeezing into the space between Petra and the fridge. "That smells great."

"Sausalito turkey cuts." Her eyebrows arched. "I hope you don't mind a little spice."

"Not at all."

"And cheddar cheese. Organic. Sharp." She peeked over her shoulder, ran the tip of her tongue across her upper lip and winked. "I have particular tastes."

"My good luck." He eyed her back when she returned her attention to the stove. He was willing to accept that peck on his cheek as a friendly kiss. But there was not an ounce of innocence in that wink. Petra was not talking about food. What game was she playing? He could show her a few moves.

He grabbed the tea tray. The only way to walk out of the tiny kitchen was to raise the tray above Petra's head. He edged behind her with his arms high. She lifted the pan off the stove and elbowed his ribs in the process.

Cups rattled on the tray. He pressed his back to the fridge. "Careful."

"Oh, sorry!" She turned to face him, hot pan in one hand, sticky spatula in the other, trapping him between her arms in that precarious position.

Seizing the opportunity, Sami lowered the tray behind her back. He leaned to press the softness of her upper body against his.

"What are you doing?" Petra whispered, fanning his face with her warm breath. Her neck and cheeks flared red, a chilli pepper invigorating his senses.

"Playing fair." He dipped his head to kiss her, but she moved her head ever so slightly, and his lips brushed the corner of her mouth instead. A groan escaped him.

Petra's entire body went rigid.

His lips hovered over hers. He waited for a response, chest squeezing tighter with each passing second, arms straining to keep the blasted tray steady in his hands. A bouquet of smells saturated the air around him. Her pleasing, pure—even saintly, yet alcohol-laced fragrance, and the spiced aroma of the mouthwatering sandwiches.

Eyes cast down, Petra froze against him. Not a coy kind of quietness, rather a cold, icy stillness. Her pale face contrasted with her red lips, so close he could sample their nectar if she gave him the green light.

Sami touched his forehead to hers and whispered, "You're killing me here."

Petra parted her lips with an audible, quick inhale. More of an unexpected hiccup than an invitation.

Her reaction confused him. Had he misread her signals? Releasing a chopped exhale, he straightened and raised his arms again to release her.

She jerked back, bumped against the stove and lifted wide eyes. "Are you okay?" Her voice came out high-pitched and unnatural.

"I could be better." Sami said, his confusion mounting. He was the one who should ask that question.

The pan in her hand tilted. She quickly slid the sandwiches onto a platter and walked out of the kitchen leaving Sami stunned.

What was that all about? He followed her to the table and set down the cursed tea tray. "Petra, I'm sorry if I—"

"Don't apologize." She cut him off and lifted the teapot to fill a cup. Her hands shook. Tea spilled onto the tray, making a small puddle.

He took over. "I got this."

She handed him the pot and sat down. Clasping her hands on the table, she lowered her head and breathed deep and slow.

Sami fumbled with the dainty pot handle and served in silence, giving her time to regain her wits. She sat statue-like, hands clasped tight enough to turn her knuckles white. She didn't want him to apologize? If she thought he wasn't imposing that kiss on her, why didn't she reciprocate? Never mind that, why this strange withdrawal? He had never encountered this kind of reaction from a woman. His confusion turned into serious concern. What was wrong?

He sat across the table. "Talk to me, Petra."

She remained silent.

Grasping her hands, he unlocked her icy fingers and wrapped them around the warm teacup. "Drink. Please."

Petra lifted her head and took a sip, with an obvious shudder.

"You need something stronger." He rose to his feet.

"Tea is fine." Her voice broke. She touched the back of his hand. "Will you please sit down?"

"Only if you eat something." He put a sandwich on her plate, hoping to energize her. She had said she was hungry, after all. Perhaps that was the reason behind her strange lethargy.

Petra bit into her sandwich and Sami dropped onto his chair. They sipped tea and exchanged crunching sounds of toasted bread. All the while, she stared into the space separating them and he considered possible ways to explain her behaviour. He tried not to give in to the notion that Petra might be a manipulative woman who thought so little of him that she would play this cat and mouse game.

An ambulance siren shrieked outside, piercing the loaded atmosphere. The shrill had faded by the time Petra emptied her plate. Natural colour returned to her face.

Refilling her cup, Sami asked, "Feel better?"

She nodded.

"What's the matter, Petra?"

"I didn't invite you up here for . . ." she pointed at the kitchen, "that."

"I didn't think you did." Sami set down the teapot, his patience running thin. "Things got out of hand." He snapped his eyes to hers. "My mistake."

She held his gaze. "Not entirely."

"Meaning?"

"I had a hand in it." She tucked loose hair strands behind her ear. "I won't demean you by pretending otherwise."

Sami emptied his lungs in a long, relieved exhale. There sat the woman he had hoped Petra would be— one he was drawn to like no other, a confident woman who didn't play silly games. He placed his elbows on the table and overlapped his hands. "Fair enough."

"I didn't plan it. I'm not that kind of woman."

"What kind might that be?"

"One who takes her faith lightly and defies cultural traditions." Petra pressed her lips together. "I don't. I was raised well despite what you may think of my patchy upbringing."

Sami waved a dismissive hand. "Petra, nothing much happened. Certainly nothing to feel guilty about."

She shook her head. "I *wanted* you to kiss me."

"I tried." He snapped back in his chair, absorbing the blow to his ego. "I can do better, I assure you."

"I don't doubt that." She slanted her moist lips in a sideways smile, her cheek denting with a tiny dimple.

Sami forced himself to stay seated. Jumping over the table to lick that dimple would scare the daylights out of her. He rubbed his chin. "So what went wrong?"

Petra sighed and collected their plates, taking her time to answer.

He waited, his gaze locked on the mark where her dimple appeared.

"The last man I kissed was my husband. And Bassam is . . . well, he's dead." She slipped out of her chair and went into the kitchen.

Sami worked the logic. Did she mean she had *forgotten* what it was like to be kissed? How to return a man's attentions? That she was too prudent to kiss a man who wasn't her husband? It wasn't even a proper kiss, for heaven's sake. And she admitted her role in creating the situation. Had she compared *him* to her dead husband? What the hell did she mean? And why would she ask if he was all right after that damn non-kiss?

Splashing sounds came from the kitchen. He rose, picked up empty cups and used cutlery. A thought struck him. He dropped everything on the table and sprinted to the kitchen.

Petra stood by the sink, rinsing dishes, head bowed.

Sami approached and turned off the faucet. "The night Bassam had his fatal heart attack, you said he was in bed, caught between the sheets."

Petra lifted her head, tears running.

Sami swallowed. Using his most tender tone, he continued. "Was that what you were doing? Were you—"

"Yes," Petra whispered.

Sami held her by the shoulders and gently turned her to face him. "You can't believe it was your fault."

"Bassam complained he was tired, and I... I didn't... pay attention."

"Jesus!" Sami drew her into a soft embrace. "You didn't know he had a heart problem. *He* didn't even know, right? You didn't cause his death, Petra."

"In my head, I know that," she said, her voice muffled.

Sami loosened his hold. She pulled away.

286

Petra rubbed her hands up and down her arms. "His defective heart couldn't handle the extreme desert weather. The doctors said it could have happened in his sleep." More tears flowed. "I think when you tried to kiss me, what you said, brought that night back."

"I'm so sorry." Sami ran his fingers through his hair and tried to recall what the hell he had said. He might have uttered something about not being able to breathe. Shit!

"I'm trying to tell you what happened is not your fault." She wiped tears with the back of her hands. "I don't want that to ruin our friendship."

"Of course not." He pulled himself to full height. Friendship? Good grief, he wasn't thinking of friendship.

"It won't happen again, okay?" Petra asked, her face full of concern, hope.

"As you wish." Sami nodded, not sure what he was agreeing to. Did she mean she wouldn't freeze if he kissed her again? Or that she wouldn't give him another chance to try? Better drop the subject for now. He would not cause this delicate woman more trauma.

Injecting easiness into his voice, he tried to sound casual, unaffected. "You said you have something to show me?"

"Oh, yes." Petra headed to the living room. She pulled out a cardboard box from the console holding the TV.

"I didn't want to show it to you before you had a chance to settle things with the girls' grandparents."

CHAPTER TWENTY-FOUR

Petra sat on the couch and placed the shoebox in her lap. Her hands had stopped shaking, but her heart rebelled against its restraints. She had done it. She had finally talked about what happened with Bassam that night, and not to a therapist, but to another man. A man she fancied. She had made progress. Mouzah would be proud of her.

Waiting for Sami to sit down, she asked, "You sold the apartment?"

"Yup." Sami sat to her right, careful to keep his knees from touching hers.

"So fast." She noticed his reserved posture. The poor man didn't know what had hit him. He had taken it well, though. He was still here. "It's been only a week since it went on the market."

"There's a waiting list of potential buyers for these kinds of apartments. It sold the same day it was listed."

"How much did it go for? If you don't mind me asking."

Sami drummed his fingers on the arm of the couch, showing his impatience. "Eight-fifty."

"Wow!" Petra couldn't bring herself to open her box yet. She needed to be sure. "Does that cover the deal you made with the girls' grandparents?"

"I used part of my savings for the rest. It's all set. Money, papers, everything. Legally, they're out of the picture."

"You have full custody?"

"It'll be official on Monday." He pinched the tip of his nose. "What's this about?"

"I asked Mouzah to FedEx me this box from Kuwait after I met your mother."

"Is she your friend from school?"

Petra felt horrible. The man was beyond confused. She tried to smile. "Mouzah is Khalid's wife."

"She was introduced to me as Umm Ahmad, not by her given name." Sami crinkled his eyebrows and pointed with his chin to the box. "So what's in there?"

Petra swiped her hand over the lid. "Everything I own of my father." She lifted the lid, rifled through the contents, and pulled out a black and white photograph. "This is a picture of my father and three of his friends. There's no date on it." She pointed at the man in the middle of the group. "That's Dad. It's the only photo I have of him. He burned everything else. Mother managed to save this one by hiding it in her passport."

"You'd think she would have saved a photo of just your father. Or a wedding picture, not him with a bunch of guys. Do you know why he burned the rest?"

"I was a child when my mother died. I didn't have—"

"You didn't have a chance to ask questions," Sami interrupted, his tone apologetic. He truly believed his father responsible for her familial situation.

"Look closely." She offered him the photograph. "Do you recognize any of the other men?"

Sami studied the grainy picture. He pointed at the man on the far left. "That's my father. This must have been taken before he left Kuwait for the States."

"What makes you think it was Kuwait?"

"See the building behind them? A standardized design for schools during the seventies and eighties. Vaughn told me our fathers went to the same high school in Kuwait." Sami tapped the photograph. "All this sand around them. This was in Kuwait."

"Flip to the back. See those initials in Arabic letters?"

"Four sets of initials."

"I can't read Arabic, but I know my alphabet," Petra said. "One is clearly for my father. *Waw* and *Seen*. Waleed Saba."

Sami turned toward the side lamp. "I can make out the initials *Ya'a* and *Ein* for my father's name, Yahya Amara. Another reads *Seen* and *Dal.*"

"S and D. And the last one?"

"It's not clear." Sami tilted the photograph. "I think the letters *Ha'a* and *Fa'a*. Or the second letter could be *Qa'af.*" Sami looked at Petra again and scratched his head. "There's a trace of other dots over that letter, I can't quite make it out."

"So the first name starts with an *H*, and the last name possibly starts with an *F*?"

Petra watched Sami examine the photograph from the front and back, waiting for the conclusion she had reached to dawn on him, too. He took too long.

"Is it possible that *Fa'a* might be a *V* instead of an *F* in English?" she prodded.

"There's no *V* in the Arabic alphabet. Some modern translations use three dots over the *fa'a* for the *V* sound."

"What name do you think the initials *H* and *V* correspond with?"

Sami rose slowly to his feet. "Hanna Vanyos!"

"*Khoury* Dahood didn't show you a picture of him?"

"No. Even if I could find one in the church files, I doubt I could match it to this old, distant photo of his face." Sami reclaimed his spot on the couch. "It has to be Vanyos. It makes sense now. They all knew each other from school."

"Maybe your mother can recognize the fourth man."

"I doubt it. We went through Dad's old albums one by one looking for something that might trigger her memory of Hanna Vanyos. It didn't help." Sami clicked his tongue. "Actually, it backfired. Mom got agitated and restless." He handed the photograph to Petra. "I didn't see anything like this one."

Resting his elbows on his knees, Sami laced his fingers under his chin and stared at the floor. Petra tucked the photograph in the box. She sat inches away from Sami, close enough to see his jaw muscles pump, and sensed him drift miles away. How to reel him back to shore?

He shifted, slung his arm over the back cushion and faced her. "Remember that big favour I said I'd ask of you?"

"You never told me what it was."

"I need you to look after my girls for a few days. A week at the most. Stay on top of Mrs. Madigan while I'm gone. Can you do that?"

"Of course. Where are you going?" Petra asked, knowing the answer beforehand and feeling guilty for giving Sami the final push.

"Where else?" Sami raised his eyebrows. "Time to find some answers."

Too wired to sleep after Sami left, Petra waited until dawn to call Mouzah and catch her at a reasonable hour on her side of the world. She cuddled under a blanket and filled her in, omitting certain embarrassing details.

"So are you fine with taking care of his girls?" Mouzah asked.

"It's more like supervising their nanny. They'll stay at home with their grandmother and Mrs. Madigan. That's the nanny's name. And I'll check on them every day."

"Oh! That is so clever," Mouzah snapped. "This Sami is very calculating."

Petra didn't appreciate her friend's tone. She forced herself to calm down. Her nerves were stretched to the limit after her emotional train wreck of an evening. She couldn't understand Mouzah's judgmental comment.

"What do you mean?"

"He is testing you."

"For what?"

Mouzah sighed into the phone. "To see if you are a good fit. He is getting ready."

"For what?" Petra repeated, yawning.

"For marriage, my friend. It is as obvious as the sun."

"How can you think that?" Petra slid further under the blanket on the couch. "Sami's going to Bethlehem to clear his father's name. Marriage is the last thing on his mind, believe me. Especially after tonight." Petra caught herself. "I mean—"

"Ooooh! What happened tonight? Tell me, tell me."

"I told him about Bassam."

"And?"

"The night he died."

"*Eeeh*?" Obviously too impatient, Mouzah switched to Arabic.

"What we were doing."

"*Ya hafith*! You talked about it? You told *him*?"

Petra pulled the blanket over her head. "I did. I don't know where I got the courage from. It just spilled out."

"How did you say it?" Mouzah squealed. "What words did you use?"

"Well, I didn't actually say much. He sort of figured it out. I think it scared him."

"What did he do? Tell me everything. Details. Details."

Petra's phone dinged with an incoming email. She quickly checked the screen. Richard Frost. She ignored it and continued, "I didn't give Sami time to say or do anything. I hit him with the info about our fathers and he shifted focus. That's when he asked for the favour."

"Something is smelly about this," Mouzah said.

"You mean fishy. What's wrong with him wanting to make sure his nieces are well taken care of in his absence? He trusts me. I have a feeling he has a hard time trusting anyone."

"If their grandmother is there, why does he need you to supervise the nanny?"

Petra hadn't explained the condition of Sami's mother to Mouzah and she wasn't about to betray Sami's confidence. She thought fast for an answer. "When your boys were little, did you ever leave them alone with your mother-in-law? You had the maids check on them, right?"

"So now you are a maid?"

Petra sprang from under the blanket. "Oh, Mouzah! Don't twist my words."

"Listen, my friend. Khalid's mother is in a wheelchair. Don't tell me Sami's mother is crippled like her."

"Mrs. Amara has . . . emotional issues. She's unreliable." Petra felt better. She hadn't lied to her friend and used the same terminology Sami used to describe his mother. Trying to deflect Mouzah, she went on, "and the correct term to use for your mother-in-law's situation is *differently abled.*"

"Different from what?" Mouzah asked, her tone showing her confusion.

"From people like you and me. It's a more socially acceptable way to describe someone in a wheelchair."

"*Weeh!*" Mouzah was clearly irritated. "I meant to say she is handicapped."

"You're missing the point. It's not politically correct to use—"

"What does politics have to do with this? I'm talking about you and Sami."

Petra relented. "Sami and I are friends."

"You can change that. If you really like him. And I know you do. *I* like him."

"You've only met him once."

"It was enough. My vision is like iron."

"Um, that makes no sense, Mouzah."

"I have a good eye for character. And I like how he treats you and your son." Mouzah sounded as if she inhaled deep through clenched teeth. "A lesser man would have tried to take advantage of your situation."

295

Petra left the couch and paced the living room. "I more than like him," she whispered. "I think... I've fallen for him."

"Then do something. Send him a clear message."

Petra stopped herself from talking about the miserable outcome of her attempt earlier. No matter how open-minded her friend was, bound by her Kuwaiti social values, Mouzah would deem her actions inappropriate. She stood by the window and gazed at the rising sun.

"It's not in me, Mouzah."

"*Illy yabi assalat, ma tfootah!*"

"I understood one word, praying. I'm afraid it's going to take more than that."

"The saying means, if you want to catch the prayer time, you will do everything you can not to let it pass."

"I hear you. But what can I do?"

"He has a good relationship with his mother, right?" Mouzah didn't wait for Petra's answer. "You said he's a good son to her. You have a chance to spend time with his mother while he's in Palestine. Win her heart, you will win his. Trust me. It works. Every time."

Petra sighed, unwilling to correct Mouzah's perception of Sami's relationship with his mother. "Listen, Elias will wake up soon. I need to get up to speed on my emails before he does."

"You know Khalid will be honoured to receive Sami for you, right?"

"Receive him?"

"To ask for your hand, my friend. Sami can talk to Khalid." Mouzah said, her tone lighthearted and airy, contrasting with the serious nature of what she was talking about. "You have no family to represent you."

Petra pressed her fingers to her temples and briefly closed her eyes. A savage headache gripped her. Mouzah was relentless. She never failed to hit the nail on the head with her brutally honest tongue. This time, the hammer slammed Petra. "I appreciate that, Mouzah. We are nowhere near such a situation—I have to go."

"Wait, Khalid is waiting for your bank account number to send the money you asked for."

"It turns out I don't need it now. I worked it out. Please thank Khalid for his generosity."

"Promise me you will think about what I said?"

"How could I not? Talk to you later."

Petra checked on Elias. He was fast asleep. She brewed a strong cup of coffee, took two pills to muffle the thumping in her head, and sat at her laptop.

The subject line of Richard's email spelled 'Urgent' in bold letters. Taking a deep breath, she steadied her nerves and clicked open his message.

CHAPTER TWENTY-FIVE

"Why do you come to *Isrrrael*?" The passport control officer at Ben Gurion Airport asked in an East European accent, sounding his *r*s from the back of his throat.

"Tourism," Sami hunched his shoulders to speak through the circular hole in the glass separating him from the officer. No need to explain the reason behind his quick visit.

"How long do you plan to stay?"

"Maybe a week." Sami said, stretching his intended visit. He needed no more than three days; travel to Jerusalem, cross over to Bethlehem, talk to Hanna Vanyos, and return to his girls.

The Israeli officer would see a three day stay as falling short of a tourist's trip. Especially with his Palestinian roots. It was common knowledge that Americans of Palestinian origins didn't get admitted into Israel as easily as other Americans.

"You don't know how long you intend to stay?" the officer asked.

"I *plan* to stay a week," Sami qualified. "I may have to cut it short if work interferes."

"What do you do?"

"I'm CEO of a construction company in Texas."

"Where will you go in *Isrrrael*?"

"The usual sites," Sami said halfheartedly. The flight over was more than enough to stretch his endurance limits. He had slept little since leaving home the day before, only a few minutes here and there, out of exhaustion. Now he had to endure this officer's suspicious gaze and dance around questions to gain entry to *his* parents' homeland.

"Where, exactly?"

"Jerusalem, Jaffa, Nazareth. You know, as much as I can squeeze in."

"Where will you stay?"

"City of Prayers Hotel. In Jerusalem."

"*Addrrress?*"

Sami pulled a slip of paper from his backpack and slipped it under the glass pane. "Here's all the information. Hotel address and reservation details."

The officer slid the paper aside without a glance. "I will name *countrrries* one by one. You tell me if you have *everrr trrraveled* to any of them." He flipped passport pages. "*Syrrria.*"

"No," Sami answered.

"Yemen."

"No."

"Lebanon," the officer continued in the dispassionate tone of an automated phone survey.

"No."

"*Morrrocco.*"

"I attended a conference in Casablanca in 2010," Sami said.

"Which *conferrrence*?"

"Middle East contemporary design and architecture."

"*Grrrandfather's* name?"

Sami blinked. "On which side?"

The officer looked up from Sami's passport. "*Father-rr's* side."

"Mousa Nassar Amara." Sami looked the officer in the eye, letting him know he understood the reason behind the question. The officer's wry smile confirmed he was aware of Sami's Palestinian roots.

"You have family in *Jerrrusalem*."

Sami clenched his jaw. Was that a question or a statement? The man's voice remained monotone and his face flat, expressionless. Good thing he had come prepared. He nodded and gave his own statement. "A second cousin."

"Name and *numberrr*."

Sami dug out another piece of paper with the information about his father's cousin which he had found scribbled in one of his father's files. As far as he knew, his father had never travelled to Palestine, so when he found the information, it grabbed his attention. A couple of days before he left Houston, he had dialled the number and ended up having a warm conversation with his cousin in Jerusalem, despite his clumsy Arabic and his cousin's mangled English. The talk was heartening and genuine, as if he had grown up with his kin, distance and time irrelevant.

He repeatedly refused his cousin's invitation to stay at his house in Jerusalem and asked him to recommend a hotel. His cousin relented after the fifth rejection and explained he would make a reservation at a hotel owned and operated by Palestinians.

Sami slipped the paper with his cousin's information to the officer.

The officer scanned it and shoved it back to him. "ID *numberrr*."

"I'm sorry?"

"*Isrrraeli* ID *numberrr* for your cousin."

"I don't have it."

The officer stared at Sami, unblinking.

"Let me call him."

Sami dialled his cousin and got voice mail. He left a message and texted his request, stating the urgency. He waved his mobile at the officer. "My cousin is not answering, but I'm sure he'll come back to me soon."

A young female soldier, her hair tucked in a bun under a khaki cap, approached the passport control officer and whispered something in his ear. He nodded at Sami. "You will go to Ramallah?"

"I might."

"You are *Arrrab*. You people are always connecting with family."

"I'm an American citizen of Palestinian origin from Ramallah." Sami let the racist remark slide and tried to keep his composure. *Do you say that to all American tourists of different backgrounds?* He wanted to ask that, then decided against it. "I was born in the U.S. There's no problem with my passport."

The officer handed Sami's passport to the woman soldier and pointed at a hall with rows of chairs behind Sami. "Find a seat."

As he was about to turn away, Sami received a text message from his cousin with the ID number. He tried to give the information to the officer, but was waved aside.

"We will call you soon."

Soon was more than three hours. Sami chose the plastic chair closest to the windows, parked his carry-on, and set down his backpack. He texted Petra to check on the twins, despite the late hour Houston-time. She texted him with a short report of their activities since he left, ending her messages with smiley faces and lollipops. She and Mrs. Madigan had taken the girls to an indoor children's jungle gym and all was well. He checked his messages for news of his mother from *Khoury* Dahood. The priest had agreed to be Sami's eyes. No messages meant no major issues with Mother.

Fingers crossed, things would remain like that.

Sami moved on to check work emails. He couldn't afford to miss a single report from Robert. He had instructed his assistant to watch Vaughn's every move, unable to shake his gut feeling not to fully trust the man. Vaughn lurked around Sami's office where he had no business. Sami's computer was password-protected, no issue there.

Sami reminded Robert to keep his vigil and not grant Vaughn access to any files locked in his desk. Sami must have the upper hand. His initial feeling of repulsion towards Vaughn hadn't waned. The jackass was up to something, and he couldn't afford to find out what it was after it was too late. Never again.

Somewhat relieved things were under control, Sami settled for people watching to clear his head. An older man in a business suit a couple of chairs to the left twirled his thumbs in his lap and stared at the linoleum floor. A woman with a white headscarf ordered her toddler to stop running in circles. She opened a bag of chips and lured him to sit beside her. Two soldiers with machine guns dangling by their sides came into the hall. They escorted the old man away, who seemed resigned, subdued. He had expected this.

Sami gazed outside the open doorway. A female officer balanced herself on a high stool across the entrance. Arriving passengers came and went with flights landing one after another. Sami lost count of how many flights. He observed a group of young

American men and women, the Florida pistol-shaped state image on the backs of their colourful shirts. They gathered near the passport control cubicles. They didn't wait too long, no more than fifteen minutes. The same officer who handled Sami's passport came out of a side door and gave them their passports. Sami caught the officer's eye on his way back.

"Soon," the officer mouthed.

Sami dug a book out of his backpack.

Two more hours passed. The toddler fell asleep in his mother's lap. She looked exhausted and must be as hungry as Sami. He set his spy novel aside and addressed her.

"How about you lay him on the chairs?" He gestured at a row of empty chairs, folding his palms on his cheek to convey his suggestion in case she didn't understand English.

The mother shook her head. She jutted her chin toward the entrance. He twisted to see what she was pointing at.

The female officer at the entrance met his gaze, letting him know they were being monitored. He nodded his understanding to the mother and picked up his book. The mother knew she wasn't allowed to let her son sleep on the chairs. She had been through this before. How many times? How many like her having to cradle their children for hours?

Sami had neared the middle of his spy novel when he heard his name being called, with instructions to go to cubicle number five. Another officer greeted him with a smile.

"Why do you come to Israel?" The bald man had a nasal New York accent.

"Tourism and possibly see family members."

"Where will you stay? Who will you see?"

Sami pointed at the East European officer he had spoken to earlier, who was sitting to the bald officer's right. "I gave that officer all the information."

"I'm the one asking now."

The officer never dropped his smile, his attitude grating. Sami mirrored the fake grin and repeated the details from his phone. The bald officer didn't write anything down, not his cousin's name, his ID number, nor the hotel information.

"Take a seat." The officer nodded. "It won't be long."

With the setting sun, Sami seriously doubted they would grant him entry into the country. He had spent the entire day at the airport. His backside was sore from sitting on the plastic chair and his stomach was growling from hunger. He contemplated his options. Contact the U.S. embassy? That would accomplish nothing. He had read too many reports of instances where Palestinian-Americans were turned away, and the U.S. embassy never interfered on their behalf.

An older female guard replaced the one at the entrance.

He picked up his backpack, grabbed his carry-on and walked out of the hall to stretch his legs in search of vending machines.

The new guard arched an eyebrow as he passed her.

He nodded at her and rolled his luggage along. No way would he let the Israelis deny him entry to his father's birthplace. No way would he leave without collecting the information he sought. And no fucking way would he set foot on a plane again today.

A soldier approached and pointed with his machine gun toward the waiting hall Sami had abandoned, not bothering to say anything. Sami understood the message and returned to his spot before he could grab a snack. He should call his cousin and let him know what was going on. His cousin would most probably be helpless to resolve the situation in the airport. If things got worse, Sami would ask him to follow up on Hanna Vanyos.

The female soldier came into the hall. She picked up Sami's backpack and pointed at his luggage. "Come with me."

Sami followed her into a small room with a plastic table and a single folding chair. No windows. Sami's chest immediately clenched.

"Those chairs out there are a joke." He pretended to stretch his back, extending his arms to get a physical sense of the space around him and hoping he didn't appear threatening to the soldier.

The soldier threw his backpack onto the table. "Sit down. Someone will come to talk to you soon."

Sami dropped on the chair. *Soon* had its own definition here. He wouldn't last ten minutes in this box. Half an hour later, the door opened. Sami breathed a sigh of short-lived relief. Two officers came in, a stocky female and a man sporting a moustache fit for a cowboy in a western movie. They crowded the small room, pushing Sami to the limit of his endurance.

An image of being shoved into his mother's cedar chest popped into his head. Sweat collected on his upper lip—the first sign of his elevated anxiety. Sami licked his lip and used the saltiness to transfer himself to a vast beach under open skies—a mental trick he had read about in a book. It worked. He prayed its effect would last until he was released from this hell.

The officers asked the same questions as before, taking turns; this time, they wrote down Sami's answers. Or at least they pretended to. He had memorized the information by now and didn't need to consult his phone or papers.

They went through his backpack and small carry-on with meticulous attention, spreading his T-shirts, underwear, socks and toiletries on the table. Sami expected them to take a jab at his white boxers from the way they exchanged smirks while they lifted each piece, and he readied himself with scathing comebacks. They passed on the opportunity, speaking Hebrew to each other. Sami understood nothing.

The stocky female officer opened Sami's laptop and turned it on. "What's your personal email address?"

"What for?"

The officer smirked. "Maybe we want to send you a welcoming message."

"Sure." Sami tried hard to bury his irritation, imagining his toes digging in the beach sand. He pointed at the pen and paper in the officer's hand. "I'll write it for you."

He scribbled an email address he used for online orders. Should they hack into his email, all they would see was his taste in books, clothes, and children's toys. The cowboy officer could order himself a dozen of those white boxers he liked so much. Sami set his mind to change his password the instant he left. If they ever let him out of here.

"You can repack your belongings now." The cowboy officer opened the door and drawled in an exaggerated southern accent, "Welcome to Israel, partner."

***

Sami crashed the instant he arrived at the hotel late at night. Waking to the melody of church bells and Muslim prayer calls, he checked his phone. Was it Sunday already? He had lost two full days getting here. He listened to his cousin's several short messages and dialled him back. Apologetic but firm, Sami turned down his cousin's lunch invitation and pushed the dinner invitation to Monday to give himself enough time in Bethlehem. He would explain the Hanna Vanyos issue to his cousin only if his investigation came up empty. At the moment, the fewer people involved in this fact-finding mission about his father's actions, the better.

His cousin kept saying he was sorry about something out of his control, but Sami didn't understand because of his poor English. Either his cousin had lost a limb in a car accident and apologized for not being able to get to Bethlehem, or the tyres of his car had been slashed. Sami hoped it was the latter and politely ended the call, sparing his cousin the need to stumble through further explanations.

Sami showered, dressed, and headed to the front desk, noticing in the daylight the boutique hotel's exceptional architecture.

The thick limestone walls, high domed ceilings, and small circular openings atop were part of a design to regulate temperatures inside rooms, typical of centuries-old Jerusalem homes. Under his feet, thick tiles with colourful geometric designs paved the floor. The tiles in high traffic areas, especially the middle of the hallway, were chipped and worn, but the ones in the corners displayed artful compositions. This two-story house must have been a single-family dwelling before it was turned into a hotel. Sami decided to research the hotel's history when he had a minute to himself. Perhaps tonight after he returned from Bethlehem.

As he took the narrow stairs down to the first floor, he admired Palestinian embroidered tapestry splashing colour on every surface, from the bedspread in his room, to curtains, pillows, and walls, where traditional women's dresses were framed and hung. Tall rectangular stained-glass windowpanes completed the bouquet of colours.

If he had been in the right frame of mind or had the time, he would have explored the entire Old City of Jerusalem, designated a UNESCO World Heritage site—an architect's dream. But he was here on a mission and his life, with its multi-layered responsibilities, beckoned him back to Houston.

The aroma of rising yeast and freshly-baked bread drew Sami to the outdoor courtyard. In its centre was a fountain surrounded by tables. Huge entwining grape vines shaded the entire space. Chandeliers of deep red grape clusters dangled and glittered in the sunlight. The soft music of stringed instruments mingled with the abrasive clatter of dishes and chairs scraping on the stone floor.

A waiter, with the classic chequered black and white *koufiyeh* draped over his shoulders, showed Sami to a table and handed him a menu.

Sami glanced at the people around him. Some had English menus. His was in Arabic. He liked that. The waiter assumed he was a local. Sami studied the menu. It carried him back to his mother's kitchen on Sunday mornings, on one of his holiday home visits as a child. On rare occasions, his mother was well enough to make breakfast for everyone. On those occasions, he felt like a normal boy.

The single laminated menu sheet had pictures. It invited him to order a plate of everything: plain falafel, or stuffed with sautéed onions; *Fouel*, the mixture of mashed fava beans in lemon, garlic, and olive oil which he had deemed its name funny as a child; a hummus dip in four varieties—with minced meat, with pine nuts, with red hot *shatta*, or plain; and *mana'eesh* of baked dough smothered with the *Akkawi* white cheese his mother always raved about. Starving and nostalgic, Sami couldn't make up his mind what he wanted.

The waiter came back with a basket of steaming pita bread and two small bowls, one filled with emerald-coloured olive oil, the other with the dried green thyme and sesame seed concoction, *zaatar*.

"*Eish bto'mor Abu Elshabab?*" The waiter asked, pencil and paper ready in hand.

Sami smiled at being addressed as 'the father of young men'. If only he could articulate his order without his choppy accent. Sami pointed at a couple of choices, hummus with roasted pine nuts and stuffed falafel, choosing not to speak so as to maintain the image of a local Palestinian which he so eagerly accepted.

311

The waiter scribbled the order in his pad and turned to leave.

Sami stopped him. "*Lamoon bilna'na' kaman.*" He ordered mint lemonade with the least number of words possible, forcing the difficult Arabic letter *Ein* deep from the bottom of his throat, a dead giveaway for anyone whose Arabic wasn't his mother tongue.

The waiter nodded, flipped one dangling edge of his *koufiyeh* onto his shoulder, and marched away.

Sami filled his lungs with fresh air. He had passed his own personal test. He fit in here. Where were those airport officers to see that?

His table, stationed at the outer edge of the courtyard, faced one of the gates in the ancient wall surrounding the Old City of Jerusalem several yards away. Camera-toting tourists in sandals, shorts and tank tops posed for pictures then strolled through the gate. Orthodox Jews, women in long skirts, men in dark trousers, flowing ear locks and yarmulkes strutted onward. Some of their children slung rifles across their small frames. Israeli soldiers stationed at the gate randomly stopped Palestinian men, women, and children. The soldiers prodded and examined bags, clothes and even shoes.

Sami made the distinction from their clothes. The majority of Palestinian women wore the folkloric dress he had seen decorating the hotel walls. His mother had insisted on wearing a similar dress at Fareed's wedding, a full-length black linen *thoub* embroidered with red stitches.

Checkered *koufiyeh*, black on white or red on white distinguished most Palestinian men. And the children—they strode defiantly, their heads lifted, eyes glaring at heavily armed soldiers.

Girls walked rigid with stiff backs, holding their mothers' hands.

Boys marched like men, square-shouldered, chins jutting.

Sami recognized that proud stance from his vantage point. He had walked in the same manner when he was a boy, to make his body seem bigger than it was, to hide his fear, to project knowledge of his rights, to express dignity.

The waiter interrupted his thoughts. Attacking the tasty meal, Sami imagined describing the scene to Petra once he returned to Houston. The first time he had met her at Mr. Faisal's office in Kuwait, she told him she dreamed of bringing Elias to Palestine to connect with his roots. How far could Elias stretch his little body if he were to pass one of those soldiers?

A soldier pulled aside a young boy of about ten or eleven. He yelled something at him in broken Arabic which Sami didn't understand. The boy pointed at the gate and screamed at the top of his lungs, "*Rayeh a beity!*"

Sami understood the last word. The boy wanted to go home.

The soldier lifted the boy's T-shirt with the muzzle of his machine gun.

Sami threw onto his plate the half-eaten falafel disc in his hand, his insides about to reject what he had eaten. He took a sip of his mint lemonade, hoping the drink would soothe his stomach.

The boy held his hand up to halt a woman rushing to his side, perhaps his mother. She stopped several steps away. People joined her. The boy took off his T-shirt, dropped it on the ground, and spread out his arms.

Two soldiers flanked their comrade and pointed at the boy's shoes. He took off his shoes, flipped them in the air and set them next to his T-shirt. One soldier pointed at the boy's jeans. He shook his head.

The soldier bellowed again, lifting his machine gun to the boy's face. The mother waved her hands and screamed. She cursed at the soldier; her fury couldn't be misunderstood. She spoke to her son, her tone softer. "*Tkhafish. Tkhafish. Khalleek rijjal,*" she repeated over and over again.

Sami's throat closed. The mother was telling her son not to be afraid, to be a man.

The boy dropped his jeans, stepped out of them, and twirled around in his boxer shorts, obviously daring the soldiers.

A woman with a big straw hat, perhaps a Japanese tourist, pushed past the gathering crowd, raising her iPad. She was filming or taking pictures. One of the soldiers stepped into her view and blocked the iPad with his hand. She quickly tucked it away.

The soldier looked around. Other people had their phones and cameras in the air, documenting the boy's utter humiliation. The soldier flicked his hand to the boy, dismissing him. The boy dressed and joined his mother. She kissed his head and patted him on the back. They disappeared through the gate.

Sami's palms hurt. Glancing at them, he realized he had been clenching his fists the entire time. His nails had dug crescent grooves into his flesh. He relaxed his fingers and ran them over his face. He had learned of his people's history from books, knew all about the atrocities, the military occupation, the confiscation of land and the Palestinian diaspora.

Years of knowledge could not impress upon him the weight of the Palestinian tragedy, as did those several minutes he spent witnessing what unravelled at that Jerusalem gate.

He signalled for the waiter to clear his table. Disgust clogged his throat. He grabbed the spoon and studied his distorted reflection on its curved surface. Did he have the same look in his eye that his father flashed every now and then when he talked about Palestine? The look that made Father stop whatever he was doing and stare into space. The same look made Mother tear-up and claim it was because of allergies. That deep painful stare articulated history in a language Sami yearned to understand. Staring at his disfigured face on the spoon's smudged surface, he saw Father's disturbed eyes. They reflected the bitter past, cruel present and bleak future.

Sami dropped the spoon and snapped his gaze back to the gate, a crusted scab covering a pulsing wound he had always known was there, but couldn't remember the incident that caused it. Was it his birth to exiled Palestinians? Thinking of the past, he had jumped beyond his thirty-two years of age in the span of this single Palestinian meal and acquired the burdened heart of an ageing Palestinian man.

He paid his tab and went to hire a car to go to Bethlehem. Seeking information from the manager, an older man at the front desk, Sami gave up on speaking Arabic. The manager recognized the Amara name as Palestinian. He gave Sami a disapproving once-over when Sami opened his mouth to declare it was his first time in Palestine.

Sami apologized for his language deficiency with one sentence, "I grew up in America."

The older man's frown deepened. Sami winced, silently acknowledging his lame excuse.

The manager recommended Mahmoud. He explained in perfect English that Mahmoud had a car with the required yellow license plate allowing him to cross through the security checkpoint at the separation wall. Mahmoud would chauffeur Sami during his stay beyond the wall and bring him back to Jerusalem in the same car.

"I might spend the entire day in Bethlehem," Sami said. "No need for Mahmoud to stick around. I'll find a way back."

"You can take a taxi or a public transportation bus. Green license plates. If the taxi driver or another passenger on the bus is held up at the checkpoint, you will have to wait, of course."

"I'll hire another private car." Sami tried a smile. "No worries."

"Cars in areas outside the 1948 occupied lands have white license plates. They are not allowed entry into Jerusalem. Make sure the car has yellow plates and the driver has the required permit to enter Jerusalem." The manager took off his thick spectacles and used the hem of his *koufiyeh* to clean them. "Otherwise, the driver has to drop you off at the checkpoint." The manager balanced his glasses on his nose. "And you will have to cross on foot."

"Got it." Sami nodded. "Yellow plates. Better than white."

The manager jerked his head, as if Sami had slapped him in the face. "Yellow plates are issued to Israelis. They can go anywhere on Palestinian land," he said through clenched teeth. "White plates are issued to Palestinians. They are barred from driving into Jerusalem." The manager leaned on his desk and raised bushy eyebrows above the rim of his glasses. "Do you get it now?"

Sami swallowed. His unfortunate choice of words had insulted this proud Palestinian, running his family home as a hotel in the heart of Jerusalem. Sami should have picked up on it when the man referred to the West Bank as outside the 1948 occupied land. In the manager's view, all Palestinian land was occupied, inside and outside Israeli borders, including the West Bank. With that defiant phrase, the manager made sure he understood that. It dawned on him that this was what his cousin had attempted to explain on the phone. His cousin didn't have the required permit to return to Jerusalem if he left. He was cut off from the rest of his family in Ramallah.

"How long a drive is it to Bethlehem?" Sami kept his tone polite and apologetic.

"Fifteen minutes. Coming back," the manager lifted his face to look at the ceiling, "you need His help."

"I'm sorry?" Sami asked, confused and off balance.

"Even with your American passport, you look Palestinian and your family name gives you away. The soldiers at the checkpoint will certainly give you a difficult time entering Jerusalem."

"I see," Sami breathed.

The manager dropped his chin to his chest. "Don't worry, that passport will protect you, young man. Up to a point, so be patient and try not to look nervous."

Sami shook his head. "I'm not nervous. I'm frustrated and . . . angry."

The manager lifted his head and finally cracked a smile. "Welcome to Palestine."

CHAPTER TWENTY-SIX

Driver Mahmoud spoke English well enough. Sami guessed that Mahmoud was his age, or maybe a bit younger, despite his white sideburns. He hopped around with jovial energy and took Sami to his once-upon-a-time white Toyota, explaining they should have left hours earlier to catch farmers harvesting olives on the way—a sight not to be missed. He laughed as if he had delivered a joke, its meaning lost to Sami. Mahmoud's cheerfulness and excitement contrasted with Sami's heavy spirits and solidified his realization that he really did *not* fit in here. He was a Palestinian born in exile, an outsider who didn't have to worry about the colour of his license plates to figure out which city he could drive to.

Weeding through Mahmoud's Arabized pronunciation of some words, Sami listened to his driver harangue him about the challenges residents of Bethlehem faced after the construction of the dividing wall, or as Mahmoud put it, the 'damn apartheid prison' wall.

Merchants had lost the influx of pilgrims who flocked to the Church the Nativity before the wall closed off routes to Bethlehem. Roadblocks and checkpoints broke up the few roads which remained passable.

Groups of Israeli settlers accompanied by armed soldiers roamed into Bethlehem from the myriad settlements surrounding the city. They strutted around insulting locals by shouting obscenities into open windows and spitting at passersby. They pulled down displayed merchandise and aggravated local shop owners. European or American tourists and clergymen in small numbers ventured in from time to time with tour guides. They purchased olive tree wooden crosses and rosaries. It wasn't enough to make a dent in the shop owners' dwindling earnings.

"Streets in the city used to be crowded, you know? Hotels always booked. Not just at Christmas and *Eastar*." Mahmoud said. "But after the damn prison wall went up, Palestinians can't go through *Al Quds* to travel between north and south anymore. They have to—what's the word?" Mahmoud drew a semi-circle in the air.

"Bypass Jerusalem," Sami offered.

"Yes, yes. Bypass *Al Quds* because they can't go without special permits. Impossible to get. Palestinians have to go through *Wadi Al Nar*, you know?"

"Valley of Fire?"

"Fire, yes. It is very dangerous and takes hours." Mahmoud snaked his hand in the air before Sami's face. "Sharp turns down the deep *wadi* . . . uh valley.

321

Look over there." Mahmoud pointed at the checkpoint they approached. "After we pass here, we will be in *Beit Lahem*. Ten minute distance. That's how long it used to take." Mahmoud shook his head. "Not anymore. Not for Palestinians who can't enter *Al Quds*. If they survive *Wadi Al Nar*, they're stuck in the *cantainar* all day, you know?"

"What's that?" Sami tried to absorb the reality Mahmoud threw at him with lightning speed.

"It used to be a small shop on a hill overlooking *Wadi Al Nar* from Abu Dis side. It looked like a shipping *cantainar*, you know?"

"Oh! A con-tain-er." Sami articulated the word.

"Yes, *cantainar*." Mahmoud shot a bewildered look. "The Israelis set a checkpoint next to it, so people warned each other about that checkpoint by the *cantainar*. The Israelis gradually made their checkpoint bigger. They forced the small shop owner to close and kicked him out. It became the *cantainar* checkpoint."

Mahmoud eased the car between concrete blocks leading to a post manned by three Israeli soldiers. A large German Shepherd perked to attention and strained against the chain tethering him to his handler's arm.

Mahmoud rolled down his window when a solider approached. He handed him his papers and Sami's passport. The soldier stared at Sami's face for several seconds, flipped pages, and returned the passport. He pointed at the back of the Toyota. Mahmoud opened the trunk.

In the side view mirror, Sami watched another soldier check contents at the rear then slam the trunk shut. The soldier by Mahmoud's window flicked his hand into the car. Mahmoud's papers flew across his chest.

"*Rooh*," the soldier said in broken dialect, unable to pronounce the last Arabic letter that sounded like someone clearing his throat.

Mahmoud gathered his papers and took off. "*Akhu Shlikkeh*," Mahmoud spit the words from the side of his mouth, away from the soldier's earshot.

Sami eyed his driver and tried to figure out what he had said. Mahmoud had cursed, something profane and ugly. Sami didn't know the exact meaning of the words, but Mahmoud's disgusted face conveyed their strength. Sami twisted to look back.

"That was quick."

"Oh, there's no problem leaving *Al Quds*." Mahmoud tucked his papers in the glove compartment by Sami's knees. "They want us to leave. The problem is returning."

"But you're a resident of Jerusalem. With an Israeli ID."

Mahmoud nodded. "For a Palestinian, there are no guarantees. Israelis refuse me entry any time they want. No reasons. You know I pay for that permit every year? You know where most of that money goes to? To build that damn prison wall." Mahmoud slammed his chest with his open palm. "They make us pay for what separates us from our families outside *Al Quds*. If they keep making life impossible, they think we will leave." Mahmoud stuck his fist upward and shook it. "*Wallah*! We will never leave our homes even if they pull our eyeballs from our heads. Never!"

"Listen, I hate to keep you from your family the rest of the day." Sami's discomfort matched the intensity of Mahmoud's oath. "Just drop me off and go back."

"No, no. It's okay. I'm used to this." Mahmoud chuckled. "I need the quiet time away from the wife, you know?"

"You have children?"

"Five boys and a girl. I hope to have another daughter next year. My Hiba needs a *sistar*."

"Six and going. That's impressive. How long have you been married?"

"Sixteen years. If the bastards didn't rob four years of my life when they jailed me in the *mu'taqal*," Mahmoud tilted his head toward Sami and laughed, "I would have made two more children. Give Palestine more sons and daughters, you know?"

Sami returned Mahmoud's jovial jab with a chuckle of his own, wondering how Mahmoud possessed the ability to laugh in these circumstances. The soldier at the checkpoint had thrown Mahmoud's papers in his face in a most insolent way. The uncertainty of whether he could return home to his kids always hung over his head. Yet, he made jokes.

Sami gazed ahead, his heart beating fast. The wall blocked the horizon to his right as they travelled parallel to it. Graffiti of the Palestinian flag and patriotic slogans decorated the twenty-five-foot high concrete barrier topped with razor wire. Observation towers equipped with cameras popped up every few feet. For the concrete to hold this height, the construction had to be at least eight feet thick. Did olive farms spread on the other side of the wall? How could farmers reach them? He got Mahmoud's sarcastic joke about seeing farmers gather their harvest now.

Sami stuck his face out of the window and breathed deep to delay a panic attack. Mahmoud was wrong; this massive structure was nothing like a prison wall, not even a maximum security prison. This divider, barrier, separator, was a weapon, an assault on human dignity and on nature itself.

Sami turned to Mahmoud. "You say you spent four years in prison?"

"It wasn't prison, friend. Prison is for criminals. It was a *mu'taqal*. You know, to silence political challenge." Mahmoud's cheek twitched. "Beatings and other stuff."

Sami nodded. He would not prod for more details. The firm tone in Mahmoud's voice made that clear.

"I took the blame for my mother." Mahmoud's face shifted into a grave and solemn expression, eyebrows knotted, lips thinned into a straight line. "No way I would let them touch my mother with their blood-stained claws."

"What happened?" Sami asked, despite himself.

"My mother is thin like me. Of my eight brothers, I'm the one who looks most like her." Mahmoud shook a fist in the air. "She is the *sistar* of men, you know."

"A sister of men," Sami repeated, confirming that he understood the compliment.

"Last Intifada, my mother was with three of her brothers. They tried to stop soldiers from arresting children returning home from school. The soldiers said one boy had a *nuggaifeh*." Mahmoud let go of the steering wheel and motioned with both hands to mimic a sling. "To throw stones, you know?"

Sami steadied the steering wheel with his left hand. "Yeah."

"It was the rubber thing the boy tied his books with." Mahmoud took control of the car. "Later that day, the soldiers shot and captured some people. Then they went to my father's house to arrest four men of the Fraikh family. Routine, you know?" Mahmoud shrugged. "It didn't matter if we did anything. Whenever something happened, the Israelis *callected* whoever they got their hands on from the Fraikh family. My uncles spent more of their lives in the *mu'taqal* than out."

Mahmoud grimaced. "Anyway, I took my mother's place to join my uncles and complete the number to four that the soldiers insisted on."

Mahmoud let go of the wheel again and stretched his arms before him. "Soldiers broke my arms in the jeep on the way to the *mu'taqal*. You don't think that stopped me from making children." Mahmoud threw his head back laughing. "I had my Hiba a year after I got out."

Sami shot his hand to the wheel again. "Be careful, man."

Mahmoud regained control. "How many children do *you* have?"

"I don't..." Sami cleared his throat. "I have two girls. Twins."

"*Sistars.* That's nice. You are lucky."

Sami turned his attention to the city's gloomy atmosphere. Mahmoud wasn't exaggerating. They drove down Bethlehem's empty streets. Open shops, but no shoppers trekking in or out. Men sat on street corners smoking. The car slowed to a stop at a traffic light. Sami caught a young man's eye. The hollowed expression on the man's face spoke of abandonment and despair. These people lived a perpetual state of Sundays, day in and day out.

"So, now we are in *Beit Lehem*. Where do you want to go?" Mahmoud asked.

"I'm looking for someone. A friend of my father. Where can we go to ask about him? His name is Hanna Vanyos."

"Well, we can start at the *Mukhtar,* you know? In the mun . . . munic—"

"Municipality?"

"Yes, that place."

"So he's like the mayor of the city?"

"Mayor? Yes. He has records about everyone here." Mahmoud stuck his head out of his window to talk to a man walking down the street. The man pointed in the distance and twisted his palm right then left. Mahmoud turned to Sami.

"The *Mukhtar* is not in town today. We will go to Abu Issa. He is the oldest man in the city. He will know about Hanna." Mahmoud offered a tired smile. "Don't worry. People's memories endure here. It is all they have left."

Abu Issa had wrinkled, net-like skin, as if he had slept for hours face down on metal mesh. The crisscrossed grooves on the old man's cheeks were so prominent, Sami had a hard time not staring at them and he struggled to concentrate on what was being said.

Hanna Vanyos had left Bethlehem.

"Hanna moved to *El Khalil* three years ago," Mahmoud said, ushering Sami out of Abu Issa's house. "Abu Issa even remembered the exact day. The day

328

Israeli *settlars* took over Hanna's house. Christmas morning."

"Does Abu Issa mean the Israeli government demolished Hanna's house?" Sami asked, fearing Mahmoud hadn't understood Abu Issa's toothless speech.

"No. Let's go. I'll explain on the way."

Driving out of Bethlehem, they followed road signs spelling Hebron in Hebrew and English, the Arabic letters of *El Khalil* scratched off the metal sheets. Mahmoud pointed at a house up a hill surrounded by barbed wire. The wire also surrounded the well-paved street leading to the house.

"That's Hanna's home. Armed Israeli *settlars* stormed in and took it over. They kicked out Hanna and his family. Now three thieves live there."

"My God!" Sami balled his fists. "I read about settlers taking over Palestinian houses. It's different when you see it on the ground. And those settlements crisscrossing the land. They're illegal."

"Yeah, right," Mahmoud said with a harsh snort.

Sami swung his head to glower at Mahmoud. "All condemned by international law. This land is supposed to be under the control of the Palestinian Authority."

"But the Israelis continue to build more *settlemants* on it, anyway." Mahmoud kept going. "El Khalil is on the other side of this hill. We have to go around. One hour, *insha Allah*."

"Why not take that road? It goes up the hill. Looks like a shortcut to me."

"That road connects Hanna's stolen house to the closest *settlemant* on top of the other hill. Only Jews can use those roads. They're patrolled by Israeli soldiers. We're not allowed on them."

"Not even cars with yellow plates?" Sami regretted his question the instant he saw Mahmoud's incredulous look.

"Only . . . Jews . . . can drive on the network of roads connecting *settlemants* together."

Did Mahmoud stop short from adding "stupid"?

"We are Palestinians." Mahmoud shifted sideways and slapped his backside. "International law *bi ijri* . . . ah, my foot. The world don't care."

CHAPTER TWENTY-SEVEN

Petra closed Dr. Seuss's *Fox In Socks* book and let the girls choose their socks to place next to their shoes for the morning. Leena picked up the first pair she touched, while Deena rummaged through the sock drawer to pull out a red pair with white laces. The girl knew what she wanted. Petra exchanged an admiring smile with Mrs. Madigan.

Petra kissed the girls goodnight, left them in their nanny's care and escorted Elias downstairs for a chat with Sami's mother before they left. She had established the routine while Sami was away. Five days, and counting.

Sami called every night. He asked for details about the girls, his mother, Mrs. Madigan, and Elias's health, yet shared nothing of his findings.

Petra refrained from asking, preferring to receive in person whatever intelligence he had gathered from Hanna Vanyos. Sami understood her unspoken wish and kept his calls short. His reserved and businesslike tone revealed things he didn't articulate. A piece of history was wedged between her and Sami. Truth created an emotional distance as vast as the ocean separating their continents. Her instinct latched onto

Sami's unspoken message, filling their conversation with uncomfortable silence. She drove herself crazy with speculation. She wrote several questioning emails which sat in her draft folder, waiting for a moment of courage that never came.

"Mama, can I have chocolate milk before we go?" Elias asked.

"May I," Petra corrected. "Go ask Mrs. Amara."

Elias ran into the family room, where Sawsan watched reruns of *Everybody Loves Raymond* every evening. "May I have chocolate milk, *aunti*?"

"Rosa will help you in the kitchen," Sawsan said, eyes riveted on the TV screen.

Elias ran out of the room.

Petra stopped herself from directing him to walk. Ever since he had recovered from surgery, his little feet moved fast as if to make up for the time he had spent lagging behind others, tired and out of breath. Petra settled into a chair and waited for the sitcom episode to end. Missing what had instigated Raymond's latest tirade, her mind wandered.

She could handle it. Whatever information Sami brought, she could absorb the blow and move on. Elias was her priority. Nothing else. Well, her job too. She needed to go to Kuwait after Sami returned, hopefully by this weekend. She had to. She would return next month for Elias's scheduled checkup.

Richard had spelled it out in several urgent emails. Her principal answered to a school board and couldn't stretch her leave any further. Her job was in jeopardy. She didn't have the luxury to be dreamy, to fantasize about pursuing a deeper relationship with Sami. His kindness had stirred her suppressed emotions. She had recklessly, selfishly, stupidly indulged them. Where was she heading? She wasn't ready for another man in her life. Definitely not for a man who, like her, was carrying hefty emotional baggage.

Had she deserted Bassam? Abandoned the memory of her child's father? Better step back. Stay safe. It was all Mouzah's fault for planting that seed in her head. As soon as Sami returned and she figured out what he had discovered, she would leave.

Sawsan chuckled.

Petra glanced at her. The woman had been nothing but nice since day one, allowing her into her house without asking questions. What had Sami said to his mother about Petra's role with the girls? Though accepting and cordial, Sawsan remained an enigma. Petra weighed every word she used with her, careful not to shatter the thin eggshell surrounding the woman.

Sawsan turned off the TV before the credits rolled. "Did you hear from my son today?"

Surprised, Petra shook her head. This was the first time Sawsan had asked *her* about Sami. "Not yet. He usually calls me around ten. You?"

"He called this morning. Always worried, that boy. I told him everything's fine here." Sawsan pointed a finger at Petra. "With you in charge."

Petra swallowed. "Oh, I promised to look in on the girls while he's away. That's it. I'm not in charge of anything."

Crossing her legs, Sawsan brought her hands close to her chest and pressed her fingertips together. "It won't work."

"The girls' routine isn't disrupted. They seem all right with him gone so far."

"It won't work." Sawsan repeated. She smoothed her gaudy sunflower skirt. "You and my son."

Petra glanced at the closed kitchen door, expecting Elias to come out any minute. "I'm not sure what you mean."

"My son is a good man. An excellent father to Fareed's children."

"He is." Petra squared her shoulders. Where was Sawsan going with this?

Sawsan pushed out of her love seat and rearranged picture frames on the fireplace mantle; both her boys smiling at the camera. "Take it from his mother." She turned to Petra. "Sami is not good husband material."

Elias bolted into the room. "Mama, can I have chocolate chip cookies?"

Petra rose to shaky feet. "No."

"Please, mama?"

334

"You know the rule. No cookies close to bedtime."

"Not even one, mama?"

"Say goodnight to Mrs. Amara. It's time to go."

Elias wrapped his arms around Sawsan's waist. "Goodnight, auntie."

Sawsan patted his head with a flat palm, as if bouncing a basketball. "I'll see you tomorrow." She peered at Petra. "We'll play hide and seek, you and I."

Her heart lodged in her throat, Petra hurried Elias into the hotel room. Sawsan Amara was not delusional, nor insane. The woman knew exactly what she was doing. *The Watchers* she talked about appeared as she wished to do her bidding when she felt insecure, her authority jeopardized. She had clearly—deliberately—threatened Petra, warned her to back off Sami.

God Almighty! Did Sawsan intend to stash Elias in one of her hiding places?

"Mama," Elias said, interrupting her anxious musings. "Tomorrow, when we go see DeLeenas, can I play with Uncle Sam's planes?"

"They're not toys." Petra helped Elias brush his teeth. "I explained that, remember? They're models to admire from a distance. Imagine them flying."

"Uncle Sam said... I can bring the... small airplanes... from the shelf," Elias said between mouth rinses. "Can I, mama? Can I?"

"He said that? I guess you *may*. But you have to be very, very careful." Petra waited for Elias to change into

335

his pyjamas. She walked him to the bed and peeled away the covers. "We may skip going to the girls' house tomorrow, though."

Elias climbed into bed. "Why, mama?"

"I thought we might go to the movies instead. *The Amazing Spider-Man*. How about it?"

Elias wiggled from under the covers and threw his arms around Petra's neck. "Yes, yes. Please, mama."

"Okay, okay."

Petra swallowed her fear. She would never take Elias to that house ever again. She would find a way to check on the girls without jeopardizing her son's safety. As soon as Sami was back, she was gone. She should start packing. Tonight.

Elias unlatched his arms and held her face between his tiny palms. "Can DeLeenas come, too?"

"It's not a movie for little girls. They won't understand it, and they certainly won't enjoy it. It'll be just the two of us." Petra tucked Elias under the covers again and handed him the astronaut he had slept with since their NASA trip.

Elias reached for Spiderman instead. "His turn."

"Goodnight, *ya oyooni*."

"I don't know that word, mama."

Petra kissed his forehead. "It means you are my eyes."

Elias closed his left eye with his hand. "Only one eye. You need the other to see me. Okay, mama?"

"Okay." She kissed him again, turned off the nightlight and closed the French doors behind her.

Dropping on the sofa, her spirits plummeted.

Years back, when her mother had visited the Amaras' house, Sawsan must have seen her as a threat. She had the presence of mind to know that the one way to get rid of a mother effectively was to threaten her child. And Sawsan succeeded. Her mother had run far from the Amaras to protect her daughter. Far enough to hide behind a different family name. That had to be the reason. What had prompted Sawsan to summon *The Watchers* to threaten her mother? What else did her mother experience in the house on that fateful visit?

Set on silent mode, Petra's mobile danced on the coffee table with an incoming call. All capital letters, Sami's name lit up the screen. She let the call go to voice mail. No way could she talk to him now and sound normal. She was a mess. Sami would sense that in her voice. He would ask questions. She couldn't tell him what his mother had said. It would be too cruel.

The phone vibrated again. Instead of leaving a message, Sami called a second time. If she didn't answer his calls, he might think something was wrong with the girls. Sure he would, the protective new father that he was. Let him call his house and talk to Mrs. Madigan. She would fill him in and set his mind at ease. What if his mother picked up?

Petra snatched her phone to answer the call. Too late. Sami had hung up. She quickly hit the call back option, but that sent her straight to his voice mail. Frustrated, she tossed the phone onto the cushion.

She paced the room. Sami would call again in a few minutes. If he asked why she hadn't picked up, she would say she was busy. No big deal. She shouldn't have answered his calls every time her phone rang. She should've let him leave a couple of messages then called him back, showed him she wasn't glued to her phone, available at a moment's notice. But that wouldn't be her, to leave him guessing, worrying about his children.

The phone drummed. Her foot struck the coffee table in her haste to reach it. Biting her lower lip to absorb the pain, she answered the call.

"Hey, Sami. I was busy. I'm sorry." She stomped her foot. Why did she apologize?

"I figured you'd be." He sounded cheerful, not what she expected.

"When are you coming back?"

"Sunday night. Very late at night. So, effectively, I'll see you Monday morning."

"Oh!" Petra sank into the sofa. Four full days.

"Something the matter?"

"No, no. Everything's fine here." She had to get off the phone before he picked up on her lies.

"What's wrong, Petra? Something happened with my girls? Mom?"

338

"Everyone's okay. I went with Mrs. Madigan and the girls to Discovery Zone downtown this afternoon. We had a great time. The girls miss you, that's all."

"I miss... everyone." Sami cleared his scratchy throat. "Has Mom acknowledged I'm gone yet?"

Petra pulled on her ponytail. Why? Why would he ask that tonight? Did this man have a sixth sense or something? She wiggled out her hair tie. "Actually, she asked me about you today. She wanted to know if you'd called me."

"I talked to her this morning, Houston time. She sounded fine."

"Well, she is. Really."

"I'm glad she's finally comfortable talking to you about me. It means she's more connected to what's going on around her. It's a healthy sign, don't you think?"

"A healthy sign. Right." Petra brought her knees to her chest. What was she doing? Lying. Participating in his mother's deception. "Listen, I have to go. Elias needs me."

"He's still up?"

"Uh, he peed in bed." She unfolded her legs and sprang off the couch. What in God's name was that? She couldn't simply say Elias woke up?

"It's been a long day, Sami. Goodnight. Let's talk tomorrow."

CHAPTER TWENTY-EIGHT

"*Ahlan*. Come in." Hanna Vanyos ushered Sami into a narrow room brightened by the midday sun. Tattered curtains permitted rays to shine through a single window and illuminate a wooden cross on the western wall. Under the cross, a frame held a picture of a young man smiling at the camera.

Sami paid little attention to the tight space. His angst at finally meeting his father's possible accomplice took over his body—his skin was damp, mouth dry, ears tuned to the thumps of Hanna's plastic slippers.

Hanna squeezed Sami's shoulder. "I can't believe Yahya's son is in my house. Here, in Palestine." He had a booming voice fit for a sports announcer; his accent had American inflections. "Have a seat."

Sami sat where Hanna pointed. His knees pushed against the edge of the coffee table placed between couches facing each other. Lifting himself higher, Sami pressed his lower back on the cushion to free his knees.

Hanna, a shorter man, had no problem lounging comfortably on the opposite couch. He stared at Sami, narrowing his eyes in concentration, as if learning detailed information to pass an exam.

Sami let him take his full measure, clasped his hands in his lap and studied him back. Despite the passing of years and a slight weight gain, Hanna matched the young man's image in Petra's photo, with his sharp pointed chin, long cheeks, caterpillar eyebrows. Hanna had aged with grace, as his straight shoulders and thick white hair testified. He had a trustworthy vibe.

"You have your father's eyes." Hanna circled a finger in the air. "But you look more like your mother."

"My brother has Dad's looks." Sami decided not to correct his reference of Fareed to the past tense.

"I'm sorry to know your father passed away." Hanna pursed his lips. "Cancer. What kind?"

"Liver." Sami answered, annoyed Hanna asked for that detail. Sami could have said anything—lung, pancreas, stomach—it didn't matter. The man wouldn't know, yet he asked. What a waste of his time. Sami needed to broach the topic, acquire the information he was after.

"How's Sawsan holding up after Yahya's death?"

"It's been . . ." Sami hesitated, searching for the right words without revealing too much of his mother's strange state, "very difficult, to say the least."

Hanna nodded. "I met Sawsan a couple of times. She's an especially delicate lady. I wish her well."

"Thank you." Sami sat straighter, racing to make connections in his head. What else did Hanna know about his mother?

Hanna flicked his eyes to the framed photo on the wall and drew an ambiguous smile that lessened the length of his cheeks and extenuated the tip of his chin. "My first son's name is Sami."

"Should I call you Abu Sami, then?"

"You can call me *ammy*. Your father and I," Hanna stuck two fingers together, "were like brothers. We made a pact to name our first boys after a close friend."

Seizing the opportunity to get to the point of this whole trip, Sami pulled out his mobile and shuffled through his photo folder to find the one he had snapped of Petra's prized possession. He showed the black and white photo image to Hanna. "Is your close friend in this picture?"

Hanna took his time studying the photo. He scowled in concentration, then used his fingers to zoom in. He scratched his nose, rubbed his chin several times, and smacked his lips.

The old man was nervous, damn nervous.

Hanna placed the phone onto the coffee table and pushed it away from him. "Did the Israelis go through your phone at any of the checkpoints?"

Sami blinked. "No."

"Not even at the airport?" Hanna sounded accusatory.

"They went through my laptop." Sami retrieved his phone. "But this picture isn't on it."

"Good." Hanna smacked his lips again. "Don't show this to anyone. Delete it before you go through

342

checkpoints when you return to Jerusalem." He ran a hand through his white hair. "I'm surprised you have it. Your father was supposed to destroy any trace of us together."

"This wasn't in my father's possession."

"Where did you find it?"

Sami shook his head. "First tell me everything. The man's full name, the Sami you named your son after. His relationship to Dad and to the other man in that picture, Waleed Saba. I want to know details. Why destroy a picture that puts you all together?"

Hanna sucked in a long inhale through rounded lips, as if savouring the pull of an invisible Cuban cigar. "Do you have children, son?"

"What does that have to do with anything?" Sami regretted his outburst, but he could no longer stomach the lack of clarity. He had come a long way not to get answers.

"If what I tell you falls in the wrong hands," Hanna pointed at Sami, "your entire family will be in grave danger."

"Let me worry about my family." Sami leaned forward. "Just tell me."

Hanna rose to his feet. "After we eat."

Sami opened his mouth to object.

Hanna cut him off. "I won't say a word until you meet my family and share our food." He flicked his palms to his sides. "*Aib, ya'ani*. You are in my home, son. I'm going to see if my wife needs anything and will be back."

Alone, Sami tried to calm down. The Arabic word *aib* meant shame. He understood that much. He would offend the old man if he didn't accept his lunch invitation. People here had their main meal at midday. He should have thought about that before imposing on the family at this time. Damn it, how could his clenched stomach handle food?

He snatched his mobile and messaged Mahmoud that he needed at least two more hours, giving his driver the option to return to his family in Jerusalem. Mahmoud responded with a short message: *I wait 4 u.*

In the distance, Sami heard two consecutive popping sounds. Was someone celebrating with champagne in the middle of the day?

A little girl dashed into the room. She plopped by Sami's side. "*Ana ismi Reema.*" She raised her hands, spreading seven fingers. "*Omry saba'ah. Seedo aalli khaleeni ma'ak.*"

Sami looked down at the seven-year-old with thick glasses, her long dark braids tied with white ribbons. *Seedo* meant grandfather. Hanna had sent his granddaughter to keep him company.

"Hi Reema. *Ana ismi* Sami."

"*Zay isim khali?*"

Reema's chestnut irises enlarged behind coke-bottle lenses; he could easily count each hair of her eyelashes.

"Yeah, like your uncle's name," Sami said absentmindedly then realized he spoke in English and translated his words. Resigning himself to the fact he would have to wait until Hanna was ready to talk, he tried to converse with Reema.

The girl grinned at his primitive Arabic, making fun of the way he pronounced some words. She showed her intelligence by speaking in short sentences for his benefit. He learned she was the youngest of Hanna's grandchildren from his only daughter. She had five uncles; all lived far away.

That popping sound resonated again, louder this time. Must be an awesome party.

Reema scooted closer to him and clung to his arm.

He smiled down at her. "*Madraseh*?" He asked to find out why she wasn't at school.

She covered her mouth with her hand, stifling a laugh. Pink nail polish painted four finger nails, not the thumb. Reema babbled something about her not turning seven yet, or that school was too far. Sami didn't quite understand.

Clanging noises and strong aromas surrounded him. His legs cramped. He got up, stretched and looked out of the window, which was on the third floor and opened to a balcony. Two huge black storage bins blocked his view to the right, the one facing outwards dotted with holes. Metal sheets covered the second bin from the top and sides. Similar bins crowded balconies and rooftops of neighbouring apartment buildings and houses. Curious, he looked back at Reema and flipped his hand in the direction of the ugly bins. "*Aish hadol?*"

Reema remained seated. "*Ashan almai.*"

Mai. Water. They were water tanks. Sami looked closer at the defective bin shielding the other. He turned to Reema again and pointed at the holes one by one, then flicked his wrist. "*Keef?*"

"*Qannasa.*" She swept a hand around the room. "*Mustawtineen.*"

Sami arched his eyebrows and lifted his shoulders, letting her know he didn't understand those words.

A crackling noise echoed outside the window. Reema dropped to the floor and crawled under the coffee table. Sami jumped back from the window and bumped against the couch. With little grace, he fell, landing on his back. Rolling onto his belly, he peered under the table to check on Reema. "You okay?"

She nodded, glasses skewed on her nose. She straightened them and edged further under the table.

He held out his hand to help her out. "Come on."

"*La'a,*" Reema whispered. She extended one arm, raised it close to her face, closed one eye, and bent her index finger several times.

Jesus! Was she telling him there were snipers?

Hanna ran into the room. "Don't worry. It's over. They hit the building next to us." He kneeled on the floor. "*Taali, ya Seedo. Tkhafeesh.*"

346

He pulled Reema into his arms and patted her hair. He laughed out loud, shaking his shoulders. A hesitant smile formed on Reema's lips.

Sami shifted into a sitting position. What the hell? Where was the amusement in all of this? He couldn't believe his eyes. "Was that sniper fire?"

Hanna gave Reema a glass of water. "Settlers. Murderous thieves from protected settlements nearby. Some amuse themselves every now and then by shooting at our water tanks." Hanna turned to him. "Please laugh, son. To show her there's nothing to be afraid of."

Sami needed a couple of seconds. There was plenty to be afraid of. Drive-by shootings banged in his head. What had this girl seen thus far? He thought of his defenseless girls waiting for him in Houston, of Elias—close to Reema's age. He forced a chuckle, mangled and unnatural.

Reema burst out with a giggle. She knew. The smart girl knew it was all a charade and she played along to please her grandfather, to put *his* mind at ease.

Hanna sat her on the couch opposite Sami and patted her hands. "Talk to her, Sami. Keep her busy. I have to check on my neighbours. I will not be long."

Reema killed her artificial giggle the instant Hanna left. She stared at Sami, her innocent face marred by the disturbed expression in her magnified eyes.

Minutes ticked. What else could he talk about with an almost seven-year-old who faced such horrors?

Reema took off her glasses and wiped their lenses with the hem of her white dress. Her careful movements showed how much she valued her glasses, as if she was handling a piece of fine jewellery. He waited for her to put them back on.

What was the Arabic word for gift? He pointed at her glasses and mimicked unwrapping a gift box. "Christmas?"

Reema shook her head.

Remembering the Arabic words for birthday, he asked, "*Eid meeladek?*"

"*La'a.*" Reema shook her head again. Taking a long breath, as if preparing to dive into a pool, Reema talked nonstop for the next five minutes, ticking her fingers one by one to reach number four.

Sami followed as much as he could, missing the meaning of several words. He understood her story in general: her grandfather had bought the new glasses after Israeli soldiers destroyed her previous pair when they came to take her father away last month. The prior pair broke the night soldiers arrested her eldest brother. The ones preceding those fell off her face and were crushed when she ran after the jeep that drove away with her father the first time he was arrested. Lastly, Reema lost her very first pair of glasses in the celebrations following the release of one of her uncles.

That was the way Reema referenced time in her short life. When and who was arrested or released. No special

Christmas gifts on her mental calendar. No birthday celebrations to mark receiving her precious seeing aid.

Sami bit the inside of his cheek. His chest caved in. Time to find Hanna, pry answers from him and get out of there. The hell with the meal invitation. Screw social restrictions. He headed to the door and opened it. He almost bumping into Hanna.

"Food's ready. Let me show you where you can wash your hands."

CHAPTER TWENTY-NINE

They ate in a room adjacent to the kitchen. Plates spread on sheets of newspaper covering a white formica table. A television box perched on a wooden shelf in one of the top corners of the room. Surprised to see an old-style CRT television set in this day and age, Sami wondered if it worked. He refrained from asking.

The room was a mass of contradictions.

A white cord dangled by the outdated TV and charged an iPhone. Small mismatched saucers, half-melted candles stuck on them, were scattered on windowsills. A shabby wooden crate held a large screen laptop with a wireless mouse. A kerosene lamp hung next to energy-saving light bulbs in the ceiling light fixture.

Sami tried to relax his stomach muscles. The main dish set before him was fit for a king. He fumbled with his fork and knife to cut flat bread smothered with aromatic onion mixture, eager to bring an end to the meal and get down to business.

"You eat *msakhan* with your hands, son," Hanna said.

"I thought so." Sami let go of his utensils, rolled up his sleeves and tore at the bread coloured red from an abundance of some spice. He hoped to God it wasn't hot. "Are these chilli peppers?"

"*Summa*'," Hanna's wife said, pretty and soft-spoken.

"That's sumac in English," Hanna added with a smile. "But you figured it out, right? It sounds the same."

His wife dropped more than half of a roasted chicken onto Sami's plate.

Reema nudged Sami with her elbow. He followed her lead and ripped the chicken apart, wrapped meat chunks with bread, and ate. He licked olive oil dripping down his fingers.

Nothing he had eaten before, in all the countries he had been to, came close to the complicated taste in his mouth: soft, butter-like chicken contrasted with chewy succulent bread and crunchy pine nuts, slightly spiced with the sweetness of sautéed onions, the tartness of sumac and a mix of spices he couldn't determine.

Sami savoured the food, feeling comfortable and warm, letting go of his early misgivings. The calm surprised him.

"You look like you've never had *msakhan* before," Hanna chuckled. "Sawsan never cooked it in America?"

Sami shook his head in denial, his mouth full.

"No pure olive oil from *Filisteen* in *Amrica*," Hanna's wife said. "No good *summa*'. Only here."

Sami nodded, leaving the woman to believe that. His mother had never cooked *msakhan* because she probably didn't have the required patience and skills, seeing how complicated the meal was, with its multi-layered flavours.

"Sawsan is a city girl," Hanna said. "Even if she tried, she wouldn't have got it right. My wife's mother was from Tulkarm, famous for *msakhan*." Hanna beamed at his wife. "She is an expert." He turned to feed his granddaughter a juicy bite. "Reema learns from the best."

"Why isn't Reema in school?"

"Not today. I had something to do this morning. I couldn't take her to school. It's too dangerous for her to walk alone. Israeli settlers and soldiers harass children on the way to and from school. And her older brothers are not . . . available."

Hanna's wife stopped chewing. Her face fell. A pained look saddened her beautiful amber eyes.

Sami bit his tongue. He would not ask what sort of harassment, where Reema's brothers were, nor inquire about her parents' whereabouts. It was none of his business. How would he respond if Hanna said they had been arrested, or worse? Better let it be.

Suppressing some burps and discretely letting a few escape, Sami scrubbed his hands clean. Had he remained in the family room, he would have fallen asleep at the table, relaxed and content. If someone told him that his hosts had put a sedative in the food, he would believe it.

There was something to be said about sharing a good meal in someone's house. Sami had to give it to social customs in this case. It made him less nervous and gave him a chance to assess his host in this intimate setting. He wished that other men had joined them, so he could better gauge the man's character as he interacted socially. The attention Hanna gave to his wife and granddaughter revealed a positive side of the man, confirming Sami's gut feeling. Hanna could be trusted.

Sami followed Hanna back to the narrow guest room and stayed away from the window.

"Bring it on, *ammy*." He referred to Hanna as uncle, following the man's suggestion. "I've shared your food. I'm ready to share your story."

Hanna closed the door to the small room and sat facing Sami. "You want to know about the man in the picture. I'll tell you. His name was Sami Daleel. From Nablus. Now you tell me how you know Waleed Saba."

"I don't know him. I know his daughter. She's the one who showed me the picture."

Hanna fished a silver Zippo lighter from his shirt pocket. "And what do you know about her father Waleed?"

Hanna's interrogative tone tested Sami's patience. "Other than that he disappeared in 1990, nothing."

Hanna nodded at the coffee table before him and flipped open the lighter with his thumb, clearly thinking of what to say next. "We were high school friends."

"In Kuwait, right?"

"Yes." Hanna snapped the lighter shut, coming back from whatever memory tunnel he had slipped into. "You know how every group has a central figure? A pole? Well, Sami Daleel was it for our group. He was the rebel, the visionary, the most outspoken. Like me, he had *Lam Shamel* papers which allowed him to spend every summer with his family in Palestine."

"I'm sorry," Sami interrupted. "What's that you and Daleel had?"

"*Lam Shamel?*" Hanna frowned. "You've never heard of the term?"

"Can't say I have." Sami had a feeling Hanna was genuinely surprised at his lack of knowledge.

"It was a special permit given to certain residents of the West Bank by the Israeli authorities when they occupied the land in '67." Hanna thumbed his chest. "Those of us who had close relatives living in the occupied territories were allowed in at times. Provided we renewed our permits every year." He flicked the Zippo open again.

"Of course, Israelis revoked permits out of the blue. Many Palestinians were denied permits without warning, reason, or cause. You know, to control the number of Palestinians inside their borders."

Sami rubbed his earlobe, wondering if his father's family had this permit.

Hanna pointed at him, as if he read his mind. "The Amaras don't have it, son. I know that for a fact. Not many Palestinian families have *Lam Shamel*. Very hard to obtain. It took years to have an application approved. The Israelis stopped the process altogether in 2003."

"You hold on to yours for dear life, I guess," Sami said.

Hanna reached across the coffee table and tapped Sami's arm. "That's an understatement. Daleel's family had it, so he spent his summer vacations in Nablus with his grandparents and returned to Kuwait with stories, first-hand knowledge of Israeli transgressions, stuff the other guys in the group only heard about from their relatives."

"How about you? You didn't have your own stories?"

"Not to the same extent. I spent my summers in a programme at the Church of the Nativity in Bethlehem. Somewhat sheltered, you might say." Hanna swept a hand in the air. "Growing up here, facing deprivation and humiliation every day hardens you. But for Sami Daleel, an outsider coming for brief visits, witnessing the barbaric behaviour of most Israeli soldiers? It was something else altogether. Infuriating."

"Makes you feel guilty," Sami exclaimed. "Knowing you'll escape it at the end of your visit."

Hanna snapped his fingers. "Right. One particular incident deeply influenced Daleel. Distinguished him from the rest of us. He watched his young cousin die at a checkpoint when soldiers prevented the ambulance she was in from passing. She was in labour and had complications. He said the soldiers kept her ambulance stalled for more than four hours. Didn't allow any cars to pass through the checkpoint." Hanna clicked the lighter once more. "So many have suffered her fate since then. But at the time, when Daleel told us the details, the look in his eyes . . . scary."

Hanna twirled his index finger in the air. "We circled him, planets around the sun. Teenagers taken by his passion, a true revolutionary." Hanna fixed his stare on a floating spot in the space separating him from Sami. "It cost him. It cost us all."

"What happened?" Sami's voice cracked. He cleared his throat. "To Daleel?"

"We were inseparable. Palestinian youth coming into manhood, feeling the burn of injustice and exile. We were angry, frustrated and wanted to do anything to change the situation. Israelis had come from Europe and taken our lands, homes owned by our families for multiple generations. We stayed up at night talking, dreaming, plotting, each in his own way. After we graduated from high school, we agreed to meet every year in Kuwait when we visited our families. I enrolled in Birzeit University."

"Near Ramallah." Sami interjected, needing to say something, anything to show Hanna he wasn't completely removed from Palestine.

"Waleed and your father studied in America," Hanna continued. "Waleed returned to Kuwait to take over the family business. And Daleel," Hanna paused, puckered his lips, adding a higher level of seriousness to what he was about to reveal. He opened and closed the damned lighter twice.

Sami held his breath in anticipation.

"Daleel joined the PFF. You know what that is?"

"Palestine Freedom Fighters."

Invisible strands knitted a web in Sami's head, one end shooting from history books he had read over the years, the other connecting with the darkened corners of this room, the lonely framed picture on the wall and the hands of the old man before him.

Sami exhaled. "One of the pseudo-military factions operating in Lebanon within Palestinian refugee camps."

"Daleel believed in armed resistance. He went to south Lebanon and trained there." Hanna slapped his thigh. "And, by God, he had the courage of the rest of us combined."

A soft knock sounded at the door. Hanna left the couch and took a tea tray from his wife's hands.

Sami briefly closed his eyes. He saw his father through new lenses, filtering out the white hairs and the reticent demeanor. Had his father been a freedom fighter?

"This is all very fascinating," he said slowly. "But how does my father fit in?"

Hanna filled short tea glasses to the rim. "Yahya believed in resistance through non-violent means. He was fascinated by the Gandhi approach."

Sami rolled down his shirt sleeves as he weighed up Hanna's words. Yeah, that sounded more like his father. Or was it? Sami knew nothing of his father's patriotic ideas. He talked about *visiting* Palestine. That was mostly it. Never a mention of where he stood on the issue of resistance.

"Daleel confided in us on his last visit to Kuwait about a plan to attack an Israeli army convoy in southern Lebanon," Hanna said.

"That must have been in the late seventies, right? Sharon invaded south Lebanon."

"The first invasion, yes." Hanna twisted his lips into a grimace. "'78."

"It brought on the Sabra and Shatila massacres." Sami scratched his head. "No, wait, that happened in the second invasion."

"In '82. The massacres of Sabra and Shatila refugee camps were committed during that second invasion." Hanna dumped two spoonfuls of sugar into each tea glass. "What I'm telling you happened in the spring of '79. Waleed was excited by Daleel's plan to attack the Israeli army in Lebanon. He offered to finance the entire operation. He had the money and the means. Your father argued with both of them. He tried to convince them not to go forward."

358

Hanna handed Sami a tea glass. "Your father truly believed that an end to the occupation could be brought about through peaceful measures. He didn't want to get tangled up with the PFF. Yahya left for America and never returned to Kuwait."

Sami tightened his fingers around the hot glass. His neck stiffened with tension, and he was aware of another vague sentiment, weak, yet gaining strength with each word Hanna added.

"Dad fled to the States?"

"Yahya didn't flee anything. He wasn't involved at all. Refused even to see Daleel before he went on his mission."

Sami burned his tongue on a sip of tea. There it was, that vague feeling brewing in his guts. It crystallized in Hanna's voice: disappointment. His father was not a freedom fighter, nor was he a supporter of one. He was passive, idealistic; in Hanna's view, a weakling.

Sami set down his glass. "Dad immigrated to the US with his parents. He wanted to finish his studies and make a decent life for himself, his family." Sami saw his words hit an invisible wall in front of Hanna and fall to the floor, the letters scattering under the couches, along with his attempt at justifying his father's actions. Or lack thereof.

"I learned from Waleed that your father borrowed money from him before he left. A large sum."

"Yes, I know. Dad tried to pay it back. Waleed disappeared before he could."

"I see."

Sami readied himself to explain the details of his father's will that had started him on this fact-finding journey to the past. He would vindicate his father to his old schoolfriend and sharer of patriotic dreams. Sami shuffled forward, eager to set things straight. His knees collided with the coffee table and hot tea spilled over his jeans. "Shit."

He jumped to his feet, pulling the wet fabric away from his skin.

"Here." Hanna quickly poured a glass of water onto Sami's legs, soothing the scald. "I'll fetch a towel."

Hanna left the room. Sami set the spilled tea glass on the table and let out a string of curses under his breath. He looked like he had peed his pants. And by the time Hanna returned with a towel, Sami had lost the initiative. He would wait until he heard the full story from Hanna, then hit him with the details of Father's dying wish to repay his debt to Waleed, restore his honour in the old man's eyes.

Dabbing at his lap, Sami asked, "What happened to Daleel? Was his mission successful?"

"Five Israeli soldiers were killed in that attack. Two of his comrades were captured. Sami Daleel was shot dead."

Sami jerked up his head. "Oh!"

"You want to know what happened to the financial wheel of the operation? Waleed Saba?"

"What?"

"On a business trip to Beirut, Waleed was assassinated."

Sami dropped on the couch. "Assassinated?"

"By Mossad."

"How do you know that? Mossad doesn't exactly go around announcing its operations."

"Maybe one of Daleel's captured comrades succumbed under torture and told them about Waleed. I don't really believe that, because these fighters are a tough, solid cadre. But it's possible. Mossad gathered intelligence from somewhere. Or someone."

Sami forgot about his wet lap, mulling over the idea that Israeli secret operatives might have killed Petra's father. "Mossad waited eleven years to assassinate Waleed?"

"Waleed's arrival in Beirut presented the perfect opportunity for them. He disappeared from his hotel room. I say they kidnapped him and buried his body somewhere."

"Wait." Sami flung the towel aside. "Waleed was an American citizen by then. His wife reported him missing to the embassy in Kuwait. The American embassy in Beirut must have conducted an investigation."

"Let's say the embassy did. What did it conclude?" Hanna swiped his empty palms together. "Nothing.

Why do you find that hard to accept? Mossad assassinate key Palestinian figures all over the world. You know your history, don't you?"

Hanna didn't wait for Sami to answer. "I'm sure you've heard of the writer Ghassan Kanafani blown up in Beirut. The cartoonist Naji al-Ali assassinated in London? These are facts. Don't tell me your father passed on his idealistic, naive thinking to you."

Sami jumped to his feet. "And just what did *you* do to support the Palestinian cause? You're quick to judge my father. You know nothing about his life."

Hanna glared at Sami, his piercing stare burning holes through Sami's quickly assembled shield.

"I *returned*, son. I came back to my homeland and planted a family here in Palestine." Hanna's eyes flickered to the framed picture on the wall. He rose and stood tall. "I lost my *son* to the cause." He advanced on Sami. "My firstborn was shot in cold blood at a checkpoint." Hanna's voice elevated several octaves. "Two of my remaining sons are in an Israeli *mu'taqal*. Tortured as we speak."

"I'm sorry—"

"Armed settlers took my home, everything I owned in one night." Hanna's voice shook with anger. "My children and grandchildren go through hell every day to survive. To make ends meet." He spread his arms to his sides.

"But here I am. And here I stay." He dropped his arms, slapping the sides of his thighs. "Staying alive? That's a heightened form of resistance, young man."

Sami ran his fingers through his hair, his anger deflated. He had mentally chastised Hanna for judging Father's actions. In reality, Sami was the one casting judgments left and right. Over things he didn't, couldn't, know anything about. He gulped for air. He was a mess. He dropped down on the couch.

"My mother said you were the one who took me and my brother to a boarding school in Chicago. You remember that?"

Rubbing his face with his palms, Hanna sat down. He emptied his tea glass and pulled a pack of Marlboros from his shirt pocket. He offered one to Sami. "You smoke?"

"No."

"Mind if I do?"

"Go ahead."

Sami minded, but he stayed quiet. He took in the details of young Sami Vanyos in the framed picture while Hanna lit a cigarette. The boy resembled his father. That pointed chin. And there was a black ribbon draped over the top corner of the frame. How had he missed it the first time he saw the picture?

"I was on a mission with a church in Dallas. Your father and I stayed in touch, of course." Hanna puffed several times. Whether the irritation it caused him was intended or not, Sami decided not to push him. Let the old man have his smoke and be done with it.

"Yahya trusted me with a yearly stipend to help disadvantaged Palestinians. It was given anonymously," Hanna said. "Tuition for a student at Birzeit university. A family needing a little push to start a modest business. Rebuilding a demolished home. Replanting uprooted olive trees. Things like that." Hanna pulled hard on his cigarette. "Yahya believed that supporting and developing social and economic infrastructure from within was key to ending military occupation."

Blowing smoke out of his nostrils, Hanna shook his head. "The way I see it, Yahya and Daleel were on opposite ends of the same spectrum."

"How did Dad send you the money? It doesn't show in any of his accounts."

"It went through my contacts at the boarding school you and your brother attended."

"The Bright Beacon Academy?"

Hanna nodded. "Part of it went to your education and part came to me. No straight link to your father. No paper trail."

"And after we graduated?"

"That was the end of our business arrangement." Hanna crushed the cigarette butt in the ashtray at the centre of the coffee table. "Your father was a cautious man." Hanna's tone hovered too close to sarcasm. "You can definitely say that about him."

Sami cocked his head. The strange stipulation in his father's will to allocate part of the company to that particular school if Petra refused her shares made sense now. It was never about donating to the school per se. It was about what went through and beyond the school. Because of his exile to the damned Bright Beacon Academy, one truly *bright* thing had come out of it. His father had fought against the occupation in his own way, helped some Palestinians defy their imposed reality and survive the injustice. As his son, he could take comfort in that.

Was that why his father insisted *he* take on the task of unravelling his will instead of Fareed? If Father wanted him to continue on the same path, why didn't he just say that, the way he had for Petra's shares? And why keep his brother out of the loop? Fareed would have donated to the church or the school without question. Father knew that about Fareed. Father also knew *he* didn't share Fareed's blind devotion.

Sami pinched the bridge of his nose. What was he missing? Why had Father brought him to this point?

"You okay, son?" Hanna asked, filling the short glasses with more tea.

"I'm fine."

"Look, I don't mean to sound harsh. Your father and I didn't see eye to eye on many things, but I do appreciate his decision to help as long as he did. He didn't completely turn his back on us."

Sami dropped his hand. That was it. Father didn't want to spoon-feed him. Father wanted him to make a decision about the Palestinian cause. He wanted it to be a choice, not an obligation to fulfil a dead father's wish, as he did with Petra. Father *trusted* him with this choice.

"Do you still have contacts there?"

"At the academy?" Hanna asked.

Sami nodded.

"Yes, why?"

"I'll find a way to restart paying that stipend. If you're willing to resume your work. Be in business with me."

"Like father, like son kind of thing, huh?"

"That's right."

Hanna's lips parted in a sad smile, the kind that held back pain. Sami saw its sting in the old man's eyes before Hanna slanted them to his son's face framed on the wall.

"You are a good son," Hanna sighed. "Yahya lives on."

Sami reached for his tea glass and took a sip to hide his discomfort. Being here with this man brought out things in him he didn't know were there. Hanna's grief weighed heavily in every syllable he uttered, darkening the room with unrelenting shadows.

Sami pressed the heel of his palm to his eye. Since his father and brother had passed away, he had been hopping about like a clown, performing tricks to solve one intractable problem after another. He hadn't stopped to grieve, to consider his losses.

Amid the disruption and turmoil brought by death, he had ignored its stark finality. He hadn't just lost his father, he had lost the chance to know the man who had always been distant, an unsolved puzzle. Now his father was gone forever, yet Hanna saw the Yahya Amara he knew living through *him*. What was he supposed to make of that?

He set down the tea glass. "About the day you took me and my brother to that boarding school. Can you tell me what happened?"

"Waleed's wife showed up at your house that day. Out of the blue." Hanna picked up his Zippo and played with it. "But your father was at work and he missed her. She told him over the phone about her husband's disappearance." Hanna lit another cigarette. "Yahya called me. I shared my suspicions about Waleed's fate in Beirut. Your father—" Hanna blew smoke from the side of his mouth. "—your father panicked."

"Excuse me?"

"He feared Mossad would come after him and his family. Why, I had no idea. He hadn't done anything. Sawsan's fragile nature didn't exactly help allay his concerns. Lots of commotion that day." Hanna balanced his cigarette on the ashtray. "Yahya wanted to protect his boys. So he asked me to—" Hanna wiggled his fingers to indicate quotation marks, "—to hide you in one of the church's exclusive private schools."

"I see." Bile rose to Sami's mouth. He forced it down. All those years, he had blamed his mother for being the reason he and Fareed were sent away. In reality, his father had done it for entirely different reasons, nothing to do with his mother's crazy ways. Deborah's presence and news of Waleed's disappearance must have pushed Mother over the edge that day. She took action the only way which made sense to her broken mind, by hiding her boys.

Hanna picked up his cigarette again. "We agreed to get rid of anything that linked us to Sami Daleel to ease your father's mind. I went back to Bethlehem right after that."

"Waleed's wife, Deborah." Sami found his voice foreign. It belonged to someone else, a man waking from a nightmare, only to find a harsher reality. "What happened to her?"

"I don't know. I think she changed her last name to protect her daughter. I never heard from her." Sucking the last bit of the cigarette, Hanna pointed at Sami. Ashes dropped on his trousers and he flicked them off. "You said you know the daughter?"

"Her name is Petra."

"And how did you get to her?"

Sami worked his jaw. "I didn't. My father found her. He spent the last years of his life searching for her."

Hanna crushed what was left of his cigarette in the ashtray to smother its burning tip. "Why?" he asked absentmindedly, as if it was an afterthought.

Sami's head pounded. Hanna didn't really care about knowing the reason behind Father's long search. It was as if his father's *actions* didn't matter.

He waited for Hanna to look at him. "To pay his share," Sami said.

"You mean pay his debt to Waleed through his daughter?"

Sami slanted his gaze aside. "That and..." He hesitated, conflicted about whether he should state the suspicion that throbbed in his head.

"What?" Hanna asked.

"I think it was Dad's way of acknowledging that his peaceful approach hadn't worked." Sami heaved a heavy sigh. "I believe... Dad did it out of defeat."

"Look at me, son."

Sami returned his gaze to Hanna, allowing him to see the agony that seared his soul.

"Look around you. We're still occupied. It's coming up to seventy years now. Daleel, mine, your father's? All of our approaches failed."

"What are you saying?"

"Whether your father abandoned his stance doesn't matter. What counts is, now that you know what happened, what are *you* prepared to do about it?"

CHAPTER THIRTY

Petra walked Elias into Vaughn's office. "Sorry I'm late."

"It's fine, Mrs. Haddad. You're here now." Vaughn closed the door behind her. "And you brought your son."

Vaughn's tone clearly showed his displeasure. Petra cringed, recoiling from him. Did he expect her to come alone? He had phoned her last night and offered to come to her place to go over some papers. She told him she would stop by the office instead. When he insisted that she come early in the morning before the office staff arrived, she agreed, thinking nothing of it. Vaughn sounded in a hurry to get things done.

Standing in his office now, trepidation curled her gut.

"Everything all right, I hope?" Vaughn asked.

"I underestimated morning rush hour." Petra held Elias by the shoulders. "Say hello to Mr. Vaughn, *ya omry.*"

Vaughn stuck out his hand. "Nice to meet you, young man."

Elias turned and buried his face in Petra's hip.

"It's not good for a boy to be shy." Vaughn clasped his hands together and went behind his desk, dismissing Elias. "Let's get to work."

The hairs on Petra's arms perked. Something was wrong. Her outgoing, trusting son wasn't shy. He was scared. She pulled Elias tighter.

"You said this was very important?"

"Yes." Vaughn sat at his desk. "Please have a seat."

"Can't it wait until Sami returns?"

"I'm afraid not. This won't take long." Vaughn pulled a folder from his files. "I just need you to sign a couple of documents."

Petra eyed the door. "What documents?"

"Routine stuff." Vaughn thrust out his chin and peered upwards, disregarding her efforts to understand. "But it will smooth things in Kuwait."

"Does it have to do with my loan?"

"No. Like I said, it clears legal glitches in Kuwait."

"Mr. Faisal handles legal issues in Kuwait for me. You need to talk to him."

"These documents require *your* signature. Faisal doesn't have a legal power of attorney. He can't sign on your behalf." Vaughn's eyes narrowed, his lips flattened, hardening the expression on his face. "You don't mind helping out, do you, Petra?"

Bile rose in her throat. The tone Vaughn used when he said her name was too familiar. As if she was hearing it from Richard Frost in Kuwait. Strange how a few words, spoken in a certain way, had the power to transport her thousands of miles away. Like Frost, Vaughn's polite facade concealed imminent danger.

She took a deep breath. Why wouldn't Vaughn wait for Sami? And why wasn't Robert, Sami's personal secretary, at this meeting?

"I spoke to Sami last night," she said. "He didn't mention signing any documents."

"Sami is not involved in this. I'm legal counsel for the company. I don't bother him with little details while he's away." Vaughn twisted his mouth sideways, expressing disapproval and even anger. "I represent the Amara interest in this partnership."

"I see. And I am the new partner."

"Now I need your approval to proceed with this."

"I feel sure I should run this by Mr. Faisal." Petra tilted her head to one side. "This can't be all that urgent, right?"

"Wrong." Vaughn tapped the folder. "If you don't sign these today. Right now. People will be out of jobs in Kuwait tomorrow."

Elias squeezed her waist, evidently disturbed by Vaughn's tone. She patted his back to reassure him. "I don't think I have anything to do with that part of the busin—"

Vaughn rose behind his desk. "What's the matter, Petra? You don't trust me?"

"Oh, not that. I just don't know anything about legal stuff." She discretely pinched Elias's arm. He cried out. She bent down and pretended to listen to Elias whisper in her ear. She lifted her head. "I'm sorry, Mr. Vaughn. Elias needs to use the restroom."

Elias looked up at her. "Mama?"

She flipped her hair to one side to hide her face from Vaughn and opened her eyes wide at Elias, giving him the signal to stay quiet. She pushed him toward the door. "We'll be right back."

"I'll show you where to go."

Petra shook her head, adding a sweet smile. Feminine power. Richard Frost's voice echoed in her head. "I know the way, Mr. Vaughn. At the end of this hall, right?"

"Yes." Vaughn plopped down in his chair. "Around the corner. Make it quick, please."

"I won't be long." She walked Elias down the hall. When she rounded the corner, she grabbed Elias's hand and sprinted.

"Mama, I don't need to go pee pee."

"I know. I know."

"Where are we going, mama?"

"To find Robert."

Good thing she had visited Sami's office before. She knew her way around this floor. Robert had once told her he was the first person in the building most mornings. She prayed today was one of those days. Approaching the glass doors to his office, her heart sank. Robert's desk was vacant.

Elias pointed to her left. "Can we go to the showroom, mama? To see the small buildings?"

Petra pulled out her phone. She would call Robert, see if he had any idea about the documents Vaughn wanted her to sign. Vaughn would become suspicious if she took too long. So what? She didn't have to return to his office. Simply walk out of the building. But what if he was telling the truth? What if people's jobs depended on her signing those papers?

Elias tugged at her arm. "Can we, mama?"

"What?" She asked, distracted, searching for Robert's number on her phone.

"Go to the showroom?"

She shook her head. "We can't go in there, *ya alby*."

"Why, mama?"

"Because the doors are locked."

"Robert can let us in." Elias ran to the doors. "He's in there. I can see him from here."

Petra turned. Slim glass panels lined the sides of the solid wooden doors. Elias peeked through the narrow windows.

She knocked quickly.

Robert opened the doors. "Mrs. Haddad? What're you doing here?"

"I don't have much time. Vaughn's waiting for me in his office. He asked me to come in to sign papers for work in Kuwait."

"This early?"

374

"Yes, well. It just dawned on me." Petra held Elias back from pushing past Robert into the showroom. "It doesn't sound right. I don't want to cause problems, but do you know anything about it?"

"No idea." Robert frowned. "Did you see the documents?"

She shook her head. "I told him Elias needed to use the restroom and got out of there."

Elias broke free from her hand and ran to the largest architectural mock-up in the center of the room. "Look, mama, tiny cars in this one. I want to stay here. I don't like that old man."

"I see Vaughn hasn't lost his charm." Robert grinned. "Go back to Vaughn's office, Mrs. Haddad. Tell him you ran into me and I offered to show Elias the viewing hall." Robert checked his watch. "Vaughn knows I come in early most days. Stall him until I bring Elias over. Don't sign anything, okay?"

She nodded. "Elias, I'm going back to Mr. Vaughn's office. You listen to Mr. Robert, *ya rohy*."

"Yes, mama."

"It'll be a few minutes," Robert said. "I need to check something."

She returned to Vaughn's office and fed him the concocted story. As she suspected, he didn't look pleased.

"Let's do this." He flipped open the folder. "No point keeping your son waiting."

Petra took a seat. "Elias loves the viewing hall. He calls it the showroom. It's going to be a problem dragging him out of there." She crossed her legs and rested her back, indicating she was in no hurry. She was never a good pretender, but she could certainly keep old Vaughn dangling for a few minutes.

"The longer I take to get Elias, the happier he'll be." She offered him a devilish grin, shifting her lips sideways. "He didn't like waking up early. This makes up for it."

Vaughn picked up his pen and clicked it several times. "Shall we?"

She rubbed her temples. "Is it possible to have a cup of coffee? I missed my usual caffeine dose in my rush here and now I have a headache."

"The break room isn't open until eight."

"Another hour. It's pretty early to be at work, isn't it?"

"Not if you want to catch people still at their desks in Kuwait." Vaughn slipped the papers across his desk toward her. "I'll have you out of here in a jiffy. Two documents, that's it."

Petra arched her eyebrows. "Do you have any ibuprofen?"

Vaughn exhaled, frustration building on his face. He clicked his pen again.

"For my headache." Petra briefly closed her eyes, partly to block Vaughn's piercing stare and partly to demonstrate she was in pain. "If I don't nip it now, it'll develop into a full-blown migraine."

Vaughn jerked open a desk drawer and rummaged through it. "I think I have a bottle of aspirin here somewhere." He slammed the drawer shut. "Not anymore."

"I may have something in my bag." She took her time going through her handbag, the same one, empty of pain-killers, that Mouzah had chastised her for in Kuwait. "I don't usually carry medicine, but I thought I saw a small bottle of Advil in here the other day. I hope I still have it."

Vaughn's pen clicked relentlessly.

She stretched the search as long as she could manage, set aside her bag and lifted her head. "No luck." Squinting at the windows, she shielded her eyes with her hand. "Could you please close the mini blinds? Bright light compounds my problem."

Vaughn jerked his chair back and stomped to the windows. He pulled so hard on the cords of the blinds, she feared he would rip them from their fastenings.

"Is this better?" He returned to his desk. "Can we do this now?"

She picked up the papers. "Let me see what this is all about."

"Just sign by the sticky yellow arrows." Vaughn rested his elbows on the desk's dusty surface. "Don't work your pretty head too hard. Increase your headache."

Petra lifted the papers to hide her face, reining in her anger. So Vaughn had finally dropped his mask, revealing his true colours. Time to show him hers. She peered at him.

"First rule of thumb, never sign anything before you read. Don't take it personally, Mr. Vaughn. You're a lawyer. I'm sure you understand."

"I'm happy to explain things. To save time." He checked the platinum and diamond-encrusted Rolex peeking out from his shirt sleeve. "It'll be the end of the business day soon in Kuwait and I need those documents on file before work resumes tomorrow."

She peeled her eyes away from the exquisite jewellery piece and thought of her puny engagement ring, bought by Bassam in instalments. Life was not fair.

"I'll ask if I have any questions. I'm a fast reader." She flipped pages. Was this written in Latin? She couldn't understand a single clause. So many legal terms.

Vaughn's pen-clicking echoed in the silence, mercilessly counting the seconds. Robert was taking too long.

Vaughn cleared his throat twice. She ignored him.

"Petra, it's to allow payment to a new contractor the company recently hired. He's to deliver construction materials in Kuwait."

"I see." She lifted her gaze off the pages. "What sort of materials?"

"Steel slabs. For the marina project, if you want to be specific." Vaughn arched one eyebrow. "Need more info?"

"I do." She looked him in the eye, forcing him to see her determination. She wasn't about to cower or back down. "What about this second document?"

"Payment authorization to release the shipment from the pier." Vaughn said, the pen in his hand about to snap. "If we don't have the steel delivered on time, work will stop."

Petra nodded. "And if there's no work, there's no pay."

"You got it." He shifted forward. "Will you sign now? We're already cutting it close as it is."

"How come you left this to the last minute? I mean, you must have known about this shipment and the work schedule ahead of time, right? Why did you wait until today?"

Vaughn curled his upper lip in an insolent sneer. "Are you going to tell me how to do my job?"

"I'm trying to understand. You said you'd be happy to explain things."

"Fine." Vaughn pointed at the papers. "I brokered a deal with this contractor in the last minute after the one we had before failed to deliver on time." He dropped his hand. "Are you satisfied now? Or do you want actual details about the shipment weight and size?"

Petra rubbed her temples. A real headache was about to start. Now she was truly pissed off, and the incessant hammering of his pen was driving her crazy. Vaughn was nervous. His concern wasn't about the work schedule in Kuwait. For him to be this edgy and insolent meant that this was personal. What did he get out of this deal? That clock-sized Rolex he kept checking exposed him. She had been right to alert Robert. What else could she do to stall or waste time?

The office door opened. Elias ran straight to her. "Mama, one of the buildings has itsy-bitsy people. And tiny trees."

"Oh, that's nice."

Robert strode in. "Good morning, Vaughn."

Vaughn gave a curt nod. "We're almost done here."

"Actually..." Robert took confident steps forward. "You *are* done."

"Get out, Robert." Vaughn said, shoving the documents into a desk drawer. "Come back in half an hour."

"Mrs. Haddad, you can go home." Robert held the door open, ignoring Vaughn. "Sorry to have troubled you this morning, but there's nothing for you to do here. Vaughn and I will take care of business."

Vaughn rose from behind his desk. "Now you wait a minute, here."

Petra sighed with relief. Tall and lanky, Robert looked like a teenager compared to Vaughn, yet he carried himself with the confidence of an informed man. A man armed with facts. She took her time gathering her bag, curious to see how things would end between the two men.

380

Vaughn pointed at Robert. "What the hell are you doing here? You have no business barging into my office."

"I just got off the phone with our project manager in Kuwait. He told me about a steel shipment." Robert kept his tone polite. "I must have missed your email about it. I don't recall running its specifics by Sami."

"Check your spam box." Vaughn's thick neck reddened around his shirt collar. "Some emails end up there."

"I did." Robert sucked a long breath. "Nothing. Your email must be floating on the dark web. Lost."

Elias tugged on Petra's skirt. "Mama, what's a dark web?"

"I'll explain later." Petra shushed Elias. Eying Vaughn's reddened face, her suspicions were confirmed. This was a man caught in a lie.

"Anyway, I spoke to Sami on the phone," Robert continued. "You know how he is when it comes to hiring new contractors. He instructed me to go over the deal and authorized me to sign if everything checks out."

"Sami authorized *you*?" Vaughn's voice shook.

"He copied you on the authorization email." Robert motioned with his hand for Petra and Elias to leave the office. "Check your inbox."

Vaughn pounded keys on his desktop keyboard.

"Well, it seems I'm not needed anymore." Petra grabbed Elias's hand and headed to the door. She turned to face Vaughn. "Let me know if you need anything else from me. I'm happy to help."

"Yeah, right." Vaughn threw his pen onto the desk. It clattered against the keyboard and landed in the wastebasket. "Thanks ever so much."

On their way out of the office, Elias tugged Robert's hand. "I lost a wheel from my Batmobile. Can you please look for it in the dark web?"

CHAPTER THIRTY-ONE

Ever since she had vowed not to take Elias to Sami's house, Petra had gone out of her way to find activities around town for the twins, keeping them busy and stimulated. When Mrs. Madigan took them home at the end of the day, they either fell asleep in the car or crashed soon after they arrived, foregoing their bedtime routine with Petra.

She convinced Sawsan to spend an entire day with her and the kids by the beach on Galveston Island and invited *Khoury* Dahood for support. The good priest obliged, though he kept his head out of the water.

On another day, they all ventured to the amusement park by Kemah pier. Petra remembered Sami had recommending the place before Elias went into hospital. It turned out to be the perfect entertainment for everyone. Sawsan seemed to enjoy the invigorating sea breeze, walking arm in arm with *Khoury* Dahood on the boardwalk.

Petra managed to keep Elias out of Sawsan's reach and maintain a watchful eye on the girls at the same time without raising Sawsan's suspicions. *Khoury* Dahood, the perfect accomplice, supported her efforts and asked no questions.

The last time she had communicated with Sami was Thursday morning after she left Vaughn's office. He had sent a text message to thank her for involving Robert. Offering no explanation, he wrote that he might have difficulty connecting over the next couple of days. Should something urgent transpire, he asked her to leave him a message on his U.S. number, which he regularly monitored.

She must have glanced at her phone a hundred times during those long days, making sure it was fully charged in case Sami was able to call. Each time she checked her phone, her frustration climbed up a notch. It mounted to full-blown anger by Sunday. Anger at herself, at her weakness and dependency.

She missed hearing his voice every night. It irked her. When had she become so attached, so fond of Sami's scratched vocal cords?

Late Sunday night, Sami texted her three words: landed in Houston.

That was it. No promises to visit after he connected with his family. No *I can't wait to see you* statements, or any declaration of any sort.

At first, she ticked off the hours until Monday noon when she expected to hear from him. Next she counted the minutes. Monday came and went with no word from him.

She forced herself not to dial his number, rationalizing that he needed time to recover from his emotionally charged and physically demanding trip across different time zones. Factor in his claustrophobia; he must have arrived in bad shape, exhausted and jet-lagged. Besides, he had a lot to catch up on at work and at home.

At least he would find his girls well and happy.

Sami's silence stretched through Tuesday. Her frustration turned to worry. What kept him away? Were the facts he had acquired in Palestine as bad as he had suspected? No matter what the situation was, it should stay in the past. Didn't he know that? Was he avoiding her, thinking she might blame him for whatever his father might have done?

She had spent a good part of her life trying to find out what happened to her father. She had uprooted kind and supportive Bassam and planted him in the hot sands of Kuwait. Chasing after her father had proved as futile as aiming for a mirage. What had it got her? A dead husband. In her quest to grasp one ghost, she had created another.

If Sami was avoiding her because of what he had discovered in Palestine, she would not ask him about it. If he ever called, that is. She would let him off the hook. Let the past rest where it belonged.

Or was he brushing her off because of his mother? Sawsan may have said something damaging about her. Anything was possible with unpredictable Sawsan.

How to tell Sami about his mother's manipulative tactics? It would only cause him more pain. It was bad enough for him, living with her mental illness, but to think—to know—she had enough presence of mind to master her hallucinations and control his life as an adult? That would truly damage him.

Perhaps she shouldn't tell him. Sawsan would not harm the girls when there was no threat to her position at home. A threat like Sami having a serious romantic relationship. Or, God help him, bringing home a wife.

She should at least warn him. That would be the responsible thing to do. Finding the right words would be a challenge. What on earth could she say that wouldn't sound like an attack on his mother?

She got on with her preparations to return to Kuwait the following week. Shopping with Elias, she hunted for perfect gifts for Mouzah and her family. Keeping Sami out of her thoughts proved difficult, and shopping kept her busy. She checked her phone less frequently while strolling through the malls, ticking off items on her to-do list. She had no idea what to buy Maryam. Her elderly neighbour had sophisticated taste and followed the latest fashion trends.

Hoping for inspiration, Petra spent Wednesday with Elias at a huge high-end mall in uptown Houston. She grasped multiple shopping bags in one hand and held onto Elias with the other, afraid he might slip away into the crowds.

It seemed people were on a mission to bump into her in their quest to find what they wanted. She shouldn't have come to this crazy mall. Sawsan had told her the Galleria was an essential part of the Houston experience. She foolishly thought she should give it a try. Big mistake. She could have easily found the same items in any of the other less crowded malls she had visited.

Her phone rang. She dumped the bags on the floor and dug out her phone.

It was Sami — finally. He had waited until Wednesday afternoon to connect with her.

She took a deep breath, intent on being firm and brisk. "Hello Sami. Welcome back."

"Oh, good. You're still talking to me."

Unsure if his tone was serious or jovial, she pushed the bags with her feet toward a bench and plopped down with Elias. "Why do you say that?"

"I should have called, but I have so much to tell you. I wanted to see you. I tried, believe me. I was on my way out the door a number of times. Had to turn around to deal with one urgent thing after another." Sami rushed his words. "Things got complicated at work and Mom's been acting weird—"

"I'm not fifteen." She cut him off. "You have priorities." She handed Elias one of the books she had bought for the plane ride. "I know I'm not at the top of the list."

"Petra, it's not like that. I'll explain when I see you. Where are you now?"

"Shopping."

"Where exactly?"

"Galleria."

"Will you meet me for lunch? I'll come to you. There's a nice French bistro by the ice rink on the first floor—"

"Sami, it's five thirty." She cut him off again. He sounded hyper, as if pumped up on gallons of coffee.

"Oh," Sami groaned into the phone. "I lost track of time. I've been working non-stop since I landed."

"Vaughn?"

"The jackass has been cutting corners with contractors in Kuwait. Pocketing money behind Dad's back. That's why our project was so far behind."

"I had a hunch. Is your Kuwaiti partner involved?"

"Sulaiman had no clue. He trusted Dad. And Dad trusted Vaughn. Damn him. He jeopardized the company's reputation. Everything Dad worked hard to establish." Sami exhaled a long audible breath, revealing his exhaustion and frustration.

"Fareed suspected something was off in the records Vaughn sent from Kuwait. He was trying to get to the bottom of it, going over the data I sent him." Sami cleared his throat. "But then the accident . . ."

The scratch in Sami's voice that she liked so much remained prominent. He sounded tired, overwhelmed.

"I can look through those books for you. I have a

master's degree in accounting, you know," she said in a lighthearted tone to ease his burden.

"God, if only I had thought about that earlier. I hired a forensic accountant to go over the books and kept Vaughn in the dark about it. You have a lot on your plate. That kind of scrutiny is time consuming." Sami paused for a breath, then continued. "Petra, you coming in as a third partner complicated things for Vaughn. The bastard thought he could have you sign whatever he needed for his shady dealings in my absence. That explains his eagerness to jump on board with Dad's will."

"You thought Vaughn was devoted to your father."

"He wore a good mask."

"I didn't let him push me around." Petra injected a smile into her tone. "I think I drove Vaughn crazy."

"You provided the proof I was probing for."

"Glad I could help. Are you going to fire Vaughn? I mean, *can* you fire him?"

"I can. And I will. Once I have complete access to his files. That's another mess I've been dealing with." Sami paused. "I really need to see you, Petra."

His tone shifted to a different level, something deeper, intimate, as if he were divulging a secret. Either that, or she truly was an infatuated fifteen-year-old who read too much between the lines.

What the devil was wrong with her? She was leaving. Returning to Kuwait. Back to the quiet life she had

389

before Sami Amara showed up with all his baggage. Some willpower she possessed. Sami was overriding it with that special murmur in his hoarse voice. It was particularly hard when he spoke her name.

"Petra, have dinner with me."

His tantalizing voice tapped a deep spot in her stomach. Damn it. Damn it.

"Tonight," he said, nudging her closer to the end of her depleting resolve.

She glanced at Elias, immersed in his book. "Elias would love to see you. Come over." She winced. "I'll order pizza."

"I was thinking we go out. You and me."

"I can't."

"Sure you can."

She twisted away from Elias and lowered her voice. "I can't leave Elias alone."

"Mrs. Madigan will watch him with the girls at my house."

"No," Petra snapped. She couldn't tell Sami why she wouldn't leave Elias in his house. Not yet. Not on the phone like this.

"I'm sure Mrs. Madigan wouldn't mind," Sami said.

Petra bit the side of her lower lip. The poor man was trying to make sense of her swift rejection. "Sorry, Sami. That's not going to work. Elias had a long day. He'll go to bed early tonight."

"Tomorrow, then. Should I tell Mrs. Madigan to expect him tomorrow evening?" Sami persisted.

"Why do we have to go out? Come over. Bring the girls."

"Petra, I have a lot to tell you. I don't feel comfortable with the kids there. Even if it's just Elias." Sami huffed a short breath, then another. "It's not a date, if that's what you're worried about."

"I'm not," she hurried to say, praying she didn't sound disappointed. "You want to tell me about Hanna Vanyos. What you learned."

"Don't you want to know?"

"Of course I do. I've been going crazy waiting for you to call." She swallowed. God! Could she sound more pathetic? Qualifying her statement, she added, "I didn't hear from you after you went to see Hanna. You've spoken to him, right?"

"Yeah, I did."

"Does he know anything about my father?"

"I'll tell you all about it when I see you. Dinner tomorrow, what do you say?"

"If I ask you to have Mrs. Madigan babysit the kids at my place, would you do it without needing to know why?"

"You're avoiding my mother. It's okay, you can say it. After the long week with her, I understand."

"I'm . . . I don't mean to be . . . difficult."

"I'll talk to Mrs. Madigan," Sami said. "I want my girls home and in bed by a decent hour, so it'll have to be early in the evening. Pick you up at six."

"Sami, hold on. Tell me one thing." She cupped her hands around the phone and dropped her voice to a whisper to keep Elias from hearing her. "Does Hanna know if my father is alive?"

"Petra, this is not the time—"

"Please." She rose to her feet, her vow not to prod Sami for answers a distant memory. She needed an end to her emotional limbo. "Just tell me. Is my father alive?"

Sami blew a long nasal breath into the phone. She waited for him to speak. He took too long. His silence spelled it all.

She sank onto the bench. "I see."

"Petra, it's complicated. Hanna has a theory. Stay where you are, I'm leaving the office as we speak."

"Don't." She wrapped her arm around Elias to hold it together. "You'll be stuck in traffic and I'm not waiting in this mall. I'm going home."

"I'll meet you there."

"I want to be alone." She swallowed a lump in her throat. "Please, Sami."

"Damn it, Petra. I didn't want you to know this way."

"I'll be okay." She pulled Elias closer, tears escaping her control. "I'll see you tomorrow."

***

Her mind in a million fragments, her movements sluggish, Petra barely managed to help Elias through bedtime rituals. She tucked him in bed, wishing she could switch off her mind and go to sleep as well. Elias pulled her close and patted her back when she kissed him goodnight. Her son somehow sensed her melancholy and reversed their roles, providing a parent's comforting touch. They snuggled together until he fell asleep.

Rising on tiptoe, she slipped out of the bedroom and closed the French doors. She stood in the dark by the living room window. Streets emptied below, slump-shouldered workers leaving their offices at the end of a long day. She stuck her hands in the pockets of her open night robe and watched car tail lights trickle away. Sadness pushed down on her, adding weight to her bones. She dropped onto the nearby Queen Anne winged chair.

This heaviness was painfully familiar. She had become disjointed like this after Bassam passed away, moved with cannon balls tied to her ankles. She was grieving again. How could she feel the loss of a father she never knew?

She wasn't totally surprised by the news Sami tried not to utter. The probability of her father being alive after all these years was minuscule. She knew that and had grown to accept his fate. So why did the certainty of his death hit her this hard? A father never registered in her memory. Knowing he was forever gone should not affect her to such a degree.

But it did. Acutely, profoundly. She mourned a father she had never known, whose love and protection she had never relished.

She clutched both knees to her chest and curled up like a baby. Everyone she was closely related to was gone, there were no relatives to watch her back. Mouzah was right when she told her she had no family left. That piece of reality which had eluded her for years crept into her lungs and lodged itself there, a new appendage constricting her air passages.

She tried to inhale. Her throat closed with a moan. Her father was dead. Now what was she supposed to do? Where was her foundation? What was her new mission?

Elias.

She had Elias.

And Elias was enough.

A soft knock sounded at the door. She buried her face in the plush cushion. Let the world go away and leave her be.

Another knock came, louder this time. Uncurling, she checked her watch. Closing in on seven thirty. She trudged to the door and looked through the peephole.

Sami stared back, as if his eyes would pierce the solid wood.

"Petra, open the door." He leaned closer to the peephole. The thick lens distorted his head to that of an alien, with egg-shaped eyes.

"I can hear you moving." He knocked again. "Please, let me in."

She pressed her forehead to the door. Why had he come? She lacked the energy to deal with him. If she didn't respond, he would go away.

"I'll stay out here all night if I have to, Petra."

She tied the belt of her night robe to cover the tank top of her pyjamas, exhaled a deep breath and unlocked the door.

"I'm fine, Sami." She blocked entry with her body, holding the door ajar with her arm extended. "I don't feel like talking."

"Good." Sami pushed the door, forcing her to drop her arm. "Because I'm not here to talk."

He kept moving forward, backing her into the room until he shut the door behind him. He wore a white shirt over black trousers. His clothes were creased in the wrong places, rumpled from all day wear. He must have come here straight from work. Expecting him to head to the window, she stepped out of his way, moving toward the centre of the room.

Sami remained by the door.

She crossed her arms over her chest. "What do you want from me, Sami?"

He slowly shook his head. "Nothing."

"If you're concerned about me, I told you. I'm fine."

He took a long stride toward her. "Yes, I remember."

"You understand? I'm all right."

Sami nodded, took another step. "Of course you are," he said softly.

She stiffened her back. "Elias and I—" she gave a defiant nod "—we'll be okay."

"I know." He approached, leaving room for a couple of steps before he bumped into her. "I'm not here for that."

His raspy voice sounded more husky. She unlocked her arms. "Why are you here?"

Sami inched forward until he towered over her. "You're not alone, Petra."

Her knees trembled. Was this man clairvoyant?

He brushed her bangs with the tips of his fingers. "A misshapen tree can grow new roots."

Her eyes stung. Not only did he know what she was thinking, how she felt, he had also memorized what she had told him about her family roots having dried out. Her father was the last possible living one she could cling to.

"I'm here." Sami's thumb lingered over her birthmark. "You steadied me when I swayed, Petra. I want to do the same for you." He dropped his hand. "If you'll let me."

She gazed into his dark eyes. How sincere was he?

"Here . . ." She placed her hand over her chest. "Here is . . . difficult right now, Sami."

"Difficult is okay by me."

She choked back tears. "I'm a mess."

He placed his hands on her shoulders, but stopped short from pulling her into an embrace. "I can handle a mess."

She let hot tears flow. It no longer mattered if he meant what he said. She needed consolation and would accept his offering.

Leaning into his broad chest, she buried her face in the crook of his neck.

Sami patted her shoulder, swept one hand down her back and circled her waist.

She wrapped her arms around his midsection, savouring his strength, absorbing his solace.

He gently lifted her into his arms, eased onto the winged chair and nestled her in his lap.

She dangled her legs over the arm of the chair, snuggling further into Sami's warm, comforting tenderness.

She gazed out of the window at a lonely flickering star. Her head rose and dipped with Sami's steady and slow breathing. Other than that, he didn't move a muscle.

After a while, several stars dotted the dark skies. It could have been minutes, or hours. Cradled in compassionate arms, she lost track of time. She tilted her head to see if Sami had fallen asleep.

His kind eyes met hers with questioning softness.

"You awake?" she foolishly asked.

"I'm here."

She dipped her head, suddenly too aware of their entwined bodies. "Tell me what you learned about my father."

"Tomorrow," Sami murmured.

"Please. I want to know now."

He exhaled, fanning her forehead with his breath. "Your father was a patriot, paid for his ideals with his life."

"Tell me everything."

Listening to Sami spill details, she endured wave after wave of intense emotions. Her insides warmed with the thought that her father was a man who valued freedom, that he longed to combat oppression and dedicated his life to it. He was a man of action, striving to restore his stolen country. The futility of his involvement in the military operation did not matter. Her father didn't stand by and watch injustice crush his people. He did *something* to try to make things right.

That was the lesson she would pass on to Elias, to align his moral compass. Her head buzzed with a rush of excitement. Her hazy mission was now crystal clear.

At the mention of her father's possible assassination, her bare feet went cold. A sobering chill gripped her entire body. Had her father known the risk of entanglement and gone ahead despite that? She had a strong notion that he would have done so, no matter what the consequences. Conflicted about how that made her feel, she concentrated on Sami's explanation, seeking clues in his tone and choice of words.

Sami seemed genuinely to admire her father's decision to step up and take action when called upon. Yet, he talked about *his* father's aversion to armed resistance with respect as well. Sami seemed to share his father's views that non-violent means were just as effective, if not more, in resisting occupation under the existing conditions. He told her of his intention to resume the arrangement his father had with Hanna to support destitute Palestinians in the occupied homelands.

"How are you going to do that from here?" She asked. "I mean, you'll be confronting a powerful Israeli lobby. You run a company that operates internationally. Isn't there a risk?"

"If I go about it the wrong way." He gave her shoulder a gentle squeeze. "I'm not foolish enough to risk my business. I won't do anything illegal, if that's what you're worried about."

"I'm sure you wouldn't."

"There are legitimate avenues. Local and international humanitarian organizations, trustworthy NGO's. Completely transparent. And Dad always made sure we chose contractors and suppliers who don't deal with Israeli entities." He squeezed her shoulder again. "Don't worry. I've given this a lot of thought."

"I know how important this is for you . . . to continue on your father's path."

"Dad believed that sustaining and aiding social and economic infrastructures is key to non-violent resistance." Sami turned his head to gaze out of the window. "From what I've seen, in face of overwhelming and oppressive military presence, boycotting Israeli goods is a powerful tool in the hands of the Palestinians world-wide. Much like the Gandhi approach with Britain and the international movement against South African apartheid." Sami's chest dipped with a deflated sigh. "Sixty-eight years of occupation and there's no damn practical solution in sight. I see Dad was right."

That was another lesson she would pass on to her boy. There were many ways to tackle transgression and expose oppression. One person could be effective, even from a distance.

A pang of jealousy pierced her heart. She didn't have the luxury of following in her father's footsteps. "I wish my father hadn't—"

"Don't, Petra." Sami interrupted, placing a finger on her lips. "Don't do this to yourself. Your father made a brave decision according to *his* convictions." Sami removed his finger, curled his hand and rested it at the base of her throat.

Tears gathered in her eyes again. Taking a long breath, she fought to hold them back. "That devotion cut his life short. But that's not what I was getting at."

"What do you mean?"

"I wish my father hadn't disappeared the way he did, without a trace. I wish I had more time with him." Her tears spilled. "To absorb his thoughts, appreciate his personality."

"Your father didn't disappear." Sami wiped her wet chin, laid his cheek on the top of her head. "He lives on through you and your son."

"Mere fragments of him. I keep grasping for that part of my heritage, and I come up empty. I don't *know* him."

"Speaking of heritage, you should've seen the house in Jerusalem where I stayed." Sami rubbed his cheek on her hair. "It was more of an art museum. Full of folkloric items. It's important to keep those kinds of traditions alive. Even here. For our future generations."

She appreciated his effort to steer the conversation away from her sad reality. Liking the direction his thoughts were headed, she tagged along. "Sounds like you have specific plans."

"Kind of," he murmured, snaking his mouth closer to her forehead.

"Tell me."

"I want to sponsor a couple of annual events in Houston."

401

His breath ruffled her eyelashes. Pleased with that particular sense of intimacy, she dropped her eyelids. "Cultural events?"

"A Palestinian cultural festival takes place ... every spring. It gives folks a chance to enjoy music and food, and discuss books. Things like that."

"Do women wear traditional dresses?" Petra asked, nudging him to keep him talking. He seemed reluctant. Or could he be falling asleep?

"The embroidery stuff?" Sami said through half a yawn. "Sure, and they sell a few, too." His head sagged to the back of the chair. "I went there once, when I happened to be in town. It was so uplifting to see children, parents and grandparents participating in dances and other activities, showing off their heritage with pride. I'll help sponsor the festival from now on. Provide the organizers with a financial boost. What do you think?"

"I think that's a great idea."

"It's a start. I'll sponsor the Palestine Film Festival, too."

"Oh, ads about the festival popped up online when I searched for the Museum of Fine Arts and Rice University Media Center. What type of movies do they offer?"

"Documentaries and independent films about Palestine and Palestinian society and identity in the diaspora. Fareed was an ardent volunteer. He raved about the ones he saw with Lora."

"Sounds interesting."

"I'm going to look into it." Sami tilted his hips and stretched his left leg.

Petra sank deeper into his lap. To cover her awkwardness, she said, "Tell me what else you saw in Palestine."

Sami talked about what he had experienced, his expressions shifting between sadness, frustration and anger. Her insides clenched when he mentioned the life Hanna's granddaughter had to endure. Sami's fingers curled into his palm as he recounted what had happened with the Israeli settler snipers. His left hand was still at her waist and his knuckles dug into her skin, but she refrained from speaking or shifting so as not to interrupt him. He seemed unaware that he was hurting her and eventually relaxed his fists when he talked about the other things Hanna had said.

She arranged a mental list of more lessons for Elias.

There wasn't much she could teach her son about his father. One of the things that had drawn her to Bassam was the fact that he was first generation Palestinian-American. But she was perplexed to find that Bassam wasn't tuned into his background, nor was he particularly interested in his history. And Bassam, nice man that he was, never quite understood her need to find her father, although he had supported her efforts.

In her naive youthful years, she thought that by marrying Bassam she would add elements to her missing composition. Reality slapped her hand and taught her that Bassam's family had failed to pass on any remnants of heritage to their son. Why was she blind to that fact when she married him? Her need to belong somewhere was too great to allow her to see she was attaching herself to a man who didn't share her cultural hunger. After she was left to raise Elias alone, in the absence of extended family members, there were too many things left out and she grabbed at every opportunity to instil a sense of tradition in her son.

"I wish my father had left me some sort of journal," she said when Sami fell silent. "I would love to know exactly what he thought and felt. In his own words."

"He was secretive for a good reason." Sami looked at her from the corner of his eye. "To shield you and your mother."

"The same reason your father had to keep you and your brother hidden away. I can't imagine how hard it must have been on Sawsan. To have both her sons sent away."

Sami stiffened under Petra. "I've been thinking about that."

"I know you have a lot on your hands right now, but try to spend more time with her."

"Ever since I knew the real reason Dad sent us away," Sami sat up, "I felt so guilty."

"Why?"

"Growing up, I blamed Mom for our banishment. Because of her fractured mind, her fricking *Watchers*."

"You were a boy. It was natural to think that way, given your circumstances. You didn't know any better." Petra patted his hand resting across her belly. "It's not like your father *could* tell you."

"Yeah, I know that now." Sami shrugged his shoulders. "I guess I have to put myself in his shoes. There's nothing I wouldn't do to guarantee my girls' safety."

Petra pursed her lips. The same went for her. That was why she had to keep Elias away from Sami's mother. Was this the right moment to tell him about Sawsan's threats?

Tilting her head back, she peered at Sami.

"This is nice." He tightened his hold on her. "Talking like this." He ran his hand up and down her arm. "Right?"

She nodded in agreement.

No. This was not the time to break the news to him about his mother's schemes to banish her. This *was* nice.

"May I ask you something?" Sami whispered. His voice tickled her ear through his chest, coming out levels deeper.

"Sure," she whispered back.

"What perfume do you favour?"

"I don't use perfumes." She lifted her head and pushed slightly away from him. "I'm much too sensitive for artificial scents." She glanced down to recognize her favourite pyjamas, a faded set she had slept in for the last three nights. She pressed her lips together, mortified.

"Is it your shampoo then?" Sami ran his hand through her hair. "You smell so lovely."

"Oh!" She relaxed, sagging into his arms. "I use a blend of aromatic oils."

"Tell me more," he said. "What kind?"

"Lavender oil and lemon or grapefruit extracts."

"Is there vanilla in the mix?"

"Yes," she said, surprised that he detected it. "But, only a hint."

"And?"

"You want specific ingredients?"

"If you don't mind."

"Sometimes I add rose water."

"Anything else?" Sami lifted a lock of her hair and brushed it under his nose, across his cheeks and chin. "I smell something fiery and icy at the same time . . . like warming earth cleansed by a melting veil of snow."

"Mud?" she squealed. "I smell like warm mud?" The bliss vanished. She scrambled to climb out of his lap. This was too weird for comfort. Swinging both feet to the floor, she twisted sideways and tried to stand. The ends of her robe, trapped under Sami's left leg, caused her to drop back onto his lap.

With a throaty groan, he lifted her clear off him. "Hell! Woman! Not mud. I'm trying to pay you a compliment." He sprang from the chair. One end of his shirt dangled from his trousers, hopelessly wrinkled.

"Ever since I met you, I've been intrigued by yo . . . your scent." He attempted and failed to tuck in the escaping shirt tail. "I'm trying to figure out what it is."

"Well, if you must know . . ." Petra adjusted the folds of her robe. "I sometimes use the essence of thyme."

Sami stopped fussing with his shirt to gape at her, looking utterly flustered. "The herb?"

"Yes."

"I thought it might be an exotic flower or something. Are you telling me that instead of going to the florist to buy you a bouquet, I'll need to head to Phoenicia to find a bunch of thyme?"

"Phoenicia?" She cracked a smile, despite herself. "Is that a trendy natural spa your lady friends favour?"

Sami returned her smile. "It's a supermarket. My *Mom* shops there for specialty foods and Mediterranean cuisine." He wagged his finger. "I'm guessing that's where I can find thyme sprigs."

"Fresh ones, if you please," Petra said with a straight face, but the clownish waggle of Sami's finger started a giggle at the base of her chest and worked its way up. How did this man know how to absorb her sorrow? She let out a laugh without the slightest reservation, feeling girlish and light. "And don't forget the biggest bottle of rose water you can find in that specialty store."

Sami knotted his eyebrows, yet amusement sparkled in his eyes. "Got it."

"Oh, Sami. Please don't show up at my door with a bouquet of fresh herbs." She fanned her face with her hands. "They'll end up on the kitchen cutting board."

He grinned, touched her elbow. "But you just said you use—"

"Oils and extracts. I order them online. Then I experiment with portions at home. You really like it?"

"Oh, I like it all right." He pulled her close to caress her cheek with his. "It truly moves me."

Petra's heart drummed faster. This man was mesmerizing her, no other way to describe what he was doing. This was too soon, too dangerous. She stepped out of his embrace. "Speaking of groceries, are you hungry? Should I fix you something to eat?"

Sami blew out a breath. "No, thanks." He checked his watch and pulled out his keys from his trouser pocket. "It's time for me to go home." He twirled a lock of her hair around his finger. "Right?"

She stared at him, reading volumes in his skeptical eyes.

His hand quivered, the keys jingled. "Should I go home, Petra?"

"Yes, you probably should."

He nodded, let go of her hair. "Yeah, thought so." He turned on his heels, headed to the door and opened the bolt. "Don't forget dinner tomorrow. Be ready at six."

"Sami, hold on a moment." Petra followed, reaching for his free hand with both of hers. "You'll bring the girls . . . with Mrs. Madigan?

"Yes." He rubbed his thumb over her wrist. "Just like we agreed, remember?"

"Right . . . of course." She tugged on his hand.

He obliged by inching closer, questioning eyes probing hers.

She stayed put, every nerve in her body titillated by simple strokes of his thumb.

Sami leaned in and buried his face in her hair. "Did I ever thank you for—" he nuzzled her ear "—taking such great care of my girls?" His voice turned husky, cozy and sexy.

"You don't—" she swallowed "—really need to."

"I'm very grateful, Petra." He straightened, tapped his keys to his thigh, showing impatience, or nervousness?

She must be confusing this man to the limits of sanity. One moment despondent and crying in his arms, the next angry and indignant, then cheerful and laughing. And now she dismissed him, yet held onto his hand and forced him to linger. What in God's name was she doing?

"I'm very grateful, too." She lifted his hand to her lips and graced it with a soft kiss. "For not leaving me alone."

"Damn it!" Sami swore under his breath, threw his keys to the floor. He held the back of her neck and bound his lips to hers.

She accepted his scorching kiss, relishing his ardour. She would allow herself a taste of Sami. Just one quick, fleeting taste.

Sami slipped his other hand from her grip, spread it over her back and deepened his passion. She responded with a welcoming warmth, savouring the sample, craving another. She crept her fingers up his nape and engulfed them in thick hair. He served what she silently asked for generously, expertly, lips soft and skilful, tongue hot and audacious. She drank in his gifts, teasing a long-standing thirst and igniting a deep yearning. Angling her head, she pulled on his hair, shamelessly seeking more.

Sami backed her to the wall. He abandoned her mouth and paid homage to her neck, artfully nibbling, a delicate teasing. Under Sami's touch, her body danced to inaudible music, intimately choreographed with his. Clutching his back, she dug her fingernails past the fabric of his shirt, into his skin. He shuddered, laid his palm to the wall and pressed his body flush against hers.

"Oh, Sami," she croaked, her voice laden with a thousand invitations. Lord, what was she doing? What was she *doing*? She moaned her weakness, her enchantment.

Sami echoed her moan and parted her night robe. He dipped his head to brand her shoulder, lick the skin at her collar bone and below.

Petra bit her lower lip to silence the objections screaming inside her head. This was too good. This man was too good. Lifting her knee, she stroked his thigh.

Sami murmured something unintelligible, grabbed her leg and hooked it around his hips. He returned his lips to hers, hand creeping under her tank top and searing the skin above her waist. His fingers stopped a fraction of a second, then gently crawled up her ribs.

"Wait," Petra gasped.

Sami groaned, withdrew his hand. "I know," he breathed into her mouth. His lips charted their way up her cheeks to her naturally marked temple. He kissed her birthmark, one dot at a time.

She held onto his shoulders. What was he talking about? He knew what?

Blowing a chopped breath, Sami lifted his head and untangled their bodies. "I've been wanting to do that for a long time." He picked up his keys and stepped back, groping for the door handle behind him. "I'm leaving."

She stepped forward, swayed, and shot her hand to the wall. "You are." She meant to confirm, but the words left her lips with a disappointed lilt.

"I can't stay, Petra. You're not that kind of woman." He shook his head. "And I won't allow myself to ignore how fragile you are right now." He opened the door and slipped away.

Petra slid to the floor, covered her face with both palms. She took a long moment to steady her heartbeat, rose and walked to the window. She gazed into the starlit night, caught the tail lights of Sami's car and watched them disappear around a distant corner.

CHAPTER THIRTY-TWO

Sami secured Deena in her car seat, checked the buckle on Leena's seat and closed the car door.

"Hurry up," his mother called out from the passenger window, waving at him to come forward.

Sami slid behind the wheel. "We have plenty of time."

"I have so much to do. I can't arrive late."

"I thought everything was set up for tomorrow's show." Sami started the engine. "What's the urgency?"

"I want to make sure *Khoury* Dahood has every painting in the right place with the best lighting. And it's an art exhibition, Sami. Not a show." Sawsan pulled a tissue from her bag and dabbed her upper lip. "I hate this humid weather." She flipped the visor mirror. "Oh, look at my hair!"

"You look great, Mom." Sami turned up the air conditioning. Tilting the rear view mirror, he checked on the girls one last time.

"My hair is a bird's nest." Sawsan slammed back the visor. "Do go, Sami."

"I'll get you there with plenty of time to spare." He readjusted the mirror and fiddled with his phone, scanning for a specific song.

"I don't understand why you brought the twins." His mother massaged her brow. "They'll ruin everything."

"I've hardly seen them since I've been back. I don't have meetings in the office this morning so this is my chance to spend some time with them."

"At my expense!" Sawsan huffed, dropping her hand to her lap.

Sami patted her hand. "*And* spend time with you."

"Leave the office early if you want to have more time with the twins tonight." She threw a quick look at the back. "Can't you see how hyper they are this morning?"

"Now, don't worry, Mom. I have things under control." He pulled in a patient breath, checked the oncoming traffic and eased the car out of the driveway. "We'll wait for you in the playground." He threw her a reassuring glance. "I won't let the girls run amok in the exhibition hall, okay?"

Sawsan placed her bag by her feet. "Fine."

"Besides, I'm going out for dinner tonight. Mrs. Madigan will keep the girls. I figured I'd give her a break this morning since she'll be on full duty tonight."

"Business dinner?"

"No. Not business."

"Really," Sawsan pursed her lips. "You have a date?"

"Yeah."

She turned her head to look out of the window. "Your friend Petra?"

"Right." He couldn't see the expression on his mother's face, but he heard disapproval in her voice. Where did that come from? Mother had spoken highly of Petra after he returned from his trip, told him how she had taken care of everybody during his absence. What had happened that prompted this objectionable tone?

He was about to prod when an orchestra of stringed instruments began playing through the car speakers.

Sawsan swung her head to face him. "*Umm Kulthum*?"

"Yep. Your favorite singer." He gently squeezed his mother's hand. "Relax. Enjoy her."

"She truly is *Kawkab al-Sharq*."

"The Planet of the East?" Sami asked.

"More like the *Sun* to Yahya." Sawsan slumped her shoulders. "Your father loved this particular song."

"I remember him retreating into the study some afternoons, listening to *Umm Kulthum's* never-ending songs." Sami swallowed. Since his father had passed away, Mother mentioned him very little, if at all. Was the plan to put her at ease with this song about to backfire? Cause her more anxiety? He should demand reimbursement from her quack therapist for the twenty thousand dollar bill he had paid this morning. Shit! Should he change the subject? Mom seemed all right, though. She *wanted* to talk about her husband.

Sami shifted gears. "I resented *Umm Kulthum* when I was a boy. On the few days Fareed and I came home

415

and Dad wasn't at work, he locked himself in his study with her albums."

"You got very mad at him once when he told you he found her voice extremely seductive." Sawsan cracked a smile. "I remember what you told him."

"Come on, tell me."

"You said you couldn't understand how a voice that was as dense as a planet's core could be seductive."

"Wow, I said that?"

She shook her head. "I never saw Yahya so offended."

"Come to think of it, it's a fairly accurate description of her voice. It's so deep." Sami matched his mother's tentative smile. He was on a good track. "What did Dad do? Yell at me? I don't recall that at all."

"Yahya wagged his finger in your face and said, *I pray one day you'll come to understand.* He told me this particular song *touched* him." She laid her hand on her chest. "Here. As if it . . . physically touched him."

Sami nodded. "*Enta Omri,*" he slowly said the name of the song. "That means *you are my age*?"

"Life." Sawsan stretched her lips into a broader smile and corrected his translation. "You are my *entire* life." Once the operatic-voiced singer started serenading, his mother closed her eyes with obvious delight.

Sami breathed a sigh of relief. Maybe the therapist knew what he was doing, after all. Avoiding the freeway, he took side streets and drove at a leisurely pace to give his mother more time to enjoy the long song with its repetitive segments.

The girls kicked their feet with the music. Sawsan became animated, singing, swaying, waving her hands. She seemed... happy. Not confused, living in *La La*-land happy. Rather, she seemed genuinely pleased with her surroundings.

He stole a moment to commit this morning to memory. Mother was all there with him - mind, body and soul. These were rare moments.

Concentrating on the lyrics, he tried to fathom their meaning, to appreciate the song's effect on his mother and his father before her. He could make out separate words: heart, joy, taste, and something about time. His mind jumped to Petra.

He had spent the night weighing up what had happened at her place. Petra was totally vulnerable in his arms. If he hadn't hauled himself away before he gave in to her intoxicating allure, he wouldn't have been able to look himself in the mirror.

Would Petra have let him go further? She asked him to stop, but her body sang a different tune. She certainly didn't freeze under his touch, allowed him to kiss her properly this time. And she undoubtedly enjoyed it. She let him know it, too.

He liked that. He liked a lot of things about Petra. A whole lot of things he shouldn't think about right now with his mother sitting next to him.

The weeping of violins in the car, combined with the legendary singer's highly emotive vocal attributes stirred something deep in his chest. A smile tickled his heart and spread to his lips. He had made progress. Petra welcomed him. His mother sang in rapture beside him. His girls were safe, dancing in their seats. His apparition of Petra as a child hadn't visited in a long while. Hopefully, it never would again. Mother hadn't mentioned her *Watchers* lately, either. And if he played his cards right, Vaughn would be out of the picture, out of the company. Soon. Work would bounce back in no time.

Sami coughed behind his closed fist, a chortle was about to escape him. Life was good.

"What's so funny?" Sawsan stopped singing to ask.

He pointed at the speaker to throw her off his mind's track. "This song is something else." He punched the air with his fist. "It has power."

"You understand the words?" She arched an eyebrow. "I'm impressed."

"Not every word. Just the gist of it."

"I didn't know you understood the Egyptian accent. If it was another song in classical Arabic, I'd be disappointed if you didn't. Tell me, what is she saying?"

He concentrated on the verse, which resonated in a rich feminine voice brimming with the vitality of an awakening forest.

"Because of you," he began to translate. "I ... forgave the past ... times?" He checked with his mother for confirmation.

She nodded.

He tilted his head to focus on the following verse. "You made me . . . forget my pains." He waved his hand in the air. "Wait, I can get this last one." He dropped his hand to grip the gearshift knob. "And with you, I forgot the bitterness."

"Well, there you go." His mother beamed. "You sure got it." She pointed at the church coming up ahead. "Oh no, the parking lot is packed. It's Thursday. What on earth is going on?"

"Bible study?" Sami offered.

"That's on Mondays." She patted the sides of her hair. "And choir practice is on Tuesdays." Her voice rose. "So many people. They shouldn't see my paintings yet."

"I'm sure *Khoury* Dahood has restricted entrance to the main hall for tomorrow's exhibition."

"Oh, I hope you're right."

Sami nodded, adding a smile. "Me too."

As their road merged with a major highway, he was caught in cross-town traffic. Drivers more intent on their phones than adhering to traffic signals tried his patience. He slammed on the brakes and suppressed a desire to curse at the stupid driver who had cut into his lane. The girls screeched from the back. Sami swiftly reached out his hand and gave their knees a reassuring pat.

His mother slapped his arm. "Pay attention to the road, Sami."

"I am, I am." Turning into the parking lot, he crawled his Lexus LS down rows teaming with SUVs and BMWs in search of a parking space.

Kicking her legs to the beat, Deena lost a shoe. "Soo," she cried.

"I'll get your shoe when we stop, sweetheart," Sami said, smiling at Deena in the rearview mirror.

"Soo. Soo," Leena repeated, even though both her shoes were still on her feet.

"Hush now," Sawsan threw over her shoulder. "Turn right, Sami. I saw a spot in the next row."

He made the turn, thinking about what to say to alleviate his mother's creeping tension. "You know what, Mom?"

"Yes?" she asked, her lips quivering to keep her smile in place.

"Even though I don't completely understand the rest of this song, I feel its fervour. It's so . . . raw. Honest. It's like *Umm Kulthum* is disclosing a well-guarded secret." He eased the car between two pickup trucks. "I can see how Dad was deeply affected by it."

"Oh, no!" Sawsan moaned. Her smile disappeared. "It's happened."

"What happened?"

She grabbed her bag, opened it and closed it right away, her lips two straight lines. A look of anger, not confusion, filled her eyes.

His heart sank. "What's wrong?"

"Your father said it." She unbuckled her seatbelt and swung her door open. The door missed the adjacent truck by an inch. "I never understood what he meant."

Sami stayed her with his hand. "What did Dad say?"

"Let me go, Sami." Clutching her bag to her chest, she squirmed in her seat. "I'm late."

Sami rubbed her hand before releasing it. "Please tell me."

"I always thought you were more like me." She opened and closed her bag several times. "It turns out you're becoming more and more like your father."

"Baba," Deena whined. "Soo."

Sami felt for the lost shoe on the floor behind his seat and handed it to Deena. "Mom, please," he pleaded. "I really don't understand."

Sawsan heaved a heavy sigh. "Yahya told me once that the day you'd grow to appreciate *Umm Kulthum*'s songs, even if you failed to grasp the full meaning of her words—" Sawsan slipped out of the car, "—is the day you'll know."

Sami leaned over the passenger seat, peered out of the car and extended an open hand. "Know what?"

"That you've fallen in love."

***

Sami shifted the tote bag on his shoulder to return Elias's welcoming hug and walked the girls into Petra's place with Mrs. Madigan right on his heels, her arms full of other tote bags.

"Mama is getting ready," Elias said. He gave the girls a tender hug and guided them around the living room.

Sami helped Mrs. Madigan set up toys and whatever she had brought in the bags now lying scattered around the room. He eyed the closed French doors, a bit thrown off track. He had run many scenarios in his head about seeing Petra tonight; none included her not greeting him at the door.

"Why did you bring their sleeping bags?" he asked Mrs. Madigan when he saw her set the pink comforters on the floor.

"In case you're late," Mrs. Madigan said. "Sleepovers are fun. I brought one for me, too."

Sami shook his head. "We won't be late."

"Yes, well." Mrs. Madigan straightened. "Just in case." The woman looked away. "Take your time. We'll be okay here."

"We should be back by nine, at the latest." He pulled the coffee table to a corner. "You have everything you need?"

"Yes, and then some. Don't worry. I worked out details with Petra on the phone this morning."

Sami's heart rate spiked. Had Petra asked Mrs. Madigan to bring the sleeping bags? Expecting they'd do something after dinner? Go somewhere? Shit! He hadn't planned on that.

Petra waltzed out of the bedroom, stunning in an elegant tight black dress and matching high heels.

422

"Hello everyone," she crooned.

Her loose auburn hair gleamed in contrast with the dark fabric that graced the tips of her shoulders, revealing a freckled neckline and adding an aura of teasing mischief to her appearance. She looked at him, her glossed lips spread into a demure smile.

Sami swallowed in his corner. Damn! She had unleashed the little black dress and he was wearing chinos. He pulled on the lapels of his sports jacket just to have something to do with his hands.

The girls flocked to Petra. She bent down to kiss their heads, giving Sami a clear view of her body profile. She straightened and addressed Mrs. Madigan.

"I childproofed the place as much as possible. Elias's Lego pieces are all in a sealed tub above the dresser in the bedroom. Oh, and I rented a couple of Disney movies. *Frozen*, *Little Mermaid*—"

"And *Lego Movie!*" Elias hopped on one foot, tugging on Mrs. Madigan's arm.

Petra waved her hand toward the kitchen. "There are fish sticks in the freezer."

"I brought snacks, movies, toys, everything we need," Mrs. Madigan said. "Don't worry. Run along. Have a good time."

Petra hugged Elias. "You're the man of the house, now. You take care of DeLeenas. Listen to Mrs. Madigan, okay?"

Elias bobbed his head. "Yes, mama. Can I wake up Elefun now?"

"Yes, go ahead."

Elias ran to a blue plastic elephant sitting on the floor by the TV stand. He grinned and flipped a switch. The elephant's trunk blew colourful paper butterflies in the air. The girls giggled and ran to catch the butterflies, with Elias leading the way.

Petra grabbed her bag off a chair and finally turned her attention to Sami. "We should go while the girls are busy."

Sami nodded, not trusting his voice. They quietly slipped out, crossed the hall and stepped into the elevator. Sami faced the doors, searching for the perfect compliment to pay Petra. *Lovely* was such a vague and flimsy word. He couldn't simply say she looked beautiful. There had to be a stronger, more descriptive word. *Angelic* was too pure and sterile. Standing by his side in that attire, Petra wasn't exactly projecting innocence.

He took too long to speak. The silence reached an uncomfortable point. What the hell was wrong with him?

"We should have taken the stairs," Petra said. "This must be torture for you."

"No, it's okay," he rushed to say. She thought he was distressed because of his claustrophobia. Thank God for small favours. He turned to face her.

424

"I like that elephant toy," he said and immediately flinched, appalled at the words which came out of his mouth. Shit! Where did that come from?

"I was afraid the girls might act up when you left." Petra switched her bag to her other shoulder. "They've never been to my place. It was the perfect distraction."

Since he had already stepped in it, he might as well make the best of this witless conversation. "Your idea or Mrs. Madigan's?"

"Mine." Petra fixed her gaze on the screen which flashed floor numbers. "Elias loved playing with it when he was their age. His Elefun spit out plastic balls."

Sami shoved one hand in his pocket, disgusted with himself. Of course Petra was annoyed. He had escaped a claustrophobic panic attack, but was behaving with asshole stupidity. He had to compliment her *toy*! It was all his mother's fault. She had totally screwed him up with her revelation this morning. And how long did it take for this goddamn elevator to travel eleven floors?

He rocked on his heels. "Actually, what I wanted to say is—"

"And those sleeping bags?" Petra interrupted, one eyebrow arched. "Your idea?"

"Mrs. Madigan's." He chewed his cheek. There was his answer. Petra hadn't told the nanny to be prepared to spend the night. This conversation wasn't getting any better, thanks to Mrs. Madigan's meddling.

"With Houston traffic and all," he said, attempting to halt the boulder rolling down the hill he was stuck on. "Mrs. Madigan figured we might get delayed."

Petra nodded. The doors opened. She stepped out and hurried before him, her heels clicking the lobby tiles. He stole a moment to admire the sway of her hips, then caught up with her and led the way to his car parked in the hotel's circular driveway.

Holding the passenger door open, he said. "Exquisite."

"Excuse me?" Petra paused, balanced on one foot, body halfway into the car.

"You look exquisite. That's what I wanted to tell you back in the elevator."

"Thank you." She dropped down onto her seat. "Can we go now?"

He closed the door and jogged around the front of the car to slide behind the wheel. He had found the right word, all right. But it was too late for it to land with the flattering splash he had hoped. She hadn't even blinked. Damn it!

He started the engine, but didn't shift into gear to drive. He looked at Petra buckling her seatbelt.

"I brought you something." He grabbed a bag from the back seat. "From Palestine."

"Oh!" Petra put her bag by her feet, placed the gift bag on her lap and pulled out pieces of colourful tissue paper, one by one. She lifted the traditionally embroidered shawl he had carefully chosen from the Old City markets.

"This design is made with the Nazareth stitch. Your father's hometown."

She shoved the bag and tissue paper to her feet, unfolded the shawl and spread it over her lap, silently inspecting the geometric designs in the dark fabric.

He turned on the light above her head. Did she like it? Why wouldn't she say anything?

"I understand each city has an identifying design," he said, to cut through the tense silence.

Petra nodded. "Each village, even," she whispered. "The designs reflect a woman's region and history." She looked up. "Thank you, Sami. This is so thoughtful."

"I just got lucky. I think it goes well with your chic dress."

She spread the shawl over her shoulders and flipped out her trapped hair, showering him with her maddening scent. "You like my new dress?"

"Oh, yes." He steadied his eyes on her, letting her see in his intoxicated gaze exactly how much he liked it. "Very much."

"More than that elephant toy?" Petra asked, her voice a bit playful.

"Touché!" Sami winced. "I guess I deserved that."

"It's okay." She smiled, turned off the light above her head. "I was nervous, too."

He caressed her cheek with the back of his fingers. "That's not the right word for what I feel."

Petra dipped her head. "You're hungry?"

"No, that's not what I have in mind, either."

"Well, I am. So, I'm thinking we'd better go."

Sami escorted Petra into the scenic lakefront restaurant nestled under thick oak trees. They followed the hostess to the table he had requested when he made the reservation. It sat in a glassed corner overlooking the lake and offered an unobstructed view of the rolling gardens.

Graceful long-necked swans and colourful ducks criss-crossed the waters and meandered between azalea bushes. The early evening sun, on its last yawn before it rested behind the horizon, cast a golden sheen over the extensive gardens.

"This is so beautiful," Petra said, wide-eyed and smiling. "As if it's a drawing from a children's story book, spectacular."

"We'll take a stroll in the grounds after dinner, if you like." Sami held back a chair and waited for her to sit down. "It'll be cool and breezy."

Petra slipped the shawl off her shoulders and folded it over her bag. "Standing on the street, you'd never know all this splendour is here."

"This place is a well-guarded secret." Sami took his seat. *Um Kulthum's* bottomless voice resonated in his head: *With you, I forgot the bitterness.*

A waiter offered the wine menu. Sami arched his brows at Petra. "What's your pleasure?"

"Red." Petra tucked hair strands behind her ear, revealing a lazy blush that climbed up her neck and painted her freckles a shade lighter than the single red rose at the centre of the table.

Sami flicked his napkin and placed it on his lap. Was this what being in love felt like? Detecting shades of a blush? Hearing songs out of nowhere?

"Do you have the Chilean Puemo Carménère?" he asked the waiter without glancing at the menu, keeping his eyes on Petra's glowing face.

"Yes, sir," the waiter said. "The 2007 vintage Concha y Toro Carmìn."

"Bring a bottle, please." Sami handed the wine list to the waiter.

Petra wet her lips. "I've never had wine from Chile."

"It's an exceptional Cabernet. Helped me through tough times while I was on a project in Santiago." Sami smiled, surprising himself. He never smiled when he remembered his catastrophic failure in Chile. Add that to the list of side effects of being in love: the inability *not* to smile.

"Does Santiago have a vibrant nightlife like Rio and Buenos Aires?" Petra asked.

"I really don't know. Worked day and night trying to salvage a project and I failed miserably."

"Failure is life's cruellest teacher." She reached for his hand and tilted her head, spilling most of her hair over one shoulder. "Sometimes things just spiral beyond our control."

"Right." Sami squeezed her hand. Petra's soft concern warmed him, bathed him in tranquillity.

The waiter arrived with the bottle of wine and pulled the cork.

Petra smiled shyly at the waiter and withdrew her hand.

Sami raised his glass to sample the wine. He swirled the velvety liquid, sniffed the released aroma and tried a sip. He gave the waiter a satisfied nod, allowing him to expertly fill their glasses.

Sami held his glass out to Petra. "Here's to delightful, thoughtful teachers."

Petra clicked her glass to his and took a sip. "Hmm. This is different. Good, different. There's an under layer of . . ." She raised her eyebrows. "Oh, what is it?"

"Herbs." Sami winked. "Thought it was fitting."

She tipped her glass to him. "This is a special place for you, isn't it?"

"How can you tell?"

"You haven't stopped smiling from the minute you stepped in here."

"A sense of the outdoors, good wine," he leaned forward, "and the company of a beautiful, intelligent woman. I cannot help but smile."

The blush under her freckles deepened, matching the red liquid sloshing around the glass in her delicate hand.

Sami settled back, radiating with satisfaction. The right compliment had elicited the most captivating response. Finally! He was back on track. "There's another reason why this place is dear to me."

"This is where you bring your ah . . . special lady friends," she said in a naughty tone, mirth dancing in her eyes.

Sami chuckled. "Fareed had his wedding reception here." He pointed to a white arbour surrounded by yellow rose bushes. "That's where he and Lora said their vows. Fareed wanted a traditional church wedding, Lora wanted this spot. As the best man, I had to talk my brother into submission."

"Smart man." Petra sipped her wine. "It's hitting you now, isn't it? The fact that your brother is gone."

Sami blew out a long breath. Her words were a straight arrow striking the bullseye of suppressed emotions. "Fareed wasn't just my brother. My annoying, God-fearing, optimistic little brother. He was my friend. My only friend." Sami sipped wine. "Growing up away from home, I watched out for him. I was one of the larger boys at school, Fareed was at the bottom of the scale."

Petra set down her glass. "You fought your fights *and* his."

431

"And then some." Sami re-aligned his knife and fork. "Fareed never took advantage of that. Always tried to hold his ground on his own, thinking he could resolve any situation by discussing it. I admired that in him. It takes guts to argue sense with a fist coming at you."

"And that's when you'd step in."

"I was the rough brother, Fareed was the sensible, kind one. Life in that all boys boarding school was far from tranquil. And home was . . ." Sami shrugged. "Well, mother didn't exactly provide a nurturing environment and Dad was a closed book." Sami caught his murky reflection on the knife's surface. "I always wondered how my brother turned out the way he did. A healthy, decent, loving family man."

"He did so because of his big brother who had his back."

Sami looked up. "I was always angry. Left little room for friendships to develop with anyone worthwhile. Then, once I was on my own, I hopped from one place to another working on construction sites." Sami stopped fussing with his knife, placed his palms down on the table to stay still. "Hard to maintain deep, lasting relationships that way."

Petra focused her gaze out of the window. "Fareed was the stable constant in your life."

"You could say that." Sami scratched his chin. Why was he talking about Fareed? He was done with the past. Time to push forward. But how? He followed Petra's gaze outside.

Shifting evening shadows crept around the arbour, preparing the romantic spot for nightfall. He flipped open his menu. Now he was conjuring poetic nonsense. Another side effect? This was too much. And why had Petra gone quiet? He hadn't blabbered that stuff out loud, had he?

He closed the menu and set it aside. "You know, it's the second time you've done that."

Petra faced him with a questioning smile. "Done what?"

"Mention my lady friends." He leaned his elbow on the table. "If you want to ask me something, go ahead and ask."

The waiter came back with a bread basket and hovered to take their orders. Petra didn't reach for her menu. "Order for me, Sami. I trust your taste."

"They have the best steaks in all of Texas here. How do you like your meat cooked?"

"Not too red, please."

"Chef's choice of filet mignon for the lady," Sami addressed the waiter. "Medium to well done. I'll go with the T-bone, medium rare. And for salad, we'll both have the Great Caesar."

"Any appetizers, sir?"

Petra grabbed a dinner roll from the bread basket. "I don't think I can handle more food."

"That's it, then." Sami dismissed the waiter.

Petra smothered a bite of bread with butter.

Sami couldn't recall dining with a woman who did that. The women he knew balked at eating butter as if it were the plague.

Petra closed her eyes, savouring the bite.

He liked that. It even turned him on. What was this woman doing to him?

He grabbed a warm roll. "So, do you have something to ask me?"

She lifted her eyes. Her rosy lips glistened with remnants of melted butter. "Not at all," she said through a sideways smile, creating a tiny dimple in one cheek.

Sami licked his lips. The same teasing morsel of a dimple that had driven him crazy the first time it made an appearance, when Petra froze in his arms, called out to him. He forced himself to stay grounded and not scare her off. But they'd come a long way since that moment.

He placed his napkin on the table, left his chair and sauntered to her side.

She looked up. "What are you doing?"

"This," he whispered, leaned over and touched his lips to her dimple, placing the softest kiss he could manage. He lifted his head. "I don't have a special lady friend, Petra. Haven't been with anyone for over three years." He straightened, caressed her cheek and slipped back into his chair.

Petra grabbed her wine glass and gulped a mouthful. Then another. "Costa Rica?" she asked.

He nodded. "You got that from the phone call you answered in Kuwait?" He shook his head. "I'm impressed."

"Adriana," Petra whispered. "I remember her name."

Sami tore a piece off his bread roll. "What did she say to you? I have to know." He popped the piece in his mouth.

"She called you handsome."

"That's it?" He mumbled, forgetting that his mouth was full. He chewed fast.

"It's not what she said. It's the *way* she said it." Petra shrugged one delicate shoulder. "I gathered there was something between you two."

"It lasted exactly four months out of the eighteen I spent in Costa Rica. I was frustrated, lonely as hell. Adriana was beautiful, driven and..." He wet his dry throat with wine. What was he doing? He should stop talking about another woman.

Petra leaned forward, one brow arched. "Attractive as hell?"

He nodded, rubbed his chin. "The kind of woman who constantly likes new things."

"I see." Petra sat back. "And after four months, this gal," Petra flicked her wrist, "this Adriana chick moved on to newer, shinier... things?"

"Bingo. She's the local liaison for the company in Costa Rica. When I made a quick stop over there to solve a pressing matter at our project early this year, I bumped into her." Sami scratched his temple. "Somehow, her interest was renewed."

Petra brought her wine glass to her lips. "And yours?"

"Not at all. The woman never touched me."

Petra coughed, caught wine droplets on her chin with her napkin. "Excuse me?"

Sami placed his hand on his chest. "Adriana never touched me here."

The waiter arrived to serve their salads. He shaved extra slivers of Parmesan cheese onto Petra's plate at her request.

Sami drummed his fingers on the table. Was she stalling? Served him right for using his mother's words from this morning. It had all made sense then. He *was* touched—deeply, seriously, in ways he had never expected. Touched by this woman sitting before him. A woman who apparently found a pile of cheese on her salad appetizing, and more interesting than looking at him.

"Would you like more cheese, ma'am?" the waiter asked, politely indicating that Petra should ask him to stop.

She shook her head. "No, thank you."

"We're fine for now." Sami dismissed the waiter.

Petra moved most of the shaved cheese to the side of her plate and ate a forkful of salad.

Sami stabbed lettuce leaves. So she *was* stalling. She had skilfully steered the conversation to this point and now she didn't want him to elaborate? Screw that.

"What I was trying to say is—"

"Look!" Petra shot up in her chair and pointed out of the window.

A peacock looked at them, his long-feathered train dragging on the ground like a cape.

"I forgot to tell you," Sami said. "Peacocks live here. Three of them. And a single peahen, I believe."

"This is magical." Petra returned to her salad. "I see why Lora insisted on this place."

The peacock issued a shrill call, drawing Petra's attention again. Wiggling his body, he fanned out his extravagant, eye-spotted tail, showing off its iridescent colours.

Petra dabbed at the corners of her eyes with the tips of her fingers. "He's magnificent!"

"He's courting. The peahen must be close by." Sami munched on lettuce and let her enjoy the show. When the peacock wobbled behind a bush, Sami held Petra's hand and brought it to his chest.

"No woman has ever touched my *heart*, Petra." He plunged onward. "Not the way you do."

Petra slipped her hand from his grip and opened her mouth, about to say something.

The waiter arrived with their main courses. Sami counted to ten until the waiter had refilled their wine glasses and left.

He waited for Petra to say what was on her mind. But she cut into her juicy steak and ate in silence. He joined her, but the tender meat in his mouth turned to rubber. Why wouldn't she say anything? Had she understood where he was going when he talked about Adriana, his heart, and all that touching crap?

He swallowed his frustration, emptied his wine glass and decided to leave it alone, give her more time. Perhaps when they strolled in the gardens afterwards, he might find the right opening again.

A pianist filled the dining hall with an enchanting classical piece. Petra pointed toward the piano and said, "How fitting!"

"What is?"

"That particular piece is from Mozart's *Magic Flute*," she said through a soft smile. "I can almost hear birds chirping."

Sami ate, drank wine and watched Petra mellow, listening to Mozart's exuberant music. Had his face lit up the same way when he heard *Umm Kulthum's* song in the car that morning?

Done with her meal, Petra wiped her mouth. "That was really exceptional. I don't think I've enjoyed a steak this much before." Her face glowed with a sweet smile. "Thank you, Sami."

"Glad you liked it." He held out the wine bottle and was about to refill her glass.

She shot out her hand. "No more, please."

"Dessert?" he asked. "Pecan pie is not to be missed."

"Oh! I wish I could. But I shouldn't." She checked her watch. "Do you think we have time to walk around the grounds before we have to leave? It's nearly eight."

"I'm sure we do." Sami motioned for the waiter to bring the bill.

"I'm going to the ladies' room." Petra grabbed her bag and shawl. "Shall I meet you outside?"

"All right." He rose and held back her chair.

Leaving her seat, Petra turned to face him. She lifted his hand, placed it on her chest and whispered, "You touch my heart, too."

CHAPTER THIRTY-THREE

Petra strolled arm in arm with Sami as they explored the lush gardens. A hesitant breeze ruffled leaves on the trees above them, but the air remained clammy. Petra's hair frizzed with the humidity and she wished she had a hair tie in her bag to lift it off her neck. The high heels gave her a hard time on the pebble stone walkways. She kept her eyes to the ground to watch each step she took. Sami's arm provided support, but she would die of embarrassment if she broke a heel or twisted an ankle. She would never forgive herself if she ruined this romantic evening, which Sami had planned to perfection.

She risked a glance at him. How was he able to keep his cool and composure? He looked unbothered by the muggy weather, unaffected by what they had both revealed to each other minutes earlier. And he hadn't said anything about what happened between them yesterday. By contrast, she was in a complete shambles.

After what had happened with Bassam on that fatal night, she doubted she would ever overcome her anxieties and allow intimacy with another man to blossom. But last night, she had responded to Sami, became enthralled by his ardour and nearly succumbed to passion. This gallant man had the patience to unravel her knots and sweep her off her feet. Where would they go from here? Should she do anything to draw him closer? What would she do if he responded in kind?

She pointed to a thick, low tree stump. "I need to sit down, please."

"Oh." Sami signaled ahead. "There's a bench on that bridge."

"This is fine." She tugged at his arm toward the natural wooden seat. "I really can't take another step in these heels."

"Hold on." Sami pulled out his mobile phone, shrugged off his jacket and carefully draped it over the jagged surface. "There. I wouldn't want your exquisite new dress to be ruined."

"Thanks." Petra subdued a smile, noting Sami's concern about his jacket, too. The garment must be special as he handled it with such care. Hugging her bag and precious shawl, Petra sat at the very edge of the makeshift chair and patted the space beside her. "I think we can both fit."

"Only way we can fit on that is if you sit on my lap," he chuckled and slipped his phone in the front pocket of his tight chinos, stretching the fabric further around his hips at her eye level.

Petra dropped her head, using her spilled hair to cover her embarrassment. The teenager with raging hormones within her was back to torment her.

Lifting her chin with a hooked finger, Sami grinned. "Happy to oblige. Want to sit on my lap?"

She shook her head, letting his finger drop. A roaring sound flooded her ears, as blood rushed to her head. She was blushing, a flaming charcoal ignited by Sami's touch. She grabbed his hand.

"I booked a flight to Kuwait for this Saturday," she blurted. There, that was a good cold shower.

He pulled his hand out of her grasp. "Why?"

"Why?" she repeated, not expecting him to ask that simple question.

"You've discovered what happened to your father. You said you were there only for that reason. Why do you want to go back to Kuwait?"

"Because my job is there. I . . . I have commitments. Obligations."

"Send in your resignation. You can teach here. With your experience, you could land a good teaching position in any of the best schools in Houston. And Elias will be close to his doctors for checkups."

"It's not that simple, Sami." She waved her hand. "I can't just quit. Richard Frost would never give me a recommendation letter, and I need that to find a position here. I'd lose my insurance, my income. I have debts. You know I have—"

"Petra, you can have a life here," Sami cut her off. "A better life for you and your son. You can get a job at the company, too. I need someone in accounting who

I can trust. You can work with me on the Palestinian festival arrangements and the other stuff we talked about. There's a lot we can do together." Sami dropped down to one knee. "I need you here."

Her heart plummeted to the ground where Sami knelt. Cold sweat drenched her back. What was he saying? He needed her to stay for her accounting and management skills? What about all that talk during dinner? And last night? Was he toying with her? She shook her head, opened her mouth but no words came out.

Sami cradled her hand in both of his. "Petra, listen to me."

His phone rang. He ignored it. "We have great medical insurance. The company will make good profits at the end of this fiscal year, despite all the setbacks."

The phone continued to ring. Petra's heart drummed faster.

Sami kept talking. "Your share will cover your debts once and for all. I'm telling you this because—"

"Answer your phone," Petra croaked, her voice dry, injured.

"Whoever it is can leave a message." Sami rubbed her cold hand. "What I'm trying to say is—"

"It could be Mrs. Madigan." Petra withdrew her hand, her eyes threatening to spill tears. "The kids."

Dropping his head, Sami blew out a breath, rose to his feet and pulled out his phone. He frowned at the screen. "It's home."

He answered the call. "What's going on, Rosa?" He cocked his head. "What's that? Slow down." He ran his hand through his hair. "All right, all right. Lock the doors. I'm on my way."

Petra sprang to her feet and picked up his jacket. "What's wrong?"

"It's Mom. She's having some sort of a breakdown." Sami punched numbers on his phone. "I need to reach her therapist."

Petra hooked her arm in his and urged him to walk. "Let's go. You can talk to him from the car."

Petra ran into the house behind Sami. Screams and smashing sounds resounded from the second floor. Sami took the stairs two at a time. Petra slipped off her high heels to catch up with him.

"Where are my boys?" Sawsan yelled from the room in the middle of the hallway.

Rosa bolted out of the room and ran into Sami's arms. "I canno do this no more, Mr. Sami."

Sami grabbed Rosa's shoulders. "What happened?"

"I donno." Rosa shook her head. "I give Mrs. the phone. Then she go crazy."

"I want my son!" Sawsan screeched. A vase flew out of the bedroom door and smashed behind Rosa.

Sami ran down the hallway, turned to Rosa. "Who was on the phone?"

"Mr. Va . . . Van."

"Vaughn?" Petra asked Rosa as she passed her. "Vaughn called Mrs. Amara?"

"*Sí, sí.* I hear her say Mr. Sami name on the phone," Rosa said and scurried downstairs.

Petra caught up with Sami.

He arrived at Sawsan's door at the right moment to deflect a flying picture frame with his elbow. "Jesus! Mom, calm down." He looked over his shoulder at Petra. "You okay?"

"Yes, yes." Petra pushed him onward. "Go to her."

Sami stepped into the bedroom, his hands raised, palms out in a defensive gesture. "I'm here, Mom. I'm here."

"I want my *other* son!" Sawsan screamed. She grabbed the side lamp.

Sami lunged at his mother, pried the lamp from her raised hand and attempted to wrap his arms around her.

Sawsan twisted sideways, fought and slapped him across the face. "How could you? How could you do that to my baby?"

"It's all right." Sami crushed her to his chest. "Everything's going to be all right." He rocked her back and forth. "I'm here, I'm here."

Sawsan continued to wail and struggle. "*The Watchers* took my baby! Where's Fareed? Bring me my baby!"

"I can't," Sami choked, tears streaming down his cheeks.

"You!" Sawsan lashed at him again, scratched his neck. "You were supposed to keep Fareed safe!"

"I tried," Sami bellowed.

Petra stopped steps away, halted by Sami's heart-wrenching, agonized cry. He withstood his mother's physical and emotional blows.

Frozen in her spot, Petra endured a pang of remorse. On the way here, while Sami was frantically trying to reach Sawsan's therapist on the phone, all she could think about was the possibility that Sawsan was faking a breakdown to ruin their date. That Sawsan knew exactly what she was doing, putting on a show to manipulate Sami. What would happen to him if he discovered that were true?

Standing in Sawsan's destroyed room, Petra witnessed the woman fall apart in her son's arms, tearing his heart out in more ways than one. Petra tried to swallow her suspicion. The woman could not be this conniving, this cruel to her own son. No mother could.

Whatever the truth, Petra had to do something. She couldn't stand there and let Sami suffer through this mayhem alone. Where was that therapist? He said he was on his way.

Petra stepped forward and laid her hand on Sawsan's shoulder.

Sawsan flinched. "What are you doing here?"

"I talked to *The Watchers*," Petra whispered.

"You did?" Sawsan blinked several times. "How?"

"They visit me sometimes. Ever since they let me go." Petra caught Sami staring at her, confused and trapped, his tortured soul grasping for a life line. She prayed she was doing the right thing. "*The Watchers* told me Fareed was okay."

Sawsan stopped struggling against Sami. She clung to his neck and buried her face in his chest. Mother and son sagged to the floor.

Petra kneeled before them. "Your baby is fine."

"Fareed is so little," Sawsan said, her voice scratched from all the screaming. "Is he safe?"

Petra cradled Sawsan's cheek in her palm, nudging her to focus. "Sami kept Fareed safe, Sawsan. He kept your baby safe."

Sami turned his head away, hiding his face from Petra. His Adam's apple jumped in his throat. A guttural sound escaped him, a stifled sob.

Petra wiped her tears. Sami blamed himself for Fareed's death. In his big brother logic, he hadn't been able to protect Fareed on the night of the accident. And Sawsan, whether mindful of that distorted notion or not, poked his open wound.

"Doctor is here." Rosa walked into the room with a short man wearing thick glasses.

He set a leather bag on the dresser and said, "It's going to be all right now, Sawsan."

Petra rose and waved Rosa out of the room before she came too close to seeing Sami unravelling. "Please wait downstairs."

The therapist approached, an injection in his hand. "Sawsan, I'm going to give you a shot. It'll make you feel better."

Sami raised his hand. "No." He tried to clear the scrape in his throat. "She's calmed down. Just help me get her to bed."

"My baby's all right," Sawsan said, letting the therapist pull her out of Sami's lap and onto her feet. "Fareed's all right."

"That's wonderful news." The therapist dropped the needle in his bag and retrieved a medicine bottle. He patted Sawsan's shoulder and guided her to her bed. "These pills will help you sleep for a while. Rest."

Sami pushed off the floor and filled a glass of water from a bottle on the nightstand. He helped his mother swallow the sedatives, tucked her under the covers and kissed her forehead. "Everything is going to be fine, Mom."

Petra withdrew from the room. She went into the kitchen to find Rosa bawling over the sink. She patted her back. "Are you okay?"

Rosa sobbed louder. "I love Mr. Sami. He a good man. But Mrs. is . . ." Rosa blew into a wad of tissues. "Difficult. *Muy, muy* difficult."

"She's sick, Rosa. And you've been a great help to both of them." Petra handed Rosa more tissues. "Sami appreciates that. He depends on you."

"I do my best." Rosa sniffed. "Where are your shoes, Miss.?"

"Oh, somewhere in the hall." Petra helped Rosa to a chair by the kitchen table. "Can you tell me what else you heard Sawsan say to Vaughn on the phone?"

Rosa shook her head. "I no listen to Mrs. talk."

"Of course you didn't." Petra patted Rosa's hand. "I was asking if you heard anything else. By chance?"

"*Sí*. I was gettin' bath ready for Mrs. and I always leave bathroom door open when I do that." Rosa rested her arms on the table. "So I can hear Mrs. if she call or need anythin'."

"How thoughtful," Petra nodded encouragingly. "And you heard Sawsan say something to Vaughn?"

Rosa leaned forward and brought her face closer to Petra's. "You lyin'."

"Excuse me?"

"Mrs. say that to Van. You lyin'."

"Oh!" Petra forced a smile to her lips. Her nerves were shot and Rosa wasn't making things any easier. She massaged her temples. "Is there more?"

"*Sí*. Mrs. say my Sami never do that."

"Do what?" Petra asked.

"I donno. That all I hear."

"Okay. Thank you." Petra left her chair. "Could you please prepare a pot of coffee for everyone?"

"*Sí*, Miss. Petra."

Petra found her bag where she had dropped it on the stairs and took out her phone. She went into the living room, kept the lights off and called Mrs. Madigan to let her know she should spend the night with the kids. Mrs. Madigan's doubtful tone aggravated her, but she let it go. Elias was happy, the twins were fine and that was all that mattered right now. She would set Mrs. Madigan straight later if she needed to.

Sami and the therapist came down the stairs and headed to the front door. The short man turned and tapped Sami's arm. "You know the drill. Make sure she has a good meal when she wakes up, then give her another dose."

Sami ran his fingers through his hair. "Yeah, I know."

"We were making progress." The therapist peered at Sami over the rim of his glasses. "You've got to find out what triggered this episode."

"I will." Sami opened the door.

"I'll come check on her tomorrow." The therapist stepped outside. "You need anything?"

"I'm fine. Thank you." Sami closed the door and stood there, very still, staring into space.

Petra didn't make a sound, certain Sami was not aware of her standing barefoot steps away in the dark. She could only see his profile—shoulders slumped, arms dangling by his sides. He looked beaten, defeated. She should give him a private moment to regroup and compose himself.

No, she shouldn't. Sami needed her. He was lost and all alone in this pandemonium, trapped, injured. She approached him from behind, circled her arms around his midsection and held him tight.

Sami hung his head. "Sorry you had to—"

"Shhh." Petra laid her cheek onto his back, inched her hands up to his chest.

"—see all that." His voice broke into a thousand pieces. He placed his hands on her entwined fingers on his chest. "I'll call you a cab."

"I'm not going anywhere."

"The kids."

"They're fine," she said. His rapid heartbeat drummed in her ear. "I just got off the phone with Mrs. Madigan. Everyone's fine." Petra bit her tongue to stop herself from saying, *everyone but you.*

Sami blew out a long breath, his ribs caved under her hands. "Come outside with me."

She unlocked her fingers, allowing him to open the door and step onto the unlit porch. She reached for the light switch.

"Leave it off." Sami touched her elbow. "Please."

Petra joined him and closed the front door behind her. The hall light filtered through the door's stained-glass window and cast dim colours over the porch. Laden skies hid stars behind heavy clouds. Shrouded by darkness, Sami kept his back to her, his face obscure. Did he fear that if she saw the depth of his pain etched on his face, she might feel sorry for him?

Pity was for the weak, and Sami was far from being a powerless man. She had come to admire his unique blend of thoughtfulness and toughness. But it was his

451

tender soul that had won her heart. And tonight, she marvelled at his resilience. To endure what his mother had piled on him since he was a boy and to grow into an honourable man testified to his strong resolve.

No, she could not pity Sami if her life depended on it. How could she make him understand that?

She reached for his hand. "How is she?"

"Asleep. Those pills wear off after four hours or so."

"I asked Rosa to make us coffee. Wash all that good wine away." Petra winced. This was not the time to make light of things. Too late. The words had left her mouth.

"Mom will be cranky and agitated when she wakes up." Sami pulled his hand out of Petra's grasp and shoved it in his pocket. "Trust me, you don't want to be here for that."

"I don't mind. I'm here for *you*."

Lifting his face to the sky, he exhaled. "This is not how I imagined tonight would end."

"Rosa told me she overheard part of your mother's conversation with Vaughn," Petra said with caution. "It seems he meant for Sawsan to break down."

"Vaughn's been a thorn in my side since day one. Had a bad feeling about him, but I've been... distracted." Sami dropped his head. "I'm about to be rid of him once and for all. I didn't expect him to stab me in the back so viciously." Sami slammed his fist to his open palm. "Should've kept a closer eye on the

452

bastard." He turned to look at Petra. "What did Rosa tell you?"

Petra finally saw Sami's face, barely illuminated by the hall light. A bloody scratch forked down his left cheek to his neck. His mother's mark. It must be stinging him badly. Dried blood caked his shirt collar. Petra tried to tear her eyes away.

"Well?" Sami nudged. "What did Rosa say?"

"Umm, Vaughn apparently..." Petra swallowed. "Your mother accused Vaughn of lying. Told him that you'd never do that. Whatever *that* is."

"I'll find out. Even if I have to choke it out of the son of a bitch," Sami spat. "Tomorrow. Once this crazy night is over."

Rosa came out carrying a coffee tray. Petra hurried to grab the tray and sent Rosa back into the house, whispering for her to fetch a first aid kit. Sami took the tray from Petra's hands and set it on a cast iron table next to a bench at the end of the porch.

Rosa returned with a red box and handed it to Petra.

"Thank you, Rosa. Please stay with Sawsan. Call us if she wakes up."

Bolts of lightning flashed in the distance. Thunder rumbled several times before angry rain poured down and splattered on the porch cover. Petra sat next to Sami, sipped coffee and watched nature try to cleanse the world around them.

She pointed at his cheek. "We should clean that."

Sami touched his open gash. "Oh, it's just a scratch."

Petra opened the first aid kit. "Well, we don't want it to get infected." She rummaged through the contents in the dim light and found alcohol swabs and antibiotic ointment. She went to work, doing the best she could by feeling around his face and neck where she couldn't see. His open collar allowed her access to most of the cut on his neck, but not all. She hesitated a second, undid the top two buttons of his shirt and pulled away the fabric to expose his entire collarbone.

Sami sucked a long breath.

"Sorry!" she whispered.

He flinched a couple of times when she dabbed his skin with alcohol, though he refrained from complaining. His silence added to her nervousness. She was hurting him, and she hated being another source of pain.

Using the tips of her fingers, she gently rubbed ointment over the cut.

"Do you want more children?" Sami asked out of the blue.

Her hand froze midway to his cheek. "Children?" Surprise echoed in her voice.

"Do you want Elias to have siblings?"

"I uh . . . always wanted Elias to have a big family." She swallowed. "So yes, I do want to have more children." She went back to work and added under her breath, "if I ever marry again."

454

Sami grabbed her hand. "You should go, Petra."

Confusion overpowered her embarrassment. An anxious giggle escaped her. "I told you, the kids are fine."

Sami pushed off the bench and stood before her. "You were right."

She stuffed the medicines into their box. "They're probably all asleep by now."

"Petra, it's best you go to Kuwait."

"I uh..." she stammered. Her heart lay somewhere around his feet. No, it was trampled under his shoes. Disappointment stopped her from breathing. Tears stung her eyes.

He pointed at the house. "What you saw in there tonight? That's *my* life." He held her face between his palms, kissed her birthmark and touched his forehead to hers. "That's not the life I want to give you."

She held his wrists and brought his hands to rest under her chin. "I know what it's like to see your mother in agony." Petra kissed his curled fingers. "I know your frustration."

Snatching his hands back, he stepped away. "You don't understand." His voice rumbled out of his chest. "My mother's sickness is... in me." Sami slammed his forehead. "Inside my head! Mom and I... we are the same."

Petra rose from her seat. "Wait, what are you saying?"

"It's too late to do anything about the twins." He rubbed his chest. "I have no control over that. God only

455

knows how they'll turn out. But I have a responsibility not to—"

"Hold on a minute." Petra tried to reach for him. He backed further away.

"I can't give you what you want, Petra." Sami shook his head. "I just can't."

CHAPTER THIRTY-FOUR

"You've completely lost me," Petra said, her voice rising. "What are you talking about?"

"I never meant for you to get hurt." Sami pulled out his keys from his pocket and placed them in her hands. "Take my car. Go home. We'll talk more tomorrow when I come for my girls." He brought her hands to his lips. "Please forgive me, Petra." He bolted toward the front door, flung it open and went into the house.

It took her a couple of seconds to catch up with him. "You don't get to shut me out." She hissed, stopping Sami from climbing further up the stairs. Crossing her arms over her chest, she tried not to raise her voice and failed. "I deserve better than this."

"Exactly!" Sami exploded, turning to face her. "You do deserve better. I'm sorry, Petra! Sorry my father dragged you into this mess." He descended the stairs as he spoke. "Sorry *I* inflicted my family on you and your son. Sorry I can't give you what you want."

"For the love of God!" Petra snapped. "What is it that you think I want?"

"Children, damn it! A stable marriage!" He took the last step down. "What else do you think I'm talking about?"

"Oh!" She unlocked her arms, deflated. Had he proposed? When? Or was this his proposal? And why was he apologizing for it? It was as if she had arrived in the middle of a movie, having missed the vital scenes.

Sami stopped in the space before her. "Petra, I'm so sorry. I should've stayed away. Should've left you alone."

"Then why the hell didn't you?" she screamed, her nerves stretched beyond limits. She had been dangling like a yo-yo since last night, bouncing from one extreme emotion to another. And now the blasted string had snapped, flinging her somewhere between disappointment and disillusionment. She shoved Sami's chest, angry and frustrated. "Tell me, damn you!"

Sami stumbled back. "Because I fell in love with you," he roared and dropped down on the steps.

Petra tried to tame her wayward pulse. This was not how a declaration of love should happen. Where was the perfect romantic moment? The sunset by the sea? The laughing seagulls and the soaring white doves?

Sami reached for her hand. "You know what comes with love?"

"Marriage. Children," she muttered, catching his trail of thought. His apology made no sense.

"Hope!" Sami squeezed her hand. "I hoped to win your heart."

"You have." Petra slumped her shoulders. God! This was all going wrong. She sounded like a child whining, rather than a grown woman declaring her love to the man she wanted to be with.

"I hoped to have a normal life with you," Sami exhaled. "I imagined I could. I forgot about—"

"You forgot about your mother's condition." Petra dropped to sit on the step below his. "You say you love me, yet you think so little of me."

Sami released her hand. "Why would you say that?"

"You think I'm weak. That I can't handle your mother's mental illness."

"Not hers, Petra." He slowly shook his head.

"I don't understand."

"There's another constant in my life apart from Fareed." Sami twisted aside and rested his back on the wooden banister. "You, Petra. You've been visiting me for a long time . . . as a child. A cute little girl running around." He waved his hand in an arch. "You used to show up at different, random times. You are *my Watcher*. What happened with Mom tonight is my own reality." He dropped his hand in his lap. "Now, do you understand?"

Petra chewed the inside of her lower lip, processing. "How do you know it's me? This child you see everywhere."

Sami touched his thumb to her birthmark. "That's how I know."

"Am I—" Petra glanced over her shoulders, "—is she here now?"

He shook his head. "She hasn't appeared in a while." He pinched the bridge of his nose and exhaled. "I thought my hallucinations had gone, now that I had solved the mystery of who you are. But tonight—"

"You saw her?" Petra interrupted, working hard to comprehend.

"No." His lips twisted into a sad smile. "I was reminded, that's all. Petra, I can't in good conscience continue this relationship. I won't drown you in a sinking marriage with an unsound man and I don't want to remain just your friend."

"Have you been clinically diagnosed?"

"I don't need someone with a degree to tell me what I already know."

"So that's it?" Petra threw her hands in the air. "You're going to run? Kick me to the curb?"

"Damn it, woman! I'm giving you a way out."

Petra rose, a pang of guilt pinched her stomach. A few days ago she had considered taking Elias away from here, planned to leave. Now she was hurt because Sami offered it. Well, he didn't offer, he had basically decided for her.

Running footsteps echoed above their heads. Rosa peered over the handrail of the stairs. "Mrs. callin' for you Mr. Sami. She cryin'."

Sami pulled himself to his feet. "I'm coming," he said to Rosa. He turned to look at Petra, the torment in his eyes unmistakable, pleading for understanding. "Can we—"

"Go, Sami." Petra jingled the car keys and snatched her shoes. "We'll talk tomorrow."

Petra squinted, trying to see past sheets of incessant rain and the harsh beams of headlights reflected off the drenched roads. The wipers at high speed barely kept the windshield clear enough for her to read traffic signs. Inside Sami's Lexus, she wiped away the tears of her own private storm.

She went over the details of the entire evening and cried some more when she recalled the flirtatious dinner. Sami wasn't romancing her, he was prepping her. All that talk was a prerequisite for disappointment. Not only did he refrain from proposing, he answered on her behalf, too. That was how much faith he had in her. He had wormed his way into her heart and her son's life. How dare he cast them aside like that? She had a say in this relationship, damn it!

Flickering red tail lights ahead pierced the layers of rain and screamed for attention. Petra slammed on the breaks. The car started to skid. An incoming van managed to avoid a collision by mere inches. The angry driver blared his horn.

Another car's headlights reflected off the rearview mirror, blinding her. Her heart slammed against her chest. She cried out and floored the accelerator. The

Lexus slid sideways and its headlights danced across a rain-swollen ditch abutting the road.

Petra struggled to keep the car between the white lines of her slippery lane. She eased on the gas and pumped the brakes, managing to bring the car to a stop on the muddy shoulder. A delivery truck sped past and honked several times, splashing her window.

She exited and wobbled on her high heels around the car to stand beside the ditch, away from the road. She checked the tyres, lifted her face to the heavens and said a little prayer. Getting into an accident in this weather while driving Sami's car would not just kill her, it would kill him. He had handed her his car keys, as he had done with Fareed on the night of his fatal accident.

How pathetic was she? She was standing in the rain worrying about Sami's feelings after narrowly escaping a violent car crash. What was wrong with her? What was wrong with him? She kicked the back tyre and screamed at the top of her lungs.

A car stopped several feet ahead. A man ran toward her, shielding his head with a newspaper. "You need help, ma'am?"

Petra shook her head. "No, thank you."

"Car stalled? I can jump it. Have the cables in my trunk."

"The car's battery is fine." She wiped water from her face. Wet and miserable, she groaned, "I'm the one who needs a jump start."

The man moved closer, extending his arm.

Alarmed, Petra jerked back. Her heels sank in the mud. About to lose her balance and slip into the ditch, she grabbed the man's elbow for support. He wrapped his arm around her waist and pulled her onto solid ground.

"Let me take you somewhere dry. There's a Denny's about a mile down the road."

Petra pushed him away and hurried to the driver's side. "I'm going home." She quickly got inside the car, locked the doors and shifted into gear to drive. She checked for oncoming traffic and manoeuvered the car onto the road. The creepy man jumped back before she could splatter him with mud.

Gripping the steering wheel like a life jacket, she attempted to calm down. Passing the creepy man's car, she caught a child's face pressed against the window. A woman looked out from the passenger seat. The guy was a family man, a decent man who had stopped to help a stranded woman.

Petra hiccupped with fresh tears. Sami was a decent man, too. What if she didn't want a way out? Sami hadn't even considered that. And what about this nonsense that he had his mother's fragmented mind? It wasn't true. His mother must have been about his age, if not younger, when she had him and Fareed. Her hallucinations caused harm to her children. Sami showed nothing but love and tenderness toward the twins. He took the right decisions to protect and nurture them.

So what if he had images of her as a child running in his head? They could be memories. Her mother brought her to the Amara house when she was little, and the whole thing ended in a traumatic episode for him. Bits and pieces of that event had lodged in his memory, and his boyish mind had tried to make sense of it all by creating connections. She didn't need a psychiatrist to tell her that.

Sami was nothing like Sawsan. Nothing!

God! Even if he were, she would take him. Yes. She would take him and give him the life he deserved.

She executed a U-turn as fast as she could manage and drove back the way she had come. Arriving at Sami's house, she parked the car in the driveway, flipped the visor mirror and tried to put herself in order. She snatched her bag and dug out tissues to wipe running mascara. Brushing her hair with her fingers, she took several calming breaths and turned to the backseat to look for her Palestinian shawl. It lay over Sami's crumpled jacket. Her lips quivered, threatening another bout of crying. She shook her head, grabbed both garments and ran to the porch using Sami's jacket for cover.

She tried the door. Open. Slipping inside, she shivered, cool air assaulting her damp skin. She discarded her muddy shoes, shook rain out of Sami's jacket and draped it over the banister knob. Something fell and clattered onto the tiled floor. A small black velvet box lay upside down. She picked it up and flipped open the top.

A diamond solitaire ring twinkled under the yellow hall lights.

Her fingers trembling, she almost dropped the box. That explained why Sami had been so careful handling his jacket in the restaurant gardens. She tried to tuck the jewellery box back in the jacket, but didn't know which pocket it had come from.

The wooden boards above her head creaked with approaching footsteps. She quickly shoved the box into the breast pocket of the jacket and stepped away.

Sami appeared at the top of the stairs. "You came back?" He ran down.

She placed her hand on the wall and stammered, "I ... I'm not going anywhere."

Sami reached the bottom and enveloped her, his embrace rough and exuberant.

She raised her hands to clutch his back. "I want—"

"Shhh," he murmured into her ear, held her tighter.

"—to work this out," she finished her sentence with difficulty, her voice muffled by his broad shoulder.

Sami pulled back barely enough to gaze into her eyes and whisper, "Oh God, so do I."

Petra pressed her lips together to stop from crying. Was that all she could do tonight? Cry? It was a good thing she was drenched head to toe, he might take her tears for rain. A shiver ran down her spine.

Sami loosened his embrace and held her by the shoulders. "You're soaking wet. Come with me." He helped her up the stairs, blanketing her with the warmth of his body.

Her shivering dwindled. "How's your mother?"

"I gave her another pill like the doctor ordered. She went back to sleep." Sami rubbed Petra's arm. "Mom will be fine in the morning. She usually doesn't remember what happens during a manic attack." He led Petra to the first room on the right of the hallway and flipped on the lights.

"Just a minute." He went into a connecting bathroom.

Dazed, Petra looked at the king-size bed dominating the facing wall. This was a bedroom. Violent shivers assaulted her body. She folded her arms around her ribs. She couldn't stop shaking.

Sami returned with a bath towel. He slipped the shawl off her shoulders and patted her arms and the ends of her hair with the towel.

"I've ruined it," Petra said, staring at the shawl crumpled by her bare feet.

"Hmmm?"

She lifted her eyes to Sami's. "My Palestinian shawl."

"I'll buy you a thousand." Sami's hands stopped patting and shifted to encircle her waist. "A shawl for every village stitch design."

Her chin trembled. "I want this one."

Sami frowned. "I'll send it to the dry cleaners in the morning."

"Thank you," she whispered, unable to hold back a sob. He must think her demented, to worry about that shawl of all things. So much for standing her ground and showing her resolve. She was about to fall apart in his hands. So *not* what Sami needed tonight.

"Let's get you out of this soaked dress before you catch a cold." He let go of her. "I'll have Rosa come help you."

"I don't need her help," Petra said, then swayed sideways.

Sami steadied her and guided her to the edge of the bed. "I'll send Rosa with something dry to change into. You going to be okay for a minute?"

Petra nodded, finding it hard to talk, breathe, think.

Sami left, closing the door behind him.

She curled her toes and rubbed her feet on the lush rug to generate heat.

A couple of minutes passed. Petra checked the time, it was barely past midnight. So much had transpired. When would this night end?

Rosa walked in with a bundle in her hands. "Oh, no Miss. Petra. You getin' sick?"

Dry and dressed in a simple cotton nightgown and thick socks, Petra slipped under a fluffy down comforter.

"I bring you a glass of wine to help you sleep," Rosa said.

"No, thank you. I don't want any." Petra snuggled deeper in bed. "I just need to rest."

Rosa collected Petra's wet clothes and headed toward the door.

"Rosa, whose room is this?"

"The guest room, Miss. Petra. But we never have guests."

A soft knock sounded at the door. "May I come in?" Sami asked.

Petra motioned for Rosa to open the door.

Sami walked in, carrying Petra's bag. "Are we good here?"

"*Sì*. Mr. Sami."

"Thank you, Rosa. That'll be all." Sami approached the bed. "I thought you might want your phone next to you in case Mrs. Madigan calls. Is it in your bag?"

Not trusting her voice to say a word, Petra nodded and pulled the covers up to her chin.

Sami removed her phone, placed it on the nightstand and laid her bag on the floor. He sat on the bed and stroked her hair. "I'll say goodnight and let you rest." He kissed her forehead. "We'll talk in the morning."

Petra switched on the light and checked her watch. Three-thirty. She had been awake tossing and turning in the big bed for some time. Exhaustion allowed her to sleep for three hours, but now she was wide awake. She sneezed, snatched a tissue from the box on the nightstand and blew her nose. She checked her phone for possible messages from Mrs. Madigan. Nothing.

An email from Richard Frost asked for her flight number and arrival time in Kuwait so he could pick her up from the airport. She responded with a quick thank you and explained that she had already made arrangements. The last thing she needed was to give Richard any sliver of hope.

A message from Mouzah on WhatsApp showed a picture of a most adorable kitten with raised paws and the words *reaching out to my girlfriend.*

Petra chuckled, sniffed and wiped her nose. How would she explain to her friend the state she was in? And what about Richard, the school and her job? Regardless of how things turned out with Sami, she should go to Kuwait, finish her contract with the school, or officially resign. Better do it in person anyway. And there was her apartment lease to take care of, her belongings to pack and ship—whatever had not been ruined by the sandstorm. Transferring Elias's school records wouldn't be a problem once she had decided on the right school for him in Houston. She should find a place to live. Where should she start? And when?

An attack of sneezing rocked her body. She peeled back the comforter and trudged to the bathroom. Turning on the lights above the mirror, she shrank with repulsion. She looked terrible, hair frizzed and tangled, face ashen, nose as red as Rudolph's. This was not the time to fall ill. Everything was off tonight. Everything.

Stepping into the bedroom, she snatched a blanket from a side chair by the window, wrapped it around her shoulders and opened the door. On tiptoe, she headed downstairs in search of a warm glass of milk to help her sleep.

Moving quickly and as quietly as she could so as not to wake Sami, Rosa or, God forbid, Sawsan, she entered the dark kitchen and aimed for the fridge. Using the light from its open door, she fished a mug from a cupboard, filled it with milk and stuck it in the microwave, hitting the stop button before the end signal beeped. Wrapping her hands around the warm mug, she turned to leave.

Faint noises grabbed her attention. She approached the glass door to the back patio and peered into the night.

Head bowed, Sami sat on a patio chair talking on the phone. Who could he be talking to at this late hour?

"I want this done quickly," Sami said. "But I want to do it right. I've coordinated with everyone involved. I'm counting on you. Don't mess up."

Petra withdrew. It sounded like he was talking business, probably on an international call. The poor man hadn't had a moment's rest tonight.

She hurried out of the kitchen and felt her way up the stairs, careful not to spill her drink. Reaching her room, she quietly closed the door and set her mug on the nightstand.

"What are you doing in my house?" Sawsan's voice came from behind.

Petra jumped. The blanket fell to the floor. She clamped a hand to her mouth to stop herself from screaming.

Sawsan walked out of the bathroom, looking ghoulish with her unkempt white hair and black night robe pinched at the waist. She advanced into the room. "Well, answer me young lady."

Petra gulped and took a moment to recover from the scare. "Sawsan, do you know who I am?"

"Of course I do, Petra," Sawsan snapped. "What I don't know is why you're wearing *my* nightgown and sleeping in *my* guest room?"

Running her hands down the front of the nightgown, Petra sniffed. "I was caught in the rain on my way back." She glanced at the door. Should she dash out and call Sami? Where on earth was Rosa?

"My dress got soaked. Rosa brought me this gown." Petra forced a smile. "I hope you don't mind."

"It's fine." Sawsan pulled on the belt of her robe. "Where's your son?"

Petra lifted her chin in defiance and injected bravado into her tone. "Safe at my place, with Mrs. Madigan and the twins."

"Good." Sawsan arched an eyebrow, settled on the side chair and crossed her legs. "Sit." She pointed at the mug. "Drink whatever that is. Let's talk."

Petra had no choice but to comply. Sawsan's calm demeanour called for reciprocation. Cooperation would keep Sawsan from flaring into another manic episode. Sitting stiffly on the bed, Petra picked up her lukewarm milk and took a sip. Should she ask Sawsan how she was feeling now? Better not. The woman sat eerily calm and composed, as if having a chat in the middle of the night were the most normal thing to do. For all she knew, Sawsan had already erased the painful events of the preceding hours from her memory.

"You said you were soaked on your way *back* here." Sawsan rocked her dangling foot, balancing on it a black slipper adorned with black feathers. "Why did you leave in the first place?"

Petra blinked several times. How was she supposed to answer that? She set down her mug. "I wanted to go home."

"But you came back. Why?"

Petra looked Sawsan in the eye. "I came back for Sami."

The feathers on Sawsan's slippers fluttered faster.

"He's having a difficult time tonight." Petra held her breath. If Sawsan prodded for details, she had no clue what to say.

Sawsan dropped her foot. "I had a feeling that was the case."

Petra rested her back on the headboard and observed Sawsan twisting her lips in concentration, connecting the dots. Waking up to a destroyed room with no recollection of what had transpired must be confusing, scary.

"My son is very taken by you," Sawsan accused.

"I'm taken by him too," Petra whispered.

"You two will not work."

"You're wrong." Petra forced a light, cajoling tone. "Why do you keep saying that? Don't you want your son to be happy?"

Sawsan unfolded her legs and pushed off the chair. She approached the foot of the bed. "Something inside him is . . . broken." Her lower lip trembled. "Because of me."

"Whatever it is," Petra said softly, "I can handle it."

"Sami needs a strong woman." Sawsan shuffled closer. "You have a weakness. You're. . . a mother. Your son will always come first."

"And you are trying to protect yours. I understand." Petra held Sawsan's hands, urged her to join her on the bed. "I promise you, I will take good care of your son." She squeezed the woman's hands. "I love him."

Sawsan shook her head. "Love is not enough."

"You know what else comes with love?" Petra drew closer and wrapped her arms around Sami's mother. "Power."

Sawsan broke out of Petra's embrace and headed for the door. "That remains to be seen."

CHAPTER THIRTY-FIVE

Sami entered the kitchen and made a beeline for the coffee machine. He filled a mug and stood in his T-shirt and pyjama bottoms, gazing out of the window. Having not slept all night, his head pounded. He drank coffee and waited for caffeine's enlivening power to jolt him awake.

The sun was on the verge of rising, about to nudge in a new world arriving on his doorstep. Today would be the beginning of the rest of his life with Petra, the woman he loved, by his side. All else would soon fade away.

He traced the scratch on his face with his thumb. Petra had witnessed his darkest moments last night. She had stayed through the chaos, entered Mother's delirious world and defended him. Similar to that ointment she used on his skin, Petra's courageous stance was a soothing salve to his wounded spirit. She hadn't flaunted his weakness, not even when he divulged his darkest secret about his hallucinations. She listened, tried to understand, then stayed put. He had bombarded her with legitimate reasons to run, and what did she do? She came back for him.

He had been ready to propose last night in the restaurant, had picked out the perfect ring and even went down on one knee. Cementing a relationship with this woman required a bold move. And he so much *wanted* to move in her direction. He was ready to break the mould his mother had pressed him into, join Petra's world of normality, be a regular guy, settle down and raise a family. He hadn't *forgotten* his mother's condition, he ignored it—ignored his as well. He persuaded himself to believe he could leave that craziness behind once he and Petra became one. Love had the power to twist logic, skew reality and bend the world to a lover's will.

Squinting at the awakening sun, he saw things with clarity now. As long as his mother remained the anchor of his stormy life, he couldn't escape her confining box, no matter how hard he tried.

And where did Petra stand on all of this?

Petra had jumped into his box. She joined him, offered to be part of *his* bizarre world. How rare, how precious was this woman?

Pursuing her was not about love anymore. It was about survival, continuity, life itself. His life. Petra was sleeping upstairs, under his roof. He would be a colossal fool if he let her leave the house without his ring on her finger. Once he showered and dressed, he would take a breakfast tray up to her room and finish what he had started before Vaughn's lies had unleashed Mother's demons.

A squirrel scurried down a tree trunk, stuffed an acorn in his mouth and climbed up again. Sami sipped from his mug. He hadn't anticipated the viciousness with which Vaughn had screwed with Mother's head. Vaughn's audacity knocked him off his feet. Did the bastard think he could throw him off his trail?

He had set the wheels in motion for Vaughn's downfall the day he discovered the thief's shady dealings. He would have to wait to deliver the final punch until the company's legal team gained full access to Vaughn's records and the software engineers unlocked his secure computer files without triggering firewalls. Lulling the asshole to stay in the office during this time had required a lot of finesse and an Oscar-winning performance by Robert.

Sami took a sip of black coffee sweetened with satisfaction. As of three o'clock this morning, he had acquired complete control of everything Vaughn had ever touched in the company. Time to unleash his wrath on the prick.

Checking his watch, he sucked in a long breath. Mother would most likely wake up around ten. Four hours from now. He would be done with Vaughn by then, return home to catch the therapist and take Petra to her place, collect the twins. Time was tight, but he could do it. He could do anything, solve any problem, now that Petra was about to be his.

He heard someone come into the kitchen behind him. "Good morning, Rosa," he said without glancing back. "Were you able to have some rest last night?"

"Not at all," Sawsan said.

Sami turned swiftly. Coffee splashed his hand. "Oh, hey Mom!" He set his mug on the breakfast table and licked his fingers. Those pills usually knocked her out for hours. What was the deal here? He approached his mother and gave her a hug. "I didn't expect you to be up at dawn."

"I didn't either. But here I am." Sawsan held his chin and examined his fresh scar. "You look like a hobo, what happened to your face? Were you in a fight?"

"A fight with a razor." Sami kissed his mother's hand. "I slipped while shaving."

"Well, of course you slipped." She pointed at his bare feet. "You never wear slippers. I told you you're bound to get hurt. How many times have we gone through this, Sami?"

Too many times, he wanted to say. Having to lie to his mother after each manic episode stretched his endurance, made him think less of himself.

"Don't worry, I'll be fine." Holding his mother by the shoulders, he escorted her out of the kitchen. "Come on, let me help you back to bed. You need to rest before your therapy session today."

"Is it Monday already?"

"Friday." Sami sighed. A juggler tossing flaming torches, he thought fast to come up with a convincing reason for the therapist's visit to the house. "Doc had to cancel your Monday session and offered to meet with you here today instead."

"Well I need to shower, fix my hair." Sawsan puckered her lips. "What time is he coming?"

"Ten-thirty. Plenty of time." They walked up the stairs and passed the guest room.

Sami lowered his voice. "I need to take care of a few things at the office, then I'll come home and we'll have lunch. What do you say?"

"I'll make *fatteh*." Sawsan patted his arm. "You love it."

"I love everything with hummus. Especially with lots of pine nuts." He let her precede him into her room. "If you don't have time, I'll order barbecue from the Goode Company. Your favourite smoked brisket."

"I'll make the time, honey. Don't have anything delivered."

"See you at noon, then," Sami said. His mother's tone dripped with sweetness, as if she were a normal, loving mother planning a meal for her family. As if last night never happened. As if she hadn't accused him of orchestrating his brother's accident.

What a strange world he lived in, and Petra was willing to be part of it. If he were a believer, he would say God was making amends for the crappy life He had piled on him so far, gifting him Petra's loving acceptance.

As Sami turned to leave, Umm Kulthum's deep voice echoed in his head: *because of you, I forgave the past times.*

"Will Petra be joining us?" Sawsan asked.

He halted at the door and turned to face his mother. "I very much want her to." He kept his smile in place, but injected a good measure of authority into his voice. "You have a problem with that?"

"Of course not."

"Good." Sami nodded. Mother's tone was sugary, the expression on her face unreadable. It didn't matter. She could say, do whatever she wanted; nothing would sway him from the path he had carved toward Petra. And after last night's events, he was certain that nothing his mother flung at Petra would scare her away, either.

He stepped out to the hallway. "Want me to send Rosa? She should be awake by now."

"I don't need her." Sawsan moved toward her bathroom. "I'll call her to fix my hair after my shower."

Sami closed the bedroom door. He hurried toward the stairs to find out where Rosa was. As he passed the guest room, the door opened. He stumbled to a stop in surprise.

"Hello there!"

Wearing her black dress and one shoe, Petra hopped on one foot trying to slip her second shoe on the other. "Oh, good. You're up."

"And you're dressed!" Sami said, trying hard to keep his gaze above her neck. Her little black dress had shrunk after it dried out.

479

"Elias called. He's upset." Petra tugged on the sides of her dress to stretch the fabric further down her thighs. "He's not used to waking up and not finding me close." She balanced her bag on her shoulder and walked fast, "Rosa was kind enough to fetch my dress and call a cab."

"What? No." Keeping in step with her, he went down the stairs. "I'll drive you myself. I need to go into the office anyway."

Petra stopped before the front door, gave him a once over and winked. "Not like that, you're not."

"Right," he chuckled, suddenly aware of his dishevelled appearance. He warmed under Petra's appraising gaze. Goddamn! One saucy look from this woman and he was tongue-tied.

Rosa came out from the kitchen. "Taxi is here. Oh, *Buenos dìas* Mr. Sami."

"Morning, Rosa. Mom's in the shower." Rosa hurried upstairs and he addressed Petra, "I'll send that cab away. Give me fifteen minutes. Tops."

"I don't want Elias to upset the girls, too." Petra grabbed the door handle. "I really need to go."

"Wait." Sami laid his hand over hers, stopping her from leaving. He glanced at his jacket hanging on the banister. "There's something I want to—"

"Let's be practical, Sami. You have a lot to deal with this morning. Let me go to the kids."

"Just hold on a minute."

"It's okay." She pecked his cheek. "We'll talk later. When we're not pressed for time."

"Fine." Sami sighed. "I promised Mom to have lunch with her and I'd love for you to join us. Can you bring the kids here at noon?"

"Sure."

He lifted Petra's hand to his lips. "Then you and I will go somewhere nice and quiet to talk."

"You got it." Petra squeezed his hand and walked out.

Sami watched her get into the backseat of the taxi. Screw this! He snatched his jacket off the banister and bolted across the porch.

He whistled for the taxi driver to stop and yanked Petra's door open. "You forgot something."

"What is it?" Petra's leg quivered, showing her impatience.

Sami kneeled before her on the driveway.

"What are you doing?" She grabbed his elbow, tried to urge him up.

"I realize this is the least romantic thing ever, but I can't let you go without asking." He pulled the black box from his jacket, opened it and looked into her eyes.

"Marry me?" His voice sank in his chest, overrun by an avalanche of emotions he hadn't anticipated. Lifting the ring from its velvety nest, his fingers trembled. "Say yes, Petra."

She let go of his elbow. Her lips spread into a smile as bright as the rising sun above their heads. She held

481

his face between her palms. "I already said it last night. Weren't you listening?"

"I wanted to make sure," he choked. Why did his voice abandon him? He slipped the ring on her finger, leaned into the taxi and touched his lips to hers.

"Mr. Sami." Rosa called out from the porch. "Someone askin' for you on the phone."

Petra slanted her mouth aside. "I should go now," she whispered.

Tasting salt on his tongue, he squeezed her newly jewelled hand and rose to his feet. "I'll see you in a few hours." Closing the door, he gave the driver the signal to take off.

Sami licked his lips and wondered where the saltiness came from. Ignoring Rosa's repeated attempts to get his attention, he ran his hand down his face. Moisture covered the inside of his palm. Damn!

Of all the things he could do at this pivotal moment in his life, there he stood, barefoot in the middle of his driveway, allowing tears to usher in his new world.

***

Sami checked the details his legal team and computer engineers had presented in the cloak-and-dagger meeting he had called for before Vaughn arrived. Satisfied everything was in order, he dismissed everyone and called Robert into his office.

"Have one of the security guards come up with Vaughn. Tell him to keep a distance, though."

"Yes, sir."

"You've tolerated a lot of abuse from this jackass. I appreciate your patience, Robert. We're almost there."

"Deceiving Vaughn with the notion that you suspected I was behind bribing officials and that crooked contractors were giving me kick-backs, not him, was ingenious," Robert said.

"Bought us the time we needed to pull everything from his grasp, didn't it?" Sami grinned. "And I may still have to fire you today."

"It's okay," Robert chortled. "I can always pursue a career in Hollywood."

The phone rang. Sami answered. "Got it." He sat behind his desk. "Vaughn's on his way up. Move along and don't come in until I call you."

Robert bumped fists with Sami. "Game on."

Vaughn sauntered into the office. "I don't have much time, Sami. I need to head to the airport soon."

"This won't take long." Sami lounged in his chair and motioned for Vaughn to take one of the leather chairs before the desk. "Where are you off to, anyway?"

"Kuwait. A number of things still need attention." Vaughn chose the chair on Sami's right. "I told Robert. He didn't let you know?"

Sami shook his head. "Nope."

"I don't understand why you still keep the boy."

"Robert made a grave mistake." Sami leaned forward. "But I'm contemplating giving him a second chance."

Vaughn slammed his palm on the surface of the desk. "God! You should've fired his sorry ass a long time ago."

Sami arched one eyebrow. "You think so?"

"Of course. He's a thief and a lousy liar."

"Actually . . ." Sami scratched his temple. "I'm considering naming Robert in the fraud charges I filed against that contractor."

Beads of sweat glistened on Vaughn's forehead. "You filed charges? When? How come I don't know about this? I'm the head of the legal department." Vaughn loosened his necktie. "This lands right in my backyard."

"Yeah, I know. I'm trying to spare you the aggravation, seeing how busy you are with a number of things and all."

"I don't think the situation warrants legal action. Soon as I return from Kuwait, I'll handle this, see where the case stands. Firing Robert should be enough to send a message."

"Oh, I disagree." Sami left his chair and rounded his desk to loom over Vaughn. He looked him straight in the eye. "I don't take betrayal lightly." Sami straightened. "Don't bother with this. I got everything under control."

"Well, obviously you don't need me. Anything else you wanted to talk about?" Vaughn glanced at his watch. "I didn't plan on coming to the office this morning."

"Neither did I." Sami squared his shoulders. "I left a terrible situation at home."

"Oh?" Vaughn squirmed, fidgeting in his seat.

"Yeah. Mom's not doing well. She told me you called her yesterday?"

"I did." Vaughn held out his open hand. "I check on her every now and then, didn't think you'd mind."

Sami leaned his backside on the desk and crossed his ankles. "I mind when you tell her lies."

"How dare you? I did no such thing!"

"Are you saying my mother is a liar?" Sami did the best he could to remain calm.

"Of course not!" Vaughn's voice rose with the redness in his face. "She may have misunderstood what I said, that's all."

Sami crossed his arms over his chest. "And what did you say about me and Fareed?"

Slamming car doors, commotion and hurried voices emanated from the parking lot.

"What exactly did you tell Mom about Fareed's accident?"

"This is ridiculous. I won't have this insulting conversation." Vaughn shot to his feet. "I have a plane to catch."

Sami unlocked his arms, standing tall. "You're not going anywhere, asshole."

485

"Hey, watch your language. Calm down. I merely told Mrs. Amara to look at the bright side of things. Having you take charge of the company after your brother's freak accident worked well for everyone."

"That's what I thought you said." Sami snatched a document from his desk and shoved it at Vaughn's chest. "You'd better hire yourself a good law firm."

"What's this?" Vaughn stared at the document.

"I'm suing you for embezzlement, financial fraud and breach of fiduciary duties."

"Who the hell do you think you are?" Vaughn growled. "You waltzed into this company not knowing your head from your ass about running a business. *I* held everything together." He reared and lashed out with a closed fist.

Sami calmly swatted the blow aside. "Agents with the FBI and SEC are cooling their heels in the lobby. Turns out offering bribes to conduct business overseas and rigging the company's books is a federal offence." Sami thrust his chin at the older man. "I know that much."

"You son of a bitch!" Vaughn snarled and swung again.

Sami dodged the punch, opened the door and spoke to Robert. "Have security escort the federal guys up. It's time. Vaughn is done."

CHAPTER THIRTY-SIX

Relieved to see Sami's car parked in the driveway, Petra ushered the kids into the house. She had prayed she would make it there after him to avoid facing Sawsan alone. She slipped off her ring and tucked it into the pocket of her pleated skirt.

Mrs. Madigan carried the girls' things in and headed straight to the kitchen.

Sami came out of the study. "There you are!" He beamed and scooped the twins into his arms, dotting their cheeks with kisses. He listened and nodded at their babbling as if he understood every word.

Petra placed her hand on Elias's shoulder and stepped toward the living room, allowing Sami to devote his attention to his nieces.

Dressed in a light grey Armani suit, Sami looked different than he had in the early morning, less rugged, but just as manly. The scar on his face and neck emphasized his masculine appeal. Petra patted her ring. This fine man was hers. How sweet was that?

Sami set down the twins and stomped his feet, pretending to run after the girls to steer them toward the kitchen. "Go say hi to grandma."

Petra shook her head. How could he be so animated and energized after last night? She could barely hold it together, pumped by the magical symptom-concealing power of DayQuil.

Sami returned, squatted before Elias and shook his hand. "Thanks for watching out for my girls, young man."

Elias beamed at Sami. "I'm going to be DeLeenas's big brother."

"You sure are." Sami flashed a look at Petra, the first since he had walked in. He held Elias by the arms and gently brought him closer. "You know what that means, Elias?"

Elias nodded. "I can call you Baba Sam."

Sami burst out laughing. "You got it." He hugged Elias, closed his eyes and held him.

Petra stood still, deeply touched by Sami's genuine warmth toward her son. She wasn't surprised, but seeing how Elias's words moved Sami was something to take note of, to savour and cherish. This affectionate man would be Elias's father. How lucky was she?

Mrs. Madigan came out of the kitchen with the girls, nodded a greeting to Sami and headed to the stairs. "Come on Elias, let's hang out in the games room until lunch is ready."

Elias tried to wiggle out of Sami's embrace. "Can I play with your airplanes?"

Sami let him go and ruffled his hair. "Go ahead, son." Rising, Sami followed everyone up the stairs with his eyes.

Petra waited. Why wouldn't he look at her? Talk to her? She stood before him, as promised, and on time.

As soon as the kids and their nanny had disappeared, Sami sprang forward and wrapped his arms around her in a tight embrace. "I've missed you."

Petra laughed in nervous relief and returned his hug, stroking his back. "Since this morning?"

"It felt like days." Sami loosened his hold and kept her nestled in his arms. Grinning, he arched his eyebrows. "A lot has happened since this morning."

"Oh, you went into the office and confronted Vaughn." She entwined her fingers behind Sami's neck. "No wonder you're so excited. How did it go?"

"Exactly as planned. But that's not the source of my excitement." He angled his head and dipped, intent on a kiss.

Petra sniffled and moved her head aside. "I'm coming down with a cold, Sami. I don't want to get you sick."

He touched his lips to her forehead instead. "Do you have a fever?"

She did feel warm. It was possible that he was the cause of the heat rising from her chest. "It's not the flu. Just a cold."

"Sorry, sweetheart." He rubbed her shoulders. "Perhaps you should be resting in bed."

"I'll be fine. It's not that bad."

He pressed her closer. "Thank you for telling Elias."

"Mrs. Madigan saw the ring on my finger and cried out her excitement in front of him. I explained what was going on. I wasn't planning on keeping it a secret." Petra gazed into Sami's misty eyes. "Were you?"

"Are you kidding me? I want to shout it from every rooftop. Hell, if I was on Twitter or Instagram, it'd be all over the globe by now." He nuzzled her neck. "God! You smell so good. Thyme and," he inhaled deep, "roses?"

"Orange blossom." Petra corrected, trying her best not to melt in his arms. She buried her face in his shoulder to hide a whimper. Sami was all hands, eager and . . . bold. His palms spread over the small of her back. His lips hit a sensitive spot behind her ear, tingling every nerve down her spine.

She peered over his shoulder at the closed kitchen door. "Sami, your mother's in the kitchen."

"So?"

"Did you tell her?"

"Hmmm," he murmured. "She knows."

Petra arched her back to create some distance, forcing him to abandon her neck. "How did she take the news?"

"Mom's been very sweet about it." Sami dipped his head again.

"Really!" Petra laid her hands on his chest to stop him. "Don't you think that's odd?"

"Yeah," Sami chuckled. "But what's *not* odd about my mother?" He eyed Petra's left hand on his chest. His

490

chuckle died. "You're not wearing it." He let go of her and stepped back.

"I wasn't sure if Sawsan . . . if I should . . ." Petra pulled the ring out of her pocket. "I didn't want to cause a scene with your mother."

Scowling, he took the ring and slid it onto her finger. "You can cause whatever scene you desire." He ignited her with a blatantly sexual, hungry look. "With me."

"Sami, I'm serious. I don't want to make trouble."

He entwined his fingers with hers. "Don't worry, I invited *Khoury* Dahood for lunch to absorb any blows. So far, we're in the clear." He pulled her toward the kitchen. "We'll sit through lunch. Then you and I will head to city hall before it closes for the day."

"Why?"

"To apply for a marriage license." Sami pushed the kitchen door open. "I'm not waiting another minute to make you my wife."

Petra stared at the coffee heart floating on top of her cappuccino froth. Sami had brought her to this busy cafe downtown after they had left the Harris County clerk's office, having barely made it there in time to have a marriage license issued. Everything had happened too fast. Sami was moving too fast. She had barely had a moment to reflect, hadn't even told Mouzah her news.

She looked up at Sami, stirring sugar into his coffee. His mother hadn't made a scene during lunch, but burst his excitement bubble by downplaying the topic. Sawsan gave her a stiff hug, a dry welcome to the family, then spent the entire meal talking with *Khoury* Dahood about her next art exhibition.

"You're so quiet," Petra said to draw Sami out.

"Change your reservation, Petra. Cancel it." He flung the spoon onto the wooden table. "Why are you insisting on flying to Kuwait tomorrow?"

"I've already lined up things. I need time to finish my work at the school, transfer Elias's papers, pack our stuff."

"What about Elias's medical follow-up here?"

"The doctor has cleared him to fly. His next appointment is in four weeks. I'll be back by then." She reached for Sami's hand. "It'll give you time to sort things out, too."

"I don't need time. Everything's in order. At work and at home. If you're worried about Mom—"

"I'm not," Petra cut him off. "I can handle Sawsan."

"I know you can. But if you're concerned about Elias, I'll hire more helpers to watch Mom. A full-time nurse."

"Oh no, Sami. I don't want to cause more disruption to her life. Elias will be at school half the day, and when he comes home I'll be there with the twins. Besides, I'm hoping we can keep Mrs. Madigan on. She's a tremendous help and the girls have gotten used to her."

"Yes, of course."

"I won't start teaching before the girls go to kindergarten." Petra played with sugar grains scattered on the table. "That way the kids and I will have the same schedule." She looked up at smiling Sami. "You're okay with my plan?"

"God, am I?" Sami's smile stretched into a wide grin. He tightened his fingers around hers. "Only if that's what you really want."

"It'll give me two years to be a stay-at-home-mom. I never had the luxury for that." She flipped her hair to drape it over one shoulder. "Sami, about what you said before? About not wanting to father children..."

"Yeah, about that—"

"Have you done anything?" she interrupted, impatient to know.

He frowned.

She pressed, "A surgical procedure that can't be reversed?"

"Oh, nothing drastic like that. I'm," he clicked his tongue, "medically intact."

"I know you're wary about having children, but I'd like a *chance*." She fanned her flaming cheeks with her palm. "If you change your mind."

"Things are not set in stone, Petra. It's a decision I made in my darkest moments. When I lost hope of ever finding an angel to stick by me." He gave her hand a gentle squeeze. "If more children is what your heart desires, I can reconsider."

"We don't have to decide right away. We have time."

He leaned closer, pinned her with a mischievous, amorous stare. "I'd be happy to try tonight, now, if you're willing."

Praying she would sound confident and flirtatious, she rolled her eyes and said, "And I want nothing more than to make you happy, of course."

"Jesus, woman! Don't tempt me." He kissed her before she could object and lounged back. "I'm serious. I don't want to wait until you come back from Kuwait to get married."

"You can catch up with me there," she suggested, finally finding the chance to say what had been revolving in her mind since *Khoury* Dahood had mentioned the subject to her after lunch. "I don't have family, but I have close friends who consider me part of theirs, and I owe them the honour of being involved in this process."

Sami rubbed his forehead. "I'm my own man. You expect me to come and talk to Khalid. Ask for his permission?"

"His blessing, Sami." She shook her head. "I don't need anyone's permission."

A waitress pulled two tables together to accommodate a group of five women next to them. They bantered over seating arrangements before finally settling.

Sami eyed the loud group, sucked his upper lip and slowly released it.

She had seen him do that before, when he formulated a plan, when he was getting ready to ask her to do something. Why was he being this difficult?

"I'll do whatever you want, don't you know that?" Sami lifted her hand to his lips. "I'll fly with you, talk to Khalid or whoever." He kissed the tips of her fingers, one by one. "I'll also travel to Palestine and properly ask for your hand from any relative you feel is right."

"Thank you," she giggled, despite herself. Sami was serious. She shouldn't make light of his considerate offer, but he was tickling her.

She took a sip of her cappuccino to arrest the mirth. "My father's relatives in Palestine are distant cousins. They know nothing about me. I'm sure they wouldn't mind stepping up. Talking to Khalid will be enough, though." She set down her cup before she spilled coffee over her lap. "I would love to take Elias to Palestine when he's older, when he can understand the history and politics of it all." She pulled in a long breath. "What do you say?"

"Sure. Anything you want." Sami locked his gaze on her mouth. "I mean it."

Exhaling, she slumped forward. "Can you travel to Kuwait a week or so after me? That way, I can prep Mouzah and Khalid, bring them up to speed."

"I'll give you a couple of days before I fly out. I have a project in Pamukkale, southwestern Turkey, that I've been meaning to check on but haven't had the chance."

Sami reached out his other hand, swiped his thumb over her upper lip and licked it. "I'll book a connecting flight to Kuwait through Istanbul."

Petra dabbed her mouth with her napkin and ran the tip of her tongue over her lip to make sure she had wiped off her milk froth moustache.

Sami fidgeted in his seat. "Please, stop that. I'm barely holding it together." He flipped her hand and peppered her open palm with soft kisses. "I'll keep myself busy for a couple of days in Turkey while you prepare Khalid. We should be back in Houston by Friday at the latest."

"I need more than a week to finalize things." Petra pushed her cappuccino cup away, trying not to be troubled by Sami's speed. "You can return to Houston whenever you want. I'll stay on until I've put my affairs in order."

"Two weeks, then."

"It'll take a week just to overcome the jet lag. I need at least three." She smiled to soften her objection. "I'll be free then, yours . . . forever."

"Fine." He kissed her hand, paused then cocked his head. "Is this your way of telling me you're apprehensive about being with me? Because you needn't worry. I'll wait until you're completely ready. But I want us to be married."

"I'm . . . I don't . . ." she stammered, catching on to his concern. Doubt sprouted in Sami's voice, and she was the one who had planted its seed. How to reassure this considerate man?

"I understand if it's much too soon for you, Petra. I'd never, ever press you."

"I know that, Sami," she whispered. "I know. What I'm saying is I need time to tie up loose ends in Kuwait." She shook her head. "That's all."

"So . . . we're . . . okay?"

Petra hesitated a second. Sami's question struck her as more wistful than inquisitive. She lifted off her seat and answered with what she hoped was an open, encouraging kiss.

"Oh, thank God!" Sami exhaled, and tried to follow with more. She stopped him, glancing at the women beside them. The three facing them stared back.

Sami groaned and resumed his mouth's seductive dance with her hand, then moved to her wrist. "Would you like a wedding?"

Petra swallowed. The idea hadn't crossed her mind. She hadn't had time to think that far. "A simple dinner will do. Unless you'd rather we plan for a small reception."

His lips hovered over her tingling skin. "Planning a wedding takes time."

"Yes, it does," Petra said, holding back her weariness. He confounded her with his passionate intensity. *Slow down, Sami. Please slow down.*

"I'm thinking a modest dinner with family and friends after a private church ceremony will be enough." She shrugged. "But I don't know anyone here, so it's really up to you."

"If it were up to me, I'd sign this certificate before a judge and whisk you on our honeymoon tonight." His husky voice played havoc with her nerves. "But if a ceremony is important for you, I'll play along." He entwined his fingers with hers and gently sucked on her knuckles. "Where would you like to go for the honeymoon?"

"I haven't—" her voice broke, Sami draining it out of her body with his proficient lips. She cleared her throat and tried again, "I don't want a honeymoon."

His hand dropped to the table. "Come again?"

"We can't leave the kids, remember?"

"Oh, yes we can. Not for long, but we can escape for a couple of weeks. Mrs. Madigan's proved herself capable of taking full charge." He shook his head. "There's no room for compromise on this, Petra. Now do you have a specific place in mind?" Leaning forward, he clicked his tongue. "Or do you still trust my taste?"

"Sami Amara, you asked me to be your wife. I believe you have exceptional taste."

***

Petra took her ring back from Mouzah. "Now, are you satisfied?"

"It's not from *Tiffany's*." Mouzah twisted her closed mouth from side to side. "But the diamond is exceptionally pure. Your Sami did good."

"Finally!" Petra rolled her eyes. "You approve. I don't understand, you've been grilling me on every detail since I arrived." She snatched one of the cushions from Mouzah's living room sofa and hugged it to her chest. "Why are you being so critical?"

"It's my job," Mouzah huffed. "I'm like your sister."

"My sister's job is not to feel happy for me?"

"*Ma yhik jismak illa thifrak.*" Mouzah sighed. "Before you ask what that means, let me do this." She scratched Petra's forearm with her long, manicured nails.

Petra arched an eyebrow, beckoned for an explanation.

"Nothing scratches your body better than your own nails," Mouzah said. "I am being your nails."

Petra threw her hands in the air. "What are you talking about?"

"I am thinking of all the details to make sure you are not missing anything important. That is my job as your sister and best friend." Mouzah slapped her lap. "Of course, I'm very happy for you. I told you this would happen, remember?"

Petra swiped her hand over the cushion. "But it's happening too fast, is that it?"

"No. It is better not to have a long engagement. And the man is ready." Mouzah started counting on

499

her fingers. "He has a successful business. He will give you a secure future. And he has a big house that will fit everyone?"

"Yes," Petra said with confidence. Sawsan would not present a problem. It was clear Sami had the upper hand in the house.

"He loves your son." Mouzah continued ticking. "And he is close and kind to his mother." She wiggled her fingers before Petra's face. "Those are all good things."

"What then? Spill what's on your mind." Petra set the cushion aside. "In English, please."

Mouzah canvassed the empty room, scooted closer and whispered, "Are *you* ready to have a husband again?"

Petra met her friend's penetrating gaze. "I didn't think I would be, but I am."

"Are you sure?"

"I'm ready." Petra averted her gaze. "I truly am."

Mouzah put her hand above her upper lip and launched a long, ear-piercing trill, warbling her tongue with incredible speed.

Khalid walked into the room. "So I have the green light to receive the man tomorrow?"

Petra covered her face with her palms. Laughing, Mouzah smothered her in a tight hug. "Go easy on him, Khalid. This is only a formality."

"*Mabrook*," Khalid simply said and left the room.

Mouzah released Petra. "You know what that word means, right?"

Petra nodded. "Khalid is congratulating me. Does that mean he won't give Sami a hard time?"

"Absolutely not," Mouzah chuckled. "Sami is flying in tonight. He will be jet-lagged and tired in the morning. Khalid will torture him, but not for too long."

Mouzah's eldest son ran into the room, carrying a McDonald's bag. "Salam." He went straight to the TV and turned it on. "I missed a game. I just want to check the score." He fiddled with the remote control and flipped channels.

Mouzah turned to Petra. "Euro Cup is all he thinks about."

The teenage boy stopped at the BBC news and turned his attention to devouring a Big Mac.

"Come, let's go online." Mouzah rose to her feet, pulling Petra up with her. "See what is *moda* for wedding dresses."

"I was thinking of a skirt suit and the special shawl Sami brought me from Palestine," Petra said. "I'm not wearing a wedding gown."

"Oh, yes you are." Mouzah placed her hand on her hip. "And a veil."

The flat screen lit up with a chaotic scene. Ambulance sirens blared. Red and white lights flashed across the night sky. Screaming people ran in all directions, some covered in blood.

A reporter's voice boomed over the rolling carnage. "Five, possibly six, detonated bombs have been reported in Istanbul. The city is in total chaos."

Petra dropped to her knees.

Mouzah slammed her chest. "*Howw, ya hafith!*"

Khalid barged into the room, shouting at his son to turn off the TV.

The boy spilled his French fries onto the floor and grabbed the remote control.

"No!" Petra shrieked, crawling closer to the screen. "They're saying one of the bombs is in the airport."

"Maybe Sami is already in the air," Khalid said. "Do you have his flight information?"

"No. I . . . I know he's . . . supposed to land in Kuwait at eleven. I don't even know which airline he flew with."

Her mobile phone chimed with Sami's special ringtone.

Petra scrambled to her feet, ran to her bag. Flipping it upside down, she spilled everything onto the couch and fished for her phone.

"Petra, can you hear me?" Sami shouted with difficulty above the rumble of gunfire.

"Sami, thank God, you're okay!" She squealed. "Where are you?"

"I'm—"

"Sami! Sami!" She screamed, fell to the floor.

"*Shino?*" Mouzah dropped beside her. "What? What?"

"Oh, God!" Petra wailed, shoved the phone into her friend's hands. "Call dropped."

Mouzah passed the phone to Khalid and wrapped her arms around Petra, rocked with her.

"That doesn't mean anything." Khalid stared at the screen. "Mobile service can be interrupted for any number of reas—"

The phone chimed again.

To be continued in FOUND IN THYME

FOUND IN THYME
By Lilas Taha

CHAPTER ONE

Sami Amara never imagined he would welcome the stench of a neglected public restroom. He ran into the farthest stall, slammed the flimsy door shut and pushed the teenage girl into the corner by the filthy toilet.

Rolls of gunfire outside competed with deafening shrieks and anguished screams. If one of the shooters assaulting the mall in Istanbul airport continued to spray bullets, the teen would at least have the protection of the chipped commode.

Sami had swept off the stunned girl standing in his path the instant he regained balance. An explosion had ripped through the café they were about to enter and spared them. Aiming for the safety of the restroom, Sami hauled the girl away from the mutilated bodies before her.

Thin, lanky and shaking violently, the teen clung to Sami's bloody shirt. He pried her hands off. Where did the blood come from? Was it hers, or his?

Someone burst through the main restroom doors.

Sami pressed his index finger to the girl's lips. He eased onto the toilet and curled his basketball frame into a fetal position. Sharp pain pierced his left side. He clenched his lips and stifled a moan. If it were people taking refuge, he would have heard crying, running, shuffling. But there was stillness, followed by deliberate footsteps.

Sami held his breath. They were trapped. Could he pounce on the shooter, disarm him before he fired his weapon? Impossible. This was not a movie. He couldn't move at lightning speed nor did he possess martial arts skills. The odds in his favour would rise if the shooter was miraculously distracted. What if he waited until the gunman approached the stall? He could slam him with the barely-standing door—throw him off balance for precious seconds. Would it be time enough to grab the teen, shield her with his body and escape? Absolutely not. He would be riddled with bullets before they reached the exit.

What would happen to his twin girls at home?

They would be orphaned. Again.

No way in hell could he let that happen. He had to survive. He needed a weapon. Nothing on him but his mobile phone, passport and his father's Parker fountain pen. The solid gold nib could inflict pain. Or could it? Panic screeched in his ears, a frantic entity clawing at his lungs. What to do? What to do?

Heavy black boots showed below the stall's dangling door. Sami met the teen's eyes. *Stay calm. Please stay calm.* The youth clamped both hands over her mouth. Sami was poised, gripping his pen as he would a dagger. This was foolish, cartoonish even, but he was desperate.

The outside restroom door creaked open. A woman said something in Turkish, unmistakable panic in her voice.

Sami jerked up his head. A mother ushering her family to safety? Run out lady, Sami wanted to yell. The teen grabbed his ankle. He pressed his fist between his teeth.

The black boots turned toward the new arrivals. Shit! Sami leapt forward, crashed against the stall's door, breaking its remaining hinge and landing it atop the shooter. Pinned to the floor, arms trapped by the door under Sami's full weight, the gunman bellowed a menacing cry and fought to throw Sami off.

Sami lashed out with his pen. Gunshots thundered by his head, shattered mirrors and reverberated around the tiles. Had any bullets hit the teen? The family? He couldn't see and he couldn't stop. His beautiful little girls needed him in Houston. Petra waited in Kuwait to become his bride.

He . . . must . . . stay . . . alive.

He ripped the pen into the shooter's masked face with all the power he could muster, aiming for his eyes, one furious blow after another, over and over and over.

The gunman howled and wailed, a crazed animal. Sami rammed and twisted the pen into the man's throat to silence him. Blood spattered Sami's face, pooled under the shooter's head and shoulders.

Where was the weapon? Was the bastard still moving?

A hand touched his back. His fist paused mid-air. He looked up. The teenager stood trembling before him, her jeans soiled. A crying mother huddled in a corner, shielding two children with her body.

Sami wiped blood and sweat from his face with his sleeve, rose and balanced on the door. He jumped on it several times. More blood seeped from the mangled gunman's wounds. He was no longer a danger, but could he have comrades lurking outside?

Sami flipped up his thumbs. "Okay?" he asked in a hushed voice.

The teenager nodded. The woman unfurled her body and checked her terrified children.

"Shhhh," he beseeched them to stop crying.

They huddled around their mother, peering at him with wide eyes. The mother patted their backs, tucked her frazzled hair strands under her colourful headscarf.

He leapt to the floor, flipped the door off and kicked the lifeless body hard. Not a twitch nor a moan came from it. He carried a tall metal trash bin to the main door and jammed it under the handle. Eyeing the assault rifle by one of the toilets, he picked it up, checked the gunman's body for extra ammo, found two full clips and tucked them under his belt. He had gone deer hunting in Texas a couple of times and fired a rifle—never a semi-automatic, but he would defend this spot no matter what. Pointing the nuzzle to the floor, he studied the AK-47, located its magazine release lever and engaged it a couple of times, unloading and reloading the clip. He could do this. He had no choice.

Emulating soldiers in movies, he slung the weapon across his shoulder to rest it on his back. He grabbed his kill by the ankles, dragged it inside one of the stalls and closed the door. No telling if the children had watched him gouge out the shooter's eyes. They didn't need to stare at the grisly carnage.

What was the shooter doing in this restroom? It was as if he had followed them. Or was he looking for someone in particular?

Pain shot through Sami's ribs as the adrenaline dissipated. He gripped his left side. Warm blood oozed from it, mingled with the congealing fluid on his hand. Shrapnel from the explosion? Or a bullet?

The mother approached, clutching clean diapers. She pointed and motioned him to lift his arm. He obliged, but failed to suppress a moan. She compressed diapers over his wound and used her scarf around his midsection to secure them in place. Her auburn hair shimmered under the florescent lights, the same reddish-brown hue as Petra's.

He swayed, and shot his right hand to the wall. He smelled baby powder. Innocence and horror mingled on his skin. What the fuck just happened?

He had killed a terrorist with his father's pen.

He slid to the floor, swung the weapon onto his lap. A black shroud floated down from the corners of the room to engulf him. He fought to keep his eyes focused. He couldn't lose consciousness. Not now. Not yet.

Acknowledgements

I'm eternally grateful to my life-companion, true friend and husband, Saad Saleh. Lending his ear, insight and support was essential in delivering me to the last word of this book.

My heartiest thanks go out to my sweet mother, Nawal for her nurturing guidance, always speaking her mind to keep me grounded. And to my adult children, Leila and Bassel for opening my eyes to the magic of life that I try to capture in my writing.

I am indebted to Roger Paulding, who continues to be my writing mentor, Bob Gregory, who understood what I wanted to write even when I didn't have the right words, Luke Chauvin, who read between the lines what I was too involved to see, and Sandra DiGiovani, who went after my adverbs.

Many in my writer's critique group offered valuable feedback and kept me on track. Special thanks to Rafael Sher and Paula Porter.

I offer my sincere thanks to the wonderful team at HBKU Press who adopted me into their supportive family, namely Fakhri Nawahda, Rima Ismael, fellow author Ghenwa Yehya, and Omar Allouba.

Paramount are all the readers, who accepted my stories into your lives. Without your interest, comments and reviews I wouldn't continue on this path. Thank you.